Copyright © The author as named on the book cover.

First Edition

The author has asserted their moral right under the Copyright, Designs and Patents Act, 1988, to be identified as the author of this work.

All Rights reserved. No part of this publication may be reproduced, copied, stored in a retrieval system, or transmitted, in any form or by any means, without the prior written consent of the copyright holder, nor be otherwise circulated in any form of binding or cover other than that in which it is published and without a similar condition being imposed on the subsequent purchaser.

For my wonderful girlfriend, Jo and my beautiful children, Ella & Max xxx

CHAPTER 1

The alarm clock let out a subtle, repetitive beep and seconds later Richard lazily threw this arm in the direction of the sound and hit the over-sized off button. A sniff and scratch closely followed by a stretch and a yawn and he slowly lifted himself upright in his bed and waited for his vision to adjust. He didn't need his vision to adjust to know the time was 6:30am though. It was the same time that he'd been getting up for the past god-knows-how-many-years. Despite the uniformity of his wake-up time he still needed the aid of his trusty digital alarm clock that had served him so well; faithfully waking him up since he'd received it as a birthday present many years before. He observed this archaic timepiece and conceded it was about time he replaced it. The white plastic casing had, over time, become a tainted yellow colour, but as Richard always thought, why replace it when it works so efficiently and loyally as it had done? Richard didn't have many friends... actually Richard didn't have *any* real friends, so inanimate items doing him a trusty service were the next best thing. He remained as loyal to them as they were to him. Flicking on his bedside light he rose from his bed. Early morning sunlight peeked through the gap where his age-old curtains met, helping to illuminate his small, but tidy bedroom. He ruffled his lank, greasy, style-less hair and surveyed his appearance in the mirror resting uneasily upon a tatty chest of drawers. Admittedly he wasn't at his best first thing in the morning, but this morning he looked particularly rough. He was beginning to regret staying up into the early hours playing "*Call of Honour*" online, but once he was in the zone it was hard to break away. Fighting for his life with his virtual comrades was far more exhilarating than his normal day-to-day life. Every night it was as much as he could do to press the off button and bring an end to these adventures. With pride, he looked upon his state-of-the-art gamers chair and his fifty-five-inch TV which dominated most of his bedroom. Having had some epic battles on his games console, he had to admit, those two gadgets had been great purchases, enhancing his playing experience all the more.

Out of his bedroom, he walked stealthily to the bathroom at the other end of the landing. He was especially careful not to wake his parents who were sleeping in another bedroom off the landing. It was more than his life's worth to wake them up at this ungodly hour. Despite being on the cusp of turning forty he was still very much ruled by his oppressive parents and at this time in the morning he was quite literally treading on eggshells. He was well-versed at knowing which floorboards creaked, and just like a less agile and less charismatic Indiana Jones, he safely navigated his way to the sanctuary of the bathroom. Once there he delicately closed the door and switched on the light. The sudden change in lighting made him wince and promptly shield his eyes. It amazed him that every morning he did exactly the same thing and, there and then, he made the same promise to himself that he'd been making since god-knows-when to fit a lower wattage lightbulb and make the transition from dark to light that little bit more agreeable. Then he remembered what his father had said last time he'd suggested changing it; *"What's the point of 'avin' a light that don't make the room look bright?"* He'd followed this by insulting Richard and reminding him that he was a complete waste of space. *Perhaps the momentary stark transition of light wasn't worth the fuss after all,* he thought to himself. He removed the virtual post-it note from his brain and shuffled his way to the toilet. Standing there emptying his bladder, he was especially careful not to splash anywhere other than the toilet bowl. No easy task with the first one of the day. He could hear his mother's nagging words already *"Ave you pissed all over the floor again? It smells bloody disgusting. Sort yourself out. You're not a little kid anymore."* She'd follow this by insulting Richard and reminding him that he was a complete waste of space. After he'd finished he tore off a bit of tissue paper and gave the toilet a quick wipe round. *Better to be safe than insulted,* he reasoned. He often wondered why he was so bothered. It wasn't like his parents ever cleaned the bathroom; that was his job. As was cleaning the rest of the house for that matter. If Cinderella had a long-lost brother, he was most certainly it. Inwardly aggrieved, as he often found himself, he moved over to the basin. Standing there washing his hands, he allowed himself another long stare in the mirror. Staring back at him was the same face he'd watch slowly age. *I'm nearly forty. How the hell did that happen?!* He had to admit though, that despite the impending onset of his fortieth birthday he didn't look too bad for his age. Martin Bradshaw who worked in his office was in his early thirties and looked considerably older than he, having lost most of his hair already and sporting a rather unnecessary paunch. In comparison, Richard was slim, but his body carried natural tone; his face had good bone structure, a strong jaw line and blue eyes that contradicted his dark hair and features. He was what could be described as surreptitiously handsome.

A quick wash and a shave later and he was tiptoeing back along the landing with the same care as before. Back in his room he began to dress himself with all the enthusiasm of a person that had been performing the same task at the same time for many years. He dug out some age-old boxer shorts that had long lost their shape, colour and elasticity. The sight of these didn't perturb him though. After all, who was going to see them apart from him, and, he reasoned, *they still did their job didn't they*? He then rummaged in his sock drawer and pulled out two odd socks, both equally worn and both displaying some comedy logo typical of a pair given at Christmas. He then put on a crumpled shirt which had been placed on the back of his games chair. It was nondescript and too baggy for his frame, as were his black trousers that did nothing to accentuate his rather pert bottom. They just hung off him like an old sack. Thank god his trusty belt purchased at Burton many moons ago kept his trousers up. At best these were functional trousers. At worst they were shapeless slacks that were bigger and baggier than they needed to be. Next he located his tie which was carefully rolled up on his chest of drawers. He was clinically efficient when putting this on. Years of practice meant he could perform this task with his eyes closed. Of everything he was currently wearing, his tie was the most expensive item. He was proud of his tie. His Grandmother, who had passed away almost a year ago, had bought it for him for his birthday a few years prior. He had loved his Gran. She was kind and caring and had always stuck up for him when his parents were being particularly spiteful towards him. She was his father's mother but she'd had no time for either of his parents, especially his mother who she regarded as a malevolent, scheming freeloader. She'd been Richard's rock, but with her no longer there to support him, he bore the brunt of their contempt on a daily basis. Finishing off this morning ritual with a final comb of his drab, uninspiring hair, he silently crept from his room, down the stairs and into the kitchen to make his breakfast. Two Shredded Wheat, a cup of coffee and a quick brush of his teeth and he was out the door.

The late spring weather offered a meagre drizzle to accompany his brisk stroll to work. Despite the dampness the sky looked like it would brighten up during his journey. He hoped there would be a rainbow to accompany his walk. He liked rainbows. For, just like a sky full of stars, he saw them as Mother Nature's gifts to us. He could've easily got the bus to work, but always insisted on walking. But it was a pleasant enough walk from his house on the outskirts of Brighton to the office where he worked in central Hove. And, settling into a steady, efficient pace, he allowed his mind to wander to thoughts of the beautiful, blonde-haired lady that he saw almost every day on his way to work. For the past couple of years this mystery woman passed the other way on his journey at pretty much the same location, by the statue of George IV that stood outside the Royal Pavilion. He could tell if he was running slightly later than usual by where they passed each other. Occasionally the lady would offer him a slight smile by way of acknowledgement. That smile – the slightest of slight smiles, would be enough to send his spirits soaring for the rest of the day. Over the many instances in which their paths had crossed he'd meticulously studied her and her beauty. If it was possible to have a crush at the age of thirty-nine, then this was his. He didn't know her name, her age, whether she was single or not. However, he did know that she had deep blue eyes, luscious thick lips, long fluttering eye lashes and a well-maintained figure that wiggled so sexily as she glided effortlessly along. She dressed immaculately and smelt so alluring that he always found himself sniffing the air after she'd passed by. If he were to look at it rationally, he'd concede that he really didn't have a chance with a woman so far out of his league as her, but fortunately rationality went missing when he thought of this mystery lady. His fantasising broke up the monotonous march to work and, just like his epic game-playing sessions on his games console; it took him away from the drabness of his day-to-day life. Before he knew it he was half-way on his journey to work and reaching the highlight of his walk. And, with the backdrop of the Royal Pavilion adding to the glamour of the moment, true to form there she was – the mystery woman – who, even from afar, looked like she'd excelled in her appearance today. Despite the earlier drizzle, which had now disappeared, her luxuriant hair looked like a professional stylist had spent an hour working on it. Her dress clung to her petit, shapely figure and the smart, spring jacket looked like a fashion designer had specifically chosen it for her to wear. He could feel his heart rate quicken as their paths got closer. Hopefully today she would notice him and smile that slight smile. She was now nearing him, and he prepared himself to look cool and seductive – a tall task dressed and looking as he did. The briskness of his walk had done nothing to aid this effect either. A small layer of sweat beaded over his reddening forehead and the earlier drizzle, which looked like it had miraculously avoided the mystery lady, had firmly made its presence felt on his hair, matting down his uninteresting mop. Thankfully, he wasn't one for checking out his own reflection in windows so he was blissfully unaware of what he was currently putting on public display. Suddenly though, as they were only twenty metres apart, he felt his nose twitch and the overwhelming urge to sneeze came over him. He tried to suppress this urge by attempting to pinch his nose, but just as he reached his hand up to his nose the most almighty sneeze cannoned out. 'AAATTCHOOO!' the sneeze reverberated. Pigeons and seagulls took to the skies and passers-by jumped in fright. The redness produced from his fast-paced walking had now been added to by the deeper scarlet of crushing embarrassment as the mystery lady looked at him still cupping a handful of his spray. Just as he looked up she silkily said, 'Bless you,' before offering him a tissue from a pack in her handbag. Resisting another urge - this time to buckle at the knees at the sound of her voice - he accepted the tissue and cleaned himself up. 'Thank you,' he said bashfully.

'No problem,' she replied, and with a skip and a wiggle she continued her journey.

Stunned, flabbergasted, and with a heart seemingly about to burst, Richard finished wiping away the last traces of his apocalyptic sneeze. He then continued his own journey. With a subtle skip in his own stride, he smiled to himself as he dreamily thought, *she said, "bless you."*

CHAPTER 2

The good cheer Richard felt during the remainder of his journey quickly vanished on arriving at his place of work. He'd grown to loathe this soul-sapping office, and as he stood there staring up at the Victorian façade, he tried to build up the enthusiasm to walk up the five steps that led up to the large, black, wooden front door. He'd worked here since he'd left school, starting at the bottom and not progressing much higher. He was still used very much in an admin role, helping and assisting those with the drive and ambition to fly up the ranks. That's not to say that he was stupid or slow - not at all. He was articulate and intelligent enough. What he lacked *was* that drive and the ambition. And that was why he could often be found at the foot of these steps, willing himself up them. With a deep, resigned breath that was held all the way up the steps, he dispiritedly embarked on another tedious working day.

To say this was a drab, uninspiring office would be a massive understatement. Even the off-white paint that decorated every wall, ceiling and door had dulled over time. Stark lighting tried its best to bring some life to the surroundings but, it fought a losing battle. This, in his view, was the dreariest place on earth. The spacious office floor had been broken up into cubicles which added to the uninviting, oppressive feel, and these cubicles were populated by his colleagues; colleagues who were mostly either morons, arseholes or devoid of any personality altogether, making him, in his own mind at least, seem like George Clooney by comparison.

Martin Bradshaw was the first to greet him as he made his way to his workstation. 'Alright Rich? You're looking particularly dynamic this morning,' he said with a smirk and a look to his peers, craving acknowledgement of this masterfully sarcastic put-down. When no one even bothered to look up from their PCs, Martin moved on, as did Richard who slumped heavily into his chair. Switching on his computer he instinctively produced an inward, involuntary groan that signified the lack of desire he held for the day ahead.

Just then Graeme Chandler, the closest thing to a friend amongst his colleagues, poked his head around Richard's PC monitor. 'Morning Rich, are you going to join us down the pub after work this evening? It's Col's birthday.' Col or Colin Jameson to give him his full name was another one of the merry band of colleagues that populated the Mulberry & Jackson Chartered Accountants office. He was relatively new to the team but had risen quickly to become the golden boy of the company. He was handsome and younger than him by a good ten years. He also possessed the sort of cockiness that he couldn't help but be envious of. One of the bosses, Christian Jackson, had taken a real shine to Colin and this too stuck in his throat. Being the archetypal wallflower, he'd been constantly overlooked for training and promotion. As each year passed he felt less and less valued. It was small wonder that he harboured a subtle, deep-rooted resentment for those that progressed.

'I wasn't planning to…' Richard replied. *What the hell else am I planning to do this evening?!* he thought to himself but instead added, 'But if I'm invited I'd like to join you.'

'I'm inviting you you silly sod. We'll go straight from work. Have your drinking head on. I reckon it could be a messy one,' Graeme said cheerfully as he sauntered over to his desk. Richard wasn't invited out very often so he was mildly excited by this invitation. He also secretly liked the fact they were going out straight from work. This gave him no opportunity to linger at home and get engrossed in another online battle on his games console. It also meant that he didn't have to try and dress up – not that he could. His wardrobe of clothes was so lacklustre that even the local YMCA would turn away his cast-offs.

His working day passed, as it always did, without anything remarkable happening. His eyes and brain ached from staring at his computer screen for long periods. His back felt hunched and decrepit from sitting in the same position for most of the day. A gratuitous stretch just wasn't enough to shake the feeling of physical inactivity that had overwhelmed his body. Everyone else in the office felt in a similar condition as they rose groggily from their workstations; everyone except a sickeningly excitable Colin, who rather crudely announced, 'Alright then! Let's get pissed!' as he marched joyfully along the office floor.

As the group of four men and two ladies marched from the office in Hove down towards the centre of town, Colin flagged a cab down. 'Who wants to jump in with me?' The two ladies were quick to join him; Pauline Matthews; a middle-aged, menopausal woman who was PA to the two owners/directors of the firm, Christian Jackson and Charlotte Mulberry. Pauline was a woman who, back in the day, would've been a real head-turner. Unfortunately, an unwanted divorce had left her bitter, resentful and man-hating. With jet black hair and a busty chest, she dressed as she might've done all those years ago and had an air about her that said, "keep your distance." She scared the hell out of him and distance was something he gave her a lot of. The other lady – and lady being a very loose approximation - was a twenty-three-year-old dizzy, overly flirtatious girl called Emma Buxton. Emma was short and plump – in fact, she was almost perfectly round, like an oversized football. From the very first day she'd joined the firm three years ago in a very junior role he had found her annoying. Her high-pitched, almost false laugh was enough to set his teeth on edge. And her mindless stupidity and lack of basic knowledge left him wondering why they'd ever employed her. But she, like him, had struggled to progress much in the time she'd been with the company and that was one of her saving graces in his mind. With the last space in the taxi quickly being taken by Martin Bradshaw, Richard and Graeme both looked at one another and contented themselves on walking the remainder of the journey. Of course, they could've taken a taxi themselves but neither even considered it. Both valuing the opportunity to stretch their legs after another relatively stationary day.

'I'm glad you're making it out tonight,' Graeme said with genuine warmth as he lit up a cigarette.

'Yeah, well, Megan Fox cancelled our date so I was at a bit of a loose end,' Richard jokingly replied.

Graeme smiled as he exhaled from his cigarette. He was the only person in the office that Richard felt comfortable enough to say anything jocular to. He had little or no rapport with any of his other colleagues. They all treated him with contempt and belittled him whenever they got the opportunity. Graeme was the only one that didn't put him down or laugh at his expense. Outside work he was a family man with a wife and two kids. In his mid-forties, with receding dark brown hair, he was quietly handsome. His dark looks gave him an almost Mediterranean complexion and in many ways his demeanour was very much one from that region. He was a very relaxed character that seemed to get on with everyone and everyone got on with him. If he wasn't quite so pleasant and easy-going Richard would've been envious of him too.

The brisk, easy walk into town finally led them to the pub where they were due to meet. At the bottom of North Street, on the outskirts of the City Centre, was a large, vacuous pub called the Pavilion Tavern or, as locals called it, The Pav Tav. With cheap drinks promotions it was typically frequented by the less refined, and class was something distinctly lacking in this establishment. But it was a good place if all you wanted to do was get mind-bendingly drunk and, if nothing else, it was lively.

Squeezing through the throng of people noisily chatting over one another, Richard and Graeme made their way through the already busy pub to the far end where the others were waiting for them. Despite the fact it was a Thursday evening it seemed the whole world and their mother was out that night. Thursday was most definitely the new Friday in this establishment. By the time they reached the others they were already two drinks behind. 'Here comes the cavalry!' Colin announced as he passed a pint and a shot of Sambuca over to each of them. Richard looked warily at Colin and accepted his drinks with a thank you. He started to sup his pint of lager but Martin Bradshaw was quick to spot the faux pas. 'You're meant to neck the shot you moron, then you can have your pint. Now get it down yer,' he said obnoxiously. Richard hesitated which was all that Martin needed to add, 'What's the worst that can happen eh? You might actually have fun!'

The others laughed raucously which made him blush furiously. He swiftly slugged the shot back and moved as far away from Martin as he could politely get away with. As they talked loudly amongst themselves, Richard scanned the room – not to check out the local talent, but just to see who else would want to spend any more than a minute in this place. Commercial pop/dance music blared out loudly from the pub's speakers making talking and, in fact thinking, pretty much impossible. Fortunately, it wasn't the sort of pub for deep thoughts. There were boisterous groups of lads shouting at one another and boisterous groups of women shouting at one another. The lads eyed up the ladies and the ladies eyed up the lads. It was that sort of pub. The short time he'd been there reminded him why he didn't go out much. If this was all there was to offer, a night playing on his console seemed far more appealing. But then, just as he was about to rejoin the others, out of the corner of his eye he spotted, what was a veritable oasis in the arid desert of this establishment. To his complete amazement he gazed upon his mystery woman majestically gliding through the crowded pub. *What the heck was she doing here?!* She looked glamorous, she looked elegant, she looked… well, far too good to be in a place like this. She drifted passed groups of lads who all turned and stared lecherously as she moved ever closer towards his direction. It took him a moment to realise that he too was staring with his mouth wide open, but by then it was too late. Martin Bradshaw had screwed up a bar receipt and, with unerring accuracy, had managed to throw it right in Richard's gaping gob. Caught by surprise, he gagged and started choking on the crumpled paper projectile that had lodged in the back of his throat. Red-faced, coughing and fighting for air, he finally managed to retrieve the receipt just as she approached him. Through watering eyes, he was greeted by the mystery lady's mildly shocked and embarrassed face as she tried to squeeze past. Her look immediately softened though when she recognised his face. In the background he could see and hear Martin and the others laughing raucously at his misfortune. But he quickly blotted out that sight and sound as he focussed solely on his mystery woman. He'd never been this close to her. Perhaps he would never be again. She smelt terrific and looked like she should be doing a cosmetic commercial with her skin so smooth and perfect. Noticing again that he was just staring at her, he triumphantly showed her the spit-ridden receipt that a moment ago had nearly caused him to choke to death. 'There it is!' he cheerfully announced – not being able to think of anything better to say.

The lady smiled and with one eyebrow seductively arching upward said, 'We really must stop meeting like this.'

Slightly more composed, he wiped his damp hand on his trouser leg and offered it to her. 'I'm so sorry, my name's Richard. We…' he started.

'We pass each other every morning,' she finished for him. Her hand felt so soft and her grip so tender he wondered if her hand was actually within his grasp. 'My name's Francesca… or Frances as my friends call me.' The tone of her voice was so friendly it completely hypnotised Richard.

'Hi Frances,' he said dreamily. 'Pleased to meet you.'

'Speaking of friends… mine are just over there.' She motioned over to a small group of ladies that had escaped his earlier scan. They too looked a bit too attractive and refined for this place but none of them, he surmised, were as attractive as Frances.

'Of course,' he said, making way for her to get past. 'See you tomorrow… Same time, same place!' he chirped as she breezed past him to join her friends. As a parting gift, Frances offered him a gentle smile which sent his heart racing.

Smiling himself now, he moved back to reluctantly join his colleagues who, he couldn't help noticing, were all standing open-mouthed. *Where was a bar receipt when he needed one?* he wondered.

'Who the hell was that?' Graeme said to him in astonishment. 'She's gorgeous.'

'Yeah, but she must be blind if she's talking to ol' Dick here.' Martin added spitefully. 'I mean, did you see that shot? That was perfect. You should've seen yourself Rich. I honestly thought you were going to die!'

Nonplussed, Richard gave Martin a daggered look that did nothing to deter Martin from laughing at him.

'Don't worry about him - he's an idiot,' Graeme said with a reassuring arm on his shoulder as he ushered him away. 'You like her don't you? – What am I saying?! – She's stunning – Any man in his right mind would fancy her… But she spoke to *you* mate.'

'I don't think she had much of a choice to be honest. I was blocking her path whilst nearly choking to death... Anyway, she's a little out of my league don't you reckon?' Richard retorted before taking a heavy swig from his pint. He was still red-faced and his eyes were a little watery, but in amongst the anger he felt towards Martin, he felt mildly elated. He glanced over at Frances who was talking to her friends. She was already attracting attention from other groups of lads stood nearby.

'Yeah, maybe, but it's good to dream,' Graeme said in Richard's ear as he went back to join the others.

In truth, dreaming was all that Richard had ever done with women. He'd never had a girlfriend; he'd never slept with a woman, and his one and only kiss worthy of mention came when he was sixteen at his school-leavers disco. The girl in question that time was an equally shy girl called Louise Baxter. She'd had long, rambling brown hair, a pretty but unremarkable face and was very much the female wallflower of their class. Their similarities had brought them together and their kiss had initially been awkward at the end of a slow dance - their only dance of the night – when they both knew it was now or never. After nearly knocking each another's teeth out as they both leant in too eagerly, they settled into a dreamy kiss that lingered well after the song they were dancing to had finished. Tongues entwined and saliva was exchanged in a fully embraced, teenager's kiss. But it was crudely ended when Chris Simmonds – that period's Martin Bradshaw – had hurled a plastic cup of dubious-looking liquid at Richard's head, showering them both and breaking them out of their blissful moment of magic. In tears, Louise had scurried off, leaving Richard standing there as Chris and his cronies laughed at him. All these years later, that moment still irked him. Many was the time he allowed his thoughts to drift to those of that kiss and to Louise. *I wonder what she's doing now…*

This current evening was passing by quickly as the drinks flowed more readily. Most rounds were accompanied by a chaser of some variety, hastening the steady descent into drunkenness. For the most part, Richard contented himself with talking to Graeme and occasionally Colin, when Martin or the women were away from him. He found he was actually having a good time and after a few drinks he had loosened right up. The pub now didn't seem such a bad choice after all. Amazingly, as he gazed over to check on Frances, she was still there too. A couple of her friends had left leaving her with just one of her companions, but she was still there and looked like she too was enjoying herself. One of the groups of lads had edged steadily closer to Frances and her friend and they looked like they were gearing up to make their move. Whilst Richard and Graeme were talking about nothing much in particular, Richard kept a keen eye on developments in Frances' vicinity. Conveniently, the toilets were situated just past she stood so it seemed like a good excuse to make small talk with her as he made his way there. The alcohol that surged through him made him feel braver than he'd normally feel and his heart began to flutter at the prospect of speaking with her again – albeit to excuse him as he made his way past her to the toilet. From his viewpoint, as he subtly looked over Graeme's shoulder, he could see the group of lads trying to engage in conversation with Frances and her friend. But to his delight he saw that they weren't having a great deal of success. *It was time.* Inhaling a deep breath, he plucked up the courage to head over in her direction. He'd loosened off his tie and he could feel a warm, alcoholic glow which gave him colour to his usually pallid face. As he started to walk he quickly became aware of how drunk he'd become. He tried to adjust his gait so he didn't appear quite as inebriated as he actually was. His eyes remained transfixed on Frances as he awkwardly marched over to where he would have to pass her. 'Sorry, excuse me,' Richard said politely as he ever-so-slightly brushed up against Frances body.

'Yes, what is it now?' she said sharply not seeing him stood behind her.

'Oh, s, sorry... I just wanted to, er, get past to... y'know, go to the toilet,' Richard said sheepishly.

Realising who it was she said, 'I'm sorry; I thought you were one of those lads over there. They're really starting to get on our nerves. To be honest you sounded far too polite to be with them.'

Richard gave an apologetic smile and eased his way past. Plodding into the men's toilet he felt slightly deflated and more drunk by the second. He found the least messy, most hygienic-looking urinal and hurried himself in order to make sure Frances didn't leave without at least a brief word of goodbye. Swaying whilst urinating vigorously, he tried to clear his head by taking some deep breaths of air. Not that the air was all that fresh in this toilet. He could hear someone heaving grievously in one of the cubicles and the smell that emanated was becoming overpowering. On finishing up, he walked over to the basins and washed his hands. The reflection staring back at him was of someone he wasn't used to seeing. This person looked a lot less troubled; a bit more dishevelled - yes, but at this precise moment that didn't seem like a bad thing. But most noticeably he looked happy. Yes, there was definitely a grin or a mischievous smirk on his face that looked like it might stay on there for a while. As he stood there admiring himself in the mirror, a man came and stood beside him to wash his hands. As they both faced the mirror, the man jokingly said, 'I bet it's hard being as pretty as you.' He meant no offense but Richard, suddenly broken out of his moment of self-admiration, coughed and abruptly left the lavatory. He was all a fluster and wasn't paying any attention to where he was going and walked straight into one of the lads who was trying, yet again, and to no avail, to chat-up Frances. Inadvertently, Richard knocked into his arm, splashing a lot of the contents of his pint glass onto the lad's shirt. 'You fuckin' idiot!' the startled and irate lad barked at him.

'I'm so sorry,' an even more flustered Richard said.

'Sorry?! I'll give you sorry. How about I smash this fuckin' glass in your face? Then you'll be sorry.'

'Look, he didn't mean it. Why don't you accept his apology and leave him alone?' Frances cut in. It was like a guardian angel coming to the rescue.

'What's he? Your date or somethin'?' the lad said incredulously. He seemed genuinely shocked that she'd taken the side of this geeky-looking misfit.

'He's got more chance of having a date with me than you,' Frances quickly retorted with probably more gusto than she'd intended. 'Now please stop being so aggressive and go back to playing with your friends.'

Shame-faced the lad was at a loss of what to do. 'Slut!' he childishly spat at Frances. She ignored the comment and tried to continue her conversation with her friend. She certainly didn't want to be intimidated by this moron. But when his comment didn't get any reaction he turned his attention back to Richard. Pushing him he firmly said, 'What are you waiting for? Get me another drink and be lively about it… Actually, wait a minute… You can get us all a round of drinks… With shots.'

'Of course,' Richard resignedly said as he started off towards the bar. Out of the corner of his eye he could see his colleagues, none of which had made any attempt to step in and back him up. Martin Bradshaw nervously laughed behind Graeme's shoulder, obviously praying for Richard to get a good hiding. Then he felt a pull on his arm.

'Hey Rich!' an excited voice said. It was the man who'd stood by him in the bathroom a moment ago. 'I *thought* it was you in the toilet. It's me, Matt… Matt Samson… From school,' he continued slowly running out of enthusiasm and realising perhaps Richard wasn't who he'd thought he was.

But then, from the depths of his booze-muddled memory, Richard recalled who he was; Matt had been his one and only friend at school. They'd lived just across the road from each other and often hung out together. He felt rude for not recognising Matt, but in fairness, Matt had changed considerably since they'd last met. At school Matt had been fairly unremarkable. Like Richard, he'd been relatively quiet and unassuming. They'd taken solace in the other's equally quiet nature. Matt had always been the one to stand up for himself and, at times, stand up for Richard too. But essentially, both of them had left school and no one had really noticed they'd been there at all. The chap that now enthusiastically greeted him seemed a complete contrast to the person he once knew. He stood there, well-groomed and well dressed - like All Saints or Diesel had just used him to model for them. His hair was dark and looked expensively styled; an easy stubble with just the faintest of grey mixed in peppered his chiselled face. It was obvious he took good care of his body; his buff physique certainly suggested so. His shoulders were broad and his arms and chest bulged out from beneath his t-shirt. As he stood there admiring the physical form of modern-day Matt, he found himself a little lost for words. But just as Matt was about to give up, he said, 'Oh yeah... Matt. How are *you*?'

'I'm...' Matt started, but before he could continue, the beer-soaked lad cut in. 'Oi, stop chatting to your boyfriend. Those drinks aren't gonna get themselves... Come on, chop chop.'

'A friend of yours Rich?' Matt said, averting his attention and not taking his eyes off the lad who'd rudely interrupted him.

Matt stood a couple of inches taller than him, and with a confidence that Richard could only dream of, he stared down the lad. Tension hung in the air as onlookers started to take a keen interest in how this scene was going to play out. It was a case of who was going to blink first and Matt had no intention of it being him. Conceding, the lad buckled and submissively said, 'He... he was just getting us a round of drinks.'

'And why would he do that?' Matt replied, his face stern and unyielding. His eyes bore into the lad who was visibly unravelling now.

'Well... h-he was going to buy us a round of drinks coz he spilt my p-pint down me,' the lad stuttered, having now completely lost his bottle. By way of trying to back up his statement, he showed the stain on his shirt caused by the spillage.

'Wait a minute, so my mate Rich has got to buy you *all* a round of drinks...' Matt started.

'With shots,' one of the lad's friends nervously chipped in.

"...with shots,' Matt continued, 'because he accidentally spilt a drink on *you*?' He paused for effect. The music in the place was still blaring away but it was as if it wasn't playing at all as the tense atmosphere hung heavily between them. 'If that's the case it seems only fair to me that my mate Rich should spill a drink on the rest of you idiots too. What do you think?' he said looking around.

'Nah you're alright mate. We were just leavin' anyway,' the now humbled lad said as he prompted his buddies to drink up. In the blink of an eye the group of lads eked towards the exit, a couple of them even saying, "excuse me," as they pushed past.

Once the lads were well out of earshot, a totally gobsmacked Richard turned to Matt and said, 'That was *amazing*!'

'Nah, that was nothing. They're just idiots. It's not hard to bring them down to size when you take the alpha-male out of the equation,' he said modestly. 'Anyway, just think of the money I just saved you on that round... I think you owe me a pint.'

'With pleasure,' Richard gratefully replied.

And just when he thought he couldn't be anymore stunned, Frances added, 'You can get me one as well if you like.'

'Of course. Would your friend like a drink too?' he asked politely. The alcohol had broken him out of his shyness, and the elation he now felt from witnessing Matt's dismissal of the beer-boys gave him a sudden shot of confidence.

Having taken all the drinks orders he strutted to the bar. Whilst he was up there, Graeme sauntered over. Unlike Richard, the effects of the copious amounts of alcohol had hardly made a mark on him. 'I'm off now mate. See you at work tomorrow. And don't be too late,' he said through a friendly smile as he shook Richard's hand and patted him on the shoulder.

Moments later Matt joined him. 'I'll give you hand with the drinks,' he said. 'I gotta say, it's great to see you Rich. You really haven't changed. When I saw you in the bogs, I thought, that's Richie Chambers; but when I spoke to you, you ran off! That did make me laugh.' Matt talked confidently and with a perfect smile emblazoned on his face. His eyes became like narrow slits when he smiled, showing just what a friendly, happy and approachable person, he was. When they were teenagers at school Matt was always giggling and joking. He'd had a mischievous streak – mainly when it was just the two of them - which had always made Richard nervous. Deep down he was just jealous that Matt had the courage to do the odd naughty thing, knowing he stood a chance of getting into trouble. Matt leaned over on the bar as Richard relayed his order to the barman. 'How do you know the ladies then?' he asked, nodding his head in the direction of Frances and her friend.

That'll be right, Richard thought, *Matt will cruise on in there with his good looks and smooth charm and Frances won't even remember she'd ever met me.* He could feel his elated mood rapidly diminish like a fast-deflating balloon. He wanted to say that Frances was his girlfriend and they were on a date or something like that to deter Matt from sweeping her off her feet. In actuality he knew he couldn't and Matt wouldn't have believed him anyway.

'The one that looks like she's off the cover off a fashion magazine – that's Frances. I walk past her every day on my way to work. Today was the first day I've ever spoken to her. The other lady's her friend. I don't know her name,' he said dejectedly as they made their way back over to the ladies.

'Don't worry mate. I can see you like her… I won't cramp your style.' Matt whispered the last part into Richard's ear. *What style?* Richard laughingly thought to himself. 'Besides, she's not my type,' Matt added with a disarming smile. Richard wasn't convinced by that last statement. *Surely Frances was everyone's type.*

Somewhat reassured but still a little sceptical, Richard handed the ladies their drinks and everyone introduced themselves to one another. Frances' friend was called Jenny. She was short and had wavy auburn coloured hair that flowed down past her shoulders. Richard thought her dark eyes and long eyelashes were very captivating and she had a genuine, friendly nature that made him instantly relax around her. They were all talking and laughing and it wasn't long before he felt happy and comfortable again. He looked over to where his colleagues had been and saw they'd all left. *Good of them to say goodbye,* he thought. He didn't linger on that thought for long though. For the first time in what seemed an eternity he was actually having fun. He really couldn't remember the last time he'd had fun that didn't involve staring at a TV screen with a games-controller in his hand. It transpired that Frances worked as a lecturer at Brighton University. When she announced that, he was taken aback; she certainly didn't look like a lecturer, but when she added that she lectured on Fashion and Fashion History it made a lot more sense. By now the alcohol was really kicking in again and his focus kept drifting. He found it harder to concentrate on the conversations which now seemed to pass him by. He stood there, sipping his pint, swaying and grinning inanely. He studied every inch of Frances as he listened to her speak. Her voice wasn't what you'd call posh but she was well spoken and every word she said was like poetry to his ears; drawing him in; entrancing him. Choosing his moments to scan her figure so he didn't appear too lecherous, he noticed her petit but shapely figure didn't seem to carry much fat, although she certainly wasn't what you'd call skinny. Her breasts were pert and proportionate to her frame, and if he looked hard enough (which he was trying so very hard not to) he could make out the pattern of her bra beneath her shirt.

'So,' Matt began, 'have either of you got boyfriends?' The unsubtle question shook Richard out of his state of bliss and he temporarily sobered up in order to hear Frances' reply. Matt returned to sipping his pint, with the same mischievous look on his face that Richard remembered him having all those years ago, while he waited for the answers to fall from the ladies' lips.

Not at all bothered by the unsubtle conversation-turner, both ladies were quick to answer. Jenny answered first. 'I'm not actually seeing anyone at the moment,' she said as she flicked Matt flirtatious look.

'I've just come out of a fairly heavy relationship.' Frances said. 'I was with my ex for eight years and I have finally got myself back to where I want to be… It's taken some time…'

'Why did you split up?' Richard found himself saying. A moment ago, he'd been staring at her bra; now he found himself staring deep into her eyes, intent on hearing her answer.

She seemed slightly taken aback and stuttered a little before saying, 'We just became different people from the people we were when we first met.' The melancholy tone of her reply told him not to press any further. There was an awkward pause and, looking at Jenny, he could see this was still a very sensitive subject.

'One for the road?' Matt quickly cut in to soften the mood.

'I've got to go,' Frances responded.

'Come on – one more,' Matt encouraged, and after the slightest of arm-twisting they all stayed for one last drink.

It had been some years since Richard had heard the *"last orders"* bell in a pub. On the very rare occasions he'd been out before he'd usually left a couple of drinks into proceedings. He'd never felt comfortable enough to stay beyond that and he'd always had a hard job letting himself go. By this stage though he was more than a few sheets to the wind; in fact, he was a whole laundry basket. The heady glow the alcohol had given his face made him look much healthier than he usually looked, and the childlike smile that was there earlier had made a reappearance. Their conversation took a sillier direction, and they now found themselves all laughing at his misfortune earlier in the day and, again, that evening. For once he found himself laughing along with those laughing at him. He had to admit that both his cataclysmic sneeze on his way to work and his near-choking-to-death experience must've looked hilarious to anyone witnessing either mishap. And he also had to admit that without both instances, he wouldn't be stood there talking to Frances, Matt and Jenny.

As they were slowly ushered out the front door of the pub by the bar exhausted staff who'd given up the will to live, the four of them all gave one another a friendly hug and kiss goodbye. The effects of the alcohol protected them from the chilly breeze that now swept around them. Richard conceded he'd had more fun in those past few hours than he'd had in the rest of his life combined, and he felt a great deal more affinity with these three than he'd felt with any other group of people before – and that included his family. Perhaps it was the ample amount of booze accentuating his feelings but he couldn't deny that feeling of belonging he'd rarely ever felt. When he came to kiss Frances goodbye he savoured every millisecond of that moment. The smell of her perfume, the look of her perfect skin and her soft, luscious lips. Lips that, although he didn't kiss them, he so wanted to. A quick kiss on the side of the cheek had to suffice. He desperately wanted to ask her out for a date as they parted but years of shyness came flooding back, drowning the new-found confidence he'd acquired that evening. The words he wanted to say, stuck in his throat and he went back to being "Richard the wallflower; the man no one noticed."

The ladies gave a final, friendly wave goodbye as they walked towards the taxi rank around the corner and Matt put his strong, muscular arm around Richard. 'Come on, let's take a stroll. We can walk off some of this alcohol,' he said.

'Suits me,' Richard replied in a very downbeat tone.

'Hey, what's up mate?'

After a lengthy pause, when Matt had almost thought Richard hadn't heard him and was about to repeat himself, Richard mumbled, 'I don't know... I had such a good time tonight. I didn't want it to end.' He felt like Cinderella running from the ball at the end of her own glorious evening; although he wasn't running – he was swaying and veering along the pavement with his hands tucked deep inside his coat pockets. The stiff breeze had started to make its presence felt and they both now felt decidedly chilly as they staggered along the road that ran past the Royal Pavilion - the grandiose and seemingly out-of-place former royal palace. He managed a passing glance to acknowledge where he was, but in truth, having lived in Brighton his entire life, he'd become a bit blasé to the beauty and splendour of this magnificent structure. His vision was more focussed down towards the few feet of pavement that stretched out in front of them.

'Why didn't you ask Frances for her number?' Matt asked.

'I don't know… I wanted to. I'm just not all that confident around women. I didn't want to give her the opportunity to say no.'

This brought a smile to Matt's face. 'You really think she'd say that? She's been wounded by whatever went on in her previous relationship – you could see that. The company of someone like you might be just what she needs.'

'Come on mate. You've seen her. She's gorgeous.'

'And?...'

'And look at me… I'm hardly Bradley Cooper.'

'Maybe she doesn't want Bradley Cooper. Maybe she goes for someone like you.'

This simple comment shook Richard out of his melancholy stupor. *I hadn't thought of it like that*. He still didn't fully believe that he was anywhere near the sort of chap that a woman like Frances would go for… but he could be. With some help from his old school chum, he felt he might be just the sort. His heart suddenly lifted and his mind began racing. A thousand thoughts filled his mind in what seemed like seconds. "Can I ask a favour?"

'Of course. Whatever you like.'

'Would you go shopping with me? – You know, sort of make me over.'

'Richie, it will be my pleasure.' Matt said happily as he gave Richard a friendly one-armed hug. 'Who's Bradley Cooper anyway?!'

CHAPTER 3

As Richard's trusty alarm clock let out it's subtle, repetitive beep next morning it sounded like the most annoying and unnecessary sound he'd ever heard. He groggily reached out to switch it off before it awoke his parents. A flashback to the previous night popped into his head. He remembered getting in around half past midnight and trying so very hard not to make any noise as he spilled through the front door. As he'd crept up the stairs, every single step seemed to creak at a volume he'd never heard before. He'd managed to make his way to the top and without the usual care, stumbled his way along the landing to the bathroom to relieve himself from the aching and overwhelming urge he had to empty his bladder. He'd swayed from side to side, forward and back, with his pee splashing noisily into the pan and sending spray all over the toilet and onto the floor. The memory made him wince. He now struggled to open his eyes which seemed as if they were glued shut and, with all the effort he could muster, tried to raise his head which felt like it was the weight of a large cannonball. There was a distinct lack of moisture in his mouth and his tongue seemed to have dried up and stuck itself to the roof of his mouth. Despite the short time he'd been awake, it was easy for him to assess his current state... he felt like complete and utter shit... Today would be a very long day.

His next mission was to make his way to the bathroom, remembering this time, to be as careful and meticulous as he usually was, and not as he cringingly remembered he'd been the previous night. The bathroom light seemed savagely bright this morning. He shielded his eyes with his hand as the light, which seemed like it was beamed straight from the sun itself, threatened to blind him permanently. Once his eyes had finally adjusted to the unnecessary brightness, he made his way over to the mirror. He had to double-take when he gazed upon the reflection staring back at him. It was now apparent that not only did he *feel* like complete and utter shit, but he *looked* like complete and utter shit too. He decided not to dwell on the view for too long and went over to the toilet to relieve himself. Staring down it was like returning to the scene of a crime. Large splashes of last nights' drunken piss were still clearly evident. After he'd finished he gave the toilet a good wipe to remove the incriminating traces and stripped down to take a quick shower. He had the vain hope that it would make him feel a bit more "with it." Unfortunately, as he dragged himself out the shower a short while later, he just felt like a damper version of the tattered sole that had entered the shower moments earlier.

As he finished getting ready for work everything he did seemed to take twice as long as it normally did. But then came the sudden realisation that he would miss his daily rendezvous with Frances. This time yesterday he hadn't even known her name. Now he knew that and lots more besides. It was now all the more important to make sure he was on time. This sudden jolt back to life triggered a shot of adrenaline that spurred him into action. He focussed and instantly felt better. Although he didn't look a million dollars, he left the house just a few minutes later than he would've normally left. The sky that greeted him couldn't have been any greyer without raining, but he barely seemed to notice. Whilst keeping up a hurried pace he munched on a slice of peanut butter on toast which did nothing to moisten his stale, parched mouth. But he was feeling better than he thought he ought to and his mind was now firmly concentrated on the mission at hand. His stride quickened in an attempt to make up the lost minutes taken from his sluggish start and before long he felt like he was on target again. Beads of sweat - and most likely alcohol - trickled down his face and his shirt began to stick to his back as he rapidly strutted along. So focussed was he though, that he barely noticed. Quicker than usual, he approached the point where their paths normally crossed – the northern entrance to the Royal Pavilion. His adrenalin was pumping hard but, as he frantically scanned everywhere, his heart dropped and he felt all the excitement and enthusiasm drain from him. *Where was she?* His paced slowed until he stood at a confused standstill. People who weren't looking for a woman they'd only just had the courage to speak to, busied past him as he stood deflated in the middle of the wide pavement. He knew that it was going to take a monumental amount of effort to get his legs moving and continue his journey to work.

The rest of the journey was walked with the heavy burden of his dark thoughts choking his mind. There was obviously a simple reason why Frances wasn't there at their usual rendezvous point, but his mind was racing with more outlandish scenarios. By the time he'd made it to work he looked and felt miserable. Unfortunately for him the first person to greet him as he reached his desk was Martin Bradshaw. 'Woah, look at what the cat dragged in.' He said this with a look, as he always did after aiming a derogatory comment at Richard, towards his imaginary audience. 'You *really* have excelled yourself today *Dick*,' he continued. 'Just when I thought you couldn't look anymore shit, you go and turn up like this – *Amazing*!'

The smarmy smirk emblazoned across Martin's face was more than Richard could bear. 'Oh, why don't you just *bugger off* you horrible little man!' he snarled. 'You're not funny; you never *have* been and you never *will* be!' The cutting put-down and its venomous delivery shocked even him, but now his adrenalin was pumping again as he stood, staring wild-eyed at the dumbstruck face of Martin Bradshaw. A few others in the office had heard this and sat there equally shocked. Nervous giggles then cut through the tension. 'Now if you've nothing else to say, get out of my way.' he finished. With that, two or three of the office juniors sitting further back laughed and clapped as a completely embarrassed Martin Bradshaw made way for Richard to pass. Richard slumped into his chair and gave Martin one last glare causing him to scurry away. Richard might be a kind-hearted soul but he'd reached his fill with the likes of Martin

Bradshaw. Years of soul-crushing put-downs had taken their toll on his self-esteem and he'd finally found the gumption to bite back. Perhaps it was the traces of last night's alcohol still filtering through his system or the fact that he was funnelling his disappointment of Frances' no show, but whatever it was, he'd swiftly seen off the office bully in thirty seconds flat… And, as he sat there with his blood pumping hard and his body shaking from the sudden surge in adrenalin, he had to confess it felt good.

Seconds later, a flabbergasted Graeme came over. 'Oh…my…GOD! Where the hell did *that* come from? That was brilliant!' he exclaimed. Then he noticed that there was more than a little bit of truth in Martin Bradshaw's comment. 'He did have a point though mate. You don't look great. I take it you stayed in the pub for a long time after I left?'

'Yes, I did. I had a really excellent night though,' Richard said in a voice that contradicted his statement.

'So, what happened?' Graeme eagerly enquired.

'I think I've discovered why I don't drink to excess – especially when I've got work to contend with next morning,' Richard sighed as he rubbed his sweat-matted hair. The adrenalin that, a moment ago, had pumped some life back into his exhausted, booze-ravaged body, had now ebbed away, leaving him feeling nauseous and clammy. His head pounded like it had its very own woodpecker pecking away inside.

Graeme looked sympathetically at the fast-unravelling form of Richard and said, 'Listen, go to the toilets and splash some water on your face and I'll get you a cup of coffee. I'll get you some paracetamol too. You look like you need them.'

In the small toilet, Richard spent a few minutes trying to compose himself. The spontaneous reaction he'd had to Martin had surprised even him. He felt elated. *Why had it taken so many years of his abuse and bullying to finally put him in his place?* He spent a moment studying the reflection looking back at him. There was no two ways about it – he looked dreadful. His eyes looked like they still had alcohol swimming around inside them; his skin was so pale that they would have to find a new, whiter shade of white to compare it to. But as he stood there remarking on his dishevelled appearance, it was this morning's quirk of character that was beginning to make him think. For so long he'd followed rules and sat idle as the world went by without him. Was this the moment when he finally took charge of his life and changed the direction it was heading? Was it now time to give life a run for its money? He was unsure where this sudden injection of motivation had come from but, to be honest, he didn't really care. Despite his physical state, inwardly, he felt terrific. Feeling a lot more positive he took a deep breath and splashed some cold water on his face before returning to his workstation. Sitting there on his desk was a cup of coffee, two paracetamol tablets and a post-it note from Graeme simply saying, "*Good on you mate.*"

Although a struggle, the rest of the day passed by mercifully quickly. His mind was filled with fast-moving thoughts of new possibilities. It was like he'd woken from a coma and was now trying to adjust to the influx of information his brain was receiving. He kept himself to himself throughout the remainder of the day, despite constantly overhearing excited chatter from other colleagues regaling his cutting dismissal of Martin. He almost felt sorry for him now. *No, wait, Martin Bradshaw is an arsehole and will always be an arsehole,* Richard reasoned. And like any bully - and that was what Martin essentially was, a bully - Martin needed putting in his place. No, he didn't feel pity for him, just a slight pang of regret that he hadn't stood up to him much sooner. As his working day reached its end, he picked up his coat, said goodbye to Graeme and wished him a good weekend. He tried to avoid eye contact with Martin Bradshaw but couldn't help looking over to where he was sat. Just as their gaze met, Martin quickly looked down to his desk, as if he were working on something vitally important.

Stepping into the fresh, late springtime air he instinctively pulled his coat tighter around him. He was feeling fatigued and this heightened his sensitivity to the cold. He was just contemplating getting on the bus to hasten his journey home when he felt a weird vibrating sensation emanating from his trouser pocket. He felt down and pulled out his mobile phone. He'd completely forgotten what it was to receive a call, and as looked at the name that appeared a smile came to his face.

'Hello Rich, how are you?' Matt's voice was upbeat and chipper; everything Richard wasn't.

'I'm good… Well, actually I'm absolutely shattered… Wait a minute; how did you know my number?' a befuddled Richard asked.

'You gave it to me last night as we walked home you numpty. I gave you my number too. I actually had to punch in the digits though as you couldn't focus on the screen enough to do it yourself.'

'Wow, how drunk was I then? I can't remember that at all.'

'Very. But don't worry. That's what's meant to happen when you drink as much as we did.' Matt could almost hear Richard ruffling his hair in puzzlement at the other end of the phone so he continued quickly. 'Listen, the reason I'm calling is I'm in town having a few after-work drinks with some lads I work with. Do you want to join us?'

In the last twenty-four hours, Richard's world had been turned upside down - and not in a bad way either as far as he could tell. He was struggling to compute everything that had happened and *was* happening right now. No one ever phoned him. It was a rare event if he ever went out. Now he was looking at the prospect of entering a pub two days in a row.

'Helloooo. Are you still there Rich?' came a slightly concerned sounding Matt.

'I'm sorry. I was miles away… er, yes, I'll come and meet you. Where?'

'We're in The King & Queen, near the Pavilion. Come join us.'

'Okie dokie, I will. See you in a bit.' He placed the phone back in his pocket and, with a sudden spring in his step, made his way to the pub.

The pub in question, The King & Queen, was a large, mock-Tudor style pub. It was large and, at the time of his entry, not very busy. It'd been a few years since he'd last been in this place but nothing had seemed to have changed; the floor was carpeted with the same threadbare carpet it had always had and the décor was still the same – complete with all the stains and scuffs. The only thing that had changed was the price of a pint. he received his change from the barman and scanned the pub for Matt. He couldn't see him but soon heard lots of laughing and loud chatter coming from where the pool table was. He walked over and was greeted by Matt who looked like he'd sunk a few pints already.

'Aaaaayy! Rich, you made it. Lads, meet a very old friend of mine, Richie Chambers. We used to go to school together.'

'You said you never went to school!' a young lad, no more than twenty-one years old said. Everyone laughed including Richard, but more out of nervousness than anything else. 'Alright Rich, I'm Adam,' the young lad said and gave Richard a strong and vigorous handshake. His hand felt rough despite his youthful age. Adam had flecks of paint on his face and brown hair and his clothes showed the tell-tale signs that he was obviously in the painting and decorating trade. He seemed genuinely friendly and had a face that said as much.

Another chap came over to greet Richard. He was a lot older, in his late fifties, with grey hair and a white stubbly beard. He had narrow eyes, sharp features and smelt strongly of cigarettes. 'Ello Rich. Good to meet you. Matt hasn't stopped talking about you all day. I'm Alan. Matt and I are working on a job together at the moment. I've known 'im years. He's a crackin' lad. Any friend o' Matt's is a friend o' mine.' Alan then gave him another strong and vigorous handshake and went back to playing pool.

There was one person that hadn't come over to say hello. He was a bulky, hard-looking character with tattoos the full length of his arms and protruding from the collar of his t-shirt. He was stood with a pool cue in his hand staring fervently at the game taking place. Richard ambled over to him and held out his hand 'Hi, I'm Richard or Rich as Matt calls me.'

The bulky chap, without looking at Richard, gave the hand a brief but firm shake, said 'Alright Richard,' then moved off to take his shot. Richard got the distinct impression that he wasn't welcome. He turned back to talk to Matt who was laughing at Alan for potting the white ball.

'I don't think your friend likes me,' Richard said nervously, nodding towards the Matt's friend who was now moving around the table to take his next shot.

'Who, Jamie? Nah, he's alright.' Matt explained. 'He just gets a bit serious when he's playing pool. We work together. We've got a building company… I told you last night.'

That would explain why Matt, who was dressed like a model last night, currently looked like a dust-covered refugee. Richard feigned remembrance so he didn't resemble someone with amnesia and took a long sip of his pint. *My god that tasted good*! he thought to himself. All day his mouth had felt like the bottom of a zookeeper's boot; the fetid flavour of a hangover had made his taste buds seem as though they were obsolete. As he took another long chug of his ice-cold lager he could feel himself coming back to life. The warm glow of alcohol brought colour back to his cheeks and in no time he'd drained the remainder of his pint and was at the bar again ordering a round for everyone else. He might not have been one for going out very often but he knew the social etiquette involved when it came to buying a drink. It would be a lot easier to be accepted by Matt's colleagues if they thought he wasn't a skinflint.

Matt followed him to the bar and leant lazily against it with his handsome face beaming an unstoppable smile. 'You look a damn sight better than you did when you first came in,' he said cheerily.

'I *feel* a damn sight better than I did when I first came in,' Richard replied.

'Did you bump into Frances today on your way to work?'

'No, I didn't,' Richard said with a slight shake of his head. 'It was probably a good thing though because I wasn't looking or feeling my best. Given my previous two meetings with her, I'd have probably thrown up on her and that's never a good look.' They both laughed.

'Yeah, I doubt she'd be so forgiving this time when she's picking carrots out of her hair!' Matt added through his giggling. They were both brought back to their teenage years when they used to make each other laugh and, once they stopped chuckling, they both gave each other a look that acknowledged just that.

As Richard looked away he saw Jamie, the bulky chap, looking intimidatingly at him. 'I'd better take the drinks over.'

'I'll give you a hand,' Matt said.

'There you go,' Richard said, handing Jamie his pint.

With a slight grunt of gratitude Jamie went back over to the pool table where he set his pint down and picked up his pool cue. 'Hope you didn't cheat whilst my back was turned you mangy old git,' he said to Alan who was quick to hold his hands up in innocence.

One pint became two, two became three and before Richard new it, he was drunk again. But fatigue was starting to set in and he decided he'd better get home whilst he could still walk. For the past hour or so he'd been swaying and on the periphery of conversations. The earlier lift the alcohol had given him had receded and now he knew the time was right to leave. Besides, he was now craving food. He hadn't really eaten much all day. Now he was ravenous. He said his goodbyes and just as he left, Matt grabbed him and said, 'Are we still meeting tomorrow?'

'I don't know…Are we?' Richard said slightly confused.

'You said you wanted to go into town on Saturday and get some new clobber and stuff.'

'Oh yes! - Sorry! I need a good night's sleep I think. My brain's all over the place. What time do you want to meet?'

'The earlier the better; before the masses turn up. Listen, let's have breakfast somewhere and then hit the shops. I'm also going to book you into my barbers too if you don't mind. Let's jazz up that sorry barnet of yours.' Matt knew from old how sensitive Richard was so quickly added, 'No offense. But you asked me to make you over and I intend to do just that.'

Richard didn't take any offense. He could never be offended by Matt. He was excited about the prospect of bringing his appearance into the twenty first century.

He left the pub just as it was beginning to get too busy. The couple of hours in which he'd been there had seen an influx of people and he was glad to be leaving now as he really didn't like over-crowded places.

Stopping off at a fast-food place on the way home, he stocked up on some much-needed carbs before he finally and wearily made it to his front door. As he put the key in the lock he let out a deep breath. He knew what awaited him once inside. He slowly and apprehensively turned the key and opened the door.

'Where the bloody 'ell 'ave you been?' were his mother's first words as he pushed open the living room door. She was a fairly rotund woman, with a chubby, red face and an auburn-coloured perm. She wore too much jewellery, none of which carried any value and poured herself into clothing that was far too tight for her lumpy frame; this figure-hugging dress was a classic example.

'I've been with Matt - remember Matt Samson from across the road?'

'Who?...oh I remember; that little runty thing. Never liked 'im...Whatchoo doin' wiv 'im?'

'I met him last night when I was out with some people from work.'

'Wait a minute. You went out?...And you had fun? 'Ere, Gerry! Our boy's only gone out and had fun!' She was shouting out to Richard's father, Gerry, who seemed to spend most of his life in a horizontal position. This time he was stretched out full-length on the tattered, red leather sofa. Richard couldn't help thinking her resembled Jabba the Hutt wearing a beer-stained vest; a look, he was grateful, wasn't on show to the public. Why his mother felt the need to shout at him when he was less than five feet away from her was beyond Richard's comprehension. Without averting his gaze from the TV, which Richard recognised to be showing "*Eastenders*" at an unnecessarily loud volume (which might now explain why his mother had been shouting), his father, just grunted, as if he'd been woken into the real world. And, with his smoke-ravaged voice said 'Is that right boy? Did you 'ave fun? We thought you was upstairs playing yer game and pullin' yer plonker.'

Richard tried to ignore that comment and escape their ridicule. His bedroom was like a sanctuary to him and right now he could feel its calling. As Richard trudged dispiritedly upstairs, he could hear his father laughing at him; his rasping cackle only stopped by a hacking cough. The overly loud TV was still blaring out with one cockney character shouting at another cockney character about something cockney related. He assumed that both cockney characters were in the same room. *Why did they have to shout at each other all the time?* he wondered.

CHAPTER 4

Even though his alarm didn't go off this morning, Richard still woke at his usual time. He was really looking forward to the day ahead and it didn't take any effort to lift himself up from his bed. He rubbed his eyes and with his customary care negotiated his way to the bathroom.

In no time he was ready. Try as he might though - and he recognised he needed to try – he knew he was fighting a losing battle to look cool and trendy. He really didn't want to look an embarrassment to Matt when they met up. A pair of poorly fitting jeans that had long lost what little shape and colour they might've originally had and a white v-neck t-shirt was as good as it was going to get unfortunately. He'd tried to brush his hair into some sort of style but he knew that as soon as he started walking the breeze and the lack of haircare over the years meant it would quickly revert to its natural state of a listless mop. As he was about to leave he looked at the kitchen clock which told him he'd been too efficient in getting ready and would have to wait a while before he left the house. It was only 7:30am. He decided to kill some time by switching on the TV and catching up on the news. Two minutes into this and he soon wished he hadn't bothered. Suicide bombings, train strikes, political codswallop and images from war-torn countries left him feeling thoroughly depressed. *Why's there never any good news to report?*

Surely the world can't be devoid of anything positive to make people aware of. He quickly switched off the TV before he found himself needing to watch a catch-up episode of *"Eastenders"* to cheer his mood. There was a reason he didn't watch the news…

He left the house with bright sunshine giving his spirits the lift they needed. Despite it being late spring, it was unseasonably warm, almost like a late summer's day. The air smelt of a million different things all exploding into life. The leaves on the trees looked an amazing emerald green and everything had a fresh, clean sheen to it. The sun felt warm on his face as he meandered his way along the long road that led into the centre of Brighton. He noticed the tulips and daffodils were still in bloom, giving their last flourish before they died back for another year. Cherry and apple trees out in full blossom also added to a wonderful, colourful scene. He couldn't help but feel cheerful with all this natural splendour filling his senses.

During his walk he passed the odd waif and stray who were making their way home from wherever they'd been partying; all of them making little or no attempt to make eye contact with him. These were creatures of the night and the bright morning light was less welcome to them. Brighton was arguably the party capital of Great Britain and it was with a large pang of regret that he'd never really used it to its potential. It was this thought that triggered him to lose himself in his own little world again; thinking of all the things he hadn't done, and a melancholy feeling came over him. He was woken from those morose thoughts when a little Jack Russell barked at him as he neared. It was a cute and lively. Richard bent down to stroke it 'Hello little fella, how are you?'

'His name's Barney,' the elderly male owner said. 'Go on, you can stroke him if you like... Don't worry, he won't bite.'

Richard offered his hand for the dog to sniff before stroking him. Barney sniffed his hand and gave it a quick nip causing him to jolt back. *I thought you said he wouldn't bite me!*

'Barney! You naughty boy!' the owner chastised the bewildered dog.

'Don't worry,' Richard said reassuringly as he carried on his journey. 'Goodbye Barney. Be a good boy,' he continued as he waved his farewell. He loved animals. He'd never been allowed a pet of his own. His parents had always told him they made too much mess and cost too much money to keep. He'd discovered at a very young age that it was pointless to argue with his parents about anything. They did a good job of ganging up on him and forcing their will upon him. He'd contented himself with pouring his love for a pet on his Gran's loveable black Labrador, Benji. When he thought of Benji he always thought of him with such love. In truth, it was the love for this dog that would give him the semblance of love his life lacked. He had been devastated when Benji had died. Old age and arthritis had caught up with him and he'd reached the point where he could barely stand. When his Gran had said she was going to take him to the vets to have him put to sleep, he had insisted on accompanying them. As Benji lay on the vet's examination table, he said his final goodbye to the dog he'd loved so dearly. Afterwards, as they stood heartbroken outside the vets, he and his Gran had sobbed in each other's arms. Only they knew what their beloved pet had meant to them. His Gran would never have another pet after that, such was the loss she'd felt. The thought still felt so fresh and vivid that he realised his eyes were moist at the recollection. He blinked and two lonely tears fell down his face. He allowed them to stay there a while before wiping their traces away.

He was nearly at his destination now. His walk had taken him through the North Lanes, a vibrant and bohemian part of town, which was slowly coming to life. Shop owners were setting up ready for a busy day ahead. He liked Brighton when it was like this. Not yet bustling, but not long in being so. It really was the calm before the storm.

He reached the café where he'd agreed to meet Matt and discovered he was unfashionably early - half an hour early to be precise. *Oh well* he thought to himself *I'll just read a newspaper whilst I wait.* He ordered a cup of tea and picked up a copy of the only available paper, The Sun. Two pages into it he had to put it down. This tabloid paper seemed to be ignorant to all the depressing news that he'd seen on the TV earlier. Fair enough it had managed to avoid these downbeat stories, but it had also miraculously avoided including anything of any substance at all – good *or* bad. Instead, they'd concentrated their efforts on news about supposed "celebrities." Despite war and famine going on in some parts of Africa and The Middle East, the front page of this newspaper concentrated their efforts on a plastic-looking, Z-list celebrity, suspected of having a boob job. This continued onto the next couple of pages. *Just how much can you write about someone having a boob job?* There was a reason he didn't read a newspaper… Instead of reading the newspaper, he contented himself with looking out the window at the eclectic array of people passing by the café. Brighton is home to some weird and wonderful inhabitants. He acknowledged he was probably the least weird and least wonderful person that currently inhabited the City. There were so many people here, that lived their lives, not caring what anyone thought, what they looked like, who they spoke to, who they kissed or shared their time with. He was having another subtle epiphany. They seemed to be coming thick and fast now. *What the hell have I been doing with my life?* he questioned. He didn't intend on growing dreadlocks, getting loads of tattoos and piercing various parts of his body, but he decided he wanted to look slightly more remarkable than he currently did. This latest realisation caused him to take a large intake of breath and without even realising, he let out a massive, involuntary sigh. 'UUuurrgggghhhhhhhh!' The collective weight of thirty-nine years of living a seemingly wasted life had inadvertently made this sigh a great deal louder than it needed to be. In fact, so audible and obvious was the sigh, that a man sitting two seats along from him, turned his head from the teacup he was about to drink from and gave him a worried look. He blushed and looked down at his own cup. Picking the paper back up, he opened it up around him. *Now, who was this celebrity again, and has she really had a boob job?*

Matt was not long in arriving. In contrast to his work attire worn the previous day, today he was back looking and dressing like a male model. Preened to within an inch of his life, Matt sat there unwittingly garnering looks from other patrons of the cafe and passers-by. Men and women, straight or gay all turned their heads on seeing him. For his part, Matt was oblivious. He was concentrating his attention on Richard and seemed as excited as him about the day ahead. As they ate breakfast they enthusiastically discussed plans for Richard's big makeover. The conversation was effortless. It was as if there'd been no wilderness years between them. They barely noticed that they'd gobbled up all their breakfast and drank their tea as they left still chuckling about old times. 'Do you trust me?' Matt said to Richard as they stepped out onto the pavement.

'Of course. Why?' Richard replied, somewhat perplexed.

'Because if I'm to make you over, you have to trust my judgement.' Matt's face was full of sincerity.

'I trust you,' Richard said with equal sincerity. 'Besides, anything you can do to improve my appearance would be better than I've currently done myself.' He stood back gesturing to his current attire.

'Excellent. How do you like the colour pink?' A big mischievous big grin stretched across Matt's face as he walked towards the first shop.

'You're joking right?... Please tell me you're joking,' Richard said as he scurried after Matt.

The North Lanes, bristling with cool boutique shops, cafés, restaurants and bars, was an area Matt knew well and shopped at regularly. He wasn't such a fan of the bigger, more commercial shops in the nearby Churchill Square shopping centre. Already, despite the relatively early hour, the streets were quite busy and Matt knew that within a couple of hours they would be heaving with hordes of people. Their first port of call was a sleek-looking tailors. The name on the sign said Gresham Blake. The mannequins at the window were dressed in some stunningly ornate looking suits and shirts. Richard stopped and gulped. He felt almost too embarrassed to walk in there with the clothes he was dressed in. Matt seeing that Richard had halted, tried to reassure him. 'Hey mate, don't worry. It'll be fine. It's not like you'll be prodded with spears when you go in there. You're going to upgrade your clobber, that's all. You'll feel a million dollars afterwards.'

'No, I'm okay,' Richard said, trying hard to convince himself as much as Matt.

'Is it the cost? I know the places I'll be taking you aren't the cheapest. We can go elsewhere if you like,' Matt said, now putting a reassuring arm on Richard's shoulder. 'Out of interest, how much have we got to play with today?'

'Enough,' Richard said as he made his way to the shop and opened the door.

'Enough?' Matt repeated with an acknowledging nod and a shrug of the shoulders as he followed Richard inside the shop.

A petit, attractive Asian lady, who herself, was immaculately dressed in a stylish suit welcomed them warmly. 'Hello sirs, how may I help you?'

Richard was like a rabbit caught in the headlights and just stared inanely at the lady.

'We're looking for a couple of suits for my friend here and perhaps a few shirts too,' Matt said speaking on behalf of a stunned Richard.

'Come with me,' The lady said. Measurements were made, suits and shirts were tried on and nearly an hour later Richard stepped out the shop with bags full of two of the sharpest suits he'd ever seen and three of the most beautifully designed fitted shirts. He even bought a couple of jazzy ties and some cufflinks to go with them. Whilst he was trying everything on and admiring himself in the mirror, he instantly felt like a different person and it was a massive wrench to put his shapeless jeans and his worn t-shirt back on. 'Where next?' he said excitedly.

'Easy tiger,' Matt replied jokingly. 'Are you ready to spend some more?'

'Let's do this!' Richard exclaimed as they marched along the road. He was like a child at Christmas. His spirits were sky-high. From one shop to another they bought and bartered. Matt was so confident that he managed to make a saving on pretty much everything they bought. His quick wit and charming nature made it easy for the shop assistants to shave off ten percent here, twenty percent there. Richard was certainly making up for lost time. He could almost feel his debit card beginning to warp and melt under the strain of so many purchases. They were both laden down with bags overfilling with clothes and footwear. Richard had now discarded his old clothing and was sporting some slim-fitting Levi's that finally did his figure some justice. A cool All Saints T-shirt worn underneath an expensive, black leather jacket was finished off with a pair of boots that he would never have had the confidence to wear before. Now he felt unbeatable. *Why had I never done this before?* he thought: a thought that was fast becoming his mantra. It was so true though. If a few hours clothes shopping had made him feel this good, it was a crying shame he hadn't got round to doing it sooner. He didn't have any time to feel any self-pity though as Matt boldly ushered him to their last port of call.

The jazzy-looking hairdressers which Matt presented with a 'Ta da' made Richard suck in a mouthful of air. Even with his new clothes he suddenly felt well out of his comfort zone. Peering through the window he observed young, effortlessly cool people with strange and flamboyant hairstyles busily cutting, colouring and styling other young and effortlessly cool people's hair. Matt, not letting Richard think more than twice, dragged him by the arm and into the salon.

To say the salon was white would've been a doing the colour white a disservice. This made the polar icecaps look grey. Richard almost had to squint to see properly and what he saw was white, neat and emphatically clean. 'Ah, the lovely Matthew, how are *you* you gorgeous man?' an overtly camp gentleman said as they entered. He looked like an eighties popstar with big, dyed blonde hair and, in keeping with his place of work, the whitest teeth Richard had ever seen. 'And who is this handsome creature with you?' he continued. He was putting the finishing touches to a marvellous hairstyle that Richard confidently knew would never suit him.

'How are you doing Curtis? This is a very old friend of mine, Rich. I want you to work your magic and give him a haircut he can be proud of.'

Curtis took a quick look at Richard's lacklustre hairdo. 'Magic I can do my darling; miracles are a little bit harder,' he said with a slight look of distain.

Richard went crimson with embarrassment but his mood quickly lifted when Curtis and Matt burst out laughing. 'I'm only kidding my love. Take a seat,' Curtis said as he beckoned them to some nearby chairs.

'Don't worry; Curtis has been cutting my hair for years. He's amazing,' Matt said reassuringly.

Moments later, with an apron fastened around his neck and Curtis standing behind him, Richard was siting nervously in the chair. With obvious trepidation etched on his face he looked more like a patient about to undergo root canal surgery than someone awaiting their hair to be restyled. Both staring at the mirror, they chatted about the task at hand. 'So my love, what shall we do with *this*?' Curtis said with extra emphasis on the "this" as he pulled his fingers through Richard's greasy, lank hair.

Richard was too embarrassed to speak so Matt quickly got up from his seat and spoke for him. 'Nothing too wild or "out there" but give him something easy to style and cool. You know what to do.' With a comforting squeeze of Richard's shoulder, he then returned to his seat.

Curtis raised a highly manicured eyebrow as if to say, "*Of course I know what to do.*" In the next three quarters of an hour, he washed and conditioned Richard's hair before he set about cutting and styling it. Conversation was interspersed with lots of tutting and shaking of the head from Curtis; obviously appalled by its current condition. Richard could offer no argument and looked somewhat embarrassed into the mirror. Seeing this, Curtis reassuringly said,

'Don't you worry my darling. We'll soon have this looking right as rain.'

As Curtis skipped around him; snipping here, combing there, Richard watched on mesmerised. Clippers followed, tidying up the back and sides and all of a sudden, with the aid of a bit hair product ruffled in for good measure, Richard looked upon the finished result.

'Wow!' was all he could muster. Curtis had indeed worked his magic. He hardly recognised the reflection staring open-mouthed back at him. Curtis stood over him, glowing with pride on seeing this dramatic transformation come to fruition. 'Thank you *so* much. It looks amazing,' he said when the ability to speak again had returned.

'You're welcome my darling. Just take good care of your hair from now on. Here, take these,' Curtis said as he handed him a selection of haircare products including shampoo, conditioner and texturing gum. 'These are on the house as you're a friend of Matthew's,' he continued as he blew a kiss to them both. Then, with nimble grace, he span on his heels and tended to the next customer.

After Richard paid and left the salon they stood outside not really knowing what to do next. They were over-laden with bags so decided to get a taxi back to Richard's, drop the bags off and then head back into town for some afternoon drinking.

As they sat in the back of the cab, Richard was literally glowing with a rush of happiness he'd never felt before. He almost felt guilty that his elation was due to some very self-indulgent consumerism.

Matt looked at his friend and smiled. 'You look like you enjoyed that.'

'I *so* did. Thank you so much,' Richard replied, unable to hide the gushiness I his voice.

'You don't have to thank me mate. You're the one that spent the money.'

'I know, but if I hadn't had met you in the pub the other day I wouldn't have even thought of going shopping like that today. I'd have been doing the same thing that I always do on a Saturday – absolutely nothing.'

'I still don't see why you need to thank me. It was your decision to go shopping – to make yourself over – not mine. You should be proud of yourself. You look great. You really do… I mean, how do you feel?' Matt already knew the answer but wanted to see Richard's face full of joy again as he gave his answer.

'I feel amazing!' he gushed again. 'I don't know how to explain it. It's like I've been put in a different body and someone has unlocked my mind. I've felt so bogged down for so long. Now I feel alive.'

'Welcome to the world,' Matt said as he firmly patted Richard on the back.

As they arrived outside Richard's home and stepped out of the taxi, he felt the need to warn Matt what he was about to walk into. He was desperately hoping that his parents might have dragged themselves out to the pub or wherever they went when they weren't slobbing around indoors, but he knew they'd be there; ready to burst his happy bubble as soon as he walked through the door. 'Listen, I don't know if you remember my parents from way back, but they haven't really changed since then, except to become fatter and more spiteful. I apologise in advance,' he said hurriedly as he put the key in the door.

Matt just chuckled. He did remember them and back then he was scared of both of them but gone were the days when he was scared of anyone anymore.

'Oi Sylv, Elvis has just entered the building! And there was me thinking 'e was dead. 'Ere come n' 'ave a look at our boy,' Richard's dad, Gerry, said through a rasping cackle. Miraculously he was standing upright with a cigarette hanging out the corner of his mouth, looking every bit the slob he was. He was wearing a tight-fitting white T-shirt with some ingrained food and drink stains plastered on it. His faded jeans, which also had their fair share of stains, hung loosely below his oversized waist, exposing a pale and repulsive belly. *No doubt the rear view of this visual treat would be revealing a butt-crack that you could park a bike in,* Richard thought as he surveyed the scene that stood before him. Patchy grey stubble peppered his flabby jowls and his equally grey hair stood out in different directions giving the impression he'd just been thrown out of an aeroplane. But, given his pudgy, untrained frame, Richard thought it would take a fairly robust aeroplane and colossal parachute to achieve such a task.

Sylvia, Richard's mum, waddled into the living room where the television was blaring out some god-awful American reality show at an ear-splitting volume. On seeing Richard standing there proudly, she burst out laughing 'Hahahaha! What the bloody 'ell do you look like?!' she said through her laughter. Richard's euphoric mood had been rapidly replaced with crushing self-consciousness. He stood there almost about to cry as his parents continued to laugh and pick holes in his new appearance.

'Well, I think he looks fantastic,' Matt said nonchalantly. He could see Richard didn't have the resolve to withstand too much more and desperately needed someone to come to his rescue.

Matt's comment had shocked Sylvia and Gerry. They soon stopped laughing. 'Oo asked you?' Gerry said aggressively. 'You're that Matt Samson ain't ya?' he said suddenly realising who stood before him. 'What, you iz boyfriend now?' he snarled as he gestured at Richard.

Matt could feel his anger rising but, taking a deep inward breath, he calmly stared deep into the angry eyes of Gerry who stood a good five or six inches below him. Even from his elevated position he could smell Gerry's rank breath which reeked of stale alcohol and cigarettes. But, retaining his poise, and despite the overwhelming urge he had to gag, he held out his hand and equally calmly said,

'Yes, I'm Matt Samson. So good of you to remember me. How are you Mr. Chambers?'

Gerry didn't know what to do so grasped Matt's hand and shook it. Gerry's hand felt podgy, cold and clammy within Matt's solid grip. He gave it a firm squeeze and waited for Gerry to notice the strength of his clasp. All the time Matt's stare bore into Gerry. Unnerved now, Gerry let go of Matt's hand and gave his own hand a subtle rub. A tense silence cut through the blaring din of the television. 'Rich, take that stuff upstairs. We've got a taxi waiting for us outside,' Matt said calmly, taking his eyes off Gerry just long enough to give Sylvia a punishing stare of her own. A moment later and Richard was back downstairs and heading towards the front door. 'Well, it's been an absolute pleasure to see the both of you again, and both looking so well too.' Matt couldn't disguise the sarcasm in his voice. Edging his way out of the room he offered them one final contemptuous glance before joining Richard outside.

They took the taxi back into town and settled in quaint pub in The South Lanes called The Cricketers. It was a pub Matt frequented regularly and liked it for its local feel and friendly service. It wasn't a big pub but it was cosy and oozed charm and character. Their taxi journey back into town had been in complete contrast to the one they'd shared to Richard's home. The high spirits and elation that Richard had exuded earlier had now been replaced by a very sombre feel. Sitting on one of the plush, pink sofas, Richard gazed morosely at his pint of lager, watching the beads of condensation slip from the top to the bottom of his glass. Matt could see Richard was mortified by his parent's behaviour and knew he had to bring him out of this mood, sooner rather than later. 'It was great to see your parents again after all this time,' he said with a wry smile.

Richard looked at Matt and saw the faint smile on his face and a smile grew across his own face. 'I'm so sorry,' he said. 'I knew they would try and put me down in front of you – that's one of their specialties. But they don't seem happy until they've completely broken my spirit. I've had it all my life.' His voice was almost ready to break with emotion.

'Why do you still live with them?' Matt responded as he took a big sup of his pint.

'Honestly, I don't know. I guess I've just got so used to living with them.'

'Right,' Matt said as he rubbed his hands together. 'Here's my advice; you've gotta move out of there as a matter of urgency. I'm telling you mate. Your parents are sucking the life out of you, and I wouldn't be surprised if they're not bleeding your bank account dry too. I don't want to speak out of turn, but they were horrible to you when I knew you all those years ago. They only seem to have got worse in the years since.' He paused and thought for a moment before saying, 'How much money have you got saved up?'

'A bit.' Richard replied somewhat taken aback by the question. 'Why's that?'

'A bit?' Matt prompted.

'A few grand,' Richard said as he took a sip of his own pint.

Matt could tell Richard was being coy and pressed him again. 'A few grand?' He was aware that he was starting to sound like a parrot but wanted to get a solid answer out of him. 'Are we talking double figures?'

'More like triple figures,' Richard said bashfully.

Matt's mouth gaped open. 'W-woah… Are you telling me you have over a hundred grand sitting in your bank account and you're still living at home with your parents?! Where… w…what… how?' he stammered. 'How did you save up that much money?'

'I don't go out much and, as you've seen, I don't spend much money on clothes. And my Gran – do you remember my Gran?' Richard paused.

'I do. Yeah, she was lovely,' Matt agreed, smiling at the recollection.

'Well, she died a year ago and willed me all her money. With the sale of the house, I received close to two hundred grand. My parents were furious and have never forgiven me; hence why they're so spiteful to me all the time.' Matt could tell Richard had never really spoken to anyone about this subject before and was almost embarrassed to being doing so now. It was obvious that Richard was far from superficial or materialistic, despite his little splurge at the shops today. Even at school Matt could remember Richard hated any attention, good or bad, being drawn to himself so he decided to try and move off the subject. He was just about to say something to alter the flow of the conversation when Richard continued, 'My parents have always put me down and belittled me. I can't recall the last time they said something nice or complimentary to me. I've just become so used to their insults that I'm pretty numb towards it all… But it hurts… It hurts a lot.'

Matt noticed tears forming in Richard's eyes but didn't say anything. He knew this was all stuff that Richard had bottled up for such a long time. He just put his hand on the back of Richard's neck to comfort him.

'I'm sorry. I don't mean to spoil our fun,' Richard said apologetically.

'Don't you worry mate. There's plenty of time to have fun… I'm sorry about your Gran though. I remember going round to her place with you after school once. She cooked us the best sausage casserole I think I've ever tasted. Then she gave us a couple of quid each to go down the shops and get some sweets – remember?' Richard nodded. He remembered it well. His Gran was always so friendly and welcoming. He used to spend as much time as he could round her cosy house where he received the love and attention his parents neglected to give him. He'd often thought that if she'd had a decent sized spare bedroom at her house he would've gone to live with her.

He wondered what his parents would've done if he had moved out. They probably wouldn't have even noticed. It was small wonder he'd lived such a sheltered life given he had them as inspirational role models. He felt a sudden jolt of anger, a bitterness, for being kept down for so long. Meeting Matt had awoken something inside him and that bitterness was rapidly being replaced by a determination to alter the path of his life before it was too late. 'Finish your pint,' he instructed Matt.

'Ok. Where are we going?' Matt replied, as he drained the remainder of his drink.

'Flat hunting,' Richard said purposefully.

CHAPTER 5

They stood outside the pub, the bright sunshine making them squint. They'd both finished their pints far too quickly and the gassy effects were making them burp under their breath. 'Do you know what you're doing? I mean do you know where to start looking?' Matt said once his burping had subsided.

'Not really,' Richard replied as he suppressed another burp. 'I guess we go to a Letting Agents and have a look at what's available.'

'Have you thought where you'd like to live? You've got quite a healthy budget. I'd suggest, with the summer on the horizon, a nice seafront flat would be a good place to start.'

'To be honest I hadn't given it a single thought until a moment ago. A seafront flat does sound lovely though. I'd like to stay fairly central to town if possible.'

'Cool. Well, let me phone a mate of mine. He runs his own Letting Agents and always has some nice places on his books. He should be there today.'

A moment later, Matt was speaking on the phone to a chap Richard overheard to be called Wayne. After he got off the phone he turned to Richard and said 'We're in business. My mate Wayne from Manley Properties is going to meet us at a flat at Palmeira Square. He's a really good fella and I completely trust him. He won't rip you off. He said he's got a flat that's just come up for rent and it would be perfect for you... Are you sure you want to do this?'

'Positive,' Richard replied confidently.

They decided to walk to the flat, along the seafront where a distinct lack of breeze made it feel almost tropical. Richard talked excitedly about the prospect of finally moving out of his parents' place. Matt, for his part, was trying to temper Richard's excitement a little by making him aware that there'd be bills to pay and he'd be living by himself for the first time in his life. He could see what huge and sudden step this would be for Richard. 'I'd sooner live by myself than with those two,' Richard said with complete contempt in reference to his parents. 'And given how much money they've fleeced off me over the years, I'm sure I won't notice the bills I'll be paying. I just can't wait to see the look on their faces when I tell them I'm moving out!'

They reached their destination just as Wayne was stepping out of his black Mercedes. 'Hello mate. How have you been?' Matt said warmly to Wayne as they greeted each other with a hug. Wayne was in his late forties or early fifties Richard guessed; he was handsome and carried a friendly, disarming smile. Once Matt had made the introductions, Richard instantly felt at ease and the three of them chatted casually about this and that as they entered the property.

The flat in question was in a serene Regency square, only five minutes' walk from where Richard worked. He was trying to think if that was a good or a bad thing as Wayne talked him through the vital statistics of the property. It was a one bedroom flat on the ground floor, and although it didn't face the sea you could easily see it from the window and it was only a short walk to the seafront. It transpired that this apartment had come onto Wayne's books that very day and he didn't expect it to be on there very long before someone snapped it up. *Yes, I'm sure he'd say that anyway,* thought Richard, but he had a strong feeling that this might well be the case in this instance. It was a gorgeous flat that had been newly decorated with neutral colours of magnolia and white. There were large windows letting lots of light flood into the living room and the high ceilings had ornate coving bordering it. The beige carpet felt new and spongy under foot. Everything felt fresh and well presented. As he walked from room to room, he felt more and more impressed and more and more at home. He noticed that in every room there was furniture and appliances installed and Wayne confirmed that the flat came fully furnished. This sealed the deal for him.

'I'll take it,' he said, stopping Wayne in the middle of his sales pitch.

'*Woah*, are you sure?' Matt said as he looked at Wayne, whose eyes had lit up. 'This is the first and only place you've seen. I just wanted you to get an idea of what's available.'

'No, this is the one. I could see a hundred more places and they wouldn't be as perfect as this. I'll take it.' Richard was beaming proudly and happily. Never before had he been so spontaneous.

A short while later they stopped off at Wayne's offices along the road where Richard filled in the relevant paperwork and paid the deposit. He was told he could move in the following weekend and this sent his emotions soaring. So much had happened in the past few days but he was just going with it. It felt like he was finally taking charge of his life and the path it was taking.

'We need celebrate,' Matt announced after they'd said their goodbyes to Wayne.

'Of course. Where shall we go?' Richard said.

They strolled back into town, walking back past the flat again where Richard wistfully stared up at his soon-to-be new place of residence. He hadn't spent more than fifteen minutes in there but it already felt like home. They walked back along the seafront where the sun was warming the backs of their necks. His new haircut had exposed more of his neck than had been on show for years. It felt naked but he welcomed the new sensation. Looking out towards the sea, it appeared like a millpond with little or no breeze to rustle up any waves. There seemed an air of hope and excitement that summer was on its way, an air that matched his contented mood.

They spent the rest of the afternoon going from one pub to another in the busy Lanes area of Brighton. Conversation was easy and free-flowing, much like the alcohol. Richard was quickly realising that despite not being a big drinker in the past, he was now making up for lost time. And making up for lost time seemed to be a big theme of those next few hours as they laughed and joked about times past. Memories came flooding back as if they were yesterday. 'Who was that old teacher that used to froth at the mouth and spray you with spit when he got angry?' Matt asked as they reminisced. 'He had awful breath too... God, what was his name?'

'*Oh yes*, what *was* his name?' Richard said, beginning to giggle.

'Mr Grayson!' they both said at the same time and burst out laughing.

'You were alright,' Matt said when the laughter subsided. 'You were a good boy, but me... He once got so angry at me that he got me up in front of the class where he shouted spit at me for a couple of minutes... When I returned to my seat I had to take my jumper off to wipe my face! I was drenched!' They both belly-laughed again.

Richard had to wipe tears away from his eyes before adding, 'Remember that girl in our class that we used to call Crab because she always seemed to walk sideways?'

'Amanda Chapman. I remember her well.' Matt said with a knowing grin.

'Wait a minute; don't tell me... you... her... noooo!' Richard said with a look of horror.

'Yep.' Matt said proudly with a wink of his eye. 'I fingered her around the back of the bike sheds.'

On hearing Matt's crass comment Richard spat out the mouthful of beer he was just about to swallow, spraying it all over Matt who tried in vain to protect himself. They both continued to laugh as Matt mopped himself with a nearby napkin. 'I'm soaked… Nearly as bad as when Mr Grayson shouted at me!' They literally couldn't stop laughing now. Every time they looked like they were about to stop they looked at each other again and laughed some more. Their sides hurt from the exertion as mild hysteria started to set in. They'd been transported back in time and were fourteen all over again. It was as they were doubled over, still giggling and wiping away more tears of laughter, that a large figure loomed over their heads. Jamie stood there unimpressed and quickly changed the mood.

'Am I missing something?' he said.

'No, we were just laughing about old times… Sorry Rich, I should've said that Jamie was joining us. Hope you don't mind,' Matt said as he slowly regained his composure.

'Why would he mind?' Jamie he said with more than a hint of intimidation.

Of course Richard minded though, but he wasn't in a position to complain. He was having so much fun with his old friend and now Jamie was going to alter those social dynamics. It didn't help that he really didn't feel comfortable around Jamie and he doubted he ever would. His intimidating physical presence seemed to be equally matched by his intimidating personality, which was devoid of any charm or warmth.

'What do you think of Rich's new…er…' said Matt as he was trying to think of the right word '…appearance?' he finished as he waved his hands towards Richard like a magician that had just performed a trick. Jamie just stood there nonplussed with his chunky arms folded across his chunky chest. 'Rich and I have spent the day getting him some new clothes and a new hair style. What do you think? I think he looks amazing.'

Still unimpressed, Jamie examined Richard, who in turn gave a shy smile as he was being observed. 'S'pose 'e looks alright. Can't say I noticed the difference to be honest,' he said unenthusiastically before changing the subject. 'So, where are we going tonight? Somewhere there's lots o' birds I 'ope. I wanna get my cock sucked tonight.'

It was the first time since he had met Jamie that he could remember him getting animated about anything. Before that last vulgar statement, he'd shown little or no emotion about anything. Obviously, the prospect of getting his cock sucked was one of the few things that truly inspired Jamie, he mused. Not a thought he'd allow himself to dwell on for long though.

'We'll just hit a few bars and see where we end up. How does that sound?' Matt said. 'Anyway, I thought you might want to take it a bit easy with Lauren ready to pop.'

'What she don't know don't hurt 'er,' Jamie replied with a smarmy grin. 'Besides, she ain't put out for ages and my bollocks are gonna burst if I don't chuck my custard up someone soon,' he continued. And with every word that spewed out of Jamie's mouth Richard liked him less and less. It seemed the looming prospect of fatherhood and the respect and welfare of his partner weren't as high a priority as "chucking his custard up someone." He'd never met Jamie's partner, Lauren, but he already pitied her.

They continued their night, but for Richard a lot of the fun had gone out of it. Jamie had become very overbearing, and the drunker he got, the more aggressive and boisterous he became. This put Richard very much on his guard. Conversations that, earlier had flowed so well and had been so enjoyable, were now stilted and uncomfortable. The only plus point was that Richard's new, enhanced appearance was drawing the attention of some amorous female admirers. It was a strange feeling for him because for so long he'd been the ugly duckling, the wallflower, and now women were casting a flirtatious eye over him. The problem was he really didn't know how to react. Jamie took the incoming looks as interest in him and kept standing in front of him, blocking his view, as he unsubtly flexed his big, tattooed biceps in his tight-fitting t-shirt. This seemed as good a deterrent as would ever be needed though. Soon Jamie was bored of frequenting the pubs where you *could* hear yourself talk and wanted to go somewhere livelier. Both Richard and Matt were quite drunk by this stage and acquiesced without complaint. Matt did want to retain some semblance of control though so suggested a place to go. 'If you want to go somewhere livelier, how about a club? There's a club on the seafront that I used to go to a few years back and they're doing an old skool house night. It might be a laugh.'

Despite Richard's drunkenness and his lowered inhibitions, he was startled when he heard the word "club" mentioned. He was wracking his beer-addled brain to think if he'd actually ever been to a nightclub before and the notion that they might be about to go to one filled him with sudden panic. 'Listen, I'm not too sure I fancy a nightclub. I've had a good night but I might head home,' he said.

'Rubbish. You're coming with us if I have to drag you there myself,' Matt said drunkenly as he pawed at Richard.

'Let 'im go home if 'e wants to go,' Jamie said.

On hearing this, something inside Richard stirred. He knew Jamie didn't really want him there and this only inspired him to change his mind. 'Ok, I'll come.' He gave Jamie a little glance and almost felt himself about to wink at him but he thought better of it. He appreciated that there were distinct limitations to his drunken bravado.

So there he found himself, queuing up to enter a nightclub. Thirty-nine years old and he'd never stepped foot in one. He struggled to fathom how that could be. The club was situated on the seafront where all the old fishing huts used to be and some still operate as such. The earlier warmth had now deserted them and a cool breeze blew off the sea making him dig his hands deep into the pockets of his new leather jacket in a vain effort to stay warm. The queue wasn't long but big enough to give him a feel for the sort of people that were looking to enter. There were a few youngsters but not as many as he was expecting. Most people seemed to be a similar age to him. He was quite surprised by that, but as Matt explained, this was a reunion of a club night that was very popular there in the late nineties. Matt seemed very excited. He bobbed from one foot to the other in nervous anticipation. Richard didn't quite share Matt's enthusiasm. He was filled with an overwhelming feeling of trepidation that one only gets when completely out of their comfort zone. A typical night for him would be spent locked in his bedroom blasting away people on his games console. He was only just coming to terms with frequenting pubs on consecutive nights. Now he was going to enter a place where the music was loud and where he might be expected to dance. That filled him with dread. He didn't know if he had any rhythm – he'd never needed to know.

As they neared the front of the queue, he observed the team that were controlling who entered the club or not. Cloaking the entrance was a collection of big, burly bouncers whose intimidating presence did nothing to calm his nerves. In front of them, welcoming those that approached was an attractive blonde-haired lady holding a clipboard, which Matt explained was the guestlist, and a tall, unconvincing drag queen. Richard couldn't help but smile when he saw Jamie's face as he noticed the drag queen. 'You didn't tell me we were going to *that* sort of a place,' Jamie remonstrated with Matt.

'What sort of place?' Matt replied with he's usual ease and grace.

'I dunno. Full of weirdos like *that*,' Jamie said gesturing towards the drag queen.

'Don't worry big guy I'm sure there'll be lots of pretty girls for you to pester,' Matt responded with a smile. 'Look, it's a very cosmopolitan, mixed night. There'll be people from all walks of life in there; gay, straight, bisexual, transvestites. The music will be brilliant and if it's anything like it was years ago, we'll have excellent time. Now if you don't want to join me – don't. I'm going in though.' Matt then turned towards the lady with the clipboard. They were now at the front of the queue.

'It doesn't bother me,' Richard said cheerfully, taking some pleasure in Jamie's obvious discomfort. Despite Richard's very sheltered life he'd always been very open-minded. A lot stemmed from the fact that his father had always been so bigoted and narrow-minded. When he saw the person his father was, he used all his views as anti-views to guide him through life. Richard was very much of the opinion that people were people no matter what their skin colour, religion or sexual orientation. But as he stood there he could almost hear his dad's rasping voice saying, *"Well, it's not natural is it? Bloomin' queers."* Richard sensed that his father and

Jamie would get on famously if they ever met. He deeply hoped they never did though.

'Right, we're on the guestlist,' Matt said turning to the other two. 'If you want to come in just confirm your names with the lovely lady and join me in there.' He then strolled towards the nightclub entrance. Richard and Jamie both looked at one another. Richard turned and gave his name to the lady and, more confidently than he actually felt, followed Matt. Jamie then begrudgingly joined the other two, frowning moodily as he did so. On the way in they were frisked – an experience that Richard had not encountered before. At first he thought they were trying to rob him and when he received a pat on the back to signify his entry, he was in a state of mild shock until Matt grabbed him by the collar of his coat and pulled him inside.

Once properly inside and having checked their coats into the cloakroom, Richard spent a moment observing his new surroundings. He had to admit, he was slightly underwhelmed. He was expecting it to be heaving with people but found it quite empty. Matt, seeing the other two's faces reassured them 'Don't worry, it'll fill up. Come on, let's get a drink.' They wandered over to the bar, got a drink and stood there in silence whilst they took in the venue.

It was a cavernous place featuring lots of chrome and bare brick. The arched ceilings had an array of lighting suspended from them and pumping house music pounded a steady beat which made

Richard's heart beat in time. As they left the bar to have a walk about, they went from one arch to another. During these meanderings, Matt enthusiastically greeted people he knew and seemed very much in his element. He politely introduced Richard and Jamie to all he met and, as everyone was so friendly, Richard felt himself relax again. Jamie, on the other hand, was looking more and more disgruntled. Richard took a sordid sense of pleasure in Jamie's obvious uncomfortableness. When Matt introduced them to an exuberant gay couple it was plain to see Jamie's distain. As Matt, and then Richard, received kisses on the cheek, Jamie backed away, regarding the couple with unbridled contempt. There was an awkward pause before Matt left them and turned to Jamie. 'What the hell was that?' he said forcefully.

'I didn't come 'ere to meet poofs and fuckin' weirdos,' Jamie replied aggressively. 'I came 'ere to meet birds.'

'Look, these are good people. I've known them for years. Seems to me, the only weirdo here is you. If you don't like it in here, fuck off someplace else. You're not going to ruin my night.'

'What, so you can spend some quality time wiv your little boyfriend?' Jamie said gesturing to Richard.

'Oh, just fuck off mate. I'll see you at work on Monday,' Matt said, having had quite enough of comments like that for one day. He stared hard at Jamie who was trying to use his size to try and intimidate him. A moment later, a very grumpy Jamie turned on his heels and went to leave. He made sure to thump into Richard's shoulder as he passed, half spinning him around, before heading to the exit.

'Sorry about that. He's not always like that,' Matt said.

'I don't want to speak out of turn, but from what little I've seen, it seems he's *always* like that,' Richard replied as he rubbed his shoulder. 'Look, I know we've only just...' he fumbled around in his mind thinking of the right word '...reconnected, and you've known Jamie a fair while, but he seems to be a complete and utter arsehole. I'm sorry but that's the way I see it.'

Matt looked down at the ground, taking in what Richard had just said to him. 'I know... you're probably right,' he resignedly admitted. 'I guess I'm just used to him now... Anyway, let's not spoil a great day. Let's get some more drinks and have a good laugh. Come on,' he said, beckoning Richard to follow.

As they walked back to the main bar Richard noticed that, whilst they'd been taking a tour of the place, the club had filled up. People were on the dancefloor and he could feel a strange sort of energy starting to flow through the club. It was whilst they were walking just out of the main room that Matt suddenly stopped Richard below a staircase and rather conspiratorially said, 'Open your mouth.'

Richard was a little bit taken aback but did what he was told. Matt put something on his tongue and told him to swallow and wash it down with his drink. Whatever it was on his tongue tasted bitter and he found it hard to swallow. After he'd finally managed to gulp it down he grimaced and asked, 'What the hell was that?'

'A pill... Well, half a pill actually,' Matt replied nonchalantly.

'What sort of pill?' Richard asked rather concerned.

Slightly puzzled, Matt said, 'Ecstasy... What did you think it would be - paracetamol?'

Richard freaked out, 'What?! You've given me drugs!' he exclaimed.

'Shhooosh.' Matt said putting a finger to Richard's lips in an effort to calm him and to not draw any attention to them. Fortunately, the pounding bass emanating from the dancefloor masked any such drama. 'Don't worry. I thought you needed to relax and enjoy yourself. You looked a little on edge.'

'What, so you thought you'd drug me?' Richard said incredulously.

'Don't be so dramatic. It's only half a pill. It's not going to do you any harm. Just go with it. Relax, enjoy the night and forget you've done it,' Matt said reassuringly.

Richard was still aggrieved but, after quick consideration, he trusted Matt not to have poisoned him. The thought of doing something illegal worried him, but it excited him too. He'd never even smoked marijuana and here he was popping pills. He decided it was too late to change anything now and was just going to "go with it." 'So, what is it going to do to me?' he asked, still sounding more than a little concerned.

'Well, be prepared because it's going to make your blood boil and your eyes pop out before you choke to death on your swollen tongue,' Matt said looking sincerely at Richard whose face was now one of abject terror. But he couldn't contain his laughter. 'Sorry mate, I shouldn't joke. That was worth it though, to see your face,' Matt said through his chuckling. Richard just stood there still in a state of shock until Matt continued, 'You'll be absolutely fine. It won't kick in for another half hour or so and when it does you'll feel the very subtle effects at first. You'll feel relaxed; you'll feel happy; I mean, it's not called ecstasy for nothing. Try not to worry and try to enjoy yourself... You trust me right?'

'Yes, I do. I just wished you told me what you were giving to me before you gave it to me.'

'And give you the chance of backing out of it? No way. Live your life my friend... before it's over.' Matt raised his arms up in the air accentuate his last comment before spinning around and heading towards the dancefloor.

Richard, still slightly stunned, was about to follow him when he noticed a familiar face standing a few metres away. *This can't be. What's she doing here?* he thought to himself. There, chatting to her friend Jenny, was Frances. He couldn't move, as if his feet were glued to the floor. His brain was having to contend with a lot at the moment and seeing Frances unexpectedly now stripped him of the ability of movement. He took a deep breath and forced his feet to move him in her direction. Jenny noticed him first and smiled causing Frances to turn to see what she was smiling at. 'Hi,' was all he could manage.

At first Frances didn't quite recognise the new and improved Richard that stood before her, but when it registered she sweetly said, 'Oh, hi Richard, I didn't expect to see you here.'

He was still struggling to get his words out as he stood there dumbfounded but eventually he said, 'I didn't expect to see me here either. W…what…why…' he stuttered as he realised that he should've just kept quiet. But a friendly smile grew across Frances face as she tried to make out what he was trying to say.

'I used to come along to this club night years ago. There are a lot of old faces here tonight. Hopefully, none of my students will be here though!' she giggled. She then looked him up and down, 'Anyway… What happened to *you*?' she said and watched Richard look bashful before adding quickly 'You look amazing!'

He didn't know what to do with such a compliment from someone so attractive. He wasn't used to receiving compliments from anyone, let alone beautiful women. 'Matt and I spent the day shopping and I got myself a hairstyle... do you like it?' he said ruffling his newly styled locks.

'I think it really suits you. You look very handsome,' Frances replied with another friendly smile and the slightest of touches on his arm. That touch and those compliments completely melted him. He didn't know if it was the ecstasy kicking in but his emotions were going through the roof.

'I was just going to get us some drinks, would you like one?' Jenny said, waking Richard out of his euphoric trance.

'Er… wait, I should get these,' he said, wiping his mouth in case he'd been drooling.

'No, you stay there and keep Frances company. What would you like?'

'Just a glass of water then if you wouldn't mind,' Richard said politely.

Jenny gave him a peculiar look as if he'd just asked for glass of cat urine and trotted off to the bar leaving him and Frances alone. He was suddenly in the unaccustomed situation of being in the sole presence of a lady; a lady he'd obsessed over for longer than was healthy. He rummaged his mind for something to say. He could see her big round eyes looking up at him expectantly. 'I didn't see you on the way to work yesterday…' was as good as he could manage.

'Yes, I took the day off. Something came up,' she said. 'Did you miss me then?'

He didn't know how best to answer this so he thought he'd stutter awkwardly instead. This made Frances smile broadly and this in turn made him blush. *Was it getting hotter in here?* he thought to himself as he pulled at the neck of his t-shirt. He somehow managed to regain his composure and say, 'Yes. Yes, I did.' His voice was full of sincerity. 'I look forward to seeing you every morning… I doubt you even notice me.' Shyly, feeling that he'd said too much, he dropped his gaze towards the floor. But to his complete amazement he felt a small kiss planted delicately on his cheek and looked up to see Frances smiling up at him. The moment seemed to stand still. Their eyes locked on one another and his heart felt like it was going to leap out of his chest.

'Here you go,' said Jenny handing Richard a bottle of water and breaking him out of the moment. 'I got you a bottle rather than a glass. It'll be easier to take on the dancefloor,' she added, seemingly oblivious of the colossal moment she'd unwittingly gate-crashed.

'Thank you very much,' Richard said politely.

'Come on,' Jenny said excitedly as she beckoned the other two towards the dancefloor.

The thought of dancing suddenly sent a shiver of fear right through Richard's body. As Frances followed Jenny willingly onto the heaving dancefloor, Richard stopped dead in his tracks as he watched everyone dancing in rhythm. *What if I can't dance?* he thought to himself. He couldn't remember if he'd danced before.

He'd never really felt the compulsion to dance before. His life at home had never given him reason to spin gleefully around the house, and work was so devoid of fun and happiness that it was as much as he could do to not fall asleep at his desk on a daily basis, let alone cut some shapes on the office floor.

Frances turned around to see Richard's frozen figure and returned to encourage him. 'Come on,' she said in a friendly tone.

'I'm... I'm not much of a dancer,' he said hesitantly. 'Perhaps I'll just watch you two for a bit.'

'Not a chance. Come on,' she said grabbing his hand and dragging him to the dancefloor. Fortunately, the dancefloor was busy enough that he didn't have a great deal of room to manoeuvre. He eased himself into it by mimicking what everyone else was doing. It was more like swaying than dancing. Initially he felt extremely self-conscious. It didn't help that he didn't know the music he was dancing to, unlike all the other people there. But, slowly, he felt more and more relaxed. He soon found he was actually enjoying it. The music, which a moment ago sounded alien to his ears, now sounded strangely familiar and effortless to move to. An easy smile grew across his face and a warm feeling coursed through his body. As one tune blended into another, he soon realised that he must've come up on his pill. His whole body, from head to toe, felt wonderfully relaxed. He raised his gaze to see if he could spot Matt. *Where had he got to?* He wanted to thank him for introducing him to the delights of ecstasy, but he was nowhere to be seen. But at that particular moment, he felt so content on the dancefloor, he didn't want to leave it. Dry ice filled the floor and flashing lights seemed to spellbind him. Lasers cut through the fog the dry ice had left behind and the thumping, almost tribal bass, beat out a steady rhythm. His vision couldn't really focus on anything for longer than a few seconds, but every so often he let his gaze rest upon Frances. *My god she's beautiful,* he thought as his smile grew ever wider. At that moment she looked up and their eyes locked.

'Someone looks happy.' She had to shout to make herself heard over the music.

'I really couldn't be happier,' he replied still smiling the widest of smiles. And then he felt a sudden and impulsive urge to kiss her. He leaned in and kissed Frances delicately on the lips. Half-expecting her to pull away, he was pleasantly surprised when she pulled him closer and kissed him back, this time harder and more passionately. He soon felt her tongue enter his mouth and their mouths locked like their eyes had done a moment earlier. Every single nerve ending seemed to feel alive and those few short seconds felt like a lifetime.

'Get a room,' he heard Jenny jokingly say and they both separated from the kiss to look bashfully at her.

'Sorry,' they both said together.

'You kids.' Jenny teased.

A slight shyness returned to Richard and he was very unsure of what to do next.

Almost reading his mind Frances said, 'Come, let's go get a drink,' before leading him by the hand again.

Richard was now breathing very deeply. The combination of the pill and the kiss had made his body and mind experience sensations they weren't used to experiencing. They settled at a bar nearest to the dancefloor. Frances gave Jenny a little wave to make sure she was ok but Jenny was so into the music and the dark, Spanish-looking guy dancing next to her that her look and wave was only a fleeting one.

'How are you feeling?' Frances enquired.

Richard gulped furiously before answering. The adrenaline and come-up off the ecstasy were almost too much for his system. 'I feel wonderful. That kiss was…' he tailed off as he blew out his cheeks in exasperation.

Frances just stood there smiling broadly and looking up at him with her big blue eyes. Richard bought them both drinks; a gin and tonic for Frances and a beer for himself. Strangely now the beer tasted different and he soon regretted ordering it. The taste for alcohol had been quashed by the ecstasy which was steadily working its magic around his system. His body was still rushing with a multitude of new sensations. 'Shall I get Jenny a drink?' Richard asked.

'I think she's ok,' Frances replied, motioning towards Jenny who was wrapped in the arms of her Spanish-looking dancing partner and enjoying her own passionate kiss. 'Get a room!' she shouted over to Jenny who offered a middle finger in response.

The club, that a couple of hours ago seemed so alien and intimidating to him, now seemed comfortable and welcoming. And the music didn't seem quite so loud now. Perhaps his ears had become accustomed to the sound levels. As he observed the dancefloor, he saw nothing but happy faces and it was yet another moment in those life-altering few days when he found himself thinking, *why hadn't I done this before?* Without even realising it, his arms had found their way around Frances. She had her back to him and her head resting on his chest. No words were spoken. None were needed. They were just taking in the moment. He'd never felt this complete; this happy. It was like being in the most beautiful dream; one that he didn't want to wake from. After a while spent in this copasetic state, he said to Frances, 'I did half a pill.' He was unsure why he felt the need to confess what he thought might be an illicit crime.

'I know,' was all she said in reply.

'You knew?' he said, slightly pulling away so he could see her face. 'How did you know?'

'It was fairly obvious. No one looks that happy without being on something... Don't worry it's no bad thing. Jenny and I did half a pill each too,' she said very matter-of-factly.

He was somewhat surprised by her admission, but now he felt even more empathic towards her. With the newfound confidence he'd discovered over the past few days, he turned her gently around to face him and kissed her with a passion that exploded from deep within him. When they finished he looked at her without the shyness that had blighted his life for so long and said, 'I'm puzzled; why me?'

She looked back at him and calmly replied, 'Because I could tell you had a kind heart. I've been with too many men who have thought far too much of themselves and too little of me; who've pushed me into a corner; who've belittled me and crushed my spirit... You always looked so gentle and kind. I've got to say though, and please don't think of me as being too superficial, but your makeover has finally done you the justice you deserve.'

He was taken aback. 'Wow, I don't know what to say.'

'Don't say anything,' she said as she leaned back in and kissed him gently on the lips.

A short while later, Richard suggested they go for a walk around the club. He was curious to see where Matt had disappeared to. They went through the double doors leading to another area of the club and he instantly recognised Matt's robust figure standing in amongst a group of other robust men. 'Look, Matt's over there,' he said to Frances as he led her by the hand and made their way over past a field of sweaty bodies. When they were only a few metres away, a large, muscular chap grabbed hold of Matt. But just as Richard was about to run over to help him out, he saw them kiss - a kiss worthy of his and Frances' a moment earlier.

CHAPTER 6

Matt opened his eyes after his kiss to find Richard staring open-mouthed, just a few yards from him. It was hard to tell who was the more shocked but it was Matt who recovered his composure first. 'How are you Rich? Are you having fun?'

With Richard still standing there gawping, Matt thought he'd better do the talking for a moment, so continued, 'Perhaps I should've told you I was gay.'

'No... no, you're alright,' Richard said as the power of speech finally returned. 'I...I just didn't realise... It really doesn't bother me, you know... you being gay an' all... you... um... erm...' he was getting flustered and Matt was starting to get some sadistic satisfaction in witnessing it.

After watching him flapping and squirming and trying to think of the right thing to say he thought he'd save his blushes by changing the subject. 'And you've met up with the lovely Frances. Hi Frances,' he said reaching out to her and giving her a one-armed hug and a kiss on the cheek. His other arm was still draped around the big muscular guy who Matt introduced as David. David was preened to perfection and had short dark hair and a hard, rugged-looking face. Richard was mesmerised by David's long, dark eyelashes which seemed longer than Frances'. For a big man, David had a very soft, almost effeminate voice. But his gentle voice was very deceptive and disguised a strong, vice-like handshake that almost broke Richard's hand into dust when he shook it. Still wincing slightly from the crippling handshake, Richard turned back to Matt and pulled him in close to whisper, 'Thank you for the ecstasy… pill…thingy. I'm having *such* a great time… thank you.'

Matt pulled away slightly to talk at normal level. 'You're more than welcome mate. I told you you'd enjoy it didn't I? Let's all do another half and go on the dancefloor,' he said enthusiastically. Frances and Richard both looked at one another before nodding their agreement.

Once on the dancefloor, Richard found it much easier to find his rhythm than he had earlier. Matt teased him as he leaned in and said, 'I didn't know you could dance.'

'Nor did I!' Richard replied. The ecstasy-induced grin was firmly plastered across his face again. Having found Jenny and her Spanish-looking friend – who, in fact wasn't from Spain, but from Bognor Regis and called Gary – the six of them danced the night away until the club finished. Bright, white lights filled the venue to signify that it was time to leave. In the stark light the club looked far less glamorous than it had a moment ago.

Having retrieved their coats they were thankful that they had them as they stepped outside. The fresh air and stiff sea breeze were quickly cooling their warm, sweaty bodies. Richard really didn't want this night to end. Despite it being 4am he felt no fatigue and was still bursting with energy. So, when Matt suggested they go back to his for a nightcap, Richard felt a leap of joy from within. Jenny and Gary kindly declined, having somewhere seemingly better to go, but much to Richard's surprise, Frances chose to accompany him back to Matt's. On the walk to the taxi rank Frances linked her arm around Richard's and snuggled deeply into his chest. This high level of contentment was all new to him and although a lot of the effects of the ecstasy had now worn off, there was no indication of this, as his contented smile was as wide as the Cheshire Cats'.

Matt's place was in the Hanover district of Brighton & Hove, just off a long, steep, steady hill called Elm Grove. Richard was impressed at how neat and tidy his place was. Matt had always been quite untidy and scruffy at school so he was amazed at how pristine he now kept everything. It was a mid-terraced house on three levels with the kitchen in the basement. And, around the central island worktop in that kitchen, they now gathered. Matt busied himself getting everyone a drink and making sure they were warm and comfortable. In the very short time since they'd reconnected, Richard had been so impressed at Matt's ability to always be thinking of someone else. It was wasn't false or forced. He genuinely cared for everyone's wellbeing. Richard felt privileged that Matt was his friend – his one and only true friend. When they were all settled, Richard asked Matt, 'So, how long have you and David been… you know… seeing each other?'

Matt and David both looked at one another and at the same time said, 'About three hours.' They then burst out laughing. This made Richard blush for he assumed they'd been an item for some time. But on seeing Frances laugh as well, he chuckled along himself. Matt could see that Richard was a bit nervous again. The ecstasy and alcohol had pretty much worn off now and his natural inhibitions were beginning to return. 'S'pose it was a bit of shock to see me kissing Big Dave here then?' Matt said to Richard as he playfully nudged David sitting next to him.

'You could say that,' Richard replied with a smile. 'I don't want to sound rude, but I never would've thought you were…' the words dried up as he realised how blunt what he was going say already sounded.

'Gay?' Matt finished for him. 'Why, because I could play football and once fingered Amanda Chapman?' They both chuckled at that. David and Frances exchanged a look as if to say, "*Who the hell's Amanda Chapman?*" Matt was now sitting forward and resting on the work surface whilst he crafted a spliff. Richard was transfixed by the nimbleness by which Matt performed this task. 'Not all gay men mince around, listening to Steps and saying, "ooh matron." Some of us work on building sites, play pool and watch the football results come in on a Saturday afternoon,' Matt said.

'So, the chaps you work with know you're gay then?' Richard enquired.

There was a slight pause before Matt replied, 'No.'

A stilted silence followed for a moment, but it seemed a lot longer than a moment before Frances asked the question Richard wanted to ask. 'Why not?'

'They don't need to know,' Matt responded rather pragmatically 'It shouldn't matter if I'm gay or not.'

'Even more reason to tell them then,' Frances said as she took a sip from her glass of wine.

Matt was starting to feel slightly uncomfortable and Richard could see this. 'Let's change the subject because it doesn't really matter.'

No, no... You're alright,' Matt said calmingly. 'Honestly, I don't know why I haven't told them. I suppose it's a very male, hetro environment that I work in. Most of the blokes I work with wouldn't bat an eyelid, but some of them would not take the news quite so well.'

Richard had a good idea of whom, in particular, Matt was referring to. 'I can imagine Jamie wouldn't be flipping cartwheels at the news.'

'That's one way of putting it,' Matt said as he licked the rolling paper and completed his well-crafted joint. 'I mean, you saw the way he was tonight. He's a complete homophobe. He'd probably lynch me.'

'Which begs the question; why's he your friend again?' Richard said jokingly but meaning it deadly seriously.

'Who's Jamie?' Frances asked.

'My business partner,' Matt explained. 'He's not as bad as I'm making him sound…'

'He is,' Richard interjected. 'And I think you're scared of him.'

'Says the man who won't stand up to his parents…' Matt fired back. Richard went a sudden shade of crimson again and there was a frosty pause in conversation. 'I stand to lose my business partner if Jamie walks away. He knows a lot of people and brings in the vast share of our work.' He paused to light the spliff and take a deep pull into his lungs. He turned to expel the smoke which left a pungent and, in Richard's view, a not unpleasant smell behind. 'The way I see it, it's more hassle to upset the applecart than to carry on with the way things are.'

So intent were they on their conversation that they hadn't noticed David had drifted off to sleep. And not a light sleep either. He suddenly let out a thunderous snore which jolted him out of his slumber and made Frances jump and spill her wine.

'Sorry, I think I may've dropped off there for a second,' David said innocently as he rubbed his bleary eyes. The other three laughed and instantly the mood lightened.

Night slowly gave way to the first rays of early morning and with it there was the realisation that it would soon be time to go home. The earlier energy Richard had felt had now given way to a contented fatigue. He was looking forward to lying down and closing his eyes. After one more drink and some mindless chit-chat, he whispered to Frances that he was going to head home. He hadn't told her that he was currently living at home with his parents so wanted to sneak off as best he could, without drawing any attention to where he was going back to.

'I'll head off too,' she whispered back. She phoned a taxi and moments later they were standing at the front door saying their goodbyes. David had not joined them, having drifted back off to sleep with his head rested on the kitchen worktop. The other three exchanged hugs and kisses.

'You don't think anything less of me then? Y'know… now you know I'm gay?' Matt asked Richard. It was the first time in the past few days that Matt had sounded unsure and not quite so confident of himself.

'Don't be silly,' Richard answered with a smile. 'It makes absolutely no difference to me and nor should it to anyone else you know. You are you and you're a wonderful person… I want to thank you so much for today. It's been the best day of my life - and I really mean that.'

'It was good to see you enjoying yourself so much. Promise me you'll keep on having fun,' Matt said with one of his charming smiles.

'Of course,' Richard nodded.

'You can start by keeping me company in the taxi,' Frances whispered into his ear. It was said so subtly and unexpectedly that at first it didn't register. When his brain caught back up with him, he turned around to look at Frances who was looking very alluringly at him. In a day of firsts this was yet another one; he'd certainly never been looked at like that before.

Stunned, he turned back to look at Matt who gave him a wink and a smile. 'Go have that fun.' He then turned to go back inside. As the taxi pulled up Frances grabbed Richard by the arm to lead him to it. Just as they were just about to step into the cab Matt called from the doorway, 'And Frances, be gentle with him.' And not for the first time that day Richard went as red as a tomato.

In the cab, despite Frances leaning contently on his shoulder and snuggling into him, He felt anxious and uneasy. Kissing was one thing; the thought of, what he'd built up in his own mind to be the Holy Grail - sex with a beautiful woman - now scared the bejesus out of him. *What if I'm no good? What if certain things don't work?* Of course, there was no guarantee that she wanted sex, but that didn't stop his overactive mind from running rampant. A thousand similar thoughts now flooded his mind until his terror was momentarily interrupted by her looking up at him and almost purring as she said, 'I had such a wonderful night.'

'So did I,' he managed to say, although he sounded totally unconvincing. The rest of the journey went by without words but a fair degree of trepidation on his part. He insisted on paying for the cab and, with his nerves fraying by the second and his heart racing as if it'd come up on another pill, he looked at Frances. *What the hell is wrong with me? She's gorgeous. What am I worried about?* he tried to reason with himself. It was reasoning that was failing miserably. He looked up at the charming Georgian townhouse that they now stood outside. *Not bad for a college lecturer,* he thought; his mind taking a momentary break from terrorising him. These thoughts were swiftly sent back into fear mode when he felt a gentle tug on his hand to beckon him inside and saw Frances looking endearingly up at him. With an aridly dry mouth and beads of sweat forming on his brow, his nervousness was now palpable. But whether it was a deep-rooted survival instinct kicking in or his brain offering him a shot of bravado, he suddenly felt a surge of much needed confidence. With a swagger James Dean would've been proud of, he strutted inside the house.

CHAPTER 7

Standing there in the hallway like a member of The Starship Enterprise, who'd just beamed down onto a strange planet, he quickly scanned his new surroundings. There was a delicious warmth that greeted him, and a pleasant scent that teased his nostrils, enticing him in. This coupled with the lingering fragrance of Frances' perfume made for an extremely alluring welcome. But as welcoming and enticing as this was, now safely through the threshold, he was again gripped by fear. His momentary bout of confidence, which had given him enough gumption to get through the door, now left him as it had found him – suddenly and without warning. A cool sweat broke out upon his back and his brain reverted back to panic mode. He was even more concerned when he looked into the large mirror in the hallway and saw a petrified space cadet staring back at him. In the glaring light the beads of sweat produced from this soon-to-be traumatic experience were highly visible. *How did I get myself into this situation? I could've stayed at home zapping my virtual enemies on my games console, but noooo; I had to be so cool. Well look where it's got you. I hope you're satisfied...* Panic had rapidly descended into senseless irrationality. He knew he was being ridiculous but he was battling a very determined and well-drilled psyche.

'Are you going to come in?' Frances said after seeing him still stood in the hallway staring worriedly at the mirror.

'Yes, I'm just…' he stopped because he didn't know what he was "just" doing. *Shitting a brick* was what he was doing but that didn't seem like an appropriate answer. Fortunately, she hadn't waited for him to finish his sentence. She'd returned to the living room, obviously waiting for him to join her.

'I've poured you a glass of wine. Come join me,' she said.

I could just quietly let myself out and this whole ordeal will be over, he thought, but he managed to suppress this momentary pang of panic and, taking a deep breath, walked unsteadily into the living room. He found Frances sitting seductively on the sofa. A woman that an hour earlier was the source of all the lust in his sexually starved life, now seemed like a praying mantis… And he was the unsuspecting insect about to get eaten alive. He was trying frantically to keep his cool and not show how scared he was, but he must've failed miserably as she asked, 'Is everything ok?... You look terrified. Please don't be… Come here – I promise I won't bite.'

He walked over to the sofa and sat down very formally next to her. He tried to avoid eye contact for the moment, instead choosing to stare straight ahead. *She'll see the terror in my eyes,* he thought. He then felt her reassuring hand on his shoulder. 'Look at me,' she said with such gentleness that he could've burst into tears.

Slowly he turned to face her, taking an eternity to do so. All the time his brain was rapidly thinking of what to say next that wouldn't make him sound like a complete fool. His voice shook as he came to the only sane conclusion and confessed, 'Look...' *deep gulp of air...* 'I've never been with a girl before... I mean a lady... I mean... well, y' know... I've never had sex before...' After he'd finished his stuttering admission he hung his head in shame.

It took a while for her to digest what he'd said and to find a suitable reply. 'Is that why you've suddenly become so frightened? Please don't worry about anything. As I said - I won't bite. We can just talk. But try and relax. I'm really not going to hurt you.'

'I know you're not. I'm just a little intimidated – not of you, but of "it." And I'm really embarrassed... Who at thirty-nine hasn't had sex?!' he said with a nervous laugh.

Frances set her wine glass down on the coffee table. 'Come here,' she said and cuddled him. To Richard, that cuddle felt even better than the kisses they'd shared earlier on that night. He'd spent his entire life starved of moments of affection. Cuddling his Gran outside the vets after her dog had died was probably as close to this moment as he could remember. That was a cuddle that was required for a totally different reason - for consolation. This one was for comfort and he immediately felt at peace again.

'Thank you,' he said after they separated from their embrace; the shakiness had now left his voice as he began to relax. He reached down and picked up the glass of wine that she had poured for him and took a long, deep glug. He couldn't help but let out an audible sigh afterwards. This sigh was borne out of relief and made her smile. He could almost feel the smile break across her face and turned around to look at her. Seeing her smile made him smile too and seeing him smile made her laugh and before they both knew it they were laughing like idiots.

'Who said I'd have sex with you anyway?' she managed to say through fits of laughter.

'It…I…I… but…' he started to stammer before she put him out of his misery and say that she was just joking. He felt happy and relieved that the brief moment of irrational terror had receded and he was back to being content beyond comparison. When their laughter subsided, he felt the need to apologise. 'I'm sorry for acting like a…' he couldn't think of the right word.

But Frances could '…Div?'

'Yes, a div,' he agreed. It was a familiar insult from his school days and one that seemed mightily appropriate at that particular moment. He nodded his head in subtle appreciation of the word and could feel that Frances was still very curious but too polite to press him on his lack of sexual experience. He couldn't look her in the eye. He sat there staring forward as he took another swig of wine to lubricate his throat before he expanded further on his admission. 'I've never had sex before because I've never really had the opportunity. I don't move in the sort of circles that bring me in contact with women. The only females I ever have contact with are the ladies in the office and they're either scary or really not worth losing "it" to.' The word "it" compensated for the word he couldn't bring himself to say – virginity. It seemed such a formal and out-of-date sort of word.

'You're forgetting about me. You see me pretty much every day on your way to work,' she said in an amazingly soft voice.

'Yes, and you always seemed completely out of my league – a dream woman; one that I had absolutely no chance with... until today.' A smile broke across his face. 'I still can't believe I'm here with you now. It's like a wonderful dream that I'm going to be woken from at any minute... I'm still baffled... Why me? – I know I've asked you this already, but I still can't get my head around it... why me when you could have the pick of any man out there?'

The question hung in the air for a moment before she took a deep glug of wine herself and said, 'I haven't told you this yet as we've only just met and it's all a bit heavy...' She paused as she tried to gather herself for what he could see was her own admission. 'I said I've just come out of an eight-year relationship, and I have. But technically I'm still married – we just haven't got divorced yet. My ex-husband's name is Mike and he was a bit of a bully. He never hit me, but at times I wish he had. It would've been preferable to the way he actually treated me. After years of his mind games, his controlling and manipulation, he left me a shell of the person I used to be.' Her voice broke slightly and Richard saw that her eyes were starting to well-up.

'Look, you don't have to talk about this if you don't want to,' he said. All of a sudden the roles had reversed and he found that he was the concerned one – the comforter.

Frances put a hand up by way of saying that this was something she wanted to say and continued. 'When we first met, he was all charm and smooth talk. He works in the City at some investment bank so he always had money to back up the promises he made, and for the first few years we were very happy. I felt so looked after in those early years. But the problems started when we tried for a baby – alas with no success. Obviously, he blamed me and started using words like "barren" to describe me. We had all the tests and nothing ever suggested there was a problem with me, but Mike wouldn't accept it. He then started sleeping around. Mainly with women he met in bars after work or the few women in his office. At first I knew nothing of it, but the signs were there and soon I became aware of what he was getting up to. But he had a power over me. And slowly but surely, over time, he'd whittled down my self-confidence. I became meek and submissive and didn't have the courage within me to confront him. I just took it. This went on for a few years until one day, after a particularly desperately low point in my life, I took an overdose…' Tears were flowing steadily down Frances' face now but she didn't seem to be aware of them. It saddened him to see her crying. 'It was more of a cry for help than a serious attempt to kill myself and it was Mike that found me. But he seemed more annoyed than sympathetic and refused to take any responsibility. He was incredulous when I challenged him on his many affairs and how unhappy he'd made me. As I lay in that hospital bed, having been examined both physically and mentally, I felt utterly alone. And it was then, at my lowest point, that I had this epiphany. It was like waking from a nightmare. I decided there and then that I'd had enough and I was going to start living my life again – on my terms… So, if you want to know why you… It's because you're everything Mike isn't. I could tell you were fairly…' She searched for the appropriate word, 'innocent… and you always looked at me with such kindness.'

'But I dress… or should I say *dressed* like a complete dork. Nobody in their right mind would be attracted to me.'

Frances let out a little laugh. She seemed relieved that Richard didn't want to focus too heavily on the deeper subjects she'd just divulged. 'I'll be honest; I thought it was the dorky look you were going for… you know, how Jarvis Cocker from Pulp used to look. Being in fashion, albeit lecturing, we're told to stand out and not follow the crowd.'

'Well, I suppose in that sense I've been a roaring success. Who'd have thought, for all those years I was a fashion icon!' His comment was tainted with sarcasm although there was genuine wonderment in his mind.

'Who said anything about being a fashion icon!' They both allowed themselves a little giggle before she broke off to say, 'You *do* look much better now - so handsome and well-groomed.'

He was still unused to receiving compliments; it sounded like she was talking about someone else. He felt himself glowing with a combination of pride and bashfulness. 'Thank you. I don't know what to say.' But he did. He moved closer to her and looked deep into her eyes. 'I think you're the most beautiful woman I've ever seen… and I know I'm not exactly an expert… but you *are* beautiful. And you're not just beautiful on the outside; you have a beautiful and caring soul too. Anyone who would look twice at me, let alone find any attraction towards me must be a sympathetic kind of person.' The last part was delivered with a cute smile; a smile that prompted Frances to grab his face with both hands and pull him towards her. Their kiss this time was passionate and frenzied. He could feel stirrings deep within him, the like he'd never felt before. The earlier shyness seemed a world away as he found himself totally absorbed by the moment. They kissed, they fondled… and there on the living room floor, they made love.

CHAPTER 8

Richard awoke on that bright Sunday morning feeling like a new man. It took him a moment to realise he wasn't in his own bed. This bed was big, luxurious and oh so comfortable He looked down at his chest and saw Frances resting peacefully upon it. If he could pick one brief snapshot of his life to frame and keep for ever it would be this one. It was a perfect picture. He ruffled his hair with his free hand as he tried to think of what time they'd finally gone to bed. It must've been daylight when they finally went to sleep. He scanned the room to see if he could find a clock that would confirm what the time was now. He delicately sat up an inch or two, being extra-especially careful not to disturb her, and spied a bedside clock that gave him the answer. It was coming up to midday. As he lay there so contentedly he allowed himself a moment to reflect and take stock of the past few days. He was usually a man of achingly mundane routine, but the last few days he'd been wildly spontaneous. He'd never wake up at midday usually. He was a creature of habit and always rose around the same time. Today he found himself waking up without much regard to the time; after making love to a beautiful woman, after having an amazing night with the same beautiful woman and his long-lost best friend. He'd been made over, he felt a slow, growing confidence building within him and was about to move into a new flat and away from his awful, oppressive parents. He was just waiting for Jeremy Beadle to spring out of the wardrobe with a big microphone in his withered hand and tell him that it was all an elaborate jape. Fortunately for him, he remembered that Mr Beadle was dead so there was little chance of that happening. He allowed his mind to bask in this oasis of happiness for a while. *Is this what life is really like?* His mind soon found itself wandering back to last night's passionate lovemaking. *What the hell was I worried about?* he mused. He'd nothing to compare it to but he felt like he gave a good account of himself. Whether it'd been the alcohol or the after-effects of the ecstasy he'd taken, but he'd been surprised by his own stamina. He'd always just expected to explode in his pants as soon as a woman went anywhere near his penis. As it happened, for once, this massive life-affirming moment more than lived up to his expectations. In fact, it may well have exceeded them. They'd started on the sofa, and then slipped onto the floor, disrobing as they went. Initially he was shy to be on the verge of nakedness, but there was something about being with Frances that seemed to make him feel comfortable and less self-conscious. Naked, they explored each other's bodies with both passion and tenderness. He'd never felt these sensations before; of lust, of love and this overwhelming feeling of being so alive. When they were finished they lay on the living room floor, their hot bodies still entwined. He couldn't help but sport the biggest, smuggest smile; a smile that Frances could sense without seeing. "Well, you've certainly popped your cherry now," she'd said. They'd both laughed; the sort of laugh that only those blissfully happy could laugh.

When she had led him upstairs to her bedroom, they initially just lay in bed. But, as their naked bodies cuddled up to one another, the urge became too great for him to resist, and a much more sensual love-making session ensued. His dormant libido had been awoken and he had the sexual appetite of a rampant twenty-year-old. In the end, she'd had to tell him she was exhausted and needed to sleep. It was only then that they'd both drifted off into a contented, satisfied slumber. And here he laid, with this beautiful lady - the object of so much of his surreptitious affection, and he really couldn't imagine ever feeling more complete. If he smoked he'd have sparked up the fattest Cuban cigar to honour the moment.

A short while later Frances roused. She looked up at Richard with a groggy but happy face. 'Hey Mister Lothario, how are you feeling?' she said in almost a whisper.

'Honestly? I'm so…so…Ahhh! I don't know! I feel amazing!' he gushed.

'I'm pleased to hear it. Do you know what would make *me* feel amazing?...'

His mind went into porno mode on hearing the suggestive way she posed that question. In a millisecond it was flooded with various sexual positions they could try out. This was abruptly brought to a halt when she answered the question for him '…A nice cup of tea.'

It took a few seconds for him to realise that the request wasn't sexual related before he chirpily said, 'Of course m' lady. Would m' lady like milk and sugar?'

'Milk, no sugar please,' Frances replied as he slipped out from under the covers. He was suddenly conscious of his nakedness and he covered the front part of his nakedness like a pre-pubescent schoolboy heading for the showers after P.E. class. Frances had rolled over and observed him with her head cradled in her hands. 'You shouldn't be so shy. You've got a lovely body. And a really sexy bum.'

He didn't know how to contend with two quick-fire compliments so joked instead 'What, this?' he said looking down at his bottom. 'Why, that's kind of you to say. I was going to ask for another one though. This one appears to have a crack in it… and it leaks occasionally.' He left the bedroom to the sweetest sound… of Frances giggling.

Making his way down to the kitchen, he took in his current surroundings. The flat was all pale grey, white and subtle beige. All of the furnishings were fluffy and comfortable; in fact, the whole house had a homely, serene feel to it. He sniffed the air and the scent that filled his nostrils was floral and fragrant. *His* home stank of cigarettes and stale booze. The furnishing in *his* home were worn and stained. After being here it was going to be a hard task to step foot back in, what he was now going to refer to, his parent's home.

He couldn't wait to move into his new place. *It'll be a long week,* he thought to himself.

Still naked and with his mind still wandering he stepped into the kitchen. The sunlight glared through the window, temporarily blinding him. He raised a lazy hand to shield his eyes and let them adjust to this sudden influx of light. When his eyes had acclimatised he saw, what appeared to be, a dark figure silhouetted just in front of him – or that's what it looked like anyway. He blinked a couple of times and wiped his eyes with his fingers and when he opened them again it was to the sound of a man's voice. 'Good morning.' The voice was strong and resonant.

Richard let out a shriek and shirked away – admittedly not the manliest response he could've mustered, but when he regained his poise and, more importantly, his focus, he could see the figure was sat on a kitchen stool with one leg folded over the other. He was broad and on closer inspection, well-dressed, with dark slick-back hair. Well-dressed was something Richard wasn't. His hands moved rapidly from his face to his groin in a belated effort to cover his modesty.

'Please don't feel you need to cover yourself up on my account,' the man said.

By this stage Richard had a fair idea who he was confronted with. 'Mike, right?' He shifted his hands to offer one of them for the man to shake.

'Pardon me if I don't, I've just seen where that hand's been.' The man's voice was calm and measured. 'But you are correct. I am Mike and I assume you've just had sex with my wife.' He then stood up and Richard suddenly felt very intimidated. Mike stood far taller than him and had the burly physique of someone who'd had played a lot of rugby in their time. Richard felt very small and very naked in comparison. Without saying anything or making any further movement, Mike had managed to make Richard feel more and more intimidated by the second. There was an uncomfortable silence where the only sound that Richard could hear was that of his heart pumping furiously in, what seemed to be, his throat. He really wasn't sure what to do next but fortunately he was rescued by his fair maiden who had silently padded down the stairs and barked, '*Mike, what the hell are you doing here?!*'

'Hello darling, I just thought I'd stop by and pick up a few bits.'

'Don't you dare "*hello darling*" me.' Frances' voice was full of anger. Richard suddenly felt very much like he was in the way. 'Get out and get out now!' she yelled.

'Woah, calm down Franny, it's still my house. I believe I'm still paying half the mortgage here.'

'And don't call me Franny either,' she said with venom. 'You don't have the right to just let yourself in now we're separated. I told you I would go to the police and get an injunction if you tried this crap again - and I will. Now, I'll give you to the count of ten to get the hell out.' Her eyes were wide and furious and they locked onto Mike's who remained very passive and controlled.

He took a moment before he replied, 'I've forgotten how sexy you are when you're angry. Look, I don't want to cause a scene. Your little naked friend here has done that himself.' He gestured towards Richard who was still standing with his hands shielding his groin and feeling as conspicuous as it was possible to be. 'Allow me to collect what I need and I'll be on my way.'

'You haven't got anything else left here. You've just come here to piss me off,' Frances said in a much more restrained manner. She'd quickly regained her composure and she didn't want to give Mike anymore ammunition to upset her. 'I'll count to ten – that should give you enough time to get what you need – and then you can bugger off. I'll get the locks changed and if you ever try and pull a stunt like this again, I'll get the police involved… The sooner the divorce goes through the better.'

'I'm sorry you feel that way, baby.' The mere word "baby" in reference to her made her skin bristle with fury, but she held her tongue and let him say his piece before she started counting. 'You know I still love you and I know I'm guilty of neglecting you a bit in the past.' His voice was smooth and sounded full of sincerity as he continued, 'If you feel the need to get back at me by sleeping with other men, I'll let you get it out of your system and I'll be there when you're past this… phase.' He said the last word with pure contempt as he waved his hand in Richard's direction, but still remained icy cool.

'One... two...' Frances started counting.

'You know what; I don't really think I do need anything now after all so I'll be off,' Mike said and held out his hand for Richard to shake. Richard didn't know what to do so, reluctantly, he went to shake it. As his hand was about to grasp Mike's, Mike suddenly shifted as if he was going to punch Richard in the stomach. Instinctively Richard went to protect himself and felt an excruciating pain and looked down to find Mike's large hand squeezing his genitals. His grip was strong and he yanked Richard closer to him and whispered menacingly into his ear, 'If you want to keep hold of these little things in my hand I suggest you never come around here again... Do you understand me?'

Richard was stood on tiptoes in a vain effort to lessen the pain. He was wincing and his teeth were gritted as he delivered his reply by way of a frantic nod. Whether he meant it or not didn't matter. He just wanted Mike's hand to stop crushing his testicles – testicles that only a few hours before were the happiest testicles in the world. Now they felt like they were as delicate as over-ripe grapes and could squish at any time.

'Let him go now!' Frances said, 'Let him go and get out!'

Mike released his grip and gave Richard a condescending slap on the cheek. Richard fell on the floor, coughing. He felt sick and dizzy as his eyes filled with water. 'Nice to meet you,' Mike said to Richard who was now curled-up in a fetal position and rolling around in agony. 'Franny, I'll see you again soon. I'm not working next week so, who knows, I might pop by again. But ciao for now.' He then calmly left the kitchen and then the house.

As soon as the door shut Frances rushed over to Richard. 'I'm *so* sorry. Are you ok?' she said as she stroked his hair.

'Well, he was charming,' Richard managed to say in an octave higher than usual. 'I can't imagine why you'd possibly want to leave him.'

'He's a complete arsehole – I'm so sorry.' She helped Richard to his feet but he was obviously in a lot of discomfort.

'That's just typical,' he said still wincing. 'I've only just started using them for the purpose they were made for and now they've been crushed and probably incapable of working.' He sucked in a few gulps of air before he said, 'If it's alright with you I'd really like to put some clothes on now.'

He was shown to the bathroom where the serenity of the room instantly soothed him. As with the rest of the house, it was decorated in delicate colours and had modern fixtures and fittings. When he felt brave enough, he looked down to inspect the damage. He was relieved to find that both testicles were still there, although he was now convinced that they were squashed and misshapen. There was no bruising or visible sign of the ordeal they'd just been put through, which belied the aching that emanated from that region. He leaned over the sink and stared into the bathroom mirror. He felt nauseous. He hadn't really expected to have his gonads crushed by an over-sized ex-husband when he woke up that morning. And the day had all started so happily and tranquilly too. It was just his luck to have finally found his state of grace; his Zen, only for a manipulative ex to bring him crashing back to reality. In an effort to subdue the enveloping wooziness, he helped himself to a shower where the warm water cascading over him soothed his body and allowed him to relax again. By the time he'd smothered himself in the fluffiest towel he'd ever felt, the rigours of the past half hour seemed like just a bad dream.

When he returned downstairs to the kitchen he found Frances still in her dressing gown, sitting with her head in her hands. It was obvious that she'd been crying but she was determined not to show him. On his arrival, she hurriedly rubbed her eyes and wandered over to the fridge in an effort to hide her face. It was too late though; he had seen her. She cut a sorrowful figure with her eyes puffed-up and her nose red and running. 'Would you like some breakfast?' she said trying to sound as chirpy as she could, but the sniffing gave her away. 'I could make you some toast. Sorry, I haven't got much in. I'm not a big breakfast person.'

He felt an overwhelming need to go over and comfort her. She suddenly seemed so fragile. He walked over to her and put his arms around her from behind and then pulled her in close to him. She seemed to melt under his embrace and it was then that he was aware of just how petit she was. She nestled her head into the crook of his arm. Richard suddenly felt like a man again. After the demeaning scenario of appearing naked in front of her ex-husband and having his balls squashed to the size of pistachios, he needed a moment of redemption like this. 'Are you ok?' he asked although it was plainly obviously that she wasn't, but he knew he had to say something.

'I'll be alright. Mike's mastered the art of getting under my skin. I can't believe that I used to love him. He's such a…' Frances searched for the right word but it was the only word that was appropriate '…bully.' She then sank, dejectedly after saying it.

'I definitely think you should get the locks changed. It's not right that he lets himself in whenever he wants,' he said in almost a whisper.

'I know. I'll do that tomorrow.' There was then a pause when he could almost hear her mind working. After a moment or two she said, 'That was the reason you didn't see me on your way to work on Friday morning. When I got home on Thursday night after seeing you in the pub, there he was waiting for me in the living room – as if he still lived here. He didn't seem to think there was anything wrong with it. I was completely taken unawares and didn't know what to do. I told him to get out but he remained so calm and didn't move an inch. He just wanted to know about my evening, who I was with etc etc… I couldn't answer quickly enough before he was firing another question at me. Telling him it was none of his business didn't seem to have any effect. Telling him to get out didn't have any effect either. He just sat there on the sofa, legs crossed, as calm as you like, grilling me like it was his right to do so.' She sounded weary and far from the fun-loving, vibrant person he'd got to know over the past few days. She now turned around to face him and looked up at him with wet, puffy eyes. 'I said I would change the locks, I said I would call the police but he didn't seem too concerned; he just sat there as bold as brass. In the end I didn't have it in me; I was just too exhausted and wanted to go to bed… So, I left him there on the sofa and switched all the lights off. I hoped he might take the hint and bugger off. But when I woke and went downstairs there he was asleep on the sofa... I just lost it. I woke him up and tried to manhandle him up off the sofa but as you've seen he's not exactly small and he seemed to take great amusement in seeing me struggle. The more wound up and frustrated I became, the more that smug smile grew across his smug fucking face. And after the amount we'd drank the night before it wasn't long before that started came back to haunt me. I had to break off from this ordeal and deal with the impending prospect of throwing up. Believe me, I was sorely tempted to throw up all over him but didn't want to get any sick on the sofa so I rushed over to the toilet as quick as I could. I made it just in time. Mike wasted no time in trying to be chivalrous, offering to hold my hair whilst I puked. It's hard to have an argument with someone whilst your head is halfway down a toilet, but I tried my best. In the end I think Mike saw the fruitlessness of his endeavours

– that or he no longer saw the attraction of someone chucking their guts up – and he made some half-hearted excuse that he had to be somewhere else and left. As soon as he left the house I just broke down and cried. I was still holding onto the toilet for dear life but I sobbed like a baby. He just upset me so much. After that I couldn't face work and spent the rest of the day curled up on the sofa feeling sorry for myself until Jenny came round after work and shook me out of my doldrums. That's when she said she was going to take me out to the nightclub last night.' Frances finished with a weary sigh, a sigh from the depths of her soul.

   Richard didn't say anything. He was just trying to take in everything Frances had just said. He couldn't help but be secretly pleased that Mike was such an arsehole. This made it so much easier to dislike him. It was now all the easier for him, Richard, to be seen as the good guy – the knight in shining armour as it were. In the absence of words he brought Frances in close again and cuddled her. He could feel the relief emanate from deep within her as her arms folding around his waist. They held that position for what seemed like an eternity; neither one wishing to pull away from the embrace.

CHAPTER 9

After a locksmith had been booked in to change the locks they both dressed and ready to make belated use of the afternoon. Richard was still in last night's clothing which carried the stale smells of the night's activities. Despite Frances trying to reassure him that he looked fine and smelt fine, Richard, who in the space of a day, had become very conscious of his appearance, was adamant he needed some fresh clothes to wear. And in keeping with his new-found spontaneity, he decided to buy a whole new outfit.

Again, the weather was unseasonably warm, and people were out in their droves. Brighton on a warm day attracts a fantastic array of people from all walks of life. Gorgeous and perfectly preened girls and boys were joined on the busy streets by the more rotund and misshapen that were poured into ill-fitting clothing. The affluent and carefree strolled obliviously past the destitute and poor. Gay, straight and everything in between rubbed shoulders; everyone with their own agenda.

Richard and Frances' first port of call was a boutique menswear shop in The South Lanes. Richard didn't protest when Frances took charge and picked him out a short-sleeved shirt and some slim-fitting trousers. He certainly wasn't going to argue with someone who taught fashion for a living, although he was a little unsure what he'd been given to try on in the changing rooms. But his concerns were allayed when he stepped out and looked upon his reflection in the mirror. He gave her a nod of satisfied acknowledgement, and after purchasing a pair of espadrilles to finish the outfit off, they left the shop to continue their day.

Richard was forced to squint due to the strong sunshine and it wasn't long before Frances was dragging him into a shop to buy some sunglasses – and not just any cheap sunglasses – a slick pair of Ray Ban Aviators. "A perma-fashion" Frances called them. He didn't think it was possible to feel any cooler, but as he walked arm in arm with Frances, he felt his gait take on a whole new strut. They meandered their way to the seafront where the sea glistened and the smell of fish & chips and freshly made doughnuts filled their nostrils. It was days like these that Brighton really was one of the best places in the country. It has a buzz – an energy - that gave the city a feel-good aura that is unsurpassed.

'Let's go to the Pier!' Frances excitedly exclaimed. She'd said it with such enthusiasm that he couldn't refuse and before he knew it he was being dragged across the busy seafront road, through a gaggle of people and found himself at the entrance of the pier. The smell of doughnuts was now too hard to resist and they eagerly purchased some to share as they strolled along the wooden walkways of the pier. The Brighton Pier (or the Palace Pier as locals called it) was constructed in 1899 and is still one of the most visited tourist attractions, not just in Brighton, but in the UK. Unnecessarily loud amusement arcades belted out all manner of sounds and music; a tide of people mooched up and down the half kilometre pier. It was tacky, it was loud, but Richard couldn't help but sport a huge, beaming smile as he walked hand in hand along with Frances. In all the time he'd been a resident of Brighton & Hove he couldn't recollect ever being on the Pier. He felt like a kid again – a kid that hadn't had the good fortune of a loving childhood. But the sun was shining and life had *very* suddenly got *very* good.

After their walk along the pier Frances suggested keeping the tourist vibe going. Their next destination was the Royal Pavilion. She'd predicted Richard must've walked past this impressive, ostentatious palace a thousand times and, like most of the residents of Brighton & Hove, never actually been inside it.

The grandness of the Royal Pavilion was breathtaking. On wandering around the many rooms and halls Richard appreciated that King George IV, who'd commissioned the building of it, certainly wasn't one to do things by halves. Each room was outlandishly decorated and remarkably different from the next. Richard's favourite was the Music Room which had a wondrously eerie feeling of history as he looked around it. He could almost imagine what had gone on in this room during the King's many parties there. Frances watched Richard's face beam in amazement. She felt a pang of pity that his life was really only starting now. She had an overwhelming feeling of sympathy and a strong desire to help him live the life he should have led. For his part, Richard was listening intently to the commentary of the tour guide who explained the extent of King George IV's extravagant parties. This was a chap who'd really lived his life and, it seemed, enjoyed every single minute of it. Richard was moved and deeply inspired. He admired the fact that he still spoken about and remembered so many years after his death. It provided him with yet another epiphanic moment. As each day passed he was becoming more and more determined to make up for lost time and live his own life to its fullest.

By the time they left the Royal Pavilion both their stomachs were rumbling noisily. They decided to find a restaurant as a matter of urgency. 'What do you fancy eating?' Frances asked.

'I'm not fussed. Surprise me,' Richard casually replied.

With a casual shrug of her shoulders, she grabbed him by the hand and led him to a nearby restaurant. He was soon sat in a small and very simple Thai restaurant. It was cramped and busy but they managed to find the only table left. Frances was expectantly waiting for him to share his thoughts. She'd guessed, correctly, that he'd never had Thai food before and was eagerly anticipating his thoughts. Sitting there he scanned the menu they'd just been handed and all the while Frances was staring at him, awaiting his reaction.

Finally, he tossed the menu down, 'Ok, I give up. What would you order because I haven't a clue what this menu says?'

Frances chuckled and asked the waiter for the English version of the menu. 'I think you need to sample a green curry,' she said pointing to it on the menu. 'You've never had Thai food?'

'Not unless it was given to me as a very small child... which I very much doubt,' Richard replied. 'I've led quite a sheltered life and that goes for the cuisine I've eaten over the years. If it was bland and tasteless then I'd probably have eaten it.'

'Well, this should be very interesting then,' Frances mused.

Moments later the waiter took their order and delivered them some Thai beer each and a bottle of water to share. Richard looked wistfully at Frances and found it hard to believe that they'd known each other for such a short time but sitting here now it was like they'd been together for years.

'Hello!' Frances said waving at Richard. He realised that he'd inadvertently been staring at her, or more accurately, through her. He gently shook his head to regain his focus and apologised. 'Don't worry,' she reassured him. 'You looked miles away. What were you thinking about?'

'Oh, nothing,' he replied. 'I just can't believe how easy your company is and how much I've enjoyed spending time with you.'

'The feeling's mutual,' she said with friendly smile.

When the food arrived they both looked down at their dishes in different ways. For Frances it was a look of real appreciation and for Richard it was a look of slight fear. 'Here it goes,' he said after taking in a deep breath of air. Mesmerised, Frances couldn't help but watch as the first mouthful hit his tongue. He coughed and quickly reached for his glass of water, draining it in seconds. It was like he'd put molten lava in his mouth. As he gasped for air like a fish out of water, Frances couldn't help but laugh and nearly sprayed him with the mouthful of food she'd been about to swallow. Other diners turned around to see them both red-faced and laughing hysterically. Some tutted, some gave disapproving looks. But they couldn't of care less. They were oblivious to anyone apart from one another and they were having fun.

After they'd finally finished their meals, which for Richard had started off as a bit of an ordeal but ended up being as enjoyable as Frances', they felt full, relaxed and in need of a sofa to lounge on. The past few days' exertions had certainly taken their toll.

They decided to head back at Frances' house and when they'd arrived there Frances seemed very edgy, as if she'd been waiting for Mike to spring up out of nowhere. Sensing this Richard had taken control and had gone to the kitchen and poured them a glass of red wine. After handing Frances hers, they both collapsed on the sofa. Richard let out a heavy sigh 'I'm really not looking forward to going home later,' he said sorrowfully.

'You don't have to. You can stay with me if you like,' Frances replied.

He could sense the pang of fear she was feeling at the thought of being left alone. 'I'd love that but I've got work tomorrow and sooner or later I've got to face my parents.' He had, over the course of the past two days, told her all about his parents including the fact that he still lived with them - a fact she'd taken in her stride – and now he found himself facing up to the looming prospect of dealing with their ridicule once again when he returned. He was also nervous about work. He knew people would be staring at him in his new suit, with his new haircut. The thought of all that attention being focused on him made him feel queasy. But if this weekend had taught him anything, it was that he should confront things head on.

'Stay with me tonight. I'll pay for you to get a cab back in the morning,' Frances said.

When she talked like that he really didn't have any answer. *What the hell?! She's asking me to stay with her. Don't be an idiot. Say yes!* Even his own mind was having a go at him now! 'Alright then. As long as you don't mind me leaving at the crack of dawn.'

A smile grew across Frances' face and they clinked glasses before they both took a long sip. Both seemed mightily relieved at Richard's agreement to stay. Frances, because she didn't want to be by herself for fear of another unexpected appearance of Mike, and Richard, because he would hopefully avoid seeing his parents before he went to work.

As they lay in bed later, with Frances resting contently on Richard's chest, both were quiet, deep in their separate thoughts. Richard was still coming to terms with all that had happened in the past few days and wondering what the next few days held in store.

And Frances was scared of what Mike might do next. He still seemed to have the power to disrupt her life and make her feel scared and fragile. *Was it fair on Richard to bring him into all this turmoil?* she wondered. Their respective thoughts swirled around their heads and, despite their obvious fatigue, sleep took its time to come. When the sound of an unfamiliar alarm clock shook him from his slumber it felt like he'd only been asleep for a few minutes. It was with a heavy heart that he left Frances lying peacefully asleep in her bed.

After dressing he left the house and climbed into the taxi which had arrived outside. He didn't notice the man sitting in the expensive BMW. A man that seconds after the taxi had disappeared from view, got out of the car and walked towards Frances' house.

CHAPTER 10

Richard stood at the front door of what he now referred to as "his parents' house." He lifted his face towards the heavens and took a deep breath, then, as quietly and carefully as he could, he turned the key and opened the door. On stepping through the threshold, he quickly felt like an intruder. To him it just didn't feel like his home anymore. The stench of nicotine and whatever that other stale smell was quickly filled his nostrils. He scanned the hallway and looked up the stairs, listening intently for any tell-tale signs of his parents awakening. It was as if he was avoiding waking a dragon but in many ways that's exactly what it was. He knew it wasn't worth the trouble to wake them. *"Where've you bin? Whatchoo bin up to? You fink yer sumink special now do ya boy?"* He could hear his Dad's voice berating him even though he was sound asleep. That thought inspired him to be extra quiet as he tiptoed his way up the stairs and into his bedroom. Once in the sanctuary of his bedroom he quickly and quietly set about sorting through the clothing he'd bought a couple of days prior. He held up one suit, then the other. Even in the dimly lit room, both suits looked lovely – far too good to waste on his office. He deliberated for a moment on wearing his usual attire; at least no one would mock him. He could be as unremarkable as he usually was. Sure, someone might make a comment of his new haircut but he could handle that. As he contemplated all this he rubbed his chin, much like any great thinker would do, and felt a few days' worth of stubble. *I need a shave,* he quickly surmised.

With expert care, he navigated his was along the landing, as skilful as ever in his ability to avoid the creaky floorboards and reached the bathroom. Confident that, as he'd been awake for quite a while now, he was fully prepared for the harsh, bright light of the bathroom... Or so he thought; the moment he pulled the light cord it was like he'd watched an atom bomb explode. Shielding his eyes from the savage brightness, he made his way over to the sink. He looked in the mirror and hardly recognised the image staring back at him. He looked completely different. Obviously, his haircut changed his appearance somewhat but there was definitely something else that looked different about him; some of the innocence his face had always carried had, over the course of the weekend disappeared, likely never to return again. It had been replaced by a more "knowing" expression. He certainly didn't see it as bad thing – quite the opposite. As he stared at his reflection he saw a man looking back at him, rather than the overgrown teenager he'd been used to observing. He did look tired though. The weekend's endeavours had certainly taken their toll, but after a shave and a shower he looked infinitely better. Taking care to style his hair with his new hair products, he regarded his appearance again in the mirror and felt a surge of confidence rush through him. With that same confidence and a satisfied smile etched on his face he opened door... and let out an impulsive scream, for there, standing right in front of him was his father, in all his glory. 'Where've you bin all weekend?' he barked aggressively.

Well, you were right about that, Richard thought, referring to his father's predictable tirade. He wouldn't have minded if that comment were born out of concern for his well-being, but it wasn't. It was born out of jealousy and spite. They just didn't want himself. But Gerry's unexpected appearance and the hostile delivery of his question caught Richard completely unawares, and he was momentarily lost for words. He'd never known his father to be up at this time and given his father's appearance, he didn't think this ungodly time of the morning did him any favours. His hair was even more messed up than usual and his gut protruded extensively from the bottom of, what seemed to be the same vest he'd been wearing for many days now. And, if it were possible, that vest carried even more stains than the last time he'd had the misfortune to see it. He looked like he'd been in a food-fight – and lost. If there was an upside to this sorry sight confronting Richard, it was that his father's gut hung so low that it screened his nether-regions which were mercifully contained in an age-old pair of grey Y-fronts. 'I... I... I've been staying at a friend's. W... what are you doing up anyway?'

He suddenly felt a hard slap across his face. 'Don't give me lip boy!' Gerry growled. The slap sent a surge pain up to his brain and tears involuntarily formed in his eyes. A moment later their bedroom door opened and another visual treat greeted him. His Mum, Sylvia stood there in her nightie and gawdy dressing gown, rubbing her eyes. She looked like she'd been pieced together with plasticine. Thankfully, her dressing gown was sparing Richard's eyes from the obvious body-carnage going on beneath. 'What's all this commotion?' she said, still rubbing her eyes. When she regained her vision she squawked, 'Where've you bin? We've been worried sick ain't we Ger'?'

'Yeah, worried, that's what we've been,' Gerry reiterated. 'You can't treat this place like a flamin' 'otel boy. Off out wiv yer boyfriend doin' god-knows-what.'

Richard stood there being chastised but inwardly his blood was beginning to boil. He wanted to tell them exactly what he thought of them but he really didn't have the time. He had to finish getting ready and get to work. He was sorely tempted to tell them that he was moving out the following weekend but he wanted to leave that pleasure until the time was right. This wasn't it. They were still rebuking him when he pushed past them. 'I'm sorry, but I haven't got time for this,' he said as he bulldozed his way past their combined podgy mass. It made his skin crawl to have touched their flabby, odorous bodies. He could hear his father's voice getting louder and more irate but he'd switched off now. He'd mastered the art of zoning out from his parent's insults. He felt his father's slipper hit him on the back of his head as he reached his bedroom and closed the door behind him. A few bangs on the door and his father gave up and returned to their bedroom. Richard breathed a sigh of relief. His adrenalin was pumping after the confrontation but that only spurred him on to get ready for work quicker. He no longer doubted what he should wear. He put on one of his new shirts, which he had to admit, felt wonderful upon his skin – not like the scratchy old shirts he used to wear to the office. Then he slipped on the trousers of his chosen suit. The suit was grey and slim fitting. They fitted perfectly. The belt he put around them was just for show. He then put on his tie – not one of his new ones, but his favourite tie - the tie his Grandmother had bought him, and then finally, and somewhat indulgently, he pulled on the suit jacket. He didn't need to look in the mirror to know whether he looked good or not. It all felt so good he just *knew* it looked good. He felt empowered; he felt strong; he felt confident… But he also felt mightily nervous about walking into the office dressed like this. But he didn't have time to stress about that now. He was running late. He left his room, crept downstairs and made himself some breakfast. After he'd polished off his Shredded Wheat and a cup of tea he quickly brushed his teeth. Before he knew it he was out the door and strutting along in his new Barker brogues.

Despite his parents trying their hardest to burst his bubble, Richard walked along with his head held high and sporting a proud smile. The sun was shining brightly which only accentuated his confident mood. As he donned his new Aviator shades he couldn't remember ever feeling like this before. He was seeing the world in a whole new way; much clearer and much more optimistically. Boldly strolling along the familiar route to work, his mind was filled with thoughts of

Frances. He wasn't concerned whether he saw her on his way to work this morning. He had seen *all* of her during the past few days. He still found it hard to believe that things had moved in the direction they had, and with such speed. Sure, he'd walked into a bit of a situation with her and her ex, but he was confident that, being the non-threatening kind of guy he was, she'd seek comfort and solace in him. Richard wasn't one to judge people but it was plainly obvious that Mike was a controlling and manipulative bully. Confrontation was something he avidly sought to avoid, but he wished he were that little bit bigger and that little bit braver so he could stand up to Mike. It made him shiver when he thought of how Mike had crushed his gonads before completely disregarding him. In his mind he recounted his meeting with Mike but this time, instead of just standing there naked and intimidated, he used some rapid kung fu moves leaving Mike with a cracked windpipe and bruised testicles of his own. Just the thought of this fictitious encounter made his adrenalin pump, but before he got too carried away he thought, *Perhaps I'd better master a martial art before playing out such fantasies.*

So caught up in his thoughts was he that he barely realised that he'd arrived at the doorstep of his office. He froze momentarily. *I could just take the day off sick. I never take the day off sick,* he thought, but an inner determination made him move up the steps and into the office.

As he made his way from the corridor, into the main office, he used all his concentration in order to keep his head up and focused on getting to his desk. But out of the corner of his eye he saw Martin Bradshaw talking to their short, plump colleague, Emma Buxton. Martin fleetingly caught his gaze but both were quick to look away and it was with great relief that Richard sunk into his chair and switched on his PC. After his upbeat strut to work and his adrenaline-fused walk into the office, his brow was beading with sweat. It was just as he mopped at his sweaty forehead that Emma Buxton came rolling into view. 'Oh, hi Richard, how are you?... I couldn't help but notice that you look rather handsome today. What's happened? – Not that I'm complaining! It's just a very impressive transformation if you don't mind me saying so.' She was in full-on flirtatious mode and even finished her last sentence with a cheeky giggle.

Richard didn't know whether to be flattered or not. His overriding compulsion was to run away from this uncomfortable situation but he didn't want to hurt Emma's feelings. He just took a big gulp and wide-eyed, politely said, 'Thank you. I thought it was time for a change.'

This only egged Emma on as she playfully stroked his arm and whispered, 'You look lovely – literally, good enough to eat.' She finished the last word with rolling her tongue across her teeth to accentuate the seductive delivery of her comment.

Richard blushed furiously and it was as much as he could do to say, 'I'd rather you didn't eat me. I might get stuck in your throat.' But as soon as he'd said it he inwardly winced and realised he really shouldn't have said anything at all.

'I wouldn't mind getting certain parts of you stuck in my throat.' she suggestively. Another flirtatious look followed. Richard sank cringingly back into his chair. 'Anyway, you know where I am. Come and find me later,' she said enticingly, putting a firm hand at the top of his thigh. He felt his entire body stiffen, including his penis which was now perilously close to Emma's hand. *Please move your hand, please move your hand, please move your hand!* he inwardly begged. Fortunately, Emma, having seemingly read his mind moved her hand away and waddled back over to her desk, but not before she gave him, what she thought at least was, one last, alluring look. He sat there for a moment; bright red and perspiring, wondering why he found himself getting aroused by Emma Buxton. Mildly flustered, he gave the office floor a quick scan to see if anyone had witnessed him getting propositioned. The only person he did see was Martin Bradshaw who again looked away as soon as their eyes met. Richard then leaned back in his chair and breathed out a massive sigh of relief. In keeping with the past few days, this morning had been a truly surreal experience. He switched on his PC, looked at the screen and tried desperately to focus; but try as he might his mind kept flashing images of the weekend's activities. It was a lot for his brain to contend with. After so many years of relative inactivity it was now dealing with a sudden influx of new sensations, emotions and worthwhile memories. His mind seemed to linger on the mental images of Frances; especially those when they'd made love. It'd been absolutely blissful; so blissful in fact that he let out an involuntary, contented sigh. It was at this moment that Graeme Chandler walked past his desk. Graeme had to do a double-take as the sight of Richard's change of appearance registered. 'Bloody hell Rich; I didn't recognise you there. What happened?! You look great!'

Awoken from his dreamy thoughts, Richard replied bashfully, 'Thanks. I just fancied a change.'

'And what a change,' Graeme enthused as he scanned Richard from top to toe. 'I'm not kidding you mate; you look amazing…I mean, that suit looks incredible… and expensive!…As do those shoes…Wow!... Look, I've got to get cracking but let's go for lunch somewhere and you can fill me with everything.'

Richard felt a proud glow wash over him as he turned his attention back to his PC and the working day ahead. But it soon became apparent that he was struggling to get motivated about work. In truth, he always struggled to get motivated about work, but after the enlightening developments of the weekend, today felt a much greater struggle than usual. He knew this would be the next thing on his agenda to address. He'd gotten so used to the routine of his working life that he hadn't appreciated how much he loathed it. He turned up, did his bit and then went home. There was nothing remarkable or dynamic in what he did or what he could do. He knew it was definitely time for a change.

And this was what he discussed with Graeme as they sat in a coffee shop later that day. He'd already filled Graeme in with all the goings-on over the previous weekend which he found a bit of a novelty. He wasn't used to talking so much about himself but Graeme was keen to know everything. Graeme had always been the only one in his office that paid any attention to him and was genuinely pleased to hear of all these life-affirming developments that had occurred over the course of one weekend. As Richard was talking it all sounded so bizarre – almost as if he were making it up, but Graeme knew what an honest person Richard was and listened intently with a big smile on his face.

'Good for you mate. It might've taken you some time but at least things are going in the right direction for you at long last. I still can't believe you bagged that Frances girl. She's gorgeous.'

Richard chuckled 'Nor can I. It's been a weird and wonderful few days but I'm not going to complain.' There was a pause in conversation before Richard then continued, 'With everything that's gone on it's really made me re-evaluate my life…'

'And so it should mate,' Graeme interjected. 'You've got to grab hold of your life with both hands. Believe me if I weren't tied down with wife and kids I'd be doing just that. I'm not saying that I resent my family or anything, but once you've had kids they anchor you down and you can't be so impulsive. You've got the luxury of having the world as your oyster. Go live your life.' The cogs started to turn in Richard's mind as it was suddenly flooded with a ream of possibilities. He stared into space as his mind wondered here, there and everywhere. Graeme wondered whether the epiphany he'd just triggered had blown a fuse in Richard's brain. 'Look, I've got to get back but I'm so glad for you. You've had to put up with a lot of shit from people like Martin and some of these other idiots in the office. Now it's time for you to spread your wings my friend…'

All that afternoon his mind wandered and many times he caught himself staring vacantly at nothing in particular. Graeme's parting words repeated again and again in his mind. He had an overriding urge to just march into his boss' office and hand in his notice, but he wasn't quite ready to be that impulsive. He had to reign himself in a little. *Let me deal with moving out of my parent's place first* he thought. *And let's see what comes of me and Frances.* He desperately wanted to send her a message to let her know he was thinking of her; to unload some of the million or so thoughts that had been engulfing his brain. It was only then that he realised that he didn't have her phone number. In the intense time he'd known her it had never crossed his mind to take her number. After all, it wasn't something he was used to doing. He'd only got Matt's number because Matt had physically put it in his phone himself. Richard cursed himself for forgetting to do the fairly obvious thing of exchanging numbers with the lady he'd been infatuated with for such a long time. He consoled himself by deciding to pop by her place on the way home. He could just about remember where she lived. *It would be spontaneous. She'd love that. Perhaps I'll buy her some flowers. Yes, that's a great idea. Richard – you're on fire today!*

All that thinking had made him thirsty so he decided to go to the watercooler and get a cup of water. He still felt very self-conscious walking through the office. Aware as he was that people were staring at him in his new suit, with his jazzy new haircut. It was with palpable relief that he made it to the watercooler, situated in a secluded alcove at the back of the office. He'd just finished gulping down a cup of water when Pauline Matthews came over to join him. He could smell her scent long before he saw her. It was an overpowering smell that made his nose twitch. She made a point of brushing herself up against him as she reached for a cup. 'Hi Richard,' she said as she looked seductively over her black-rimmed spectacles. Kitted out in her stock PA outfit of high-heals and figure-hugging black dress Richard couldn't deny that, for her age, she looked very alluring. He also couldn't deny that she scared the shit out of him. This was as close as he'd ever been to her and, not for the first time that day, he was feeling a trifle uncomfortable. 'You look…' she paused whilst she thought of the suitable adjective, '…different.' *Well, she could've been a bit more descriptive,* he thought as he absorbed, what he assumed, was a compliment. He tried to edge his way past Pauline, smiling inanely in an effort to disguise his desire to get the hell out of there. 'Not so fast,' Pauline said in a domineering voice. 'Do I intimidate you Richard?' she asked as she looked intently into his eyes.

Richard stood open-mouthed, not knowing what the best answer to this question would be. After what seemed like an eternity he managed to reply 'I…I…Well…If …If I'm honest… Yes…Yes you do.'

This seemed to amuse Pauline. A smile grew across her face as she said, 'Do y'know, you're the talk of the office? Even Charlotte has made note of your new appearance.'

The thought of one his bosses even paying him the slightest regard sent a surge of pride through him. 'It's only a haircut and a suit,' Richard said modestly.

'Don't play it down Richard,' Pauline said as she put a hand gently on his chest. 'It's been noted… And not just by Charlotte...'

He was all in a fluster again and he could feel nervous sweat forming on his forehead and on his back. His obvious distress seemed only to inspire Pauline who upped the stakes by leaning in even closer and whispering in his ear, 'I want you…' she paused to let the words resonate in his mind. Richard's eyes grew as wide as saucers as she continued '…I want you to come to Charlotte's office at the end of the day.' Richard again gulped and was trying hard to think of something to say before Pauline put him out of his misery. 'Don't worry Richard. Charlotte wants to speak with you.' She was enjoying seeing him squirm and as seductively as she'd arrived, she moved away and turned on her heels. '5pm Richard. Don't be late,' she said in a voice loud enough for the entire office to hear which prompted heads to rise from workstations like meerkats. Richard stood there red-faced and sweating, with a subtle bulge forming in the front of his trousers. *Down boy, down,* he subconsciously told his ever-ready penis. He could really do without parading back to his desk with a highly noticeable boner trying to poke out his trousers. He took a deep breath a tried to compose himself. After another cup of water, he strolled back and sank into his chair. *What a day!* He wasn't used to women propositioning him or even being suggestive towards him, but all of a sudden he'd become a babe-magnet. Well, perhaps babe-magnet was a bit of an exaggeration going by his new-found office fan-club, but it was still uncharted territory for him. He also knew he'd be fretting his way through the last couple of hours wondering what Charlotte Mulberry might want with him. Surely she didn't want to have her wicked way with him too. But she was happily married with two teenage children, so he very much doubted that.

When 5 o'clock came, he rose groggily from his seat and he made his way to Charlotte Mulberry's office. Outside her office he found Pauline Matthews sitting at her desk. When she saw him, she smiled and jokingly said, '*Ohh* Richard, you *came.*' She seemed to be proud of her suggestive double-entendre, but Richard was more concerned with what was waiting for him through the door ahead of him and chose to ignore Pauline altogether. A moment later, with Pauline slightly hurt that he hadn't reacted to her comment; Richard was ushered into Charlotte's office. This office, in contrast with the rest of the rooms in the office was painted in warmer, darker tones, giving it a more homely feel. There was a couple of, what looked like, old and expensive paintings on the walls, along with some certificates which took pride of place just behind where Charlotte sat. He felt like he was seeing the headmaster at school. In all the time he'd worked for Mulberry & Jackson he calculated that he'd only really spoken to either owner a handful of times. He stood there for a short time, scanning the room until Charlotte Mulberry looked up from her paperwork. She was only a few years older than him but the way she carried herself and presented herself made that age gap seem far larger. Expensive spectacles framed a plain, austere face and greying, styled hair fell easily onto her slim shoulders. Despite her small size, she still carried that air of authority that frightened him to his core. 'Ah, Richard, thank you for coming to see me. Please, take a seat.' He sat in one of the two seats just in front of Charlotte's desk and tried to act casually, although inside he felt like he was about to explode. His heart felt like it was about to pop it was beating so fast as he waited to hear what she had to say. Charlotte, in contrast, was the epitome of calmness. Her actions, along with the way she spoke were so measured and precise as to be hypnotic.. There was pregnant pause that seemed almost deafening to him. Finally, she said, 'So… Richard, I imagine you're wondering why I have called you into see me…' Richard was about to say something when Charlotte continued, 'Martin Bradshaw came to me and said that you had an altercation with him last Friday…' Again, Richard was about to say something but the words stuck in his throat. It didn't matter though as Charlotte wasn't waiting for an explanation from him. She continued again, 'I am glad you put that man in his place. It's been a long time coming. Obviously, I said I'd speak with you but that was a matter of formality.' She could see from Richard's panic-stricken face that he was mortified to have been brought in front of his boss over a matter such as this so she reassuringly added, 'Don't worry Richard, you're not in trouble - quite the opposite. If ever there was a man that needed putting in his place it's Martin Bradshaw. If he weren't so good at what he did we'd have gotten rid of him a long time ago. He has a spiteful nature that doesn't belong in any work environment, but I think you have done something that has been a long time in coming.'

Richard didn't really know what to say. When Charlotte had started speaking he was crumbling; now he felt a great sense of relief. 'It wasn't my intention to have a go at Martin as ferociously as I did,' he said, and in truth he still felt a little guilty for snapping back at Martin in the way he had, but as Charlotte had just reassured him, it was for the greater good. Now Martin would think twice before picking on, not just him, but his colleagues too.

Charlotte observed Richard for a moment, picking up on all his nervous movements. She was smiling though which made him relax a little and he realised she wasn't the scary lady he'd built her up to be. 'But, right or wrong, this little episode has brought you to my attention. For many years you were quite an unremarkable cog in the wheel that makes this company work so well.' *If ever there was a back-handed compliment then that was it,* Richard mused. He couldn't argue with that appraisal though. He'd spent a vast majority of his adult life being unremarkable. 'I think both Christian and I have been waiting for you to kick into life. I'm sure our predecessors who initially recruited you thought the same thing: You come across as a very pleasant, polite person but you lack a bit of… how can I put it?... *Oomph*: but looking at you sat before me now, it looks like you've certainly gone through some kind of metamorphosis and I must say that it's good to see. May I ask how old you are?'

'Thirty-nine… well, actually I'll be forty in a couple of days.'

'Really?' she said, somewhat surprised by Richard's answer. 'I thought you were younger than that. Oh, well, well done you. You must tell me the secret to your youthful looks.' She said this with, what looked to Richard, a wink and a smile. *Is she flirting with me? God I hope not.* Richard felt like he was squirming in his seat and there was an uncomfortable pause before she continued, 'Aaaanyway, your job role is not befitting a person of your age. You cover a position that someone on work experience could do and I want to give you the opportunity to progress. Better late than never eh?.. Now, I know your qualifications limit you somewhat, but the role I have in mind doesn't require you to have qualifications. As you're probably aware Colin Jameson has just qualified and will moving up the ranks here and this leaves a void to be filled. Along with his other duties he also managed the office for us, keeping everything running smoothly... Would this role appeal to you?' Richard was completely taken off guard and mouthed words that didn't leave his lips. He'd thought he was brought here for a telling off not to be offered a promotion. 'I don't expect you to give me an answer right away. Have a think about it and give me an answer in a couple of weeks... When you're back from your holiday...'

Richard sat confused. *What holiday?*

Charlotte could see he was puzzled by her final statement, as she expected him to be so decided to enlighten him. 'I've looked at your attendance record since you've been with us and see that you only been off sick once in all the years you've been with us - and that was a week you had off for flu.' Richard remembered that well. He'd been bedridden for an entire week. Although neither of his parents had lifted a finger to help him as he sweat and fitfully tossed and turned in his bed whilst he battled the fever. Although he hadn't been in a fit state and was still as weak as a kitten he'd returned to work as soon as he could stand upright again. 'You've also only ever taken a fraction of your holiday entitlement so that's why I'm giving you a little sabbatical. Take the time to go away and enjoy yourself. Come back with a clear head and be ready to accept my offer of office manager. You'll answer directly to me and have responsibility and an increase in wage that reflects this.'

Richard was gobsmacked. He didn't know what to say. Along with this bombshell his mind was also racing at the thought of what he was going to do with this unexpected time off. It reminded him of the Christmas holidays when the office was shut for a week between Christmas and New Year. A week at home with his parents was like a punishment he didn't deserve. He'd spend most of that week upstairs in his bedroom blasting people away on his games console. After what seemed like a ludicrous amount of time he stood up and managed to say, 'Thank you. I really don't know what to say.' He realised he was smiling. After years of obscurity, he'd finally been noticed and rewarded for his service to the company.

Charlotte returned the smile. 'It's a pleasure. See you in a couple of weeks.'

Richard rose from his seat, shook Charlotte's delicate hand and floated out of the office. Although it had been a highly surprising meeting it had been very much in keeping with the past few days. He decided he needed to share this news with Frances right away and skipped out of the office still beaming like a child as he made his way to her house.

CHAPTER 11

Stepping outside the office, Richard breathed in the air, filled with the scent of summer coming to life. The sun was shining so brightly that he quickly slipped on his new shades. His head was spinning with the news he'd just received. Sure, he was scared stiff about what this new job role would entail, especially the prospect of having to keep Martin Bradshaw in line. That was going to be tough, but he was excited about having new things to do. His life had become so routine and humdrum that he was on the verge of turning into a robot. Data entry, filing and research had become so mind-numbingly mundane that he was surprised he'd lasted as long as he had without going insane. He was also caught up in thoughts of how best to spend his time off. He certainly didn't want to be at his parent's place for the rest of the week. Maybe he should blow the dust off his passport – a passport he'd never used but renewed every ten years nonetheless – and book a holiday. He'd never been abroad. Perhaps now was the time to step foot on a plane and see what else was out there. Travelling, like almost everything else had always scared him. The thought of being on a plane made him feel uneasy, but he inwardly debated with himself and concluded that everyday millions of people board aeroplanes and fly to their destinations without a problem. Besides, he was going to ask Frances if she wanted to accompany him. She gave him confidence and made him feel far braver than he actually was.

As he strolled along the road he was woken from his drifting thoughts when he stumbled over an outstretched leg of a homeless man who was lying along the wall of a shop. Apologising, Richard looked down at the man who he'd nearly tripped over and a sudden wave a pity rolled over him. The man was probably in his late forties but looked a lot older due to his unruly beard and wild, unkempt, grey hair. He was cradling a young, mangy puppy that looked, like he did, that he needed a good bath, a comb and a belly full of food.

'No, I'm sorry,' the man apologised slightly flustered. 'I'm always in the way and it doesn't help that I've got these bleedin' long legs of mine.'

Richard surveyed the man again and had to agree, he did have incredibly long legs. 'Please, don't worry about it,' he said and was about to set off on his journey again when something compelled him to stop a moment. Richard, dressed as he was, and with all the money in his bank account, couldn't help but wonder how this chap that lay before him got to where he was now. They weren't too far apart in age, but something must have gone awry to lead him to where he now found himself; looking up at Richard; a shy, far from dynamic person; who, up until a week ago hadn't lived a single day of his life. Richard crouched down by the man and instantly wished he hadn't. An overpowering smell of body odour and god-knows-what-else, bit into his nostrils. Not wishing to appear rude, he held his breath whilst he acclimatised to the stench. *It's not his fault,* he reasoned. It saddened him all the more that the man probably couldn't do much about the way he smelled, as much as he couldn't really help being in the tattered, dirty clothes that he wore. 'What's your dog's name?' Richard asked.

'Who, her?' the man responded, somewhat shocked that anyone had actually stopped to talk to him. 'I 'aven't given 'er a name yet. Only found 'er a couple of hours ago. I rescued 'er from some other homeless guy along the road 'ere. He didn't want 'er no more. He couldn't care for 'er anyway. He's always pissed out of his 'ead... She's better off wiv me...' The man looked at the puppy adoringly and stroked behind its ear. The puppy looked to be a cross between lots of different breeds but was mightily cute nonetheless. She seemed to be relishing the caring touch of the man.

'Well, you should give her a name,' Richard said kindly. 'What's *your* name?' he added.

The man appeared to think for a moment, as if he'd forgotten what his name actually was. 'My name is Jeremy - or Jez. Jez is what my friends call me... or called me... I don't have any friends anymore.' He seemed genuinely sad as he delivered the last sentence.

'Hello Jez, I'm Richard... Or Rich as my friend calls me,' he said as he held out his hand for Jez to shake.

A smile grew across Jez's face and he sat up and repositioned himself before taking Richard's soft, clean hand in his rough and grubby one. 'Pleased to meet you Rich... Thanks for stopping and talking to me. Most people just scowl as they walk past. Some teenagers even spit at me.'

'That's horrible… How long have you been sleeping rough?'

'Longer than I care to remember,' Jez replied. 'I've got used to it now. When I first slept on the streets…'

'What brought you to sleep rough – If you don't mind me asking?' Richard cut in. He was genuinely fascinated.

'Oh, er, well, my marriage broke down – my fault. I was an arsehole and used to gamble all the time. My missus just 'ad enough. Don't blame 'er at all. She was lovely. She really loved me too. She just couldn't take it no more… Anyway, when we split I got a place of my own but quickly realised I couldn't afford it. My parents are long gone and I didn't have any other family I could turn to, so I moved out and sofa-hopped at friends' places until they got tired of 'aving me there. Then I lost my job… I used to work in this warehouse distributing stuff, but when they went out of business I just didn't have the qualifications or experience to find another job. My friends had all turned their backs on me – I think I was a bit of an unwelcome burden to them. And my ex had moved on with some other fella. I don't know where she is these days but I hope she's happy. God knows I didn't make 'er happy…' Jez tailed off as he stared wistfully at nothing much in particular. 'So,' he said after a moment's reflection, 'I had nowhere else to go. Initially, I slept in parks - on benches, but they can be a bit scary at night. I got beaten up a few times when other homeless people wanted my bench and once I woke up to a load of kids kicking the 'ell out of me. Now I either sleep in doorways or on the street itself. It's much safer. And now I've also got this little thing to look after too,' he said pointing at the doe-eyed puppy adoringly looking up at him.'

'So, what are you going to call her?' Richard asked. He felt the need to get Jez off the subject of his past. He could tell it was hard for him to summarise the downfall of his life.

Jez thought for a moment. 'Betty… She looks like a Betty don't y'think?'

'Yes, I like that… Betty. You're right, it suits her.' And right on cue Betty looked up at Richard. She seemingly knew this was now her name – and approved of it.

'It's the same name as an Auntie I used to 'ave too. She was kind and used to spoil me rotten. It's a good name.' Jez said, pleased with himself.

Richard felt a great deal of sympathy for Jez. He appreciated that if things were a little different it could just as well be him sat there on the street. There was a lot of regret and remorse that emanated from the tone and feeling of Jez's backstory. He reached into his jacket pocket and retrieved his wallet. He pulled out a crisp twenty-pound note and handed it to Jez, but just as Jez was about to take it he asked nervously, 'You won't just spend it on booze or, you know, whatever else?'

Jez's eyes lit up and he smiled a huge smile. 'Blimey, that's really generous of you, but I tell you what; if you don't trust me to spend it wisely…'

'No!.. I didn't mean it like that. I…' Richard said flustered and embarrassed. He *did* mean it like that, but that was beside the point. He hadn't wanted to upset Jez.

Fortunately, Jez hadn't taken it to heart. 'Don't worry. I'd ask the same question if I were you. But if you'd rather see what the money is spent on you can pop to the shops and buy me something. You'd be doing me an even bigger favour as I'm not really dressed for the shops anyway,' he said as he gestured to his grey, shabby attire.

Richard mulled over Jez's suggestion. He'd gone this far and, although he was eager to get on and see Frances, he agreed. 'Ok, wait here,' he said and inwardly cringed.

'Yeah, I don't think I've got any other plans at the moment,' Jez said jokingly, seeing Richard's innocent misjudgement of words.

'Right, I'll be back in a jiffy,' Richard said and scurried off to the nearby shops. There was a wide array of choice and he quickly found he wasn't content with just buying Jez and Betty just a few items of food. He soon found himself going from shop to shop and it was twenty minutes later when he arrived back to where Jez and Betty still sat; arms laden with bags of shopping.

'Wow,' said Jez, shocked. 'I thought you'd done a runner.' His eyes stared at the bags bursting with items. 'Obviously not… Is this all for me?' he asked, his eyes misting up with tears of pure joy.

'For both of you,' Richard replied, nodding towards Betty. 'I think I might've got a bit carried away.'

'We won't complain, will we Betty?' Jez was now stood up, still cradling Betty, and Richard was now aware of just how tall Jez was. He towered over Richard. He stared at the bags like a young boy waiting to open his Christmas presents. Richard handed the bags to Jez as Jez handed Betty over to him. Richard tentatively held the scraggly puppy at arm's length whilst Jez rummaged through the bags of goodies. In there he found a rucksack complete with sleeping bag, sleeping mat and torch; a dog bowl with enough dog food for a few days; a large bottle of water; toothpaste and toothbrush; a hairbrush and wet wipes; an assortment of snacks and fruit and last but not least, a change of clothing, albeit camping clothing with some robust walking boots. As Jez finished wading through the bags, he looked back at Richard with tears streaking his dirty face; the tears making visible tracks as they fell down his cheeks. 'Are you sure this is all for us? It must've cost you a small fortune,' he asked with a voice choked with emotion. A satisfied smile broke across Richard's face. 'I don't know what to say. Really. It's the kindest thing anyone has ever done for me…'

'My pleasure… But please promise me two things… Firstly, don't just sell this stuff for some booze or a hit…'

Jez shook his head vigorously. 'I've never done drugs and I don't touch booze no more. It 'elped bring me to where I am now, so you got no worries there.'

This answer seemed to satisfy Richard. 'And secondly, look after this one here,' he said as he handed Betty back to Jez like someone handling a pressure-sensitive bomb.

'Of course. We'll be alright won't we Betts?' Jez replied as he buried his face in her fur. 'I can't thank you enough Rich. Thank you… Thank you.' He then gave Richard a look that was so sincere and full of appreciation that Richard could've cried himself. Instead, he looked down at the ground. He felt proud of himself though and pleased that he could have an impact on someone else's fortunes. There was no guarantee that Jez wouldn't just sell all the stuff, abandon Betty and get rip-roaringly drunk in a local park, but he doubted that very much. There was a sincerity and genuine warmness about Jez. Richard just hoped his donation was enough to set them on a better path.

'I'll say goodbye then,' Richard said. 'I've got to be somewhere, but it's been really good to meet you and Betty.'

'Well, it's been a real pleasure to meet you too and thanks again for all this stuff. It's unbelievable…I, I just don't…' Jez tailed off.

Richard bashfully waved the words of thanks away, but secretly it was filling his heart that Jez was so happy. 'Look after yourselves,' he said as he turned and continued his journey. As he walked along the road he felt a mixture of emotions; excitement at seeing Frances; pride that he'd done a good deed; and sadness at Jez's predicament. It was yet another reminder to him that he really had to seize the day.

When he arrived at the front door of Frances' house it somehow looked different and he wondered whether he'd got the right place. The door looked like the one he'd entered through before though so he took another deep breath and, using the brass doorknocker, knocked firmly on the door… There was no answer so he knocked again - this time a little louder. He left a lengthy pause before he knocked once more. After the third knock he stepped back and looked up at the house for any signs of life. As his eyes scanned the windows he was sure he saw one of the curtains upstairs twitch. *One last try*. This produced the same results as before, so with his mind thinking of various scenarios as to where Frances may be or why she wasn't answering the door, he walked away.

With Frances' no show, the upbeat feeling that had been flowing through him was now quickly disappearing. He couldn't face the soul-shattering experience of returning to his parent's home – that really would finish him off - so he decided to give Matt a call. The phone rang for quite some time before Matt picked it up. 'Hello mate. How are you?' Matt said chirpily. 'How did you get on with Frances the other night?'

There was slight pause whilst Richard thought how much he should divulge. *Should I tell him that I had fantastic sex with Frances? Should I tell him I met Frances' husband? Should I tell him that that same husband almost crushed my testicles in his hand?*

The pause was all Matt needed. '*Yeaaah*! Go on my son!'

Richard went crimson down the other end of the phone. 'Where are you? Can we meet up? I could do with a chat.'

'Sure mate. Is everything ok?' Matt replied.

'Yes, I think so. Where are you?'

'At mine. Come round. I'll do us some dinner.'

Half an hour later, Richard arrived at Matt's house. Matt was dressed casually in jogging bottoms and an old t-shirt, but he still looked effortlessly cool. Richard was dressed in his smart suit, smart shoes and funky haircut. He felt massively overdressed, flustered and far from cool. 'You look like you need a drink,' Matt said as he ushered Richard inside.

As they made their way downstairs to the kitchen, the aroma of whatever Matt was cooking filled Richard's nostrils. His tummy instantly rumbled at the prospect of some tasty food. Matt handed Richard a bottle of ice-cold beer from the fridge. 'I'm cooking chicken casserole. Hope that's ok with you?' he said as he sat on one of the kitchen stools.

'It smells delicious. How did it go with Big Dave? Are you going to see him again?'

'Yeah, he was a brute - lots of fun though. I s'pose I might see him again,' Matt said flippantly. 'So, how's it with you?'

Richard took a deep breath to compose himself before filling in Matt with all that had happened since he'd left his place. And it wasn't until he started relaying the information that he realised just how much *had* happened in that relatively short time. He told him about having sex with Frances – his first sexual experience; meeting Mike and his ordeal after meeting him. He told him about being propositioned by Emma Buxton; about being offered a promotion and, finally, finding Frances either not in or choosing to not to answer the door to him. He chose not to divulge his meeting with Jez. That he kept for himself. Besides, he didn't want to gloat about doing something charitable.

After Richard had finished, Matt just sat there and said, 'Wow… That's an eventful thirty-six hours… That Mike sounds like a proper bell-end.'

'Oh, he is, trust me,' Richard agreed.

'So, how are your cobblers now?' Matt enquired, unable to keep a smile from creeping across his face.

A smile spread across Richard's face too as he answered, 'Yeah, they're still there. I can't say I'd recommend the experience though.'

'You'd be surprised. I know a few chaps who'd pay good money for that.' They both chuckled and Matt rose to potter around the kitchen and prepare dinner. He moved around the kitchen with ease. It was obvious to Richard that cooking was something Matt knew how to do and loved doing. Richard was very envious as he'd never cooked anything of any complexity and any cooking he did do was usually done with the aid of a microwave.

As they sat there eating, Matt's home-cooked chicken casserole it took him back to when he used to visit his Gran's. In the same way as he felt safe and looked after at his Gran's, he felt the same here at Matt's. 'So, what are you going to do with your time off? Matt asked 'You can come and work with me if you like. I'll show you what a real day's work is.'

'No, you're alright. I don't think I could manage even an hour working onsite with you… I don't know what to do. I don't want to stay at home or I'll have to deal with my parents who are getting worse – if that's actually possible. I can't go to work because it's meant to be my sabbatical and how desperate would that look if I just rocked up tomorrow… I just don't know. I thought about going away on holiday but I've never been abroad before…'

'What? *Never?!*' Matt said incredulously.

'Nope… I know it's hard to believe, but who would I have gone on holiday with? Until you bowled back into my life I didn't really know anyone well enough to go on holiday with them.'

'Didn't you ever go away with your parents?'

'Ha ha – no,' Richard replied sarcastically. 'The only place they'd ever take me was the pub when I was too young to leave at home by myself. And then I'd be left in the beer garden on my own waiting for them to return, drunk as skunks. Anyway, having thought some more about it, I'm moving into the flat on Saturday so I can't go away.'

'You know you can go away for just a few days? You don't have to go for a full week. Perhaps you should go away somewhere hot and chill out on a beach for a few days. And when you come back you can move straight into your new pad... Speaking of which; I'll give you a hand moving on Saturday if you like. Your stuff should all fit in my van shouldn't it?'

'Are you sure? Yeah, that'd be great. Thanks so much. To be honest I hadn't thought that far ahead. I'm still a bit apprehensive about telling my parents that I'm leaving.'

'I think they'll have a good idea when they see us carrying your stuff down the stairs!' More laughing ensued. 'Seriously though, go away, get some sun – God knows you need it!'

Richard blushed but he had to admit that there were mole rats with better suntans than him. 'Maybe I will then.' The thought was already beginning to scare him. After a lengthy pause he asked, 'Would you come with me?'

'I'd love to mate, but I can't. I've got too much on at work.' Matt saw Richard's face drop on hearing his reply and felt awful. 'I'm sorry.'

'Don't worry. I understand.'

There was a silence that followed that must've felt like the most uncomfortable silence Matt had ever endured because he leapt from his seat and said, 'Oh, what the hell! Go on then. I'll have to speak with Jamie but I'm sure they can cope without me for a few days. Where do you fancy going?'

'I don't know. I've never really thought about it.'

'Come on, there must be places that you want to see,' Matt urged.

Richard thought for a moment. 'Barbados,' he blurted.

'Maybe another time,' Matt answered, trying hard not to burst Richard's bubble. 'How about somewhere a little closer? Otherwise, we'll be spending more time travelling than we will actually sunbathing. Think of somewhere in Europe.'

Matt could hear Richard's mind working and after a painful amount of time he said 'Spain?'

'Spain's good. It's a big country though; anywhere specific?'

'Honestly, I don't know. Have you got any suggestions?' Richard asked.

'Ok, what about Ibiza? It'll be just before the season starts there so it won't be too rowdy yet, and the weather will be good – just the right temperature. You don't want anywhere too hot or your lily-white skin will just blister,' Matt joked.

'Great,' Richard said. A mixture of excitement and trepidation instantly flushed through him.

'We'll need to get your passport,' Matt said.

'Ok.'

'Whilst we're at it we might as well pick up the rest of your stuff. What do you reckon?'

Richard heaved a heavy sigh. The prospect of what was to come felt daunting. He wasn't looking forward to the obvious showdown he knew he'd have to have with his parents. They were going to be as cruel and spiteful as they possibly could be when they discovered he was leaving them. Their meal ticket and focus of so much of their vitriol would leave them the lonely, heartless people that they were, but he couldn't help but feel responsible for them. For so long he'd been under their spell and it was going to be a huge wrench to leave them behind. 'Yes, I guess that makes sense,' he resignedly said.

Matt could see the concern etched on Richard's face. 'Don't worry mate. I'll be with you. I won't let them bully you… Right, finish your dinner; we'd better get a shimmy on.'

After the plates were cleared, Matt rapidly cleared his van of tools and equipment, and before Richard had chance to have any second thoughts, they were driving towards his parent's house. Richard was lost in thought and staring gormlessly out of the side window. He was awoken out of his reverie by Matt who asked, 'So what are you going to do about Frances?'

'I'm not sure. I mean, we got on so well over the weekend, and I'm sure I saw her from behind the curtains. If only I'd taken her number or she'd taken mine...' Richard tailed off. This time last week he'd had none of his current dilemmas. He hadn't been worrying about women or worrying about upsetting his parents because he wasn't moving out. Life had suddenly got complicated and dealing with heavy emotions wasn't something he was used to.

'To be fair I had to literally put my number in your phone for you to have mine.'

'Yes, I suppose me and mobile phones are just starting to get used to one another. I do know I desperately want to see her again... I'm really worried about her. Her ex is very overbearing and controlling.'

'Has he ever got violent with her?' Matt asked.

'No - Well, she says he hasn't and I believe her. But I *do* think he's beating her up psychologically. You know how she was when we met her in the bar last week and in the club on Saturday? - All effervescent and confident. Well, she's a shadow of that person when he's around. He's broken her before and I think he might again.'

I tell you what; if we've got time, we'll swing by hers on the way back and check up on her. Is that cool?'

'Yeah, that'll be good. Thank you.'

'No worries… Now let's get your stuff.'

CHAPTER 12

As Richard opened the door and stood in the hallway he winced for they were hit by a wall of noise emanating from TV the living room. *"Eastenders"* was playing out in full force with one abrasive cockney character saying, or rather shouting at another cockney character, "You're bang aaat of order! You can't bar me."

"I told yer before. Ger aaata my pub!" a female cockney character was shouting back. So loud was the TV that Richard sensed his parents hadn't heard them enter. He wondered if they'd notice if he tiptoed upstairs, cleaned out his room and then left. It certainly would save a lot of drama. But Matt didn't give him the choice. Seeing Richard's hesitation, he brushed past him and bowled into the living room. His sudden appearance made Gerry and Sylvia jump out of their seats; well, as much as two rotund slobs lying horizontally on sticky red leather sofas could jump. 'Fackin' 'ell! Yer scared the fackin' life outta me!' Gerry yelled. Sylvia was pressing her podgy hand to her podgy chest and looked like she was about to faint.

Matt couldn't help but smile. He knew he'd caught them completely off guard and he was now in full control of the situation. 'Please, don't get up. I'm helping Richard move out...' He let the words sink in before continuing, 'And, before you ask, not in with me. No, he's got a lovely flat on the seafront to move in to. He's also got a beautiful new girlfriend – just in case you had any lingering doubts he was gay...I, on the other hand, *am* gay... Yes, Gerry; your son is friends with one of those awful, abominable homosexuals. How *very dare* he!' Matt was enjoying himself and Richard watched in astonishment as Gerry and Sylvia stared open-mouthed whilst Matt continued. 'You really should be proud of the way your son has turned out; and all in spite of your best efforts to undermine him and constantly put him down... Now, we're going to clear out his room; I don't expect you to help – in fact, we don't want it. Stay there like the sloths you are, watching shit TV, and we'll be gone before you can wrench your blubbery bodies up from those god-awful sofas.' With that he turned around, winked at a gobsmacked Richard, and dragged him out the room and up the stairs. As they left they could hear Gerry and Sylvia trying to scramble up from their sofas; both trying frantically to comprehend the torrent of quick-fire information that had just been delivered.

Upstairs, Matt and Richard hurriedly gathered together Richard's possessions. Matt couldn't help but acknowledge that his room had hardly changed since the last time he'd visited it, all those years ago. Richard, for his part, just wanted to get out of there as quickly as possible and decided to leave most of his old clothes behind, choosing to concentrate on the new clothes he'd purchased at the weekend. He had a momentary dilemma of whether to take his trusty alarm clock. There was no doubt that the dated time piece would look well out of place in the new flat but he couldn't bring himself to leave it behind. With the plasma TV carefully taken down from the wall and the bracket with it, they shuttled his belongings into Matt's van. They only needed three runs each and, as they closed the back doors of the van after their third and final run, they both looked at one another. Richard knew he had to go back in there and say farewell to his folks. He couldn't expect Matt to do *that* for him. 'I'd best... you know... say goodbye,' he said.

'Ok. Just don't take any shit off them. Remember, you don't owe them anything.'

Richard was aware the clock was ticking and really didn't want to say anything at all but they were his parents; he felt they at least deserved a goodbye; then it would be up to them how they wanted to be after that.

'Right then, I'll be off,' he said as entered the living room. He found that both his parents hadn't actually moved from their respective sofas. The TV was still belting out at full volume. Neither had looked away from the screen when Richard entered and, for a second, he wondered if he'd suddenly become invisible. 'Ok then... goodbye.' he said as he turned around to leave.

No sooner had he made a move out the living room door than his father said, 'So, that's it? All those years lookin' after yer and that's the gratitude yer give us?!' Gerry was now stood on his swollen feet having risen like a badly cooked pie from the sofa. 'Me and yer poor muvva 'ave done the best we could to bring yer up proper – and this is how yer repay us – by deserting us when we need yer most?'

The last comment was as much as Richard could stand. 'What?! You and Mum have been sponging off me for years. You've belittled me, bullied me, and starved me of any love and affection for as long as I can remember. You both deserve each other because no one else would want you. You're vile, *vile* people and you wonder why I'm leaving you? Just look at yourselves! It's just a wonder it's taken me so long to move out.' His voice was now raised and the reaction had stopped Gerry in his tracks, but just like a tag-team of out-of-shape heavyweight wrestlers, Sylvia came to his rescue and stood up as quickly as Richard had ever seen her move.

'Yer can't speak to yer farver like that yer ungrateful little shit. 'E's a good man and e's always done right by yer...' she began before Richard stopped her in *her* tracks.

'Oh, *do shut up* Mum. Dad's a lazy oaf. He's never had a single thought for anyone other than himself. Just like you.'

'Y y, yer...' Sylvia stood stone-faced and stammering and as stunned as Gerry.

'Oh yes I bloody well *can*. I've put up with the pair of you for far too long and now I'm going to live *my* life; out of the shadow of you two. You know, I couldn't care less what you think of me anymore; whether you're disappointed or whatever. Over the years you've managed to trample on me and make feel small. Not anymore though. Not… any… more.' The last part was delivered with tired determination; a determination that he'd only just realised he had. So caught-up in what he was saying that he hadn't realised he'd begun to cry. He only noticed when his eyes were so full of tears that he couldn't see. He blinked and the tears flowed down his cheeks.

His mother smirked at his obvious upset. 'Aaah, poor baby. Yer gonna cry now?... Yer pathetic. Yer fink yer somefink special, wiv yer fancy cloves, but yer ain't. Now go on; get the 'ell outta my 'ouse!... Yer no son of mine!' she raged as she pushed him towards the door. Not needing any further encouragement, Richard turned and left; his mother still trying to cuff him about the head with her fleshy hand as he did. The last words he heard his mother bellow were 'And don't come back!'

Richard made it into the refuge of Matt's van and heaved a huge sigh of relief. 'Well, I think that went better than expected.' he said as he brushed the remnants of his tears away from his eyes.

'Are you ok?' Matt asked.

'Yeah, I'll be alright,' Richard sighed. 'Can we get out of here now please?'

Matt started his van and began driving away. Richard allowed himself one last look at his parents who were stood looking flabby and aggressive at the doorway. He felt hollow. He wasn't used to releasing so much emotion. He'd always imagined one day standing up to his parents and he'd always expected to feel elated afterwards; but he didn't. He felt as empty and alone as he'd ever felt.

'I'm proud of you mate,' Matt said. 'I know it doesn't feel like it at the moment, but you did a very brave thing tonight.'

'I don't feel brave,' Richard sniffed. 'I don't know what I feel to be honest.'

'Look, the hard part's done. You might not think it now but you're about to start a whole new life, and in that new life you're going to feel a whole lot better about yourself... Now, where does Frances live?'

When they arrived outside Frances' house they saw a light on. 'She must be in this time,' Matt said.

Richard didn't feel so up for all this now but tiredly said, 'See you in a bit,' as he stepped out of the van.

They were lonely footsteps he trudged as he made his way up Frances' garden path. He stood there for a moment before wearily knocking on the door... He waited anxiously but there was no answer; so, he knocked again, this time more vigorously... Again, there was no answer. He was about to walk away when he thought he'd just peer through the letterbox and when he did he saw a pair of legs at the end of the hallway.

'What the *fuck* do you think you're doing!' he heard what must only have been Mike's voice roar. Richard rapidly pulled away from the door and edged back towards the front gate. Just as he opened the gate and got to the other side of it Mike, dressed much more casually than the last time Richard had met him, thundered out of the front door.

'What did I tell you would happen if you came around here again?!' Mike yelled.

Richard was frozen with fear and it was with great relief that he heard Matt's van door open just behind him. He now stood next to Richard which immediately stopped Mike from pursuing Richard any further. 'Yeah? What are you gonna do then big boy?' Matt said confidently. He wasn't quite as tall as Mike but he stood there with such presence that Mike wasn't going to challenge him.

'He knows what'll happen…' Mike said, pointing an angry finger at Richard who was now cowering behind Matt. 'I didn't expect him to bring his minder with him… Now if you don't mind, could you both fuck *right* off, out of my sight.' Mike's tone was less aggressive but still full of authority. There was definitely the feeling of a stand-off as neither party knew quite what to do next. A couple curtains twitched in neighbouring houses as they strained to see what the commotion was in this, usually quiet street.

'My friend would like to talk to Frances and then we'll be on our way. Is she there?' Matt asked.

'He's not going anywhere near my wife. In fact, if you both don't bugger off right away I'm calling the police.'

'Call the police then,' Matt replied assuredly. 'And I'll tell them that you've been psychologically abusing your wife.'

'*What?!* What the fuck do you know about my life?' Mike barked aggressively. But his answer belied the fact that he knew he was no longer in full control of this argument. Just as another stand-off was about to ensue, Frances came to the door. She looked tired and haggard. It was obvious to Richard that she'd spent a lot of time crying. 'Go back inside,' Mike told Frances but she carried on walking past him and made her way to Richard.

'Let me speak with him,' she said to Mike, who had no choice but to acquiesce.

Richard could've cried himself when he saw her. She looked small and frail. With red, puffy eyes and unkempt hair she was far from the glamorous lady he'd been used to seeing on his journeys to work. 'Are you ok?' he said in a tone only a little louder than a whisper. His eyes kept flitting towards Mike, making sure he wasn't getting closer or eavesdropping.

'Not really… Look, I really don't think you should see me anymore… I know, it's been fun but I've decided to give Mike one last chance. We're going to see if we can work things out.'

Richard could feel the blood drain from his body and his heart momentarily stop beating. As if it had sensed the mood of the moment, the skies grew darker and a cool breeze kicked up. For a minute he didn't know what to say. From everything he'd heard about Mike and actually seen for himself, he knew this wasn't a very pleasant man. For Frances to go back to him would be a massive mistake in his opinion. 'Really?' he said when he'd had time to process what had just been said. 'You don't look so happy about it. Are you sure you want this?' He could see Mike straining his head in an effort to see what was going on. Fortunately, Matt was stood looking straight at Mike, making sure he didn't move an inch.

'You don't want to get involved with someone like me. You don't deserve all the stress and drama that a relationship with me would bring… Just go.' The last two words were like a dagger in his heart.

'I don't understand. We had such a lovely weekend. W…w… why?' Richard stood there baffled with fresh tears starting to well-up in his eyes. He looked longingly at Frances but she couldn't meet his gaze. She hung her head and stared down at the ground. He knew there was nothing else he could say to change her mind but pulled a torn piece of paper and, making sure that Mike couldn't see, handed it to her. It contained his eleven-digit mobile number which he'd scrawled down in Matt's van on their journey to Frances'. 'In case you change your mind or just need to chat,' he said. Frances took the piece of paper but continued to look down, unable to give him the look he craved.

Dejectedly, he turned and returned to the van where Matt joined him a second later. 'I see what you mean about Mike,' Matt said, not wanting to upset Richard by discussing Frances' rejection of him. 'He's a proper arsehole.'

Richard said nothing in reply. He just stared out of the passenger window as a few spots of rain started to land on it.

When they finally got back they unloaded Matt's van in eerie silence. Matt could see that Richard was brooding – and for good reason; in the space of an hour, he'd been rejected by his parents and the lady he'd obsessed over for the past two years. There wasn't much Matt felt he could say to console him. But once all the unpacking had been done they went downstairs to the kitchen where Matt handed Richard a cold beer from the fridge and put a comforting arm around him. 'Let's book a holiday,' he said in an encouraging tone. And, like a stroppy teenager breaking out of a mood, Richard begrudgingly followed Matt over to his laptop. Matt knew it was fairly useless asking Richard any questions about exactly where he wanted to go so he took charge and within fifteen minutes he'd booked flights to Ibiza and accommodation there. Feeling rather chuffed with himself he turned to Richard and, giving him a friendly slap on the cheek, said, 'Cheer up Richie Boy, we're going on holiday.'

CHAPTER 13

It was with a jolt that Richard awoke early next morning. He felt Matt's strong hand pushing on his shoulder like a physical alarm clock. 'C'mon mate. You'd best get ready. The taxi's gonna be here in half an hour.' He'd slept like a log in Matt's spare bedroom. The bed was infinitely more comfortable than the one he'd abandoned at his parents, and with the emotional fatigue of the day he'd had no problems falling into a deep, all-consuming sleep. As his eyes adjusted he could make out that it wasn't quite light yet. Even though he was used to getting up early for work on a daily basis, this seemed an ungodly time to wake up. He guessed it was about 4am as he remembered Matt booking the cab right after he'd called Jamie to say he was going to take a few days off. Jamie hadn't taken the news too well but Matt had placated him by saying it was important and that he would make up the time over the coming months. Being equal business-partners, there wasn't much Jamie could do or say in response. But that didn't stop Jamie reacting petulantly and putting the phone down on Matt. They had packed the previous night. Or to be more precise, Matt had packed the previous night. Richard had stood by superfluously as he watched Matt organise clothes, footwear and toiletries into two small suitcases. Matt had supplied Richard with all the clothes he was going to need for their few days in the sun. Although bigger built than Richard, an impromptu fashion show revealed that some of Matt's clothing would fit more than adequately. Richard, for his part, had absolutely no idea what he was supposed to wear. Matt had got increasingly excited during the course of the evening. After they'd booked the holiday he'd spent another half an hour trawling the internet to show him pictures and videos of Ibiza, to give him an idea of what to expect. Richard had been somewhat intimidated by what was shown; lots of beautiful, tanned people all smiling and having fun. They all looked like they belonged there. He didn't feel like he'd fit in at all and would stand out like a sore thumb; but after trying on some of Matt's clothes he had to admit he looked much more the part. He was rather nervous about the prospect of exposing his pale, unconditioned body but Matt reassured him that not everyone out there is bronzed and chiselled. It transpired that Matt had been to Ibiza more times than he could remember and therefor Richard trusted his judgement and took comfort in his reassurance. It was hard for Richard not to be carried away by Matt's enthusiasm. After a few more beers he'd started to share Matt's excitement. But his mind kept drifting back to thoughts of Frances and how desperately sad she'd looked. In the very short time they'd spent together his feelings for her had blossomed and he felt what could only be described as love for her. He felt this feeling all the more now she was gone and his heart ached. It was a most peculiar feeling for him to have to come to terms with.

After a quick shower and groom, he hurriedly put on some casual clothing for the journey ahead. Matt had adopted the role of travel guru now; an all-knowing being that guided Richard along this new and exciting experience, making sure he was fully prepared for what was to come. 'Two things that you must not forget: your passport and your wallet. Everything else can be bought out there if need be,' Matt said in a sagely tone. He was calm and organised – everything that Richard wasn't.

As they left the house and stepped into the taxi the sun was just beginning to rise and they could hear the birds were chirping happily away. Matt asked Richard to double-check that he had everything and wasn't the least surprised when a panic-stricken Richard had to rush back inside to pick up his passport.

Both were sat in the back of the sleek, salubrious taxi and looked wistfully out of their respective windows. The roads were pretty much empty of any other cars at that time of the morning and it took no time at all to reach Gatwick airport. The banal chit-chat provided by the cheerful cabby made the journey breeze by. By the time they got their bags out of the boot and headed to the entrance, the sun was making an appearance and Richard could tell it was going to be a beautiful day. Almost reading Richard's mind, Matt put an arm on Richard's shoulder and said, 'It's going to be even nicer where we're going.'

As they entered the bustling airport, Richard suddenly felt overwhelmed by the sheer volume of people scurrying around; seemingly all knowing where they were going and what they were meant to be doing. As he stood there, dumbfounded, trying to make sense of all the information boards he felt Matt's strong grip tug in the direction of the check-in desk. Fortunately, there was barely any queue awaiting them and after checking their bags in and receiving their boarding passes they were off to security. Standing there in the queue, preparing for their turn to pass through the scanners and searches, Richard felt suspiciously guilty. Guilty of what he did not know. He looked around and there were lots of other people carrying the same troubled looks on their faces; all feeling guilty of a crime they hadn't committed. As he approached the scanner he could feel his heart racing. Matt, who was stood behind him, whispered, 'Don't worry, it's fine,' and after one last pat of his pockets Richard stepped through the scanner and heard the sound he'd been dreading – the beep that signified he was either a shoe-bomber or a drugs-mule. A large, shaven headed security guard ushered Richard towards him and told him to remove his new converse trainers and have them scanned. He could feel his face redden but was relieved to see he wasn't the only one who'd failed this test; an elderly lady who could barely walk had the same problem. The frail octogenarian didn't really fit the image of a terrorist or a smuggler and Richard was puzzled that they'd made such an effort to make her remove her shoes and give her such a thorough frisk. He stood transfixed waiting to see, if indeed, she was the arch criminal they were looking for. Mercifully, they both got the all-clear and he joined back up with Matt who, like him, was now adjusting himself and putting his possessions back in his pockets.

Safely through the rigmarole of security they were swept along with the tide of people, through duty free. Sales assistants sprung out from stalls selling a wide array perfumes, makeup and spirits, trying to tempt unsuspecting travellers with their offers. Somewhat relieved to make it out from the mayhem of duty-free they gathered themselves in the large open-plan plaza. Richard still felt like he'd just beamed down onto some strange new planet. He took a moment to observe his surroundings, taking in the swarm of people which came from a large cross section of society. You had the business professional; sharp-suited and organised. These people knew exactly what they were doing and where they were meant to be. They seemed oblivious to other travellers and held themselves with a sagacious coolness; then there was the 21st century family; all overweight but still eating furiously whilst they huffed and puffed their way from shop to shop; there was the young couple who were off for what must be their first holiday together judging by the many love-bites on their necks; there were the many families whose parents looked stressed and exhausted whilst the kids ran feral. Just watching these people made Richard tired. He wondered whether a week's holiday to sunnier climbs would be enough to offer these parents some respite from their daily drudgery.

After a quick trawl through one of the duty-free shops and having both purchased some alluringly smelling and expensive eau de toilette, they inevitably wandered into a large, noisy pub. 'Let's start as we mean to go on,' Matt said enthusiastically as they stood at the long bar.

'But it's 5:30 in the morning,' Richard reasoned.

''And?...'

'Fair enough,' Richard said with a shrug of his shoulders. They both ordered a pint of lager and a full English breakfast before searching for a place to sit. Richard was revelling in the novelty of everything. Drinking a pint of lager at this time of the morning was right up there in the novelty stakes and, along with another pint soon after, he was beginning to feel decidedly tipsy. His tired mind started to wander and he soon found his thoughts drifting to those of Frances. He couldn't shake the image of her stood there looking so sad and vulnerable. And in the background was the looming figure of Mike who now had suppressive control over her again. For so long his thoughts of Frances were just lustful and unrealistic; now his thoughts had substance and feeling. He felt her sadness and he felt powerless to help her. Just as he was about to start wallowing Matt brought him out of his doldrums. 'I know what you're thinking about – I do, but I don't want you thinking about her. We're going away and we're going to have fun. If you like we can formulate a plan to deal with things when we get back, but for now I want you to have some fun – let yourself go and embrace what's going to be an amazing few days. Can you do that for me?'

Richard, embarrassed to be found out so easily, conceded, 'Of course – I'm sorry.'

'Don't be sorry,' Matt said sympathetically. 'Just enjoy yourself. Things'll work themselves out. Try not worry.' In order to change the subject, he decided to move onto a topic they both knew well - their school days. 'Do you know who I saw the other day?... Chris Simmonds.'

Richard was slightly puzzled why Matt had suddenly lurched onto the subject of Chris Simmonds - the school bully who had terrorised pretty much everyone at their school all those years ago - but he was prepared to go along with it and see where this was heading. 'Oh, what was he up to?'

'This'll make you laugh… Guess what he does now?' Matt asked with an excited smile growing across his face.

'I don't know… a bouncer? An enforcer for some big crime boss?'

'Ha-ha,' Matt giggled. 'Nope, he's a traffic warden!'

The look of shock on Richard's face was priceless, but he shouldn't have been that surprised. 'Well, I suppose he's certainly got the right credentials to be one,' he said as he took a sip from his pint.

'Yep, no doubt about that; he always was a complete and utter tosspot.' Matt added and Richard almost spat his mouthful out as he tried to suppress his laughter. They were in fits of childish giggles now as Matt acknowledged the change of subject had had the desired effect. 'He was going to put a ticket on my van as it was parked on some double-yellow-lines outside a job we we've been working on. I strolled up to him - he didn't recognise me. When I told him who I was he looked shocked and told me he'd turn a blind eye on this occasion. He certainly wasn't as menacing as he used to be - in fact, quite the opposite. He seemed much smaller and he had a proper beer-belly on him now, but you could tell he's still a right tosspot.'

'Yes, that'll never leave him,' Richard agreed. 'I guess some jobs find certain people… *That* job is made to measure for Chris Simmonds.'

'Speaking of jobs, what are you going to do with your job offer?' Matt asked once their chuckling had subsided.

'I don't know. I suppose I've got two weeks to make up my mind… I've never been responsible for anything other than myself so it's a bit daunting to suddenly be in charge of that office. In all honesty I don't actually like many people in my office. There's a chap called Graeme who's really nice but apart that they're either dull or annoying… Or both!'

'Perhaps a complete change is what you need,' Matt suggested. He was keen to plant the seed in Richard's mind. He could tell that his current place of work wasn't going to keep his recent metamorphosis going. In the past few days since their reconnection, they'd easily slotted back into the friendship they'd shared during their school years. For Richard, these had been tough years; he hadn't really enjoyed school and had struggled to fit in. Matt's similar disposition meant they'd bonded with one another, and in turn, survived high school. Richard felt so pleased to be back in touch with the only real friend he'd ever really had.

When their boarding gate was called they gulped down the remainder of their drinks and marched the convoluted route to get there. All the way, Richard was firing questions at Matt on what he should expect to encounter in the coming days. By the time they'd made it to the gate it felt as if they'd walked halfway to Ibiza already such was its remoteness. They were both red-faced and short of breath as they handed over their passports and boarding passes to the ladies at the check-in gate.

Not long after, they boarded the plane. Richard could feel his heart beating frantically and it was with mild panic that he took his seat. Of all the things that awaited him on this short holiday, flying was the thing that scared him most. It was totally irrational but he couldn't help himself. He was trying desperately to give off the impression that he was cool, calm and collected, but he obviously must've failed with this facade as Matt reassuringly said, 'Try to relax. You've got nothing to worry about. Do you know how many planes fly every day with no problems?... Thousands. Just enjoy the experience.' Matt continued to try and preoccupy Richard with any sort of conversation, from old tales of their school days to random observations of their fellow passengers. Towards the back of the plane there was a rowdy group of lads who had obviously started early. The poor flight attendants were trying in vain to get them to sit down as the lads shouted boisterously at one another. It was going to be a long flight for the cabin crew and the other passengers having to endure them for the entire journey. Despite the commotion going on in the background and Matt's attempts to divert his attention, Richard could feel himself getting light-headed and clammy. *God I hope I don't pass out.* This was his last thought as his head flopped to the side and landed on Matt's shoulder. He awoke with a dry mouth and a bleary focus moments later. Matt, slightly worried, tried coaxing him back to consciousness. 'Hey, wake up sleepy-head.' He was aware that Richard's fainting had drawn the attention of a few nearby passengers so he tried to play-down the incident.

The colour quickly returned to Richard's face when the embarrassment of the situation hit home. He looked around sheepishly at the other passengers who were now staring at him. He was still a bit confused as he asked Matt, 'How long was I out for?'

Matt could quickly see there was an opportunity to make something out of this situation. 'The whole flight; we've literally just landed,' he said sincerely.

'*Really*?!' Richard said in an unnecessarily high-pitched voice. Now he was even more confused. It only felt like he was out for a second or two.

'Yeah, you were snoring and everything. These poor passengers had to sit through all that noise,' Matt added as he delivered a surreptitious wink to one of the neighbouring passengers. Richard's colour was returning fast now. He was now as red as a tomato as he timidly tried to sink into his seat. Just then he heard the engines erupt and the plane thrust forward. He immediately sat bolt upright and his eyes went as wide as saucers. He looked like a bush baby that had been bitten on its backside. He turned to look at Matt for reassurance but he offered none. Matt just sat there with the mischievous look of a man who couldn't quite disguise his amusement. As the plane lifted into the air, Richard felt like screaming, but instead fainted again. He awoke to the sound of Matt laughing hysterically along with the few others who'd just witnessed him pass out. *Ha bloody ha,* Richard thought as he rose once again from Matt's shoulder.

When they landed it was a far calmer Richard that gripped his seat as if his life depended on it. A few glasses of wine during the flight had suppressed his overwhelming fear of flying. Not that it was entirely noticeable to Matt as he watched Richard's white-knuckled hold on the arm rests, his gritted teeth and eye-bulging stare.

It was on shaky legs that Richard left the plane and stood at the top of the steps the awaiting shuttle bus. Standing there like an intrepid explorer having just discovered an uncharted forest, he was hit by a warmth he'd never experienced before. Although only midmorning, the temperature was already deliciously warm. His nose twitched at the unfamiliar smells that accompanied this heat, but none of these new sensations were unwelcome - quite the opposite; with eyes closed he embraced his new environment before continuing his walk down the steps. He felt infinitely better. He felt alive.

The long queue of people at passport control were hurried through by the uninterested staff who gave each passport a cursory glance before handing it back. In no time they had their luggage and were sat in the back of a cab being driven by the smelliest man Richard had ever had the misfortune to smell. The overpowering stench of body odour made his nose twitch again and this time not in a good way. He soon found himself winding the window down and sticking his head out of it, craving the fresh air that blasted his face as they travelled along.

When they reached their hotel, Matt paid the stinky taxi driver, and, knowing that he didn't speak a word of English said, 'Adios my smelly friend. Try and have a wash at some point.' Not quite understanding what'd just said to him, the driver smiled obliviously and waved them off. 'My god that man stank!' Matt blurted out when taxi driver had driven away. 'It made my eyes water!'

'No arguments there,' Richard agreed. 'He smelt worse than…' he rummaged his brain for the name he was looking for. '…Jason Price!' they both said at the same time. Jason Price being the token smelly kid from their old school days.

'Yeah, he could kick up a stink too, but he smelt more of piss and biscuits than of B.O... I'd forgotten all about Jason Price until you mentioned him... I wonder he's doing now?' Matt said.

'Probably smelling of piss and biscuits,' Richard replied as they picked up their bags and entered the hotel.

Walking through the white and luxurious lobby Richard spun around, taking everything in. There were beautiful people sauntering around wearing next to nothing. Their tanned torsos were in stark contrast to his pasty body. He was now feeling slightly nervous about parading around in his swimwear.

Checking-in, it became apparent that this was no cheap hotel. Richard had never stayed in a hotel before. At least he couldn't remember ever staying in one. A hotel of this calibre was beyond his wildest dreams and as they entered their suite he nearly gasped, for out of the large terrace windows was a breathtaking view of the old town of Ibiza staring back at them.

Matt looked at the unbridled joy that had spread across Richard's face and let him take in the moment. 'Not bad eh?'

Richard was still speechless. He felt like crying. This was a world that hadn't exist to him a week ago. Now he was feeding his senses with sights, sounds and experiences of the highest calibre. 'It's... it's... amazing.' he gushed when he finally composed himself. The suite was white, clean and modern. All the fixtures and fittings were top of the range. The whiteness was broken up by occasional creams and light greys making it feel very homely too. He walked around the suite open-mouthed gasping from time to time as he discovered yet another marvel to feast his eyes upon.

'You think this is amazing? Come with me,' Matt said as he made his way out onto the terrace. Like an excited child, Richard followed Matt. Stepping out onto the spacious terrace he was again hit by a wall of heat, but he was now starting to get used it. He stood there for a few seconds waiting for his eyes to adjust to the searing sunshine and when they did he saw Matt standing by a small swimming pool. Richards's mouth gaped open. 'It's cool isn't it?' Matt said.

'That's our own pool?!' Richard gasped disbelievingly.

'It sure is my friend. The way I saw it, you'd never been on holiday, so you've got to make up for lost time. I got a great deal on this suite so I thought, "why the hell not?"' Matt's face was beaming as wide a smile as Richard's now. He was equally excited but seeing the sheer joy and surprise on Richard's face made him feel even happier. Matt let Richard stand there in shocked amazement a while longer before waking him from his joyful trance. 'C'mon let's unpack, get our shorts on and have a few drinks by the main pool.'

'Can't we just stay around here in *our* pool?' Richard asked; impending self-consciousness rapidly bursting his bubble.

'No, because then we'll just have one another to feast our eyes on and, I like you, but I don't just want your ugly mug to look at.

There're a lot of beautiful people down there and we should be meeting them.'

Put like that Richard didn't have much of an argument, so, taking a deep breath, he set about unpacking and changing into his swim shorts. Standing there in his vest, shorts and flip-flops, he surveyed his awkward image in the full-length mirror and felt very much exposed.

Matt saw this and reassuringly said, 'Look mate, don't worry. You look great and after a couple of drinks you're not going to give two shits what you *do* look like. Try and relax.' And with that they left the suite and made their way to the pool.

The swimming pool was large and inviting. With the heat of the day really starting to kick in, Richard knew it wouldn't be long before he would be jumping into it to cool down. He also knew that submerged in the water he would feel a lot less self-conscious about his body. It was strange that he felt this way as only a couple of days ago he was parading around as naked as the day he was born in Frances' company. Now it was like he'd slipped back into being the old Richard. She'd given him confidence; he knew this now. As much as Matt had massaged his ego there was nothing like a beautiful woman complimenting him to make him feel good about himself. It wasn't long before two outlandish cocktails arrived and Richard nearly choked on the first sip as he spied the bill.

'It's alright buddy, I'll get these,' Matt said, allowing Richard to enjoy the rest of his drink.

'Is everything so expensive over here?' Richard asked.

'In a five-star hotel like this, yes. Don't worry though; you can't put a price on a good time; and that's exactly what we're going to have... We'll spend the day chilling by the pool; have a bit of lunch and then we'll take a nap before heading out tonight. How does that sound?'

Richard didn't have a better plan for the day and Matt's plan did sound pretty effortless so he just nodded his agreement and took another pull from the straw sticking out of his delicious cocktail.

And the day *was* effortless. Richard's earlier inhibitions were swiftly put to the back of his mind as more cocktails and the warming sun completely relaxed him. Every so often he'd slink into the pool to cool down and, it was as he was bobbing around, taking in the beautiful surroundings of the hotel and view out to the Dalt Vila, that he realised it had been so many years since he'd last been swimming. He'd learnt, like many kids do, at school. His parents had never taken him swimming, so it was with great determination and perseverance that he'd learnt with the aid of his P.E. teacher. He'd forgotten how wonderful it felt to float - a simple sensation, but one he hadn't experienced for such a long time. Laying there on his back with the hot sun warming his face; a broad, contented smile clearly visible on his face, there was no hiding the joy this evoked. Seeing this, Matt smiled. But it was with a tinge of sadness as he thought how sheltered Richard's life had been and how much he'd missed out on. When they were younger Richard had always seemed defenceless and innocent compared to all the other boys in their year. He'd been an easy target for the harder kids like Chris Simmonds who'd tried to oppress him and make him feel smaller than he already felt. Many was the time that Matt had stepped in and stopped Richard from taking an unwarranted thumping. Seeing Richard floating on his back with a blissful smile spread wide across his face made Matt feel so happy. Richard was finally experiencing what it was like to feel some semblance of contentment.

They spent most of the day either in the pool or by the pool. By the time they stumbled back to their suite they were clearly feeling the effects of the many cocktails and beers they'd consumed. Sensibly they'd also drunk a fair amount of water too and even managed some pasta for lunch. This had just about kept them on an even keel but, as they both fell face down on their respective beds, they were in dire need of a catnap if they were to make it out that evening.

An hour later they groggily rose from their slumber. Richard's head was pounding. The sun and the alcohol had taken their toll, but Matt wasn't going to let Richard take a backward step. 'Come on, get yourself showered and ready. We're going to watch the sunset,' he announced enthusiastically as he handed him a bottle of water.

A few greedy gulps of water later, Richard jumped in the shower. Switching on the taps, he immediately had to turn the temperature right down, for, despite having smothered himself in high factor suntan lotion, his pale skin - which had done its best to reflect the sun - had absorbed more than its fair share of its rays. He looked down at the suntan marks and had to laugh. It looked like he still had a pair of shorts on. His lily-white skin had gone a pig shade of pink and was extremely sore to touch. With obvious discomfort and great care to not tear his paper-thin skin, he shuffled his way out of the shower cubicle and wrapped himself in one of the soft, plump towels. But the towel might as well have been made from barbed wire as he recoiled at its touch.

'You might want to put some aftersun lotion on when you get out of the shower,' Matt called out from the living room.

No shit Sherlock, winced Richard as he endeavoured to dry his red-raw body.

He was still grimacing as they sat in the back of the cab which hurtled along the motorway that links Ibiza town to San Antonio. His clothes stuck to sunburnt body and every tiny movement felt like a claw ripping across his skin. Matt couldn't contain his amusement. 'You might have to take it a little easier in the sun tomorrow,' he said through a fast-breaking smile.

'You think so?' Richard replied sarcastically.

'Lots of aftersun and lots of water is what you need my friend. You'll be fine tomorrow. Believe me, when you see this sunset you're not going to feel your sunburn.'

Richard already began to feel more comfortable and was excited at the prospect of witnessing a gorgeous sunset. He gazed out the window as, up ahead, the town of San Antonio came into view. Matt had already briefed him, saying that San Antonio wasn't the classiest part of the island. The notorious West End was situated there; a network of narrow streets where bars offering cheap drinks backed onto one another. The clientele of these establishments weren't the most refined people on the planet either, but Matt did say that, with his highly noticeable English suntan, he should fit in well there.

A short while later, after the taxi had weaved its way through the winding streets, they were dropped outside a bar with a large sign saying Café Mambo. They paid the driver and rather than head straight to the bar, they walked to a nearby shop where Matt purchased some beers. Richard followed behind, slightly baffled as to why they were getting take-out beers when they had perfectly good bars to sit in.

Sitting there perched on the rocks just in front of Café del Mar - another popular sunset bar that was situated right next door to Café Mambo – Matt explained that drinks in Café del Mar were expensive and for a fraction of the cost, you could share the same view and listen to the chilled beats being pumped out of the speakers. 'I'm no skinflint, but why pay any more money than you have to?' he explained. Despite it being quite early in the season the rocky beach was full of people with a similar idea. The music playing behind them was chilled and ambient and offered the perfect soundtrack to what their eyes feasted upon. Everyone transfixed by the glowing solar orb inching its way down to the horizon. Richard could clearly see it move its way closer and closer downwards. Slowly, a reverent hush seemed to shroud the crowd congregated there. The music played was so slow and mellow that it was just the occasional sound and beat. Richard could feel his entire body tingle in anticipation of the final part of the sunset. It really felt magical; there was no doubting it was one of the most beautiful and enchanting experiences he'd ever witnessed. He felt like he was glowing, right through his body to the depths of his soul - and that wasn't just his now-forgotten sunburn. As the sun kissed the sea on the horizon he felt himself inwardly gasp. The sky was now a radiant shade of pink, orange and purple. Quite unexpectedly, some of the contingent offered a round of applause in appreciation and Richard found himself applauding too. Within a couple of minutes, the sun had disappeared from view and the temperature seemed to drop with it. Rubbing his shoulders, Matt got up and gave Richard a friendly little kick, 'Let's go get some dinner.'

They strolled through the vibrant streets until they came to the Marina where Matt ushered Richard into to a very welcoming restaurant called Villa Mercedes. It looked vibrant and busy and

Richard wondered if they even had space for them. When the attractive hostess came over and cheerfully greeted them he was quite staggered to hear Matt converse with her in Spanish. She then showed them to a table on a balcony that overlooked the rest of the restaurant. It was a beautiful spot with views of the marina and from their elevated position he could see all the other people there to dine and enjoy the cocktails. One chap caught Richard's eye. A grey-haired man who looked to be in his mid-fifties was stood by the bar. He was surrounded by young, pretty people; both girls and boys, who were captivated by his presence. There was lots of laughter coming from the assembled group as the man stood there confidently holding court. 'Is that chap famous?' Richard asked Matt.

Matt turned his attention to where Richard motioned and with a shake of his head said, 'No, I don't think so. He's probably just rich.'

Acknowledging Matt's blasé answer Richard decided to see what was on the menu. As he was doing so another pretty waitress came to take their drinks order. The waitress was effortlessly tanned, ridiculously slim and had a heavily tattooed body which was clearly evident through her skimpy, loose-fitting top. He'd never seen a female with so many tattoos but he couldn't deny it really suited her. She was still extremely feminine and her long dark hair flowed over her olive-skinned shoulders everytime she moved her head. Her blue eyes captivated Richard who now realised he was staring open-mouthed at her. He was awoken from his trance by her affectionately touching his hand and giggling before moving away.

'Hellloooo, are you alright there mate?' Matt said with a smile on his face.

'Sorry, but she was spellbinding,' Richard replied in complete awe.

'Spellbinding!' Matt repeated jokingly 'That's a great way to describe the lovely Eva. I'll tell her; she'll be most flattered.'

'You know her? She's gorgeous,' Richard gushed.

'I've been coming here for years and they retain the same staff year on year. She's a nice girl but well out of your league,' Matt joked with a subtle wink.

'No no... I, um, wasn't... you know...' Richard babbled suddenly embarrassed.

Matt just laughed. 'Only kidding mate. If you want her you go for it.'

Slightly more composed Richard said, 'No, you're right. She *is* well out of my league.' And then his mind momentarily wandered to thoughts of Frances and how he'd always felt *she* was well out of his league. 'I just haven't ever seen a woman who looks like that before. Y'know, that alluring.'

'" Spellbinding *and* alluring"; well, someone brought their dictionary with them didn't they?'

Richard blushed but he knew Matt was only teasing. 'Anyway, did I miss something? Did we actually order drinks?'

'Yeah, I ordered us two cocktails. You would've taken too long to decide so I took charge. I hope you don't mind?'

'No, not at all,' Richard replied. Matt was right, he would've taken an age to decide what to drink. He liked the fact that Matt took a lot of the decision making away from him. Pretty much everything he was experiencing was new to him anyway and he trusted Matt's judgement.

When the very *spellbinding* and *alluring* Eva returned with the drinks, Richard tried with all his might not to stare at her but it was futile; he soon found himself gazing dreamily into her big blue eyes. So transfixed was he that he didn't notice Matt, who was speaking fluent Spanish, order both his and Richard's food. Eva smiled sweetly, span on her heels and left Richard staring at thin air. 'I've ordered us the fillet steak, medium rare,' Matt said in an effort to break Richard out of his most recent trance.

Shaking his head to regain his focus Richard said, 'I didn't know you could speak Spanish.'

'You didn't ask.' Matt replied nonchalantly. 'I've picked up bits and pieces of the language over time and I find that if you can at least make the effort they will help you out.'

'Will you teach me some please?' Richard asked. And for the next quarter of an hour they sat repeating basic Spanish phrases. 'Por-fa-vor… Por-fa-vor… Por-fa-vor… Grass-ee-as… Grass-ee-as… Grass-ee-as…' Every so often Eva would look over and give them a gentle smile. Richard would try to smile back but then shyly turn away and go back to repeating what was being taught.

When Eva brought their meals, she placed the plates down in front of them and conversed a little with Matt. Eva then let out a gasp and said, 'Lo siento! Lo siento!' - A phrase that Richard recognised from the few words and phrases they'd just been repeating. Both Matt and Eva laughed aloud and Richard looked on gormlessly, wondering what could've possibly been so funny. Before she left she gave Richard a kiss on the cheek and said 'I'm so sorry. You're very sweet,' before she turned and left them to their dinner.

Matt was still chuckling when Richard enquired, 'So, what was so funny?'

Wiping away tears of laughter, Matt composed himself before saying, 'She thought you were…' he started laughing again. '…mentally challenged.' He then broke down into hysterical laughter again. It took a while for him to gather himself enough to speak again but when he did he explained that, because Richard had been staring inanely, drooling and saying basic words very slowly and repetitively, she thought Matt was his carer.

Richard sat there nonplussed, failing to see the funny side to all this. *I don't think I'll be asking for her number,* he thought. He consoled himself by tucking into his steak which was cooked to perfection; not that he'd ever had another fillet steak to compare it to, but he couldn't imagine anything tasting quite as good as this steak tasted. This was washed down with a couple of large glasses of red wine and, with a full belly, he could feel himself properly relax. On finishing, Richard contentedly sat back in his seat and folded his arms behind his head and said, 'Ok, what shall we do now?'

Whilst they thought about their next plan of action, they decided to go down to the bar and order themselves another cocktail. Richard was beginning to show the signs of what they'd already consumed. The combination of a good meal, wine, cocktails, an overdose of sunshine - along with an early start to the day had made their presence felt. On seeing Richard wobble from one foot to another, Matt directed him over to a beautiful chillout area, the other side of the restaurant where some enticing daybeds were located. He perched Richard on the edge of one of the beds then held his drink whilst he helped him recline into a more horizontal position. Despite it being designated a chillout area it was decidedly noisy and, through his semi-blurred vision, Richard could see that the gentleman he'd observed earlier from the balcony was still holding court. There were fifteen or so people gathered around him, all looking admiringly at him, like he was some kind of messiah. Everything he said was greeted by raucous laughter and no other person attempted to take the conversation away from him. Half an hour later the group dispersed, enthusiastically talking of where they were going next, leaving the gentleman all by himself. Standing there alone, he suddenly cut a forlorn figure. Matt felt a flash of pity for him. He quickly decided to go over a chat to him and, making sure that Richard was ok, did so. 'You seem popular,' Matt said, suddenly appreciating that it sounded very blunt.

The gentleman didn't seem too bothered though. He just shrugged his shoulders. 'Not anymore.' He had a bottle of expensive champagne in an ice bucket and from that he poured Matt a glass and handed it to him. 'I'll never drink all of this by myself... My name's Greg – Greg Stanford,' he said as he offered his other hand for Matt to shake.

'Cheers Greg – that's very kind of you... I'm Matt Samson, and over there is an old friend of mine, Richie Chambers,' Matt said motioning over to the swaying form of Richard who was staring gormlessly into space.

'He doesn't look that old,' Greg said jokingly. 'A bit simple maybe, but not old.'

'Yeah, that has been mentioned this evening. Is it alright to bring him over?'

'Of course,' Greg said cheerfully, 'the more the merrier.'

Matt walked over and returned with Richard. He introduced Richard to Greg and the three of them spent the next hour talking and laughing. Greg was slightly portly and had a reddish complexion, although Richard doubted his appearance, unlike his, was caused by too much sun, but rather a lot of good living. His grey/white hair was cropped short as was his beard and he wore a loose-fitting linen shirt and trousers. Straight away it was easy to see why people were so easily enthralled by Greg. He was extremely charismatic and seemed to have a never-ending number of anecdotes on pretty much every subject. Richard and Matt found themselves entranced by his every word; much like the people he'd been holding court to a moment ago. Those people, it transpired, were some of Greg's employees who worked at his recruitment company in London. They were enjoying the last night of their company incentive trip in which he'd treated them to a fun-filled few days for hitting their quarterly targets.

'They're a good bunch,' Greg explained. 'They're wild, but when it comes to work they're on point. Anyone who doesn't buy into that ethos soon gets found out. Most only last a couple of years before they move on, but in those two years they learn a lot and can *earn* a lot too. They'll all go out tonight; party like it's their last night on earth and get the early flight back in the morning. All of them will be at their desks first thing tomorrow and back in work-mode.' Greg had a confident, measured way of speaking, like someone who was used standing in front of people and being the centre of attention. Richard had hardly said a word. He was in complete awe of Greg who they discovered was a self-made millionaire, having grown up on a fairly rough council estate in Bristol. He was now CEO of one of the most dynamic recruitment companies in London. He had houses in London, the South of France and a large villa there in Ibiza. He had a private jet and his own yacht moored in Ibiza Town. 'I don't know what you have planned for tomorrow but if you like you can join me on my boat. I'm going out anyway and it'd be good to have some company.'

Matt and Richard sat open-mouthed before Matt finally replied, 'Really?! That'd be amazing. Wouldn't it Rich?'

Richard suddenly sprang to life, 'Yes, absolutely... As long as you don't mind.'

'I just invited you didn't I? Of course I don't mind! You seem like good chaps. Be there at ten o'clock... And don't be late.'

'How will we know which boat's yours?' Matt asked.

'It's on the main jetty of the Botafoch Marina. It's a white Sunseeker and called Aveline,' Greg said before downing the last of his glass of champagne. 'I'll see you boys tomorrow morning. Have fun tonight.'

He left them standing there, stunned and not knowing quite what to say. It took a moment before what he'd just said had sunken in and when it did they broke out in euphoric laughter; both of them patting the other in congratulations. 'We're going on a speedboat tomorrow?!' Richard said in amazement.

'Not just a speedboat – a Sunseeker,' Matt replied. 'Tomorrow will be awesome!' he continued, not disguising his excitement.

When their elation had subsided, they decided to head back to their hotel. By the time they stepped out of the taxi, Richard was on his last legs. He groggily walked beside Matt towards the hotel's lifts as the stark lighting through reception temporarily blinded him. He was grateful to get into their suite where the lighting was more subtle. Despite being on the verge of exhaustion, he perked up a little once inside. He was immediately drawn to the terrace and after a confused battle with the terrace doors he managed to stumble out there. The view instantly took his breath away. At night, the vista that presented itself was even more spectacular than it had been in the day. Through his alcohol-tainted vision he saw the lights from Ibiza Old Town twinkle majestically and reflect onto the waters of the nearby harbour. He manoeuvred over to the far side of the terrace so he could rest upon the balcony and let out an involuntary sigh, giving a good indication of just how content he was. Matt joined him on the balcony and put a strong arm on his shoulder. No words were necessary. They just absorbed the view and appreciated this beautiful, intimate moment.

CHAPTER 14

Richard awoke next morning to the sound of Matt singing energetically in the living room. He wasn't sure what song it was but it sounded mightily jolly. Hearing Richard stir, Matt bounded into the room and gave him a close-up rendition of his singing. Fully expecting Richard to duet with him, the hairbrush that Matt was using for a microphone was then thrust towards Richard's face. Richard was certainly not ready for this and his bemused face told Matt all he needed to know. Undeterred, Matt wheeled away and sang to himself in Richard's mirror. Every now and again he would turn and point to Richard causing him to take a step back and fall back on the bed. It was patently clear to Richard that Matt was pumped up for today's trip on the boat. It was equally clear, more so now than ever before, that Matt was very much gay. He'd never really noticed any of the obvious, stereotypical gay mannerisms and traits when he saw Matt, but he did now. Matt was evidently relaxed enough in Richard's company to let himself be the person he was. But Richard still wasn't quite awake enough to contend with Matt's exuberance. He rubbed his eyes, yawned and hoisted himself off the bed. Walking over to the mirror, which Matt had now vacated, he stared at the tired looking reflection of himself. As jaded as he looked though, he also looked a lot less troubled. The bright pink glow provided by the previous day's overindulgent sunbathing had brought much needed colour to his features. He looked well; he looked happy; he looked alive. As he headed for the shower he allowed himself a little grin in acknowledgement of this.

After taking care not to aggravate his still sore body whilst getting ready, he joined Matt out on the terrace. Dressed in smart blue board shorts and a loose-fitting, v-neck t-shirt, he didn't feel so self-conscious about today's attire.

Bright blue skies and warm sunshine greeted them as they made their way to the marina where the good ship Aveline was moored. Despite what they'd both imagined it didn't take a great deal of searching to locate Greg's boat. To be nearer the truth, a ship would be a closer approximation, and with dance music blasting from it, it definitely stood out. Greg was dancing around on the deck with a lithe, bikini clad, blonde-haired lady. He twirled her around this way and that until she spun dizzily onto one of the sofas. Giggling, she tried in vain to rise from it. It was only then that Greg noticed Richard and Matt stood below. 'Ahoy me hearties!' he bellowed down to them. They both shared a look. It was quite clear to them that Greg was more than a little bit merry already. Their host staggered over to the ramp. 'Come aboard lads – don't be scared,' he beckoned.

With Matt leading they made their way onto the boat. The blonde lady was still sprawled out on the padded leather sofa and was struggling to get back up. She looked like a new-born giraffe trying to stand for the first time. Her hair was wild and covered her face.

When she finally rose and brushed the hair from her face, she stood right in front of Matt and Richard. Richard was slightly amazed at how tall the lady was, but when he looked down, he appreciated that most of her unnatural height was due to the ridiculously high heels she was wearing. How she stood up in them, let alone danced in them was a marvel in itself. *Not the most practical sea-faring attire,* he thought.

She held out a perfectly manicure hand and, in a strongly tinged Eastern European accent, said, 'Hello, my name Sandy.' Richard very much doubted that was her actual name but took her hand and shook it delicately as he introduced himself. As he held her hand he observed her face which looked like a strong wind had blown its skin back; making it appear almost plastic. Her lips were large, puffy things that appeared to have been stuck onto her mouth. He thought she looked like she'd got her mouth caught in the vacuum cleaner hose whilst trying to kiss it.

'Yes, Sandy is a very popular lady on these shores,' Greg said with a mischievous chuckle.

Matt and Richard shared another glance at one another, as if to say, '*Yeah, I bet she is.*'

'Come; let me introduce you to the others,' Greg said, ushering them further onto the boat. If Sandy were anything to go by, they were somewhat dubious as to who else they would find. They walked into a living area which was bigger than most apartments.

There, two more bikini clad women rose from a table, sniffing and wiping their noses. 'Let me introduce Roxy and... sorry what's your name again?' Greg said to one of the ladies.

'Cassandra,' the lady said in strangely accented English. It was hard to make out where Cassandra was from but she definitely wasn't English or Spanish. Cassandra was pale-skinned, red-haired, tall and slender. She had a naturally pretty face and didn't wear much makeup, which was in stark contrast to Roxy who stood beside her. She stood slightly shorter than Cassandra but both girls wore high heels akin to Sandy. Roxy was buxom, heavily tattooed and had a scary looking, heavily made-up face. With short, spikey hair she instantly intimidated Richard. When she vigorously shook his hand it was as if a burly rugby player had done so, and he was glad when she finally relinquished her grip.

Greg then walked them up a small staircase to the top deck where a long-haired, olive-skinned man turned to offer them a friendly smile. 'This is Paolo. He's Italian, but don't hold that against him,' he joked as he gave Paolo a playful cuddle. Another firm, rough-handed handshake followed and Matt and Richard were left to take in the luxuriousness of the yacht. The boat was immaculate. Expensive wood and leather decorated both the interior and exterior of the boat. The deck looked so new and clean that Richard wondered if anyone had ever stepped foot on it. 'Right, we're going to set off in a bit,' Greg announced as he rubbed his hands together excitedly. 'Girls, you might want to take those daft shoes off! You don't want to fall overboard!' he shouted down the stairs. 'Mad tarts; wearing those onboard,' he whispered to Richard and Matt. Greg then scuttled off down the stairs to untie the boat and raced back onboard. He seemed full of life and put Richard to shame with his boundless energy.

'Do you need a hand with anything?' Matt asked as Greg sped past them.

'No, me and Paolo have got this covered,' Greg replied. 'Haven't we my friend?' he shouted towards the Italian skipper who was deep in concentration.

Slowly, they felt the boat pulling away from its mooring. As Paolo carefully navigated his way out of the marina Greg returned back to them. He was perspiring after his momentary call to action but sported a beaming smile that quickly put the boys at ease. 'Well, here we jolly well go,' he said enthusiastically. 'Let's go have a drink.'

They followed him back down the stairs where the ladies were slouched around the table, giggling. The boat had its very own bar and Greg seemed to revel in playing the host. In no time at all he'd concocted some rather ostentatious cocktails and handed them to Richard and Matt. Before taking a deep glug from his glass of champagne, he cheerfully toasted them. 'It's good to have you aboard. Thanks for joining us.'

'Are you kidding?! Thanks for inviting us,' Matt replied.

'If you want any of that stuff, just push the girls out the way,' Greg said as he gestured to the mountainous pile of cocaine set upon the mirror in the centre of the table. 'If you don't get in there quick, those vultures will devour it all.'

'I'm alright for the moment,' Matt said. 'Do you want to have a go Rich?'

Richard, who had felt like he'd been caught in the middle of a whirlwind since he'd arrived onboard, stood there trying to mouth a reply, but all that came out were incomprehensible sounds.

'Go on boys, don't be shy,' Greg cajoled.

'It's a bit early for that isn't it?' Matt said.

'Depends if you've been to sleep or not,' Greg replied with a playful wink. 'Go on, get stuck in.'

Not wanting to appear rude, Matt made his way over to the table. 'C'mon Rich,' he said.

Richard stood there deliberating. He was curious to know how cocaine might affect him but he was equally apprehensive. Matt had already taken a big sniff through the silver tube and handed it to Richard, making up his mind for him. 'Don't worry mate, it's proper stuff,' he whispered. 'Just close one nostril and take a big pull along the line I've set out for you.'

Richard took the tube and made his way over to the table. He was still trying to maintain a semblance of coolness in what he was doing - like he did this all the time. Sat in his way were two of the ladies, Roxy and Sandy. 'Er, ex… excuse me please,' Richard shyly muttered.

'Why sweetie, what have you done?' Roxy replied jokingly in a loud American accent. The other girls giggled and for once Richard was pleased of his red, sunburnt face as it masked the embarrassed blushing that followed. 'Only kiddin' with ya sweetie. C'mon in – join the party.'

Richard smiled his thanks and squeezed between Roxy and Sandy. He nervously placed the silver tube to his nostril and leant over the table. Holding his finger to his other nostril he sniffed up the line of cocaine which seemed to travel past his sinuses and straight to the back of his eye-socket. He instinctively wanted to cough but managed to suppress the impulse. He didn't think Greg would be too impressed if he blew the remainder of the pile off the table.

'Good lad,' Greg said from the other side of the room. He was twirling around dancing to the house music that he'd just put on. For an older guy, Richard noticed Greg moved with a rhythm and energy he could only dream of. Although, the exuberance of his dancing was causing his drink to spill out from his champagne flute and onto the plush, white carpet that covered most of the floor. But Greg didn't seem aware and probably didn't care anyway; he was too focussed on having a good time. The cocaine that Richard had consumed was now dribbling down the back of his throat and making him feel nauseous. He quickly gulped down a couple of large mouthfuls of his cocktail and felt better. He was still waiting to see what the effects of the cocaine would be. Images of Pete Docherty and Amy Winehouse messed up on drugs suddenly flashed into his head adding to his trepidation. Just the thought of what might happen made his heart beat faster. To calm those nerves, he took another couple of glugs of his cocktail and found he'd almost drained it. With a subtle burp he made his way back over to Greg and Matt who were dancing merrily by the bar. Looking out the tinted window he could see that they'd cleared the marina now and he felt the boat surge forward as it sped up.

'Woooo!' Greg cheered as the sudden thrust of the boat unbalanced him sending one last splash of champagne onto the expensive carpet. 'Time for a top-up!' he said as he took himself behind the bar. 'Tell me Richard, you don't seem to say much. Are you ok?'

Richard wasn't expecting the question so, whilst trying to think of an adequate response, he just stood there gormlessly trying to mouth an answer that didn't come.

'Ahh, don't worry. Coke does that to me too sometimes. It's meant to make you more sociable but ends up shutting you up. I mean, that stuff's like rocket fuel. Not like the shit you get back home.' Greg had obviously mistaken Richard for some kind of a coke-fiend.

Richard just smiled his agreement and turned to Matt who was still dancing around. 'This is amazing isn't it?! I mean, a couple of days ago we were slaving away at work; now we're on a millionaire's yacht in Ibiza. It's magic!' Matt said with a look of unbridled joy emblazoned on his face.

Richard struggled to share Matt's excitement. He was well out of his comfort zone and the cocaine had started to work its magic. A drug infused rush coursed through his body and he felt jittery and on edge. This was a lot different to the feeling of ecstasy and he wasn't sure whether he liked it. Ecstasy relaxed him and made him feel delightful; cocaine, it seemed, gave him an anxious, unsettled feeling and, once Greg handed him another masterfully made cocktail, he decided to get some fresh air out on the deck.

Stepping outside, the sun was bright and made him instinctively shield his eyes. He then remembered he had his sunglasses in his pocket and put them on. *That's better,* he thought. He was away from the noisy lounge where the music was blaring loudly. The ladies had joined Greg and Matt dancing around and there were lots of whoops and shrieks coming from inside. Richard stood on the deck and supped his cocktail quickly. The alcohol began to calm him down, and slowly he started to enjoy the experience. Looking out onto the blue waters and the Dalt Vila, standing majestically overlooking the harbour, the old fortress town captivated Richard. He thought about all the history it contained and, as his mind wandered, thought melancholically of how little a legacy he'd leave. *If I died tomorrow no one would even notice I'd been here.* But just before he got too morose Matt burst out from the sliding doors. Accompanying him was Cassandra, holding onto Matt's arm. 'Are you ok buddy?' Matt said.

'Yes. Sorry, I just needed some air,' Richard replied.

Matt nodded his understanding and stayed put but released Cassandra from his arm. She gracefully tiptoed her way towards a slightly intimidated Richard who found himself involuntarily taking a step backwards. 'I can make you feel better,' she said seductively in tone so quiet that Richard pitched forward slightly to hear her. He could see Matt grinning broadly in the background before he stepped back into the lounge, closing the sliding door behind him. With the door shut, the music was again supressed so only a dull bass rhythm emanated from within. As Cassandra moved ever closer, Richard found his heart beating faster than a young rabbit's. True, some of that might've been due to the overpowering effect of the rocket fuel cocaine, but Cassandra's sudden presence hadn't given him any time to prepare himself. He'd gone from a state of gloom to one of impromptu arousal. The fight or flight instinct of his body had just jumped overboard leaving him to think what the hell to do now. Cassandra, close enough now for him to smell her subtle fragrance, reached out and held his arm. Her hands felt soft and warm on his skin and the gentleness of her touch made his heart leap. He was frightened to say anything in case nothing more than an inaudible squeak came out. Although quite tall, without her dangerously high heels on she still stood shorter than Richard, and so gazed endearingly up at him. And, pulling herself in even closer, she rested her head on his shoulder. He gulped a gulp a condemned man would've been proud of and took an inward breath that was so deep that Cassandra momentarily slipped from her resting position. Pulling herself back up - closer this time - and with an accent he still couldn't quite place said, 'Why are you so tense? Do I make you nervous?'

'No, no... Well yes... A little,' he stammered.

'You have nothing to be tense about. I won't bite... Yet.'

The last comment did nothing to calm his nervous disposition and he could feel himself inadvertently trying to pull away from Cassandra's clutches. It was hot now, blisteringly hot, and he started to feel like he was melting. Almost taking pity on him, Cassandra wiped the film of sweat that had begun to materialise on his brow. 'Do you want to join me in the Jacuzzi?' she said seductively. 'It'll calm you down... Please, come with me.'

He really couldn't think of a reason not to join her and, on seeing her captivating figure from behind as she strode away, he soon found himself following her up the stairs to the Jacuzzi like a loyal dog.

The Jacuzzi was bubbling away like a boiling cauldron as he watched Cassandra elegantly step into it. She submerged herself completely and as she came back up her red hair clung to her face, forcing her to sweep it back. The sun glistened off her pale skin and it was only then he realised how green her eyes were. She was completely enchanting. She was so enchanting in fact that Richard found himself staring open-mouthed at her. 'Well, are you going to join me in here or just stand there and stare?' she said in a friendly but suggestive manner.

Shaking himself back to reality, he made his way over to the Jacuzzi. Without any of the elegance that Cassandra had showed, he removed his t-shirt like an escape artist trying free himself from his straitjacket. He wasn't sure how he'd managed it, but his arms now stuck up in the air and his head was completely covered.

'Do you need a hand?' Cassandra giggled.

'No, no, I've got this,' came his muffled reply, and with a few more wriggles he freed himself and tossed the t-shirt on the deck. He then flicked off one flipflop and then the other, but unfortunately the latter was removed with such gusto that it flew into the Jacuzzi, just missing Cassandra as she ducked for cover. 'Oh, I'm so sorry!' he quickly apologised.

Cassandra was too busy laughing to respond to the apology initially. When she stopped laughing she beckoned Richard to join her. 'You Englishmen are completely crazy.'

Crazy? Richard thought. He'd never been referred to as crazy before. Standing there in his swim shorts he suddenly felt vulnerable. Bare-chested, Cassandra could see Richard's sun-burnt torso and he could feel her pity for him in the look she gave. 'I know I know; I should've used a stronger factor,' he said, embarrassed.

'As I said, you English are crazy,' she replied.

Richard made his way over and stepped into the Jacuzzi, opting to sit opposite Cassandra. He was surprised by how warm the water was. Slowly sitting down, he let the bubbles tickle his chin but he felt an urge to leap back out. The water didn't relax him; it made him feel even more hot and bothered. Being hot in a hot Jacuzzi just wasn't what was needed right now. His discomfort was further compounded when he felt Cassandra's foot work its way up his inner thigh towards his groin. Instinctively he flinched.

'Don't be afraid,' she said as she moved across the water to sit on his lap facing him. She put her long arms around his neck and moved in to kiss him. Despite the last few days' eye-opening developments, being hit on by an attractive woman so blatantly came as quite a shock to him. But he didn't want to seem completely rude so tried his best not to reel from her advances. As their lips met he could smell the alcohol and cigarettes on her breath but this was overtaken by the taste of her lip gloss and saliva. Her tongue moved vigorously within his mouth and she let out a subtle moan as their kiss became more passionate. But as wonderful as all this felt, in his head he felt like he was betraying Frances. Cassandra's kiss was certainly full-on and fervent but it didn't have the same feeling as when he'd kissed Frances. Sensing something wasn't quite right, Cassandra pulled away. 'Is something the matter?' she asked.

'No, nothing's the matter,' he replied.

'You've got a girlfriend? A wife maybe?... I understand. But I won't tell if you don't.'

'I'm sorry; I'm just not used to this.'

'What kissing?' Cassandra said incredulously.

Richard wanted to say, *"well, actually yes,"* but felt embarrassed to do so, so settled for, 'No, having a Jacuzzi with a lady I've only just met.'

This seemed to wound Cassandra a little and she pulled away, sinking back into the water.

He felt compelled to expand on his apology. 'I suppose I do have someone back home, although she no longer wants to be with me.' He could hear the sorrow in his own voice and realised how ridiculous he sounded. He'd only been with Frances for a weekend – hardly the romance of a lifetime; but he had nothing to compare it to and the feelings he felt for Frances were raw and strong. He understood now, what he felt for Frances was love and it had hurt him that she'd rejected him.

Seeing the sudden sadness in Richard's face, Cassandra moved back across towards him, this time sitting next to him. She put a hand on his leg but not in an effort to arouse him; it was to reassure him. 'You love her, right?' she said.

'Yes. Yes, I do.' he said resignedly.

'I used to love someone,' she began wistfully. 'He was a lovely man called Jerome. We were very much in love, but one day he told me he'd been with someone else. He was very sorry and said it was a big mistake, but said he wanted to be honest with me. I was devastated and told him to leave... It was the last time I ever saw him. He was so upset that he took himself back home to Holland where I think he still is. I expected him to get together with this other woman but he never did – at least I'm pretty sure he never did... I still have some of his stuff. He never picked it up. I think he was too ashamed or embarrassed to see me. I do miss him though. He's the only man I've ever truly loved. I was so sad after our break-up that I came over here and started working in bars. That didn't pay enough so I started selling drugs, but when I started doing more drugs than I was selling I got into this. This pays well and, apart from the odd gentleman that isn't a gentleman like you, it's a good lifestyle.'

Richard looked at Cassandra who was staring emptily into the distance. There was no sign of tears but he could tell she felt a sadness as she told her story. 'I'm sorry to hear that.' He tried to get her off the subject. 'May I ask where you're from? I've been trying to place your accent but for the life of me I can't quite locate it.'

Cassandra broke out of her stupor and giggled, 'A lot of people have the same problem, don't worry. My mother was Irish – from Cork; my father was Danish, from a small town just outside Copenhagen, and I grew up there and later, in the north-east of Scotland. He worked on the oil rigs and my Mother worked in bars and sang in a folk band.'

'No wonder I couldn't place the accent,' Richard said, half-chuckling. 'I suppose you get your skin tone from your Mum then?'

'You'd think so, but my Father was the pale one. He had fair skin and even fairer hair. My Mother was dark haired and blue-eyed. She was a stunning woman.'

'Was?'

'She died a year after I came here. One day she found a lump on her breast, two months later she was dead. I didn't even get to see her before she died. I just didn't have enough money to pay to get home.' Her voice tailed off as the sadness returned to her. 'That's when I went a little off the rails…And this is not the place you want to be when you go off the rails. Drugs, alcohol and parties are easy to come by, and for a couple of years I was a real mess.'

Richard suddenly felt sympathy for Cassandra and instinctively put his arm around her. He wanted her to feel safe, not sad and vulnerable. He himself no longer felt uncomfortable, either in his surroundings or in Cassandra's presence. She could sense this and nestled into his cuddle. She gazed up at him, 'You're a sweetie. I wish all the men I met were like you…She's a lucky lady,' she said.

'Who is?' Richard asked.

'Whoever has your heart.'

'Yeah, but she doesn't want to be with me anymore,' he said, conscious that he was really making it sound like he'd been in some sort of long-term relationship. He'd never had to deal with these emotions before and just talking about them and facing up to his feelings stung.

'Then she's crazier than you… Good men are a hard to find and I can tell you're a very good man.'

'What makes you so sure I'm such a good man?'

'I see enough men who think they're all that - big egos and small cocks. Strutting around like they're something special. Only interested in themselves and not caring about anyone else. Straight away I could tell you had manners and you've shown me you're a sensitive soul. You're kind and gentle. These are wonderful qualities. Don't ever change. Don't ever try and be someone you're not. Stay true to yourself and good things will find you.'

'Thank you,' said Richard bashfully, a surge of pride soaring through him. He'd always only been himself. He'd never really had anyone to play up to. He never possessed an ego. But that said, it was nice to have an attractive lady sing his praises. 'May I ask you a question? And you don't have to answer it if you don't want to…'

'Do I like what I do?' Cassandra guessed correctly and Richard nodded his agreement. 'Everyone wants to know the answer to that question and I surprise them by saying yes, I really *do* enjoy what I do. It's not like I'm going to be doing this forever, but it suits me right now.' She saw the quizzical look Richard bored into her and laughed. 'What are you looking at me like that for? I like sex! I might as well get paid for having it; and I get paid decent money – certainly, a lot more than working in a crummy bar. A couple more years and I'll have enough money saved to afford to buy my own place. And who knows, I might just meet the man of my dreams along the way.'

Richard, who was on the other end of the spectrum when it came to sexual experiences, was enthralled by the freedom Cassandra showed when talking. She didn't have any inhibitions or hang-ups about who she was or what she did. Sure, she had a fragile side to her but, either she was very good at protecting herself or she'd become accustomed to shutting out certain feelings. Either way he could tell she was very good at making sure that she didn't get hurt or think too heavily about things. He guessed she was in her mid to late twenties and with her spirit he imagined she would do exactly what she planned. She'd set herself up for the future and have a good time doing so. He was in awe of her confidence and the fact that she really didn't care what other people might think. She lived life on her terms and he found that highly admirable.

For a time after, Richard and Cassandra sat contently cuddled in the Jacuzzi and that was exactly where Greg and Matt found them. 'Heeeey! Someone looks more relaxed,' Matt said enthusiastically, waking them out of their state of bliss.

'I hope our lovely Cassandra has been looking after you,' Greg said with a wink.

Before Richard had chance to relay the truth of what *had* actually gone on between the two of them, Cassandra clicked into gear. 'I certainly have. This boy has got some stamina I can tell you,' she said as she effortlessly straddled him. She left him with a big wet kiss that took him completely unawares before she rose from the water. As she did so she took Richard's hand and gently pulled him to his feet. All of the time they'd been in the Jacuzzi he hadn't been aware of where they were or where they were heading. Now he could see an idyllic island surrounded by the bluest water he'd ever seen. The sun's reflection bounced off the water's surface and, even though he was wearing his sunglasses, he still had to squint a little.

'Welcome to Formentera,' Greg proudly announced. Richard half expected Greg to reveal that he owned the island, but instead he ushered them down the steps to where a little dingy was waiting to take them ashore. The ladies stayed on the yacht as Paolo helped the others into the dingy. After a short transfer they came ashore in a little bay where a few busy restaurants were bustling with tourists seeking a place to dine. There didn't seem to be space anywhere, but from out of nowhere a waiter exposed a table that was right at the front of a rustic looking restaurant with whitewashed beams and crisp linen drapes. Greg whispered in the waiter's ear and a moment later a bottle of champagne was theatrically produced and expertly opened. With a subtle pop, the cork was removed and the champagne poured into their flutes. They clinked glasses and toasted themselves, and not for the first time in the past few days, Richard had to pinch himself to see if he was dreaming. This was a million miles away from the world he'd spent most of his life drudging through. Sitting back in his chair, he allowed himself a moment of appreciation. Although he was experiencing the unfamiliar feeling of loss - the loss of a woman he had strong feelings for, and the loss of his parents who, he openly admitted, didn't love him or have a shred of compassion for him - this moment made that momentarily disappear. His heart filled with a warmth it wasn't used to experiencing. With his sunglasses on and a contented smile etched across his face he looked the epitome of chilled-out. Greg nudged Matt and said, 'Your friend doesn't say much but he sure looks happy. He looks like the cat that got the cream.'

'I'm sure the lovely Cassandra had a little something to do with him looking like that,' Matt replied. 'Isn't that right Rich?'

Richard broke out of his dreamlike state and refocussed. He was still smiling as he said, 'Cassandra certainly is a charming lady.'

'Well, she's brought a smile to your face, that's for sure,' Matt said. Even Richard allowed himself a wry smile at that. He wasn't yet ready to divulge the truth that, actually, nothing had really gone on except talking and cuddling.

They sat there chatting away for some time. A chilled, delectable bottle of Sancerre soon replaced the champagne and for the first time in his life Richard sampled lobster. When Greg explained how they cooked the lobster Richard was slightly perturbed; he felt pity for the poor thing, but he couldn't deny how good that poor thing tasted. Each mouthful was a conflict for his conscience to deal with and he was glad when the alcohol kicked in, slowly diluting his dilemma. Mopping at his mouth with his napkin, there was absolutely no doubting that had been an amazing culinary experience. After this, beans on toast and fish fingers with oven chips might not cut it anymore.

Conversation during this sumptuous lunch was easy. Greg again regaled them with hilarious anecdotes of wild nights out, women he'd slept with and failed businesses he'd owned. Richard was amazed at how courageous Greg was when it came to business. He didn't seem to mind failing. He just dusted himself off and started again. And here he was now; a successful millionaire with all the trimmings that went with it. He was inspirational. There was no other way to put it. Richard felt an urge to start his own company and embark on the road to becoming the next Richard Branson. It was yet another wake-up call in the fast-growing list of wake-up calls he'd received over the past few days. When the time came to leave the restaurant, Greg paid the bill - which included a hefty tip for the waiter - and they made their way to where Paulo waited for them in the little dingy. Richard was feeling almost euphoric now. This was a little slice of heaven; the beach, the clear blue water, the yacht that waited for them and all the other things that had made this a truly memorable day.

Back onboard the boat the ladies were waiting for them. Cassandra greeted Richard with a kiss planted firmly on his lips. Her arms draped around his neck and, unlike earlier, he felt completely comfortable with it. The wine had mellowed him and taken the edge off the cocaine. He now felt ready to join the party. Greg made that decision all the easier with his boundless enthusiasm. He wanted everyone there to enjoy themselves and this included dancing around to the music he'd just turned up so it drowned out all other sound. There were drinks handed out and everyone took their turn hoovering up another line of cocaine. Gone were Richard's concerns that he might be on the fast-track to habitual drug taking. No more images of him lying on a piss-stained mattress with a needle sticking out of his arm. He found the cocaine, just like the ecstasy had, accentuated what he was already feeling. He could feel it surging around his system, energising him and making him feel blithe and confident. Everyone was laughing, giggling and dancing as the yacht pulled out of the bay and headed out to sea. Richard couldn't imagine ever feeling quite so carefree and alive as he did right at that moment. His mind seemed clear of anything other than the euphoria he was experiencing.

A short while later, and without much warning, Greg turned the music down causing everyone to stop dancing and wonder what the reason was for suspending their revelry. Greg beamed as he swigged a healthy gulp of champagne from his glass and cleared his throat. 'It's been brought to my attention that it's a certain someone's birthday today…' Greg paused for effect as Matt put a heavy arm on Richard's shoulder. With that all the girls swarmed around Richard and showered him with kisses. Greg then orchestrated a loud and tuneless rendition of "*Happy Birthday*" leaving Richard crimson-faced but sporting an unstoppable grin. The music was then turned back up and they spent the next half an hour bouncing around in a gleeful haze as the boat smoothly navigated its way back towards Ibiza.   Cassandra took it upon herself to dance closest to Richard, now uninhibited by his inhibitions. No longer self-conscious, he danced freely and with newfound rhythm. Cassandra seemed genuinely attracted to him and their two bodies entwined as their faces moved tantalisingly close to one another. It all felt very instinctive. Perhaps it had always been within him, somewhere deep inside, and only now had he realised it. All the time Matt was being entertained by the other ladies. He wasn't fussed that they weren't his type; he had his top off and danced with the same abandon as his friend. Occasionally the boys exchanged looks and smiles of mild disbelief as Greg hopped around with the energy of a young boy. He was in his element - the archetypal founder of the feast.

Richard felt the boat slowing right down and Greg walked over to the doors and slid them open. 'Come take a look,' he said as he beckoned them to follow. As Richard stepped outside, his eyes took some time to adjust to the stark sunlight, but there to their left was a huge rocky island that towered eerily above them. It was like something from science fiction movie. 'This, my friends is Es Vedra. Magnificent isn't it?' Greg beamed. He was extremely proud to show off this natural wonder - as if he'd paid for it to be there. It certainly made Richard stand there in awe. It seemed with every minute that passed there was more and more that was being revealed to him. The boat continued to move slowly past the island and eventually out of its oppressive shadow. A moment later, they stopped in a beautifully clear expanse of water. The sun beat down furiously on them. Richard wondered if he'd ever been this hot in his life and it was with great relief that Greg said, 'Who's up for a dip in the sea?' He then stepped up to the side of the yacht and without a pause, threw himself in headfirst - not so much of a dive, more of an aimless, sideways jump. The others ran to see Greg rise from the water and waving to everyone to join him. 'Come on in. The water's lovely!'

Matt didn't need any encouragement. Making sure his phone and wallet were out of his shorts, he leapt clean over the side, just managing to miss Greg who was still rubbing salty water from his eyes. 'Woooooh!' Matt yelled as he resurfaced. 'Come on Richie boy!' he called up.

The ladies all turned to him expectantly, giving him little choice but to empty his pockets and edge his way, a lot less confidently than Matt had approached the same task. He stepped up onto the side with unsteady legs. *My god that's a lot further down than I thought,* he pondered. With the eyes of the ladies boring into him, he took a deep breath and tried to remember what he did when he'd last dived into water. This again was back during his school days. *"Point your hands towards the water and the rest of you will follow,"* he remembered his PE teacher saying. With eyes closed, he pointed his hands forward, and with a small leap, fell towards the inviting blue water… The sound of his belly hitting the water first sounded like a big slap. The ladies all turned away and cringed. Greg and Matt both looked at one another with mild concern. When Richard rose from the water he was holding his stomach and struggling for breath. Matt seeing that he was otherwise alright laughed, 'Nice dive Tom Daley!'

Still rubbing his bright red tummy, Richard managed a slight smile, 'Ha-ha, thanks for the sympathy.'

'Are you ladies joining us?' Greg called up.

'No chance sweet-cheeks,' Roxy shouted back. 'With this amount of makeup on I'd cause an oil slick. You boys enjoy yourselves.'

'I'm just fine here thank you,' said Sandy.

Then, without any warning at all, Richard glimpsed the slim figure of Cassandra elegantly dive towards the water. Unlike him, she barely made a splash as she entered and, as she re-emerged and brushed her out of her eyes, he appreciated how effortlessly attractive she was. She then swam over to him, put her long arms around him and planted the softest, wettest kiss upon his lips. Not for the first time, Matt and Greg shared a knowing look with one another.

'That was the worst dive I've ever seen,' Cassandra said quietly when their lips parted.

'Thanks,' Richard replied with a smile. 'That one didn't quite go to plan.'

'Good job you're cute,' she said before kissing him again.

They floated about in the water for another ten minutes. Richard loved the sensation of the cool water on his skin. It took the heat out of his body. Everything seemed to sparkle: the sun on the water, the sheen on their bodies, Cassandra's eyes. This was a whole new world to him. Before this, life felt dull and grey. Colours now radiated and warmed his soul deep within. As he kissed Cassandra again he marvelled at how this attractive woman was anywhere near him. Of course, he knew she was being paid to be there but he felt that she was going beyond the call of duty. The way she was around him was very intimate. As if to prove that point she swam up behind him and hugged him with strength of feeling of someone that was truly content. Richard leaned around and said, 'Are you okay?'

'Of course. Why wouldn't I be?'

'Can I ask a question? – And don't take this the wrong way.'

'Fire away.'

'Okay… Do you actually like me or is this all part of the act?'

'Are you complaining?' Cassandra said with a sassy look.

'No, no, but the way you kiss me and the…' he was cut off by her kissing him passionately again. When she pulled away he gulped and took a deep breath. 'Yeah, like that.'

'Don't think so much darling. Just enjoy it for what it is. It's a perfect day. Don't question it.'

Richard couldn't argue. It certainly *had* been a perfect day. He hadn't woken up this morning with any real preconceptions of how the day would pan out, but even if he'd let his imagination run rampant, he couldn't have planned a more perfect day than had been had so far.

Having re-boarded the yacht and dried themselves off they set off into open water at a slow but steady rate. Soaking up the sun's rays on the sundeck, they devoured more devilishly strong cocktails. Richard was beginning to feel the pace now. His head was starting to feel heavy, as were his eyelids. Conversation started to pass him by.

He sat there grinning inanely, laughing occasionally when everyone else did for fear of being found out. The others were more seasoned drinkers than he was. For Richard this was still fairly new ground. Cassandra, seemingly reading his mannerisms, moved closer to him, sitting behind him on his mat. She folded her arms and legs around him and Richard allowed himself to completely relax into her enveloping embrace. His head rested on her breasts and she tenderly kissed his forehead as he looked innocently into her eyes. The others were still talking noisily over the top over them as she whispered into his ear, 'Wanna have a lay down?'

A puzzled look came over Richard's face. 'I thought I *was* lying down?' he said genuinely confused.

'With me, silly,' she giggled. 'On a bed… In private.'

Richard was already extremely comfortable cradled in Cassandra's body, but the loud talking of the others was starting to hurt his ears. Roxy's voice in particular had gone up a few decibels and the whining American accent had started to grate a little. 'Mmmm, yes that sounds like a good idea,' he mumbled, nodding. It had taken a great deal of effort to say that with its nodded accompaniment; it was going to take a superhuman effort to raise his lethargic body up and off Cassandra. Awkwardly they both tried to prize their hot, sweaty bodies apart. When they finally detached, Richard wondered if they had actually torn the skin off one another. His legs felt decidedly unsteady as he rose and Cassandra helped support his cumbersome frame like a punched-out boxer.

'Whoops,' said Greg. 'Someone looks he's had one too many cocktails.'

'Are you alright Rich?' Matt said half laughing, half concerned.

'He'll be ok,' Cassandra cut in. 'He's just going to have lie down.' She still had hold of Richard's arm but had stopped supporting him quite as much. Like a parent letting go of their kid's bike when they first ride without stabilisers, Cassandra released her grip on Richard's arm, and with mild trepidation, she watched him try to navigate his way past the others.

All of a sudden, every footstep was placed as precisely as if he were stepping through a minefield. If he wasn't before, he was now glaringly aware of how drunk he was. This provided great amusement to the others though who were transfixed, intrigued to know if Richard was going to succeed in his epic journey, or whether gravity and alcohol were going to win the day. Richard kept apologising to no one in particular as he wobbled from one unsteady leg to another. 'Sorry, sorry…hmmm, sorry.' This was occasionally followed by a little giggle or a supressed hiccup.

Cassandra couldn't watch anymore and, taking pity on him, grabbed hold of Richard, and with all the strength she possessed, hauled him clear of the others.

Not for the first time since he'd rekindled his friendship with Richard, Matt found himself uttering the words, 'Be gentle with him,' jokingly to Cassandra.

Still trying to stabilise Richard's burdensome frame, Cassandra flashed Matt an unimpressed look. 'Doesn't look like I'll have much choice does it?'

The others roared with laughter as did Richard, not really knowing what he was laughing at.

By the time Cassandra had manhandled Richard into one of the luxuriously decorated cabins, she was exhausted. She flopped onto the pristine and indulgent bed. Without her to support him, Richard involuntarily followed suit. They both lay there a moment; Cassandra panting furiously, Richard hiccupping and burping. 'That was a lot harder than it looked,' Richard mumbled.

Cassandra sat upright and looked incredulously at prone figure of Richard. 'You're not wrong there,' she said breathlessly. 'Come on, let's get you comfortable.' She then dragged him into the middle of the bed before collapsing beside him.

'Sorry,' Richard muttered. No sooner had he apologised for the umpteenth time than he broke into a deep, reverberating snore. Alcohol and exhaustion had got the better of him and it wasn't too long before Cassandra gave in to her own fatigue.

They were awoken later by a loud thumping on the cabin door. 'Oi, get up loverboy. You gotta see this,' Matt called out.

Sluggishly, Richard ruffled his hair and rose - not so much like a salmon; more like a geriatric worm - from the comfort of the soft bed and Cassandra's arm that was draped around his midriff. He looked down at Cassandra as he tried to piece together how he'd ended up in this unfamiliar environment with an unfamiliar bed companion. Like chunks of a jigsaw, his mind slotted together his immediate memory for him. With it came, a warm glow of endearment nestled in his soul to the prostrate figure lying peacefully there in the bed.

He joined the others on the deck where, for once, there was hushed quiet. 'What's going on?' he asked.

'That,' said Matt pointing to the crimson sun moving gently towards the horizon.

It was totally mesmerizing. If he thought the sunset yesterday was breathtaking, then the sight that greeted him now surpassed that. 'Oh my god,' he said in complete awe.

'Have you ever seen anything so beautiful?' Matt whispered.

There were no words for Richard to reply with. He just stood there in silent awe with Greg, Sandy, Roxy and Matt, transfixed by the fast-descending sun.

'It's stunning isn't' it?' Cassandra whispered in a voice so quiet it was barely audible. She'd moved silently behind him, wrapped her arms around his waist and cuddled into his frame. 'Nothing beats an Ibiza sunset.'

Richard could feel a sudden surge of contentment swiftly followed by a surge of arousal. This was largely due to Cassandra, whose hand had wondered towards his crotch. She was gently stroking the outline of his penis through his shorts and he was now completely at her mercy. Not that he minded. Although, he was thankful that everyone else was still mesmerised by the setting sun. Without turning, he walked Cassandra backwards. No one noticed them stumble back into the cabin where they embraced with a passionate kiss. Cassandra's bikini was now on the floor to the wonderment of Richard. He couldn't recall removing it and hadn't seen her do it either. But he conceded that she was probably well-versed in the removal of clothing. Fervently they kissed and, as their tongues entwined, He could feel her nimble fingers untying the cord of his shorts. They soon fell to the floor leaving him completely naked. She moved her mouth from his lips to his cheek, then to his neck, working her way down his body. He could feel himself shudder and stiffen as her mouth found its way to the stiffest part of his body. He quietly gasped as she took him. It was more than he could cope with. He didn't want to explode this early into proceedings, so sheepishly he pulled himself away and moved his hands down to cover his modesty. 'I'm sorry,' he said breathlessly. 'Give me a moment.'

'Have I done something wrong?' Cassandra said as she rose and retreated a few steps back. Richard could now see her slender figure in its entirety. She really was a sight to behold.

'No, not at all. Quite the opposite. I just need a moment.' He could see that she looked a little hurt so continued to reassure her. 'Really, you didn't do anything wrong. If anything, you're too lovely and what you were doing was also too lovely. I nearly... you know...' he motioned with his eyes to what his hands were trying to conceal. 'There and then.'

He suddenly cut a bashful figure and it was now Cassandra's turn to reassure him. 'That was the desired effect sweetie.'

'I know,' Richard countered. 'I'm just not used to...' he waved his hands around as he fumbled for the right words, exposing himself to Cassandra, 'This,' he finished for want of a better thing to say.

'You definitely worry too much if you're worrying about "*this*."' Cassandra replied mimicking his gesture. There was a smile in her delivery though and Richard felt relaxed again.

'I'm sorry,' he said again.

'Stop apologising. There's nothing to apologise for. I think it's sweet... But if you don't come back here this second I *will* start to get annoyed.'

Richard smiled and made his way back over to her. But just as he was about to reach out towards her, his mobile, that had escaped his pocket as his shorts had fallen to the floor, rang. He couldn't resist looking down to see who was calling him. So unaccustomed to receiving calls, he could only think of two people who might be doing so. One was on the boat just a few metres away from him, on the other side of the door.

Who's calling you?' Cassandra enquired, seeing the sudden distraction to their intimate moment.

Slightly dumfounded, Richard reached down to pick up his phone. 'It's Frances,' he said.

CHAPTER 15

'H..h...hello,' Richard said tentatively, answering the phone. He had instantly been taken into another world as he waited for the voice to respond on the other end of the line. It seemed like an eternity but when the reply came he could've melted.

'Hi...' It was all Frances said. But the way she said it gave so much away. Richard could hear the delicateness and remorse in its delivery. He completely forgot that he was stood naked next to Cassandra with a fast-diminishing erection.

'Are you ok?'

Again, there was a lengthy pause before Frances replied, 'No, not really...'

He could hear her sniff afterwards and it was obvious that she'd been crying and probably crying a lot. 'What's up?' his voice was full of concern but in truth he felt utterly helpless.

After another long pause Frances was just about to speak when he heard Mike's angry voice rumble in the background 'Look, I've got to go. I'll...' and the phone cut off abruptly.

'Hello... hello,' he called in vain. Panicked, he dialled Frances' number but it went straight to voicemail. He tried again with the same result. His head was spinning and he didn't know what to do.

'What's up babe?' Cassandra's voice came as if it were from a dream.

'Er, well… it… it was Frances,' he said, still somewhat shocked.

'I take it Frances is the chick you were telling me about?'

Richard nodded as he stared vacantly at the floor.

Recognising their passionate moment had passed, Cassandra walked over to the large inbuilt mirrored wardrobe and pulled out a luxurious white bathrobe. Wrapping it around her she took out another and brought it over to Richard who was still staring at the floor. 'Put this on,' she said tenderly. After he'd put it on they both sat on the edge of the bed; a bed that a moment ago had nearly been used for an entirely different purpose than just sitting on. 'Are you alright? You don't look it.'

'I'm just a bit stunned. I didn't think I'd ever hear from her again, and now I have, I'm just really worried for her.' His voice was distant and touched with emotion. He was still staring down at the floor.

Cassandra put her hand on his chin and pulled his face upwards. 'Look at me.' Reluctantly he met her gaze. 'You love her – I can see that. And she knows that. Why else would she call you?... You need to do something about it.' There was a determination in her delivery that she hoped would transfer to him.

'She sounded scared. Her husband was there and…'

'Woah, you never mentioned she was *married*!' Cassandra cut in.

Richard stuttered and fumbled for words. 'She is… But she's not – I can't really explain.'

'Either she is or she isn't?'

'Well, in that case she *is* married…' he said as he rose from the bed and began pacing agitatedly around the room. 'But she was separated when I met her and very recently she got back with her psycho husband.'

'How long were you seeing each other?' Cassandra enquired in a softer tone aimed at calming Richard down.

In a split second he thought of a multitude of answers to give in response and all would've sounded a lot more credible than the truth, but the truth is exactly what he delivered; the cold hard, non-embellished truth. He told her how they'd spent the past two years passing each other in the street; how Matt had popped up from out of nowhere and they'd rekindled their friendship; how he'd had a physical and physiological makeover courtesy of Matt; how he'd fallen in love with Frances and how she had spurned him to return to her awful husband… And all this in under a week! He felt exhausted as he conveyed the last of his tale and wearily sat back down on the bed. His head fell into his hands and he suddenly cut a sad, deflated figure.

Cassandra, although in a mild state of shock at what she'd just heard, put her arm around Richard's shoulder. Initially she didn't know what to say. It was a lot to take in and far from the usual stories she was accustomed to hearing from clients. But, after a moment's consolation and shoulder-rubbing she knew just what he needed hear. 'You know what you gotta do?.. You've gotta go rescue her; rescue her from that bastard, Mike.'

A short while later, Richard strode out of the cabin, dressed and determined. The yacht was coming into the Marina and the others were milling around the deck, tidying up the empty glasses. Surveying the mess, it looked like there'd been a much larger party than just the six of them. Everyone else looked drunk and weary. Matt had a spliff hanging out of the corner of his mouth as he carried two half-empty champagne flutes, one with a cigarette butt swimming in it. 'Alright Romeo?' he said cheekily, which made a large chunk of ash fall from his spliff. Richard noticed that Matt had eyes that could smile even when his mouth was unable to do so.

'Frances called me,' Richard said rather matter-of-factly.

Matt nodded his head in recognition and set the glasses down where they were being collected. His hands now free, he removed the spliff from his mouth and exhaled a large cloud of smoke which momentarily obscured them from one another. 'What did she say?' he asked, seemingly unsurprised by Richard's news.

Richard coughed as the smoke hit the back of his throat. 'She didn't really say much. She sounded scared and upset though. I could hear Mike in the background and then the phone went dead. Now her phone just goes straight to answerphone... I'm really worried about her.'

Matt took a moment to contemplate what Richard had said before he replied. 'I know what you'll want to do; you'll want to head back right now and rescue her from the clutches of "Evil Mike," but I'd advise against that. You could be walking into something that you can't control. It's their business... And he's a big bastard. Upset "Evil Mike" and you might find more than just your love-spuds being strangled by him this time.'

A flashback of Mike squeezing the life out of his testicles entered Richard's head and he winced at the memory. Matt did have a point, but Richard knew that he couldn't just wait on the sidelines. He knew full well what Mike was capable of and wondered if he was physically bullying Frances as well as emotionally bullying her. The thought of Mike striking or beating Frances made his blood rise and with gritted determination he said, 'I'm going to help Frances... I can't not.'

'Well...' Matt said as he inhaled the last drag of his spliff before stubbing it out in a nearby ashtray, 'If you're going I guess I'd better go with you.' He then placed a firm and reassuring hand on Richard's shoulder.

Night-time had descended and a plethora of lights illuminated the marina as they stood on deck saying their farewells. Richard couldn't help but think back on what a wonderful day it had been. It was with a very heavy heart that he kissed Cassandra goodbye. She looked genuinely sad to see him leave and the sincerity in her eyes confirmed to him that it hadn't just been an act. 'Thanks for an amazing day,' he said quietly as they stood, not quite knowing how to be with each other now.

'No, thank *you*... You know what? I think you may have just about restored my faith in men... Come here.' She held her arms open, beckoning him in. They embraced in hug that felt so warm and contented. 'She's a real lucky lady. I hope it all works out for you,' she whispered before lifting his head and planting a kiss on his lips that started off soft and gentle and finished firm and passionate. As they finally separated, Richard stood with eyes still closed in a state of sheer delight. His mind emptied of everything bar that delicious kiss.

'Awww you two,' Roxy gushed, breaking Richard out his dreamlike state. For a moment he contemplated just staying where he was. *What am I doing? Going back to a domestic situation that might not be a situation at all?* For all he knew everything could be sorted out between Frances and Mike and he would be kicked into touch again - and if Mike had anything to do with it that could be quite literally. His mind, that a second ago, had been blissfully empty of any meaningful thought, was now doing cartwheels with all the possibilities which suddenly presented themselves.

Cassandra, sensing Richard's inner turmoil decided to help him out. 'Go and get your lady… I'm not the one for you, Hun… But she is,' she said in a voice as tender as the kiss she left on his forehead.

Richard nodded his reluctant agreement. He knew Cassandra was right. Frances was two years in the making; Cassandra had been some sort of bizarre dream that he was now starting to wake from. The day itself had been one he'd never forget. The multitude of new sensations his body and mind had experienced had profoundly affected him in a very positive way. He now wanted to experience even more. There was a whole world of new and wonderful things to encounter and he was adamant he would make up for lost time. He was also adamant that he didn't want to experience all of it on his own. He wanted someone he loved to share them with; and that someone was Frances.

Richard and Matt said their final goodbyes to Roxy and Sandy who both seemed like they wanted to party some more and who both offered exuberant farewells. They saved their final goodbye for their extremely generous host, Greg, who throughout the day had made them feel so special, welcomed and looked after. Not once had Greg made them seem like they were freeloaders. He just seemed to enjoy life as much as he possibly could and he wanted to share it with other people. Richard admired his carefree manner. No doubt he was a shrewd businessman; how could he not be when he owned a yacht like his? And he hadn't been shy in telling them of his past failings. He'd been very philosophical when, at lunch, he mentioned his previous companies that had gone bust, but as he said, it had brought him to where he was right now. In a week of discovery, Richard had to acknowledge that Greg had made a huge impact on him. 'Thank you so much for having us onboard today,' Matt said. 'It's been unbelievable, truly it has. Give me a shout when you're back in London and we'll meet up.'

'Think nothing of it. It's been a pleasure,' Greg said with a tired but happy smile creased across his face. 'You boys take care and Matt, remember what we talked about.'

Richard wondered for a second what Greg meant but thought he'd ask at a later juncture. As they trudged wearily down the gangplank, Richard allowed himself one last glance at Cassandra, who in her own way had made a lasting impression on him. She lived her life by her rules and didn't give a damn what other people thought. She waved fondly at him and he responded with a subtle wave of his own. There was definitely a mutual affection there and perhaps he had just left his mark on her too. All in all, Ibiza had been a real eye-opener; like a dream within a dream. Their whistle-stop trip had more than provided him with the desire to come back and see what else this beautiful island had to offer.

They didn't talk much on the walk back to the hotel. Both were wrapped up in their own thoughts; reflecting on the day just had, and for Richard, what awaited him when he returned back home. His mind was fading from what had been, to what was about to happen. A kaleidoscope of thoughts now bounced around in his head; not one of them could he focus on for more than a second before another one came charging in. Visions of the weekend he'd had with Frances; the attraction, the laughing, the dancing, the lovemaking, her face, her body, her tears, her fragileness, Mike, Mike's grasp around his testicles – he winced again – her voice on the phone, the fear in her voice; all these thoughts were on a constant spin-cycle and without even realising it he found himself back in the hotel suite with Matt helping to pack his bag. 'Come on mate. I've got us on the late flight but we need to be at the airport like now.'

Richard was baffled. Matt must've sorted out the flights on his phone whilst they were strolling back to the hotel. It woke him out of his Frances-induced-trance though and he sprung into life. 'Are you sure you don't want to stay on? We've still got this place for another couple of nights.'

'Don't worry mate. I can come back another time. The only reason we're here now is because of you. It's been an amazing couple of days but I don't want you having to confront that ogre on your own. Speaking of which, we need to formulate a plan because we can't just turn up on their doorstep at 4am.'

All packed, they checked out of the hotel and jumped into a waiting taxi. 'Buenas noches cabelleros, a donde?' the female taxi driver said in a gravelly, sultry voice.

'El aeropurto por favor,' Matt replied. 'y rapido por favor.'

It still made Richard marvel how easily Matt spoke in Spanish. He felt pig-ignorant for not knowing more Spanish himself. Not that it seemed to matter at that moment as the driver said, 'English?'

'Si – er yes,' Matt answered.

'Why the rush to get to the airport?'

'My friend here is going to rescue his woman from the clutches of an evil man,' Matt said theatrically.

'Que'?' the lady said confused, looking into the rear-view mirror. Richard could see she was a strikingly beautiful woman: dark hair, dark skin and an intimidating look.

'My friend is in love,' Matt said trying to simplify things.

'Aaaah,' she said almost wistfully. 'I was in love once…'

Both Matt and Richard leaned in to see where this conversation was going but after a lengthy pause they realised that she didn't intend on expanding on her comment. Looking at one another first Matt finally asked, 'So what happened?'

'He was a bastardo,' she said bluntly. Again, Matt and Richard exchanged a subtle look at one another. Without any prompting this time she continued, 'I loved him so much but he was nasty to me. He cheat on me and used to hit me. Once he even put me in hospital… And you know the stupid thing? I still went back to him! Can you believe? How loco was I?'

Matt was just about to speak again but Richard responded first. 'Sorry to hear that. There are a lot of horrible people out there…'

'No, no, not lots of horrible people. Lots of good people… A few horrible people. I just fell in love with a horrible person,' the lady said as she weaved her way speedily through traffic.

It was a good way of looking at it, Richard thought. There were indeed many more good people than horrible people. He'd just been unfortunate enough to spend a lot of time with people that could only be described as horrible; his parents, Martin Bradshaw - they had done their best to chip away at his self-esteem, and it was a minor miracle that he'd turned out without any deep-rooted issues. For sure he'd retreated into himself and the man he could have been had been stifled by the over-bearing and bullying nature of these people, but he could hold his head up high that he hadn't let it suppress the kind-hearted and caring person he was. Again, his mind wandered back to his dear Gran who, more than anyone, had made sure he *did* grow up with some love and affection and values of right and wrong.

'What is your name?' Matt asked.

'Eva.'

'Pleased to meet you Eva. This is Richard and I'm Matt... Can I ask, where is this man now? – your husband I mean?'

'He was not my husband. He was my boyfriend for many years. It took a long time to get over him; you know, he messed up my head. It took me a long time to even look at another man… Because I was scared the same thing would happen again.'

Matt nodded. 'That's understandable. Are you happy now?'

'Always happy now. I love my man Raul,' Eva pointed to a faded, curled-up photo that was wedged in the car sun-visor. They both had to squint but could make out a bespectacled, geeky chap holding a timid-looking Chihuahua. If ever a man didn't really fit a macho name it was Raul, but Eva was still beaming with pride and this was proof enough that it's not always about looks and what's on the outside; there's a lot to be said for the person inside.

Eva dropped them at the departures section of the airport. 'Good luck with your woman,' she said to Richard before slamming her foot down hard on the accelerator and speeding off. They could still smell her pungent perfume long after she'd gone. Wearily they picked up their bags and walked towards check-in.

From the doorway there looked to be no queue and the staff looked like they were about to close the desk. They ran to the desk and planted their passports in front of the charmless Spanish man who viewed them with a heavy dose of disapproval. 'You just about made it,' he said in an equally disapproving tone.

'Just is good enough,' Matt said with a cheeky smile.

This comment did nothing to change the man's dour demeanour. 'We prefer that you check in with plenty of time to spare.'

'So would we but…' Matt started and then saw the disapproving man look up and give him an even more disapproving look. He thought better of finishing his sentence. 'Sorry,' he said sheepishly instead. On receiving their passports, the man cheerfully announced, 'I'm sorry too… Your flight is delayed by four hours. Have a good flight.'

As they sat upstairs in the bar, having walked defeatedly through security, the looming prospect of trying to occupy themselves for the four-hour delay slowly chipped away at the euphoria of the day they'd just experienced. It sent Richard into an emotional meltdown, worrying about Frances. Every second feeling like it was another second that Frances was in danger.

'Nothing we can do mate,' Matt said matter-of-factly. But he knew how uneasy Richard was so he tried to calm him down. He'd watched him trying to call Frances so many times that his phone was nearly out of battery. 'Let's play cards,' he suggested.

'I'm not sure I want to. Besides, we don't have any,' Richard replied.

'Mmmm if only there was a large over-sized shop in here…' Matt mused sarcastically as his attention turned to the duty-free shop which sold all manner of souvenir tat.

Matt returned five minutes later with a set of playing cards with scenic shots of Ibiza on them. Richard spent a while scanning through the cards and observed what a beautiful island it was. He definitely wanted to return - hopefully with Frances. *Ahh Frances,* his thoughts nosedived towards images of her again. Her fragile, defeated figure; her tear-soaked face; her pitiful look. Why couldn't he envisage her sexy figure; her smooth, beautiful face; her kind, confident look? This, after all, was the mental picture that'd been etched in his mind for the past couple of years, but, try as he might, the beaten-down image of Frances was the one that wouldn't leave his mind.

'Hey, loverboy,' Matt said awakening Richard from his doldrums, 'are we playing cards or getting all maudlin?'

Reluctantly, Richard handed Matt the cards to shuffle. This he did with all the nimble dexterity of a street magician. Richard wasn't surprised though; it seemed there wasn't anything that Matt wasn't good at. Despite most card games being largely based on luck he fully expected to get a good hiding playing whatever game they were about to play.

'So, what are we playing?' Matt asked as he thumped the cards on the table with purpose. When he was greeted by silence he cheerfully said, 'Let's play Shithead.'

A puzzled look spread over Richard's face. 'That's not even a card game,' he said.

'It is.'

'No it isn't.'

'Oh yes it is,' Matt said and he turned to the man seated directly behind him. 'Excuse me, sorry to bother you, but do you know of a card game called Shithead?' The man nodded and the man's girlfriend seated across from him concurred too. 'Everyone knows Shithead. You've lived a very sheltered life my friend. It's high time you were introduced to the wonders of Shithead.' Matt explained the rules and invited the man and his girlfriend to join them, and within a couple of hands Richard was up to speed. The aim of the game was to get rid of your cards and not be the last one – a.k.a. the Shithead. But the real aim of the game for Matt was to take Richard's mind off the impending showdown with Frances and, more worryingly, Mike. And, for the next four hours they played hand after hand and the time passed by quicker than they could've thought possible. Before they knew it they were sat on the flight and about to take off. By now, both Richard and Matt were exhausted and were asleep before the plane started to taxi its way onto the runway. Richard's head rested on Matt's broad shoulder and they looked quite the contented couple as the plane took flight; taking them back home; taking Richard closer to Frances.

CHAPTER 16

Richard and Matt woke groggily as the plane touched down. For Richard, the flight was in complete contrast to journey out there. He'd been far too tired to even begin to worry about the flight this time round. They simultaneously rubbed their aching necks and stretched out their legs - not that there was much legroom to do so - and as the plane pulled slowly up to the jetty he could see everyone's hands hovering over their seatbelts like cowboys about to draw revolvers in a gunfight. Some literally could not wait the last few seconds and the clicking of a hundred seatbelts unleashed all manner of weird and wonderful people from their seats. All looked haggard and grouchy; some sported uneven, painful-looking suntans that even Richard grimaced at.

Once off the plane and into the airport, there appeared to be an unofficial race to see who could get to passport control the quickest. A highly athletic power-walker would've struggled to keep up, but both Richard and Matt felt compelled to keep pace or be overtaken by the fast-strutting cavalcade of people. This quickly awoke Richard from his drowsiness as he remembered why they came back from Ibiza two days early. Frances. The name was emblazoned on his mind and this only hastened his pace. With Matt struggling to keep up, they soon found themselves out in front and the first to reach the passport desk. Arriving there slightly breathless and with a trickle of sweat running down his back, a look of mild smugness swept over Richard. He'd never won a race before and although this was hardly the Olympic 100 metres final, he felt triumphant as he looked at those filling in behind him. Matt allowed himself a wry grin knowing full well what was going through Richard's head. But it was good to see him without the pained look of someone on a lovelorn mission.

From passport control they went to collect their luggage and despite being first at the conveyor belt waiting for their bags to arrive, another subliminal contest had materialised; that of, who could stand closest to the conveyor belt without actually falling onto it and block anyone else's view of their bag. Irritable people hell-bent on making it abundantly clear to one another that they were indeed irritable and in the mood to be helpful or courteous. This was a contest that Richard's timid but respectful demeanour wasn't suited to and he waited patiently in the background. But Matt seemed to have seen his bag and with a couple of "excuse me's" he piled through a group of people that weren't going to move without the unsubtle use of brute force.

'Oi, watch it mate,' said the large, disgruntled, lobster-red, shaven-headed man.

Matt placed the case down that turned out wasn't his, turned to the man and calmly said, 'I'm sorry, but I did say excuse me a couple of times, and perhaps, if you hadn't been standing so close to the belt I wouldn't need to barge through you.' This amazingly seemed enough to placate the man and moments later Matt returned with both their cases.

'You really aren't scared of anyone are you?' Richard asked.

'There's a time for manners and there's a time to be a bit forceful… that was a time for the latter,' Matt replied confidently. 'Speaking of being forceful, have you mapped out in your head how you think things are going to go when you arrive on Frances' doorstep?'

'I've thought of little else.'

'It *is* Thursday; won't he be at work?'

'Yes, I know, but I remember he said he had the week off work. I remember that as he'd just released his grip from my balls. Funny how certain things remind you of certain things.' Richard was trying to deflect the seriousness of the looming confrontation.

'Have you tried calling again?' Matt asked.

'Only a few hundred times. It just keeps going to voicemail. I'm really worried.'

'I know you are but try not to worry. We'll sort it… What about phoning the police?'

'It's a possibility I suppose, but Mike will easily charm his way out of it. Anyway, I need to see Frances for myself; to make sure she's ok.'

They walked in comparative silence to the rendezvous point with their taxi driver. He held a sign with poorly scrawled writing saying "Mr Rickard Chalmers" on it. *It's close enough,* thought Richard, who had never had a driver waiting for him before. It was yet another reason he felt such fondness towards Matt. He hadn't even mentioned that he'd booked a taxi, let alone one which would have the driver waiting for them. The short, pot-bellied driver offered to take their cases, but the boys were happy just to keep walking towards the car park where the taxi was parked. They both felt if they stopped now they wouldn't get going again. The thought of the car's comfortable back seat was a very enticing prospect. When they arrived at the car, a sleek, white Mercedes C Class, they fell into the plump leather seats. The driver, seeing their overwhelming tiredness, didn't utter a word on the journey back to Matt's house, allowing them to succumb to more much needed sleep.

Matt felt the car reach its destination and awoke with the bland, metallic taste in his mouth that seems to accompany broken sleep. He tried his best to rouse himself in an enthusiastic manner but he couldn't help feeling like an extra from a zombie movie. 'Thank you,' he said groggily to the taxi driver as he rubbed his face with both hands in a vain attempt to wake himself up. He was just walking towards his front door when he realised that Richard was still fast asleep in the back of the cab. Matt observed the comatose form of Richard, head pressed on the passenger window and his mouth slightly agape. 'Wakey wakey, rise and shine,' Matt said in a voice that contradicted its intention.

Richard squinted, rubbed his eyes and yawned ferociously. It was as much as he could do to raise his weary frame from the comfort and warmth of the car. He mumbled an inaudible word of thanks to the driver before he drove away leaving them stood outside Matt's front door. As Matt searched for his door keys, Richard scanned the skies. Gone were the clear blue sky of Ibiza; they'd been replaced by a deep, grey blanket of dankness. It didn't seem to be raining, but Richard felt like he was getting decidedly damp. A chill made its presence felt and he was glad to get through the front door. They shuffled inside with all the vigour of asthmatic tortoises. It was only then that Richard queried, 'Weren't we meant to go to Frances'?'

'It's 6am. Unless you want to massively piss *her* off as well as that bulky, knob-end husband of hers, I'd suggest we wait a few hours. With any luck Mike will be at the shops or on the toilet or something,' Matt reasoned.

Richard liked the sound of that. The thought of confronting Mike right now was really starting to lose its appeal. The bravery he'd felt a few hours ago had diminished leaving him shrinking back into himself. In truth he felt too exhausted to do much at all. His eyes were struggling to stay open and he was on the verge of falling back to sleep standing up when Matt suggested he have a lay down in the spare room. As much as he wanted to be heroic and go rescue his damsel in distress he couldn't think of anything right now other than laying down in a darkened room. Seconds after his head hit the pillow he settled into another deep sleep.

Waking a couple of hours later, although not feeling particularly spritely, he felt infinitely better and less spaced-out than he had when he'd laid down. Matt was already up and making coffee. 'I was just going to wake you,' he said in a voice much more his own. It seemed the sleep had done Matt a world of good too. He looked preened and ready for anything. 'Are you up for this?' he said, handing Richard his cup.

Richard struggled to hold the cup which was so hot it felt like he was holding a rock of magma. He set the cup on the kitchen island just before the heat became unbearable and paused before saying, 'No... but then again, I don't think I ever will be.' He was right of course. This wasn't a moment he could prepare for. It was one that he knew he just had to deal with as events unfolded. The only thing he knew he had to do was turn up on Frances' doorstep. After that, who knew what would happen.

They both sat a little subdued whilst they sipped and slurped their scolding cups of coffee. Richard knew why he was brooding but he couldn't quite work out why Matt was so quiet and thoughtful. 'What are you thinking about?' he asked.

Almost like being snapped out of a trance Matt broke from his thousand-yard stare and pondered for a moment. 'I was thinking about the offer Greg made to me when we were on his boat yesterday.'

'Oh yes, what was the offer?'

'Well, he offered me the contract on his mansion rebuild. He's got a huge pad in Virginia Water that he wants completely redeveloped. He said at the moment it's some tired Mock Tudor carbuncle. He wants it torn down and rebuilt from the ground on up. It's a massive project. I'll need to speak to Jamie about it as it'll take us away from a few other jobs we're working on.'

'That's amazing. So, he just trusted the fact that you were a competent enough builder?'

'I showed him some photos of other projects we've done and he loved them. He also said he needed someone he liked and trusted to oversee the rebuild. He's had his fingers burnt by some rogue builders in the past, so for him it's more about the people than the size of the company.'

'And that includes Jamie?' Richard asked knowing exactly what he was asking.

'Look, I know you don't like him, but…'

'I don't like him because he's not a very nice person,' Richard cut in.

'He's not that bad. He's just a bit basic in his opinions.'

This made Richard snort. 'I've only just met him, but there's not one thing that man has said or done that redeems his character. He's repugnant and if he found out about you – your sexuality – he wouldn't like it one bit.'

'You might be right there.'

'I know I'm right,' Richard replied confidently.

'Ok clever-clogs, what would you have me do?'

'Be brave; tell him. Tell him you're gay. Tell him you like men. Tell him you like to sleep with men.' Richard's nonchalant answer was received with stoney silence. Matt was growing increasingly uncomfortable with the conversation. Agitated, he rose from his stool and began pacing around the kitchen. And to drive the point home further Richard said, 'In the past week you've taught me to face up to my fears and to confront the people I was scared to stand up to, and I thank you for that, I really do... But perhaps you should practice what you preach.'

Matt flinched a little when the last sentence was delivered. He stopped pacing and took a deep breath to calm himself down. 'You're right. You said to me earlier that I'm not scared of anyone, and in most cases you'd be right, but with Jamie I probably am. Not just because he's my business partner and I'm worried that if he is *that* disgusted he'll ostracise me from all the people we know in the trade…' There was a lengthy pause as Matt pondered whether to divulge the next piece of information. He breathed in another large gulp of air and continued. 'Around five years ago I was out with Jamie in town and he got into an argument at a taxi rank with a gay couple who were stood in front of us. I say an argument, but it wasn't really. The couple had obviously had a good night and were kissing and cuddling; pretty harmless stuff, but Jamie couldn't hide his distain. He started saying things under his breath, but loud enough that the couple would hear him. Stuff like, "It's enough to make you sick" and "fucking queers," that sort of thing. I was trying to get him to be quiet and when the couple turned around and reacted, I recognised one of them as I'd… y'know… been with him a few months previous. His name was Andre. He recognised me too and his angry face softened, but just as he was about to say something, Jamie just laid into him. It was horrible. There was only us at the taxi rank and no taxi had shown up, so it was up to me and this chap's boyfriend/partner, whatever he was to him, to try and drag Jamie off Andre who lying spark-out on the floor. Jamie was still raining punches down on the poor lad and his face was a bloody mess. The boyfriend was just screaming hysterically, begging me to get Jamie to stop. When I finally managed to prize Jamie away, he was wild-eyed and almost frothing. I told him to get going before the police turned up and we both ran off… I could hear Jamie laughing as he ran ahead... I could also hear the boyfriend sobbing as he cradled Andre in his arms… I felt so ashamed of what I'd witnessed, but I felt even more ashamed that I never said anything to the police. I spent the next couple of weeks waiting for the police to turn up asking questions but they never did. The attack – described as "a sickening homophobic attack" - made the local TV news, but the CCTV footage was grainy and unclear. And still I didn't come forward. After a month or so it just got forgotten about. Jamie was completely remorseless and even seemed proud of what he'd done and that it'd made the news. The guy's a total psycho, but I've known him a long time and he's been a good friend to me. But after that, thoughts of telling him about me went right out the window.'

Richard didn't know what to say after that confession. It saddened him to hear what he'd just heard. There was a little bit of Matt that had gone down in his heady estimation. He knew that Matt must've been completely torn up by what had happened, and he could understand the emotional turmoil surrounding his "friendship" with Jamie. What it had done though, was make him dislike Jamie even more. He felt that this story more than justified his feelings towards Jamie. 'I'm sorry... But surely this is even more reason to tell him or just distance yourself from him altogether. Why don't you take up Greg's offer and use it as a fresh start?'

Matt seemed not to have heard Richard's comment. He was looking forlornly at the floor. 'You know what the worst thing about it was?... I saw Andre a year or so later - Brighton's gay scene is very incestuous and you tend to bump into ex's all the time – and when he saw me he had a look of... I don't know...something somewhere between fear and hatred. I couldn't look him in the eye. I just left in case he started talking to me. And all the time, I had this sense of relief that I hadn't given him my number and he didn't know where I lived. Perhaps nothing would've happened with the police but I was so scared that, if they caught up with Jamie and it went to court, the subject of my sexuality would've come up… I know, totally selfish, and whatever you thought of me as some sort of brave, compassionate guy, I'm not. I'm a coward.'

'You're not a coward,' Richard said gently. 'You're a lovely bloke. You've shown me that enough times in the past week. I can see now how difficult it must be to confront Jamie on this… Look, I won't mention it anymore. It's your business and…'

'No…' Matt cut in. His voice wavered ever so slightly and his poise was now most certainly compromised. 'You're absolutely right to challenge me on this. I feel ashamed that I've never "come out" to my friends and colleagues and…' he paused, again thinking of whether to go on, before deciding it was too late to stop now. The pregnant pause hung in the air, but Richard knew what he was about to say.

'Parents?'

Matt nodded sullenly. 'I told my Mum years ago and she took the news in her stride. She said she loved me if I was straight, gay, green, purple or blue. I was her son and as long as I was happy, that was the most important thing.'

This brought a sympathetic smile to Richard's face. He remembered Matt's Mother, Joyce. She was a lovely lady who seemed to live in the shadow of Matt's father, Barry, a great hulking man with tattooed forearms and hands like catcher's mitts. He was a devout West Ham United supporter and builder in his own right. It had been many years since Richard had last seen them and he was curious as to what they were like now. 'I liked your Mum.' he said in an effort to lighten the mood. 'Your Dad... well, he scared living daylights out of me.'

'Yeah, a lot of people were scared of my Dad. "Big Bad Barry" he was known as by his mates. He's a good bloke but he's old skool. I made Mum promise she wouldn't tell him... And I would tell him in my own time... That was fifteen years ago. I guess I have the same problem with my Dad as I have with Jamie. I don't want to upset the applecart.'

'Does your Dad still work in the building trade?' Richard asked.

'No, he had to give it all up some time ago. His back gave up on him and he got very depressed. He couldn't deal with the fact he wasn't fit and strong enough to work. He took to drinking a lot and upsetting my Mum. They spilt up a few years later and it was not long after that that I came out to my Mum.'

'Do you still see your Dad?'

'Yeah, not that often, but every other month or so, we'll meet up in his local pub and have a few pints, talk about football and he'll ask me about my Mum; whether she's ok, whether she misses him; the same questions he's asked me since they separated. It's sad really. He never moved on after their split. He lives in a council flat and claims disability allowance - y'know, for his back which is totally buggered now. He can't walk too far these days and when he does he's hunched over with a stick propping him up. He's not the big scary bear of a man you remember… But he's my Dad and I love him. I just want him to be proud of me which I think he is.'

Richard didn't want to say anything. He didn't want to tell Matt that he thought he should come out to his Dad too. He was conscious that he might start to sound like a broken record; telling Matt, who was self-assured and had gone this far in life doing things his way, that he should be confronting the subject of his sexuality head-on. What did he know about being gay in the 21st century? He felt a great deal of compassion for Matt now though, as he must feel incomplete. And Matt must have a perpetual nagging worry that his illicit secret would somehow spill out to those he thought might shun him. But, rather than pursue the conversation any longer, they finished their coffees in silence, both absorbed in their own thoughts.

After the cups were collected and placed in the sink, Richard was shaken out of those thoughts by Matt announcing, 'Right, let's do this.'

Ready or not, Richard took a deep breath and followed Matt up the stairs, his heart beating that bit faster now.

CHAPTER 17

8:33am the digital clock in Matt's van read. They'd sat there in his van, parked at the end of the road, for exactly four minutes without saying a word; with Richard inwardly trying to pluck up the courage to step foot out into the dank and dismal morning. The walk to Frances' front door was only twenty metres or so, but he might as well have been at the foot of Mount Everest, looking up at its distant peaks. He was racking his overflowing mind to think of excuses not to go. *Maybe Matt was right. Maybe she and Mike are fine. Maybe I'm worrying unduly and maybe Mike will beat the living shit out of me when he answers the door.* He was fidgeting and starting to annoy Matt.

'Just get out there!.. Please,' Matt blurted. The tension had become unbearable. 'Sorry, but the longer you leave it the worse it's going to be.' He instantly felt bad for Richard who wasn't suited to confrontation. 'Look, I've got a good view of you and I'll be out this door as soon as I see any problems. But this is something you've got to do… So, do it.'

Those stern words were still ringing in his head as he opened the van door and shakily stepped out into the persistent drizzle. With all the enthusiasm of a man walking to the gallows he strode slowly to the front door of Frances' home. His recently styled hair hadn't been touched that morning and was now weighed down by the damp drizzle. He was still in last night's clothes and he had a fetid, rank taste in his mouth, having not brushed his teeth since the previous morning. He admitted he probably should've done more to appeal to Frances, but he hoped she'd just be relieved to see him. And there he stood, on the doorstep, not quite knowing what to do next. He pressed his ear up against the door to hear if there was anything audible he could pick out; to give him a clue as to where both Frances and Mike were. He was just about to move his ear away when he heard Mike's distant voice sounding like it was coming from upstairs. He couldn't make out quite what he was saying but he heard Frances' tired voice answer in reply. She sounded like she was close by the front door. This prompted him into action. He knocked the subtlest of knocks on the large, wooden door. So subtle was the knock, that after waiting for thirty seconds and not hearing Frances' footsteps coming to the door, he decided to knock a little louder. Unfortunately, his adrenalin had got the better of him and the knock was much louder than he meant it to be. He could hear Mike's voice bark, 'Get that, and if it's one of those begging charity bastards tell them to fuck off and get a real job.' He then heard Frances coming to the door, and with no time to compose himself, she opened it. It was hard to tell who was the more surprised. Given that Richard had planned to be there, you'd have thought he wouldn't have nearly screamed at the sight of Frances. Frances, although in a state of shock at the unexpected visit of Richard on her doorstep, quickly hushed him by putting her soft hand against his mouth. 'What are you doing here?' she whispered frantically.

Richard tried to reply but Frances' hand was still covering his mouth. The best he could manage was a muffled mumble which was sufficient to make Frances slowly remove her hand which she moved towards her own mouth in "shush" signal. She was obviously petrified. She looked tired, scared and dishevelled, and it melted his heart. 'I'm here to take you back with me,' he whispered so quietly that he had to repeat what he'd said. On second hearing she stood there for a moment as Richard's words registered.

All of a sudden, Mike's booming voice bellowed from up the stairs, 'If you can't get rid of them. Just give them a couple of quid. Hopefully, that'll get the scrounging bastards off our doorstep.'

Frances knew she'd have to say or do something. 'Ok,' she called up the stairs in an unsteady voice. 'I'll just see if I can find my purse.' She then turned her attention back to Richard. She looked completely torn but knew she had to act swiftly. 'Wait here,' she told him and quickly turned to go about whatever business she was about to go on.

Richard reached out and grabbed her arm. 'Where's Mike?' he asked in a hushed tone.

'Don't worry, he's in the bath. He's only just got in there and he likes a good soak. Now wait here. I'm just going to grab a few things.' She then turned and bounded up the stairs. *Who has a bath first thing in the morning?* Richard thought to himself. But before he could allow himself to marvel over Mike's bathing habits any further, Frances came flying back down the stairs with a bag stuffed with clothes fighting to get out. 'Right, let's go,' she said as she flew past him and up the garden path. 'Come on!'

'What about the door?' Richard said gesturing towards the open front door that she'd neglected to close in her hasty getaway. She ran back and closed it with enough force for Mike to hear, then turned and ran with Richard to the van. As they both fell into the passenger seat she began to cry. Whilst Matt sped his van into life, passing the house they just liberated Frances from, Richard sat stunned, not knowing what to do. Frances was shaking and Matt looked down at her and then looked at Richard. 'Well, comfort her for Christ's sake!'

Richard tentatively wrapped his arm around Frances shoulder and he could feel her momentarily flinch from his touch before giving way to his embrace. 'Thank you… Thank you,' she sobbed.

Arriving back at Matt's house, they congregated downstairs in the kitchen. Matt sprang into life and had the kettle boiling; three teas set up and had wrapped a big, fluffy blanket around Frances as she made her way shakily to one of the stools that encircled the kitchen island.

Richard felt close to tears himself but knew he needed to appear strong for her sake. Inside he was bristling with rage that Mike could've driven her into this state. He couldn't think of anything to say and when he did speak he really wished he hadn't said anything at all. 'Are you ok?' he said and instantly winced.

It did raise a slight smile from Frances though. 'Never better,' she said, seeing that he was only trying to comfort her. 'Thank you.'

Matt was still faffing. 'I'll run you a nice, hot bath,' he said and disappeared upstairs leaving Richard and Frances alone. There was a long, stony silence made all the more uncomfortable by Richard not quite knowing how to act. Now that Frances was sat on the stool wrapped in the large blanket he felt somewhat superfluous. He could hear the thumping footsteps of Matt upstairs as he prepared Frances' bath. It seemed that having a bath in the morning was all the rage. *Who'd have thought?* Richard mused.

All of a sudden Frances' timid voice broke him out of his ruminations. 'I'm sorry.'

'What are you sorry for? Don't worry. I'll make sure you're safe and happy and…'

'Oh, bless you. You've no idea how lovely you are…' She broke off and cried for a moment. 'He won't be happy when he discovers that I've gone. He's lost the plot and he's dangerous; far more dangerous than I ever thought he could ever be. He won't stop until he finds me. And when he does…'

'What did he do to you?' Richard asked, a tinge of anger in his voice.

Frances just shook her head. Tears trickled down her cheeks.

'I'm sorry; you don't have to talk about it.'

Again, Frances shook her head and Richard heard an audible gulp as she prepared to speak. But before she could utter anything, Matt thundered down the stairs. He was in overdrive. He rapidly finished making the cups of tea and delivered them to the others, before flopping into one of the stools opposite Frances. 'Your bath is running,' he said panting. 'I'm sorry, the water pressure here is pitiful. It takes a month of Sundays to fill the bath!'

'Thank you,' Frances said as she wrapped her hands around the warm mug of steaming tea. 'Thank you both.'

Richard was still waiting to see if Frances was going to divulge any more information of what had happened. She'd just been about to speak when Matt had charged in, but now she seemed content to keep her council. It nagged at him. He wanted to know. But then again, he didn't want to know. Hearing the truth of what Frances had endured in the time since he'd last seen her would make him angry and upset; upset that, whilst he was having fun in the sun in Ibiza and frolicking with another lady, she was being belittled, beaten down and emotionally abused. That was bad enough, but what if she'd been physically abused too. Just thinking about it made his blood boil. *She will tell me about it when she's ready,* he reasoned.

They sat in silence as they sipped their tea; contemplating, lost in their own thoughts. Almost apologetically, Frances rose from her stool and motioned upstairs, presuming the bath must've now run. Matt nodded his agreement it should be ready now, and then, unlike Matt, she slunk noiselessly up the stairs. Once he was sure she was out of earshot he whispered, 'Did she say anything about... y'know Mike – what he'd done?'

Richard shook his head in reply. He felt useless just sat there. A sudden compulsion made him get up and start to follow Frances upstairs.

'Just leave her for a moment,' Matt said gently.

'I can't. You've seen her. She's so fragile she might dissolve in the water. I've got to... I don't know. I've got to speak to her. I need to know what's gone on.'

Outside the bathroom door, he stood for a moment, listening to the subtle splashes as Frances soaked her body. Gently, he knocked on the door. 'Can I come in?'

'I'd rather you didn't,' Frances replied.

The reply surprised Richard. 'Why... Why not?... I just want to see you.'

'You can see me in a moment. I shan't be long.' Her stuffy nose gave her a voice that barely sounded like the Frances he knew. He was just about to turn dejectedly away when she asked, 'Can you do me a favour? Could you bring my bag up from the kitchen please? Just leave it outside the door... Thank you so much.'

He bounded down the stairs, got the bag and swiftly returned. 'Here you go. I've left your bag just outside the door. Can I get you anything else?' For a moment there was no word from Frances and Richard's heart jumped. *What if she's done something awful? What if she's tried to top herself again?* His mind raced and impulsively he banged on the door. 'Frances!... Frances! Open up! Open Up!'

To his relief he heard a sudden lurch of water as Frances emerged from the bath and opened the door. 'What's up?!' she said panic-stricken. A plump, white towel was loosely wrapped around her body. Richard's eyes inadvertently looked down on her glistening, shapely legs. Water trickled down her smooth skin and he cursed himself for getting aroused at a time when she was so fragile and vulnerable. Taking his mind from such thoughts, he forced his eyes to gaze upon her scared and troubled face. He noticed she'd obviously been submerged in the water as her hair was wet and slicked back which he also deduced was the reason why she couldn't hear him knocking. He now felt foolish and was in the process of trying to formulate an apology for startling her, but she'd read his mind.

'You thought I was doing myself harm?' There was a heavy pause. 'I've been there before and it's not a good place to be in, but I'm damned if I'm going to let Mike drag me to those depths again… Please don't worry. I'll be alright.' Her voice was now a lot more her own. Less scared and more determined.

Embarrassed, Richard's gaze dropped again, this time towards the floor, but it was Frances' soft hand that stopped it falling that low. Her gentle touch on his chin brought his face upwards to where their eyes met… as did their lips. Her kiss was soft and wet and his tongue soon found its way subtly into her mouth. The kiss lingered longer than it should have given the seriousness of recent moments. When they detached they both shared a coy look at one another. During their kiss, the towel had slipped ever so slightly and it was then that he noticed a purple mark on the side of her body. He looked at Frances and a sudden look of terror fell upon her face, as if she had been caught in the act of doing something she shouldn't. He looked again at the mark, but Frances pulled the towel up around her to hide it. He looked into her eyes and saw fresh tears begin to fill them. She faintly shook her head as if to warn him not to pursue things any further. He couldn't stop looking into her eyes; eyes which now carried so much sorrow. He felt a mixture of anger and pity. 'Show me,' he said in a quiet, cracked voice.

Frances shook her head again.

'Please.'

Frances thought for a moment, then acquiesced. She slowly lowered the towel, revealing her body; a body which was peppered with bruises of various colours and sizes. Richard stared at them; he studied each and every bruise. He gently turned her around where more bruises greeted his eyes. His eyes fixed on one injury worse than the others; a cut – not deep, but long, that was at the top of her buttocks. Tears were now filling his eyes and he drew the towel back to cover the marks and conceal Frances' shame. She was now quietly weeping. 'I told you; he's dangerous.'

All Richard could do was pull her towards him and hold her tight. With her face pressed firmly into his chest he could feel her crying but there was no sound, just the convulsive movements of her sobbing.

CHAPTER 18

Richard sat on the kitchen stool, stewing - just like the cup of tea he'd neglected to drink. He was brimming with an anger he never knew he possessed. Matt sat opposite, almost frightened to say anything. He'd never seen Richard like this before. Back in their school days he'd never been one to show emotion. Even when he knew people had gotten to him he never displayed the slightest hint of anger. He just seemed to absorb it – take it all in and hide it away. He'd always marvelled at his capacity to do that – to endure. Matt was different in that way. He'd always stood up for himself, even when it meant receiving an inevitable kick-in. But this was a Richard he barely recognised. This was a seething Richard. He hadn't the courage to ask him what had happened upstairs. He deduced from Richard's demeanour that she'd explained what had gone on in their time apart. Of all the new feelings Richard was experiencing since their reunion, Matt assumed anger was the one he'd find hardest to channel. He decided to brave it and ask, 'Do you wanna talk about it?'

For a moment Richard couldn't bring himself to reply. He just bit his lip and simmered. When he did speak his voice almost broke with emotion. 'That...' he shook his head as he searched for the right word. But no word presented itself which would fully do justice to Mike and what he'd done to Frances. 'He beat her,' he continued.

'She's got bruises all over her body… And he's cut her with a knife... I'm so angry. I know I haven't got it in me to stand up to a man like him, but if I could, I would. I've never wanted to hurt anyone in my life before, but that bastard deserves nothing better than a taste of his own medicine… I… He…' Richard was too irate to finish a sentence. With his teeth and fists firmly clenched, he cut a very frustrated and aggravated figure.

Matt saw this and rose from his stool and went over to calm him down. 'What an arsehole,' was all he could muster as he put arm around him. He could feel Richard shaking with fury; adrenaline was coursing through his body. 'We need to go to the police and report him.'

'Yeah, without a doubt. Something needs to be done.'

'I don't want to go to the police.' Frances' voice arrived before she did.

Richard and Matt both looked up towards the stairs to see Frances delicately walking down them. They shared a puzzled look at one another before Richard said, 'You've got to go to the police. Look what he's done to you.'

'I'm not going to the police,' she reiterated.

Baffled, Richard was at a loss for words. 'Why wouldn't you report him? He can't get away with that.'

Matt placed a reassuring hand on Richard's arm. He could see now wasn't the right time to press the matter. 'Can I get you anything?' he asked Frances politely.

'No, thank you. The bath was just what I needed though,' she said equally politely as she drifted past them and sat on one of the stools.

Richard could see she'd applied some makeup. Her face looked less tired and puffy and her eyes, although still a little red, seemed less frightened and tearful. It was as if the makeup had provided her a mask to hide behind. She had a regained poise, an air of austerity. Richard offered her a sympathetic smile to which Frances replied with a nod. She was trying to hold herself together and he knew the slightest thing might unravel this hard work.

'You could sit in the lounge upstairs if you like,' Matt said cheerfully. There's probably bugger all on the TV, but…'

Frances took a deep breath. 'Good idea,' she said and walked back up the stairs. Matt and Richard followed.

The living room wasn't big but it was cosy. Matt had decorated and furnished the room in a minimalist but homely way. Artwork and photos adorned the walls and shelves. The photos were of Matt with his parents and out with friends. It was a minute snapshot, a window into his life. Matt switched on the large flatscreen TV and tried to find something that wasn't going to be too taxing to watch. He settled on an antiques programme and passed the controller to Richard. 'I'll leave you two to relax. Make yourselves at home.

There's stuff in the fridge so feel free to make yourselves some breakfast,' he said.

'Where are you going?' Richard said, slightly concerned.

'Just out… There's something I need to do.' With that he left the room.

Richard stood puzzled and looked at Frances who was making herself comfortable on the sofa. She looked agitated; more so than he did so he sat down next to her. They sat there for a moment, awkwardly, having seemingly forgotten how to be around each other. 'Look, I'm sorry about … the police thing. I'm not going to tell you to do anything you don't want to do.' He said all this without looking at her, instead his gaze was directed toward the grey, thick-pile carpet; a carpet which looked like it had never been set foot on before.

Frances sighed a heavy sigh. 'I can't go to the police… Mike's father is some big-wig in Sussex Police. I was never good enough for his beloved Michael and when he discovered we couldn't have kids; he pretty much washed his hands of me. I never liked him anyway so no loss there, but I can imagine if Mike were ever charged with any offense it would be swiftly brushed under the carpet.' She let out another prolonged sigh to accentuate her tiredness of the situation. 'He's also got photos and a video of me doing cocaine at a party many years ago. He's always threatened to share it with my University and even my parents if it came to it. I know it sounds trivial but I can't allow him to do that. I really love my job and I really love my parents, and they would disown me if they knew. They're very backward when it comes to that sort of thing. All things considered – and believe me, I've considered it - it really isn't worth the hassle and turmoil.'

Richard turned and lifted his head to find her just staring straight ahead whilst she spoke; almost as if she were in a trance. 'But that's bribery,' he said incredulously. 'You said he never hit you, but I've seen what that man is capable of now.'

'That was a new thing for him,' Frances replied calmly. 'We were in the kitchen and he was telling me how he'd changed; how happy we were going to be together and then the subject strayed on to you - you'd really got under his skin - and his mood suddenly darkened. He became enraged – more so than ever before - and the less bothered I was with what he was saying, the more volatile he became. I was completely shocked when he hit me first time. I think he was too, but once he'd hit me once I don't think it mattered to him anymore. He just kept pummelling by body like he was hitting a punch bag. I was struggling for breath but I just blocked out the pain and took it. *He* was the one crying once he'd finished. When I got up I could feel he'd done some damage but I didn't want to give him the satisfaction of seeing that he'd hurt me in any way. It was as I was making my way out of the kitchen that I felt a sting across the top of my bum. I turned around to see him holding this super-sharp kitchen knife. I turned around further to see that he'd slashed right through one of my favourite tops.' She laughed. 'Can you believe that? After all he'd just done, I was more upset about the top he'd just ruined... I just gave him a filthy look and went to the bathroom to inspect the damage. I was shocked and furious but couldn't help myself from crying. I could hear Mike crying outside too. He was sobbing, saying he was sorry; it wouldn't happen ever again, blah blah blah. The funny thing was – if there was a funny thing in this sorry state of affairs - I'd never seen or heard Mike cry before. He'd always maintained an air of coolness – or rather coldness about him, even when he was being spiteful or demeaning...' She paused for a moment and turned to face him. They were now looking intently into each other's eyes. Richard felt a compulsion to look away. Frances was now the epitome of composure. It was as if all that she'd just said was trivial but it had also had some therapeutic affect to be talking about it. Frances' stoic demeanour put Richard a little more at ease. He was still very angry with Mike but Frances now appeared to be on top of things. 'When I called you yesterday I knew you'd come for me,' she continued. 'You're like my knight in shining armour. I'm so sorry for all I've put you through. I don't know why I let Mike anywhere near me again…'

'Yeah, what happened there?' Richard said, a baffled expression on his face.

Frances puffed out her cheeks in exasperation. 'Honestly, I don't know. Mike has a way of manipulating my emotions. He worms his way back in and then sets about eating away at my self-esteem, making me think I need him. It's very contrived and he's an expert at it. He knows exactly which buttons to press, but after what's happened this time, that's it. I want nothing more to do with him. If he wants the house, he can have the bloody house. God only knows what I'm going to do now, but I can't tell you how relieved I am to be out of there and away from him.'

Richard was new to relationships but there was a voice inside of him crying, *surely not all relationships are this dramatic!* A week ago, he didn't even know what love would feel like. Now he'd had a crash-course in the ups and downs of modern relationships. He couldn't help but feel his life was that much less complicated without the turmoil that Frances' love had brought him. But he also knew he wouldn't change the fact that he'd met and fallen in love with her. As he looked into her big, blue - and slightly bloodshot – eyes, his heart ached with the feelings he felt for her. He reached out to pull her face closer to his and their lips touched ever so gently. It was barely a kiss but he could feel Frances tremble slightly. Richard persevered though and kissed her fuller and more passionately. Just as they were starting to get lost in the moment, Matt poked his head around the door. 'See you lovebirds later. Won't be too long,' he said before leaving the house.

Richard was about to ask Matt where he was off to when he heard the front door shut behind him. The mood broken, they adjusted themselves on the sofa and focussed their attention on the TV. Richard wasn't one for watching TV and certainly not daytime TV.

Instead, he picked up the Sky remote and instantly wished he hadn't. The menu was something he'd never encountered before, with a whole array of dramas, entertainment, documentaries, sports and movies. 'What would you like to watch?' he asked Frances as he looked worryingly at the remote control, desperately trying to look like he knew what he was doing with it.

'I'm not fussed. Perhaps see what movies are on?'

Richard fumbled with the controls and found his way onto the movies menu and was greeted with more sub-menus. He tried to think what Frances would like to watch. *I can't imagine she'd want to watch an epic war film or a sci-fi fantasy. Romance, that should do it... Mind you she's just come out of traumatic relationship... ooohhh...* His brain was in meltdown. The simple task of choosing something to watch had become an ordeal. Frances intuitively sensed this and gently relieved him of the remote control and the overwhelming responsibility of what to watch. In less than ten seconds she had chosen "The Devil Wears Prada," which definitely seemed her sort of film.

'I've seen it a hundred times but it's easy viewing,' she said calmly, setting the remote down on the arm of the sofa. She then pulled Richard closer and together they snuggled down into a more comfortable position. Slouched on the sofa, Richard instantly forgot about the stresses and tribulations of the past few hours. Back was the warm wash of contentment he'd felt when he and Frances first got together. Frances must have felt safe and content too, as, when he looked, she's drifted off to sleep; her body limp and heaving gently up and down with restful breaths. He looked back up at the TV. His eyes grew heavy and, just as the opening titles for the movie came up, he closed them. The sleep that came was deep and much needed.

What seemed like many hours later, they were abruptly woken by the front door closing. In stepped Matt with a badly bruised and swollen face. His left eye was almost closed due to the swelling. 'Well, that went well,' he announced with mock cheer.

Richard and Frances were still trying to come to terms with being awake. Frances rubbed her eyes and did a doubletake at the sight of Matt's beaten face. Stunned, Richard just sat there. 'What the hell happened to you?' he said when the power of speech returned to him.

'Well, I took your advice and had a chat with Jamie and… well, "came out" to him... It's fair to say he didn't take it too well.'

Richard was struggling to comprehend whether Matt was upset, relieved or still in shock.

Frances kicked into life. 'I'll get you some ice for your eye. That doesn't look good,' she said as she inspected Matt's eye before leaving for the kitchen.

Richard felt an overwhelming pang of guilt for inspiring Matt into his decision to confront Jamie. Matt, seeing the worry etched on Richard's face placated him. 'Don't worry mate. I'm fine. You're right though; he really *is* an arsehole.' Matt's easy smile emerged but seemed out of place amongst the ugly swollenness and bruising.

It was now Richard's turn to utter the words, 'Do you want to talk about it?'

'I don't know how much there is to say,' Matt began. 'I caught up with Jamie and the other lads on a job we're working on the other side of town. I took him to one side and, after a bit of skirting around the subject, I just blurted it out. To say he was irate would be an understatement. At first he didn't know what to do – I think he thought I was joking. Then, when the penny dropped and he saw I was serious, he went ballistic. Before I knew it he'd punched me in the face,' Matt pointed to his swollen eye 'and then he was on top of me, reigning punches down on me. I think I went unconscious for a bit and the next thing I knew the lads were trying to drag him off of me. He was full of venom, saying all sorts of nasty stuff. The rest of the lads were in shock - as much at seeing the violence as the news that'd preceded it… I doubt I'll be going back to work with them,' Matt shrugged.

Richard thought Matt was taking this all very rationally. It prompted him to say 'Are you sure you're ok? I mean, your face doesn't look good. Perhaps we should go to the hospital.'

'I'm fine, just a little upset that he took it that way, but to be honest, he was only ever going to react like that. He's a savage.'

Richard couldn't help but stare at Matt's face which looked grotesque. He wondered what it actually felt like underneath all that swelling.

Matt was just about to say something when he felt his phone vibrate in his pocket. Looking down at it he saw it was a long, expletive-ridden text message from Jamie. Matt was struggling to read through his swollen eye so he passed the phone to Richard.

Richard marvelled at the poor grammar and numerous misspellings. 'Are you sure that some of these are actually words? He's got to be making them up.'

Matt allowed himself a little chuckle. 'I'm sure *he* knows what he means.' He received the phone back from Richard. 'Looks like that offer from Greg has come at just the right time,' he said with an attempted smile as he placed the phone back in his pocket.

Frances returned to the room carrying a tray with three cups of tea and a bag of frozen peas. 'You should go to the hospital,' she said.

'So should you,' Matt replied with another deformed smile; a smile that was returned by Frances. They'd both been through their own, personal ordeals and didn't want to extend these ordeals further by sitting in A&E for hours on end. Matt was about to say something when his phone buzzed again. This time it was ringing and Matt cringed as he pulled it back out of his pocket. He didn't want to hear another torrent of abuse from an irate homophobe. Fortunately, as he looked down at the phone with his good eye – the eye that wasn't rapidly closing due to the savage bruising – he saw it was from one of his other colleagues, Alan. He answered the call and lifted a finger to signify that he wouldn't be a minute whilst he took the call outside. France and Richard were left sipping their tea and wondering what was being said. They could hear the odd word but couldn't put it into context. They just exchanged nervous glances at one another until Matt re-joined them back in the living room. He stood before them at a loss for words. Eventually he puffed out his cheeks and said, 'That was Alan… one of my team. He told me that he and the rest of the boys were disgusted with Jamie and have said they won't work for him anymore. They'll only work for me.' Matt's voice broke as he delivered the last sentence. Choked with the emotion of the last hour and more so, the culmination of the clandestine nature he'd kept his working life for so many years. His eyes filled with tears and, once full, they fell down his cheeks.

Richard couldn't tell if he was happy or sad. He supposed it was a huge relief that this issue he'd been scared to confront was finally out in the open. He got up from the sofa to comfort Matt; an action he instantly felt awkward doing. He'd never properly hugged a man in that fashion before and as he opened his arms Matt could also sense this awkwardness. 'I'm alright mate, but thanks,' he said, but after a moment's thought he added, 'Ah, who am I kiddin? Come here,' and reached out his arms, taking Richard in his strong embrace.

They stayed like that for a moment; two friends who'd lost contact for such a long time, hugging like those wilderness years had never existed. Frances looked on with real empathy. It was a sweet moment which tugged at her heartstrings, particularly after what she'd endured in the past few days. 'Can I join?' she said in small voice. The boys opened their arms and received her into the fold.

CHAPTER 19

'Are you getting excited?' Matt asked Richard as they sat around the kitchen island. They'd just finished lunch and all contributed to its creation - a cobbled together pasta dish - in which all three of them escaped into their own little worlds as they performed their various culinary tasks. 'Are you getting excited Rich?' Matt repeated when no response was forthcoming.

'Erm... Excited about what?' came Richard's vacant reply.

'You're moving into your new place on Saturday. Or had you forgotten?' Matt said as he clumsily sipped his glass of red wine. In fairness to Richard, it was hard to understand Matt as his speech sounded quite mumbled. His lips had swollen up considerably and he'd regretted putting chilli in with the pasta sauce. This had done nothing to soothe his cut lips.

Richard had heard Matt well enough though. He was just miles away as he slipped subtle glances in Frances' direction. She was looking more and more like the Frances he had fantasised over for such a long time. She carried a more relaxed look now; less scared and tired, more cheerful. Richard could tell she felt safe here, and in a bizarre way, Matt's own assault meant she had someone that could totally appreciate the physical pain she'd had to endure. 'I'll be honest; I haven't given it any thought. What with... y'know, everything that's gone on, I've kind of forgotten.'

'Well, you better start getting excited Richie Boy! It's a big step moving into you own place and living on your own.'

Richard, who a second ago hadn't thought about moving into his new place, was now thinking of nothing else. He visibly whitened. The whole concept of moving into his new home now scared the bejesus out of him. He'd always lived with his parents, and whilst they weren't much company and treated him with absolute contempt, they were still there. It daunted him to think that he would have a whole apartment all to himself. No overbearing, under-caring parents to ridicule him – to chastise him for making too much noise as he walked past their room early in the morning or leaving the toilet with unintentional piss stains around it. As bad as they were – and they *were* very bad – he was almost going to miss the company they'd provided. Sure, they were lazy and bigoted, slovenly and vulgar, but they were company. His mind raced as he imagined his life, all by himself in his neutrally decorated apartment; the rain pattering on the window and only mind-numbing TV on in the background to give him company. Obviously, he still had his games console to keep him occupied, but, strangely, since his life had suddenly sprung into life, he had no desire to play on that anymore. He wanted to live in the real world.

Almost sensing what he was thinking about, Frances gently grasped his hand. 'I'll come and visit,' she said with a kind smile. The comment made him beam and he reciprocated by giving her a look of pure contentment. 'I can even help you move if you like,' she continued. 'It's not like I've got anything else better to do!'

'Thank you, I'll take you up on your offer, although there's not much to move.'

'Yes,' Matt agreed, 'a church mouse has got more belongings that poor lil' Richie here.' He gave Richard a playful squeeze of the cheek which made him blush.

'Have you thought what you're going to do? Where you're going to stay?' Matt asked Frances. He felt it was an opportune time to broach the subject. The mood had lifted somewhat and the dramas of the morning were slowly beginning to fade. By no means were they dealt with, but there was definitely a feeling that they could begin to discuss things without the earlier trepidation.

'You could stay with me if you need to,' Richard said shyly.

Frances smiled another kind smile. 'That's very sweet,' she said. 'But we've only just met. Let's enjoy ourselves and get to know one another properly before we move in together.'

Richard, all flustered, tried to correct her. 'No, I only meant temporarily. Y'know, until you get things sorted and…' He tailed off but hoped Frances knew what he meant.

'Thank you. I'll be ok. I'll see if Jen will take me in for a bit. She's only got a one-bedroom place but I've stayed there enough in the past.' She sighed, 'But I've got to sort things out with Mike before I do anything else. He's not going to take any of this well.'

'Do you want me to go with you to pick up your stuff or see if we can kick him out?' Matt suggested.

'Looking like you do?' Frances said with her eyebrow raised in question. 'I appreciate the offer, but I'll figure something out.'

'Seriously, I mean it. Why should he stay in your place after what he's done to you?'

All of a sudden Frances wasn't quite as ready to confront this subject as she thought she was. She sighed a significant sigh that made it quite clear that she was feeling uncomfortable with the current conversation. 'More importantly, it looks like we have the day to ourselves. What shall we do about that?' she said with forced cheer.

A quick glance shared between the boys and they surreptitiously agreed to join Frances in a move away from serious matters.

'Well, after the day I've already had I fancy getting mind-bendingly drunk… Anyone else?' Matt said. 'We can sit in the garden; I'll make us cocktails; we can smoke some weed and have a proper chilled one.'

At first Richard wasn't sure if he was serious. He wished Matt would go to the hospital. With all the swelling, cuts and bruising his face looked decidedly ugly. That wasn't something anyone could ever say about Matt's face. Even at school he'd been a handsome chap, bordering on looking effeminate he was so pretty. He was sometimes teased about his "girly looks" by Chris Simmonds and other school bullies. This more often than not resulted in confrontations and scuffles with these boys. Matt was that sort of lad; the sort to not take any grief off anyone. Ironically, in this case, that is exactly what he'd done. He'd taken a beating off Jamie – an obvious bully. Perhaps, Richard thought, it was what Matt had wanted; the physical pain to provide a little closure to all the secrecy and hiding from what he actually was. Since reconnecting with him, Matt had always seemed positive and happy, but there also seemed like there was something nagging in the back of his mind, stopping him from being fully content. As cathartic as all this might seem to Matt though, Richard still wished he'd get his injuries looked at. This was also an opinion he could level at Frances, but he knew she'd not go to hospital either.

Stepping into Matt's garden, it was to a change in the weather which was now vastly improved from earlier that morning. The bright, beaming sun had burnt away the mist and grey clouds. Radiant sunlight and warm air now greeted them. It was blissful. Matt struggled to get his sunglasses over his swollen face but after much persistence managed to do so. It didn't look comfortable to Richard though. 'Are you sure you don't…' he started saying before stopping himself. *He's a big boy and can look after himself,* he reasoned. Standing there in the full glow of the sun, Richard marvelled at how beautiful Matt's garden was. Like the rest of his home, it was minimalist and thoroughly well maintained. A neat lawn was broken up by Japanese-style ornaments, grasses and manicured scrubs. There was decking and paving in various sections and a summer house at the end of the garden. Richard could see that through his bruised and bloated face, Matt was beaming with pride. 'Did you do all this?... It's incredible.'

'Isn't it just?' Frances agreed. They both looked around like they were entering an enchanted forest.

'Yeah, this is my baby,' Matt said with a proud smile bulging through his puffy lips. 'Mi casa, es tu casa mis amigos.' Not an easy phrase for him to pronounce in his current state.

'Impressive, really impressive,' Richard nodded, and he wasn't referring to Matt's grasp of Spanish.

'If you like that, you'll love this…' Matt said as he led them excitedly to the end of the garden where, on the decking, there was smart rattan furniture set out in front of the summer house. He opened the door to the summer house and there in front of them were some DJ decks and a small bar. It was nicely decorated and finished off with fairy lights and a disco ball.

'The neighbours must love you,' Richard said.

'Ah shush,' Matt replied, although through his swollen lips it sounded like he blew a raspberry. 'My neighbours are lovely. I don't have many parties and if I do they never bat an eyelid. I'm lucky in that respect. He motioned to the decks. 'Fancy a go?'

'I wouldn't know where to start,' Richard replied.

'It's easy. Just cue up a tune and press play.' Matt switched things on, pressed a few buttons and all of sudden pumping house music pounded out of the elegant speakers.

Richard found himself covering his ears, but Frances pushed past him and got behind the decks. 'I'll have a go,' she said with hint of mischievousness. For the next few minutes Matt stood over her as he showed her the ropes, but it soon became apparent she didn't need much direction. Matt and Richard both looked at one another in surprise and appreciation. 'Wow, are you sure you've never spun the wheels o' steel before?' Matt said.

'I might have,' Frances replied as she cued up another track. When it mixed in perfectly from the last one she turned and gave him a subtle wink.

'You, my dear, are just full of surprises aren't you?' Matt said, stepping away from her. 'I think my job here is done.' He then went to the bar where he pulled out a few spirits, mixers. In no time at all he concocted three perfectly crafted cocktails and handed them to the others. Frances was now in the zone and thoroughly enjoying herself. 'She's great. I can see why you obsessed about her all these years,' he said to Richard.

'Well, I wouldn't say I obsessed over her, but...' Richard began to bashfully reply, but saw Matt sceptically looking down through his sunglasses. 'Oh, alright; perhaps I did obsess about her a little bit. She *is* wonderful though isn't she?'

'She's definitely that mate. And if I were straight I'd be taking her off your hands.' Matt gave Richard a playful nudge and then rubbed his own temple as a sudden jab of pain struck him.

Richard looked at Matt with grave concern. 'Are you sure you're alright?'

Matt held onto Richard's arm as the wave of pain slowly subsided. 'Nah, I'm fine. Don't worry about me,' he said unconvincingly. He took a big swig from his cocktail and walked out into the warm, summer sun. 'This is the life isn't?' he slurred as he raised his arms up to the sky.

'What was that? I couldn't hear you properly. You're not drunk already are you?' Richard said in a voice somewhere between joking and worry.

Matt half-turned as if he were about to reply. His glass dropped from his hand and, with his legs buckling beneath him, he fell face first onto the grass.

Shocked, Richard didn't know what to do. 'Oh my god,' were words that sounded as if they came from someone else's mouth, but they were his. Instinct suddenly kicked in and he rushed over to the prostate figure of Matt lying unconscious on the ground. 'Frances!' he shouted. 'Frances!'

Just as stunned as Richard was, Frances looked up from the decks and let out a scream, 'Oh no, oh no, oh no!' was all she could say. Hurriedly she shut off the music and scurried to join Richard by Matt's side. 'Quick, call an ambulance!'

Richard fumbled in his pocket for his phone. He dialled as quickly as he could. 'Where are we? What's this address?' he asked Frances frantically.

Frances took off into the house and found a letter addressed to Matt. She called the address out to Richard. He was near crying as he spoke to the operator. When he finished he sat there crestfallen, stroking Matt's hair and speaking words of comfort to him.

Frances stood pale-faced, in a state of shock. In the past week there'd been many moments of tribulation, but this was by far the most shocking. 'How long will they be?' she said in a faraway voice.

'They didn't say, just said they'd be here as soon as possible,' he replied before returning to comfort Matt, who still seemed to be breathing ok, but showing no other signs of life.

When the ambulance arrived, things seemed to happen in a blur. Richard found himself answering questions without thinking. It was as if it were happening to someone else. A rapid ambulance journey delivered them to the Sussex County Hospital where, because of

Matt's injuries, they'd both had to give a statement to the police. Stunned, shell-shocked and wondering what the hell was going on, they now sat outside a hospital ward awaiting news on Matt's condition. Conversation was limited as they both tried to contend with the past hours' drama. After a while one of the nurses came out and explained that Matt had a blood clot around the brain caused by the injuries sustained in his assault. She explained they needed to act quickly.

'Will he die?' Richard blurted out before the nurse had finished.

There was a pregnant pause before the lady spoke and it did nothing to settle Richard's nerves. 'We think we've caught this in good time – and that is largely due to your actions. It was a good job you were there with him when he collapsed because time really is of the essence… We're going to perform a procedure called a Thrombectomy. It involves inserting a catheter into his groin. We'll pass a small device through this catheter, into the artery in the brain. The blood clot can then be removed using this device, or, if needed, through suction.'

This was all gibberish to Richard. 'So, he's not going to die?' he asked again.

'We're confident the procedure is going to be successful and Matthew will make a good recovery. There's always a chance of complications though, so I just want you to be made aware of that, but, in answer to your question, no, Matthew is not going to die.'

Richard exhaled a huge puff of air. Frances smiled and hugged him. 'Blimey, I thought I'd lost him there,' he said through Frances hair. 'That'd be just my luck; we've just reconnected after all these years and then he goes and dies on me!'

Frances let out a relieved laugh. 'What a day,' she said with a sigh.

'Can we see him quickly?' Richard asked.

'Well, you shouldn't really, but if you're really quick you can poke your heads in before we take him to theatre.'

As they peered around the curtain they could've been excused for thinking that Matt was indeed dead. It was only the steady beep of the heart monitor and the barely noticeable rise and fall of his chest that suggested otherwise. He looked so peaceful Richard thought. His face still carried the bruises, cuts and swelling but it was completely at peace. He drew up close to Matt's ear and whispered, 'Good luck buddy. We'll be thinking of you.'

He looked up at Frances who smiled sweetly. 'C'mon, we best let them get on with it,' she said. They thanked the nurse and went back to the waiting room where they slumped wearily onto the hard, plastic chairs. 'What a day,' Frances said again.

'What a week,' Richard added. It was true. For him, his life had only really started a week ago when he'd met Matt fortuitously in the pub. It was also the same day he'd finally spoken to Frances. A great deal had happened in the time since. It felt like a life within a life, full of a wide range of emotions, drama and upheaval. As he sat there contemplating what had led him to where he was now, it wasn't with the slightest hint of regret. He'd finally seen for himself that there was a whole wide world out there and, yes, it could be brutal and scary at times, but it is also beautiful, wonderful and fulfilling. He decided he owed it to Matt and to himself to live his life to the fullest he possibly could. No more hiding in the shadows; no more letting life pass him by. He needed to cherish life; to embrace it and most importantly, to live it.

CHAPTER 20

Richard and Frances were woken by a different nurse; a gentle-sounding Indian lady whose voice drifted into their dreams and pulled them back into the real world, and the now bustling waiting room. They had no clue how long they'd been asleep and were momentarily baffled as to where they were. Richard couldn't actually recall deciding to fall asleep. He was still in wonderment when the nurse softly said, 'I thought you'd like to know, that the procedure went very well. Matthew is stable but heavily sedated. He'll be somewhat confused when he wakes, but if you'd like to pop in a have a look, you're more than welcome. I just wanted to make you aware that he'll probably be unresponsive, but that's nothing to worry about.'

They groggily thanked the nurse and allowed themselves a moment to adjust to being awake. Both of them were stiff from their slumber and rose like two zombies from the hard, plastic seats they'd been slumped upon. Stretching and yawning, oblivious of the new array of people that were sat around them, they slowly made their way out of the waiting room and into the adjoining corridor. The lights seemed unnecessarily bright and a nondescript stale smell blended with disinfectant and cleaning fluid, synonymous with hospitals, invaded their nostrils. Richard looked at his phone which informed him that it was eight o'clock in the evening. The area they were in didn't have any windows so it was hard to gauge what the weather was doing or if the sun was still as bright as it was earlier. But bright was everything Richard wasn't feeling. His whole body ached and judging by the way Frances shuffled along beside him, so did hers. 'Why don't you see someone whilst you're here?' he said.

'I'm ok,' she said in reply. 'Besides, I think they've got more important things to deal with than my few bruises.'

'But you might have a cracked rib and who knows what else.'

'If I do have a cracked rib there's nothing they can do for it... The bruises will be gone in a few days and, in truth, I really don't want all the fuss that their questions might unveil. I'll admit, it's been a wake-up call – if I needed another – and one that I'm going to take good heed of, so please don't worry about me.' She paused as if tired of her own conversation and let out a large sigh before continuing. 'Today really shocked me – and I'm not talking about what happened to me now. Seeing Matt return with his face all beaten up and then seeing him on the ground... I honestly thought he was dead.' She put a hand up to her mouth and shook her head.

Richard instinctively put his arm around her and pulled her in to his chest. 'I know,' he said. 'I haven't had chance to process a lot of what's gone on this past few week, but what happened today... I, I don't...'

Frances looked up at him with her deep blue eyes, which were also red and bloodshot. 'Shall we get out of here? We can tell them where we're going and give them your number if they need us.'

'Where are we going?' he asked.

'Anywhere but here.'

Five minutes later they were stood outside the hospital entrance with the evening sunshine partially blinding them. Fresh, sea air and the sound of nearby traffic quickly filled their senses. Still groggy from their impromptu nap, and somewhat shell-shocked from the day's events, they strolled aimlessly down the road. 'Let's walk along the seafront,' Frances suggested.

Richard didn't need to agree. With a quickening pace, he found himself led like a puppy on a short lead. 'What's the rush?' he asked.

'I just want to see the sea. And I want to see the sunset.' Frances replied, now awoken and bursting with newfound energy. Weaving through the quiet streets of Kemp Town, a bohemian, arty district of Brighton, where Georgian buildings had long since been converted into flats, they quickly found themselves on the seafront road. Dodging across the fast-moving traffic and a further walk down some steep stone steps and they were on the beachfront. This part of the seafront was never quite so busy. With no shops or bars in the vicinity, and away from the humdrum of the city centre, it was a much more sedate part of town. Here, a wide expanse of pebbly beach stretched out towards the sea. Frances seemed a lot more settled once they'd reached there, but she continued to lead Richard toward the shore. Trudging ungracefully over the pebbles she found a spot five metres from the sea and sat herself down. Richard, on the verge of falling over, sat down heavily next to her. Not looking at him, she felt for his hand to hold and clasped it in her own. Her eyes were fixed over to the West where the Palace Pier, with its bright lights twinkling along the length it, seemed to completely captivate her gaze. The sun was just beginning to edge its way down behind it, where, in the next half hour it would touch the sea, then disappear from view. She was completely quiet as were most things around them. Waves gently and repetitively rolling in, dragging the pebbles up and down the shore, the only the sound to be heard. It was truly calming and therapeutic given and was all the more so given the trauma of the day. For Richard, this was third perfect sunset he'd witnessed in as many days, but, because he was sharing it with Frances, and with all that had gone that day, it felt the most stirring. His feelings for her at that moment were soaring. He wondered if there was anything he should say then realised that no words were necessary. Just that sound and that sight were all that were needed. Not wishing to disturb the moment they shared, he carefully wrapped his arm around her. She then allowed her head to loll onto his shoulder. Given the chaos of the day, this was serenely beautiful. He could hear her breathing slow to a steady, relaxed rhythm. Despite all her recent distress, as he looked at her profile, she cut a stoic figure. He truly admired her and it was just another reason why he'd fallen so deeply in love with her so quickly and so readily. And there they sat watching the sun inch its way towards the horizon. It grew redder and redder until it lost itself behind a layer of low cloud. He thought that this might be their cue to leave, but as he went to pull himself up, Frances gripped his arm to encourage him to remain where he was.

'It's not over yet,' she said in a mellow, faraway tone. 'This sunset has more treats to offer.'

Sure enough, over the next fifteen minutes, the sky and clouds went through a rich and vivid metamorphosis. Richard felt his heart fill-up - like everything was suddenly alright in the world. When the last throes of sunlight had dissolved, a noticeable chill replaced the warm, early summer air. Slowly, Frances rose from the pebbles, brushing her skirt with her hand. With her, rose Richard, still a little uncertain of what to say and when indeed to start speaking again.

'That was beautiful,' she said wistfully.

Richard nodded a silent nod of agreement. 'Where shall we go now? Back to the hospital?'

'No, I've had enough of hospitals for one day.'

'Where then?'

'Let's just walk… Let's just walk and see where our legs take us.'

Richard followed, but a pang of uneasiness settled in the back of his mind. They strolled along the still busy seafront hand-in-hand with no words uttered between them, passing the Palace Pier with all its glittering lights. Frances was looking around, taking in all the sights and sounds. She had a peaceful grin emblazoned on her face which made him afraid to speak and break her out of her copacetic state. Crossing the bustling, busy road they meandered their way through The South Lanes; and still no words were said. As the approached the Royal Pavilion, Richard couldn't stand the strange silence that had settled between them anymore. He had an urge to say something - anything at all to break up, what was, in his mind at least, the unnatural quietness between them. After all, with everything that had happened to them in that day and the previous few days, he had a million questions bouncing around his head. 'Fancy a drink in the Pavilion Tavern?' he blurted out cheerily and instantly wished he'd thought of something a little more in-keeping with the mood of the moment. Still, he'd said it and he couldn't unsay it, so he backed himself up. 'It's where we... you know, first chatted and...'

Frances took an eternity to acknowledge his question and then, when she did it was with a nondescript sound that signified she didn't want to go for a drink there.

'Are... Are you ok?' Richard questioned. 'Have I done something wrong?'

This comment finally seemed to break Frances out of her trance. They stopped dead. Still smiling, she turned to him. 'No, no there's nothing wrong… *You've* certainly done nothing wrong. I don't know… Sitting there, watching that sunset, I almost came out of myself; like I was looking down on myself and seeing what Mike had done and how he'd made me feel. And that sunset seemed to drag all the hurt and fear out of me… And you know what?.. I don't feel scared anymore.' Her voice was so measured and calm that he was disappointed when she'd finished speaking.

'Well, it certainly was a wonderful sunset,' he replied for want of a better response.

They continued their stroll, both lost in their own thoughts. Frances' comment had a lovely sense of finality to it. She seemed completely at peace. Richard on the other hand, was far from at peace. His mind was racing with thoughts of those chaotic past twelve hours. He was also still trying to process all the memories and experiences of the past week. And in amongst all those thoughts was the impending prospect of moving into his new flat, which was starting to fill him with dread.

After half an hour of aimless wandering through the lanes and streets of Brighton, they somehow, almost instinctively, found their way back to Matt's house. Subconsciously they both realised they now needed his house as sanctuary from their respective destituteness.

Entering the house, they felt like intruders returning to the scene of a crime. Only a few hours before, they'd left it panic-stricken and traumatized. Making their way down to the kitchen, an eerie quiet had replaced the earlier vibrant atmosphere there.

'Fancy a cuppa?' Frances said. These were her first words in a while and Richard had almost gotten used to the silence. He nodded his head, being not quite ready to open his mouth just yet. As Frances busied herself making the tea, he wandered around, taking in all the things he hadn't noticed on his previous visits to Matt's. The artwork on the walls was fairly unremarkable and "arty" to his untrained eyes. It probably all cost a pretty penny, but the one picture that did catch his eye was a canvas of a photo of Matt with his mother and father. It looked like it was taken quite recently and it struck him how different Matt's parents looked from the people he remembered from years back. They'd all come together for whatever reason and in that picture they looked so happy that Richard felt himself smiling back at it.

'Here you go,' Frances said, presenting Richard with a steaming cup of tea. Her sudden appearance behind him made him jump. 'Sorry, I didn't mean to startle you.'

'Don't worry; I think I'm still a little on edge… You know, after everything that went on. Being here feels weird without Matt.'

'It's certainly been a bizarre ol' day,' Frances agreed as she slumped onto one of the kitchen stools.

Richard shuffled over and plonked himself down on a stool opposite her; the rigours of the day seemingly catching up with him as they had her. They both sat there for a moment, warming their hands on the hot ceramics of the mugs.

After a moment of individual contemplation, and without any warning, he blurted out, 'I have something to confess to you...' The words hung there and were a surprise to him too. Shaken out of her catatonic state Frances looked attentively into his eyes. He suddenly regretted opening his mouth; but it was too late now. He paused for longer than was comfortable and looked deep into his tea for reassurance; for wisdom and who knows what else. He sighed heavily then began his confession. 'I want to say... Well, when I was away in Ibiza...' He was searching for the best way to say what he wanted to say without upsetting Frances.

This was evidently a big thing for him and Frances could feel the strain that he had put himself under. 'You slept with another woman?' she offered.

Richard, abruptly shaken out of his guilt-ridden admission said, 'Yes...Well, no, not, y'know... Not everything.' It had been weighing heavily on his mind since he'd received the call from Frances on Greg's yacht. In actuality he'd done nothing wrong. At that particular moment in time, he and Frances weren't together. She had spurned him and, inconceivably, taken Mike back. But it had still laden him with guilt, nonetheless. He'd wanted to say something from the first moment they were back in touch, but with everything that had gone on since they'd picked her up, there'd never been the right time. In hindsight, he acknowledged that this didn't feel like a very opportune time to divulge this information either, but it was said now and he awaited her reaction.

Frances, for her part, was surprised to feel a slight shudder of jealousy run through her, but she quickly regained her composure. 'Look, don't worry about it. It was bound to happen. You've just discovered that you're attractive to other people. Your libido must be through the roof and...' she paused, suddenly thinking of something. 'Was she beautiful? Did you fall for her?' She was surprised again; this time to hear those insecure words fall out of her mouth.

Richard felt like he was under interrogation and knew he needed his answer to be reassuring and not the slightest bit antagonising. 'She… She,' he stuttered. Another pause as he tried to regain *his* composure. 'Her name was Cassandra, and yes, she was beautiful. She was tall, slim, red-haired…'

'I only asked if she was beautiful; I'm not after her vital statistics,' Frances said rather caustically. She was surprising herself with everything she said at the moment and had to acknowledge, her feathers had been well and truly ruffled.

'Sorry,' he said sheepishly. 'I just wanted you to know… I thought I wasn't going to hear from you ever again and…'

'No, *I'm* sorry. I've no right to question you on who you can see. You're right; you didn't know if you'd ever hear from me again – I get it. I suppose I'm just being selfish. In my head I thought you might be crying in a darkened room, not kicking back in Ibiza… I'm sorry for the way I treated you – that wasn't fair – I just had a moment of weakness and Mike seized upon it.' Frances paused and sucked in a big lungful of air before she continued. 'Thank you for telling me this, but really, it's unimportant in the great scheme of things. Right now, I really need your friendship…'

The word "friendship" and its delivery were a dagger to Richard's heart. True, he didn't have many friends, so Frances' friendship should be highly regarded, but he wanted more than that and Frances must've known that. He loved her; he r*eally* loved her and talk of friendship felt hollow and patronising. 'Is that how you see me? As a friend?' he asked not able to mask the hurt in his voice.

'Are you *not* my friend?' she replied.

'Of course, but... I don't know… I thought you felt the same way about me; I thought you loved me.' He was stunningly aware of how fragile and immature he now sounded.

'I do really care about you,' she said with all the compassion she could muster. 'I think you're amazing, and you've been there for me. You've shown me affection when I needed it most and, again, I'm sorry that I hurt you and went back to *him*. But I wasn't in the right headspace when we met, and I'm even further away from being there now… I just need some time to get over things and feel strong again... Do you understand? I'm not trying to be a selfish bitch, but I am trying to look after myself and not hurt you again in the process.'

With every word that Frances spoke, Richard could feel himself sinking a little lower. By the end of her speech his heart was on the floor and shattered into a million pieces. It took all the effort he could muster to look her in the eye and reply, 'Yes, I understand.' His voice was shrouded in emotion and he was thankful for the cup of tea which became a convenient prop to mask his sadness. He sipped noisily to fill the heavy atmosphere that had settled between them. His eyes looked forlornly toward the ground. Like young child scolded for some indiscretion, he hung his head low to hide the hurt on his face He could fill the weight of two tears which had formed and was scared to blink in case they fell and gave away his reaction. With a suffocating silence seemingly contaminating the space between them, Frances drained her tea and rose from the stool to rinse her cup. 'Could you ever love me?' he asked in a broken voice.

'Maybe,' she replied. 'Just not right now.'

CHAPTER 21

Richard woke up on the sofa in Matt's living room; the overly efficient central heating rousing him hot and bothered. He kicked off the large, heavy blanket that Frances must've covered him with before she went to sleep in Matt's spare room. He'd skulked onto the sofa, still licking his wounds from the second rejection from Frances in a week. Despite his mind cartwheeling with the emotions churning inside of him, he'd fallen asleep without problem. Exhaustion had superseded everything else and he'd succumbed to his over-powering weariness. That was until he was awoken with a dry mouth and a steady thumping in his head. The morning light was starting to invade the room through the expensive blinds, but he guessed it was still very early. He sat himself up, rubbed his temples and then the back of his neck; his body stiff from the unfamiliar sleeping position he'd adopted on Matt's couch. He tried to alleviate the achiness with a long stretch as he rose, but the sudden exertion caused him to feel light-headed and he struggled to stay upright. Whilst he waited for blood to return to his brain, he tried to remember if he had anything planned today. Obviously, he was going to pay a visit to Matt in hospital, but visiting times were fairly rigid, and he wondered to fill the rest of the day. A moment or two later and he surmised thinking was a tiring business and he flopped back down on the sofa. He contemplated struggling back to sleep there on the sofa when he heard Frances' voice call out to him from the spare room.

'Why don't you come and lie here with me. There's plenty of room.'

Still brooding, he considered his options for a moment, and with all the fake reluctance he could muster, crept up the stairs to the spare room.

Despite bright light flooding the rest of the house, the spare room, with its blackout blind ably doing its job, resembled the black hole of Calcutta as he entered it and he immediately regretted closing the door behind him. But, still wanting to maintain a degree of aloofness and present the aura of someone who could handle anything - including walking into a pitch-black room, he shuffled tentatively towards where he thought the bed was, whacked his knee on the bedside table and let out an involuntary yelp. *Not cool buddy. Not cool.*

'What are you doing?' Frances whispered impatiently. Richard shrewdly followed the sound of her voice. With his shins hitting the bed, he fell onto it. As he lay himself down and settled in the bed, he became conscious that he no longer knew how to behave around Frances. In the past week he'd slowly become used to giving in to his feelings; both with her and Casandra. Now he had to restrain himself. He did the only thing he could do in his position; he lay on his side, on the absolute edge of his side of the bed, leaving a ridiculously large gap between the two of them. The duvet made him hot and bothered again, but he didn't want to fidget. He was playing it cool – or so he thought. Frances broke him out of his strop. 'I could really do with a cuddle if you have one going,' she said coyly.

He instantly felt foolish, but not wishing to lose too much face, took his time turning over and curling around Frances' petit frame. Despite the warmth under the duvet, her body felt cold and she almost seemed to be shivering. Instinctively, he wrapped his arm around her midriff and pulled himself in close. Frances wriggled in closer and he could feel himself getting hard. *Not now. I'm trying to be aloof*, he willed himself, but it was no use.

'Oh, good morning. Someone's pleased to see me,' Frances said in a quiet, playful tone.

Busted! Well, thank you very much, he inwardly reprimanded his unruly penis. He seemed to have all the control over his penis as a rampant adolescent. He was about to roll away again when Frances' arm clamped around him.

'Don't worry about it. I'll take it as a compliment.' And with his rock-hard erection pressed up against her pert bottom, they fell back to sleep.

Richard awoke when Frances shuffled from their embrace and got out of bed. She stood, stretched and walked to the door. On its opening, light swamped the room and, turning his position, he could make out Frances: her blonde hair wild and unkempt, no makeup and wearing a loose-fitting t-shirt of Matt's. *God, I fancy her,* he thought. He was even less sure of how to behave around her now. Should he carry on being standoffish? Should he try to woo her once again; he was unsure he had the charm or knowhow to woo her. He just ruffled his hair and breathed in a heavy draw of air through his nostrils.

'I'm going to jump in the shower and then do you fancy going out for breakfast?' she said chirpily.

Half an hour later, they were walking down the road towards town. Again, the weather had blessed them with a beautiful sunny day. The sweet scent of apple blossom and cut grass filled the air and they found themselves sniffing up the succulent aroma. As they walked Frances felt out for Richard's hand and grasped it. As much as Richard was still smarting from his rebuffing, he couldn't help but grip her hand tightly. He felt a pulse of warmness surge through him and a smile return to his face. In that moment he reasoned that he was just going to take what moments Frances offered him, in the hope that they would one day lead him back to her completely.

'You seem happier,' Frances said noticing Richard's mood lifting.

'It's a nice day and I'm holding your hand,' he replied nonchalantly.

'I thought you weren't talking to me?'

'Well, I am now,' he said confidently, lifting his face up to the sky. His eyes almost closed in blissful appreciation of the air he breathed. *I could get used to these days of leisure,* he mused.

With few words shared between them, they walked with an air of contentment to a funky-looking café; a popular choice for some of Brighton's more eclectic inhabitants. It never ceased to amaze Richard how many people didn't look like they worked but still had money. Brighton was a hive for small, independent business owners, the self-employed, the start-up generation. People whose day began and finished when they said it did; people who were driven, self-motivated and industrious. Ingenuity oozed out of every pour of them. Richard admired their proactive spirit, but right now, as they seated themselves down in the crowded café, he noticed how "dressed-down" they all were. Some looked like they'd literally come out in their pyjamas. Others looked like they'd got dressed in the dark with odd items of clothing paired with other odd items of clothing with no concern to what they looked like. He had to admit he admired that too. There was a buzzy vibrancy in the chatter that pervaded the café. The waiting staff hurried around, taking the orders, delivering skinny lattes and wildly exotic breakfasts.

'Earth calling Richard; come in Richard,' Frances joked as she waved for hand in front of his face.

Richard shook his head and focussed his attention back on the beautiful features of Frances who sat opposite him. In spite of all the trauma she'd endured, she looked radiant. 'Sorry, I lost myself there for a second,' he said with a smile. 'Shall we order?.. What would you recommend?' He scanned the menu and was taken aback at the wide range of options the café offered and how expensive a breakfast was in a trendy establishment such as this. Obviously, sticking a couple of well-chosen adjectives in front of the "locally sourced" food was a clever way to add a few pounds to the cost.

Having ordered, Frances reached across the table and grasped Richard's hand. Her small hand felt so soft and cold. Richard instinctively found himself rubbing her hand with his, in an effort to warm it up. 'Don't worry about it,' she said. Y'know what they say, cold hands…'

'Warm heart,' Richard finished. He beamed her a friendly smile. Of all the emotions he'd experienced recently, compassion was the one that came easiest to him. He'd always been a very caring, sensitive person, but now he had a focus - or focuses if he included Matt. The thought of Matt suddenly shook him from this tender moment. 'I need to tell Matt's parents about him being in hospital!' he blurted.

Frances, without even flinching from Richard's outburst, calmly said, 'Have you got their phone numbers?'

Richard thought for a moment. 'No,' he said with a shake of his head.

'Do you know where they live?'

Again, he shook his head.

'Well then, you can't contact them. If Matt is awake and is compos mentis when we visit him later we'll ask him if he wants us to contact them.'

'What do you mean "*if* he wants us to contact them?" Surely we've got to let them know?'

'Maybe Matt wouldn't want to worry them. I've only known him a week, but he seems to be the sort of person who just gets on with things.'

Richard was perplexed. If he were a parent he'd want to know if his child were in hospital, but he could see Frances' point of view. Matt definitely was the sort of person to keep any hurt or distress from anyone he cared about. He decided to drop the subject for the time being. There was nothing he could do at that present time anyway.

'So, moving day tomorrow!' Frances said excitedly.

Boom! he was thrown from one quandary to another. He was trying so hard to subdue his anxieties about moving into his new place, but Frances' innocently meant comment sent his pulse racing again. Cold sweat prickled the back of his neck; his mouth dried up and, clearly unnerved, he reached for the full glass of water in front of him. Greedily, he gulped away its contents. Then, wiping his brow and licking his lips, he tried to speak.

'Anyone would think you're *not* looking forward to it,' Frances said with a wry smile. She couldn't help but find the funny side in Richard's first world problem. 'Look on the bright side; at least you have a place to move into. That reminds me; may I use your phone? I'm going to give Jen a call.'

'Of course,' he said fumbling in his pocket. He was still a little rattled and all fingers and thumbs. In his haste and with an overdose of clumsiness, he nearly dropped the phone on the floor as he handed it to Frances.

She blew him a kiss as she took the phone from his clammy grasp. She went outside to make the call as the steady din of many conversations taking place at the same time made it difficult to hear.

With Frances out of view, Richard, not for the first time that day, puffed out his cheeks. During the past week he'd gone with the flow and embraced everything that had come his way. Very soon he'd officially fly the nest and he was worried if he could cope with this impending independence. On the flipside, when he thought about it, he'd been independent for years. His parents supported him as much as paper walking stick. He'd been living an isolated life for so long he reasoned that this shouldn't be the ordeal he was now making it. That simple reasoning seemed enough to calm him. Having placated his anxiety, for the time being at least, he looked around again to see Frances returning from her phone call. 'All good?' he asked.

'Yes, all good. She couldn't talk for long as she's at work, but she said I can stay with her and we'll sort out getting my stuff or kicking Mike out in the next few days. Jen's cool. I don't know where I'd be without her.'

'Yeah, she seemed lovely. You're lucky to have a friend like her.' There was noticeable sadness in his voice.

Frances intuitively read this and delicately said, 'Matt will be ok. It's great that you've rekindled your friendship after all these years. And as soon as he's fit and well again you'll pick up where you left off.'

'Yeah, you're right.' He stared off into the distance as he spoke. 'It's weird, but although we're certainly not the same people that went to school together, we've slotted right back into the sort of friendship we had back then. He always looked out for me then too. I remember once, we must have been about thirteen or fourteen, Chris Simmonds – this bully from our high school - and his gang had confronted me in the corridors. They were picking on me and wanted to take my schoolbooks. I was sticking up for myself as I always did, but this just encouraged them and they were pushing and kicking me. From out of nowhere Matt came charging in – and Chris Simmonds was a big lad, as were most of his gang; so, to do this without any consideration for himself was so reckless and brave. Matt could fight too but against that lot he didn't stand a chance. He took a bit of a beating before one of the teachers saw what was going on and broke it up. I've never forgotten that. I've never forgotten how selfless he was and how ready he was to put himself in harm's way for those he cared about.'

'So, what happened after you left school? Why did you drift apart?' Frances was intrigued. She hadn't heard Richard open up too much in their short time of knowing one another. He'd obviously been starved of the opportunity to do so and perhaps this was all deep-rooted stuff that he needed to unload.

'We stayed in contact for a bit, but I got a job working at the accountants I still work for and Matt got a YTS apprenticeship with a local building company. Our lives changed so much. His colleagues became his new friends, whereas my colleagues became people that I quickly began to resent and avoid.'

The waitress temporarily interrupted their conversation as she delivered their breakfasts. For Frances it was eggs benedict and Richard ordered their take on a full English - as healthy a full English as could be made. Nothing was fried and the baked beans even came in their own little pot. He was unsure of the logic in this. It was unnecessary washing up in his opinion. It did look delicious though and he was aware that over the past few days he hadn't eaten much. Judging by the way Frances had got stuck into her breakfast, he wasn't the only one feeling ravenous. With a complete pause to their discussion, they both ate greedily like they hadn't eaten in months. Washing it down with a coffee and orange juice, the task was completed in a time fitting a professional food eating contest. Contentedly, they both relaxed back in their chairs whilst their stomachs digested.

'So, tell me; why didn't you leave?' Frances said, continuing their conversation.

'Leave where?' Richard asked, his mind trying to tune back in. 'Oh, you mean why didn't I leave the accountants?... I ask myself that now. I suppose I was scared… unambitious… I don't know, you get used to doing something, falling into the same routine day in, day out, and before you know it you've been there twenty odd years and haven't done anything of any note with your life. Meeting Matt again kinda kick-started things… And meeting you,' he concluded, bashfully looking back down at the table.

Frances allowed herself a kind smile although Richard wasn't meeting her gaze. 'What are you going to do now then? With your working situation I mean.'

'I got offered a promotion of sorts the other day. Sorry, I was going to tell you before but, y'know, other things got in the way.'

'Wow, that's amazing!' Frances exclaimed.

'Yeah, I suppose it is,' Richard said unenthusiastically. 'I'm just not sure I want it though. I don't think I ever want to go back to that office ever again. I've got another week to decide, but apart from a chap called Graeme, there's no one else I would want to spend more than two seconds with, let alone be in an office all day with. This past week has given me a whole new perspective on life and what I want to do.'

'What *do* you want to do?'

'I really don't know,' he said unable to stop a smile breaking across his face, aware that he wasn't as certain as he was making himself out to be.

'Well, like you said; you've got some time to decide. A lot has happened to you in a very short space of time. Maybe you should use this time to take stock of it all. That's what I'm planning on doing.' Frances looked at Richard who now met her gaze with a wounded look. 'I know you didn't like hearing that I only wanted your friendship. What you did for me yesterday took courage and I thank you so much for that, but I really need to sort my head out after everything that's gone on. Do you understand that? I can't go from one relationship into another; especially as the one with Mike was so toxic. He took so much from me. You've helped give me the strength to move on, and the only way I can continue to move on is by getting things sorted up here.' She tapped the side of her head to emphasise her point. 'And in here.' Then laid her hand on her heart. Her face was desperately sincere, pleading with him not to feel rejected; to make the greatest effort not to upset him.

After a lengthy pause, a resigned Richard looked equally sincerely into Frances' eyes. 'Yeah, I get it… It doesn't make it any easier to take though. I fell for you and when you can't have what you want - or should I say, when things don't go the way you want them to, it's tough; tough on me... But, if you want a friend you have one in me. I'll be there for you, whenever you need me.'

She could've cried there and then when she saw the emotion brimming inside of him. She could see he was trying so hard to disguise his disappointment. She could literally *feel* the love that he held for her. 'Thank you,' she said delicately. 'You're a handsome, sweet, beautiful man. I knew this before we'd even properly met.'

'But I was dressed like I'd just come out of a jumble sale and looked, well… not very sexy, let's just say that.'

'True, but I could see you from within. You have a good soul. That shines right through. That's more attractive than any item of clothing or hairstyle. Don't ever lose that. Keep being you.'

Richard still looked deflated but he offered Frances a weary smile by way of acquiescence. 'Shall we get out of here? I fancy a walk.'

Frances smiled and nodded. Full, they rose groggily from their seats and walked over to the counter where they paid their bill. Outside the café Richard stretched and yawned in an effort to shake off the crushing weight of disappointment. A disappointment he was determined not to show Frances.

With no particular agenda, they meandered arm in arm through the fast-busying streets and lanes of the city centre. Occasionally they'd stop by a shop and point at something that had caught their eye. All the time, Richard could feel such a strong emotional pull towards Frances but he kept his feelings in check and made sure he was keeping his side of the bargain. He was just enjoying being that close to her; close enough to smell her perfume which had now become his most favourite aroma. He couldn't get enough of it. When he wasn't talking he was surreptitiously sniffing the air and pulling in as much of her scent as he could. The warm sunshine on their faces added to this feeling of well-being and contentment. There seemed to be an overall feeling of happiness in the air. When they looked and smiled at passing strangers, their friendly smile was reciprocated. The faint hum of the occasional bee or a butterfly fluttering around the buddleias in the gardens of The North Laine town houses convinced them that summer was well on its way. So lost in their own thoughts and enjoying the carefree vibe they'd readily relaxed into, they'd forgotten a lot of the upheaval that awaited them. It was only when Richard spied the time on a clock in a shop window that they were jolted back to the real world. The clock read 1:28pm. 'We need to visit Matt in bit,' he said. 'Shall we grab a bite to eat first and then make our way up there?'

'Yes, that sounds like a good idea. I think my appetite has returned with a vengeance,' Frances replied. 'What do you fancy?'

Richard stopped in his tracks and looked up as if he were still sniffing the scented aroma of Frances perfume. A moment's deliberation later and he said, 'I fancy a burger,' with an excited smile on his face. His appetite had returned too and despite the well-portioned breakfast he'd devoured only a few hours earlier, he was ready to satisfy his hunger again. He felt bad for feeling this way as he was far from a gluttonous person and was well aware that there were people in the world far hungrier than him, but right now his mind was firmly locked on thoughts of a juicy burger with melted cheese oozing out the side and spilling lettuce with each bite.

They found an upscale burger joint in The South Lanes and there they sat, piling the most succulent burger on the menu into their hungry mouths. Frances was not normally one for fast food, upscale or not, but she had to agree that this really hit the spot. Their burgers sat heavily in their stomachs as they left the restaurant. They allowed themselves to follow their feet which guided them towards the seafront where they spied the familiar landmark of the Palace Pier. Going hand in hand with this sight was the alluring smell of doughnuts and fish & chips, but even Richard's rampant appetite couldn't take on more food just yet. Bright blue sky continued to fill their landscape but all these sensory delights fell into the background. Their earlier contented mood had dissipated, replaced by one more sombre. The image of Matt lying motionless in his hospital bed as the various monitors beeped and blinked now invaded their thoughts.

On arriving at the hospital ward their hearts jumped as there was no sign of Matt. Momentary panic filled Richard but Frances spoke to one of the nurses and were told he'd been moved to another ward.

Relieved, they snaked their back through the rabbit warren of wards and corridors and almost stumbled on the one that Matt was now in. After announcing their arrival to the small, squat nurse at the ward's reception they were shown to his cubicle which was surrounded by seven other cubicles occupied by patients in various stages of recovery. There were no windows but it was starkly lit. They stood looking down at Matt who was resting soundly. The reassuring rhythm of the heart monitors gave Richard cause to relax. Matt's face was still badly bruised and swollen. The bruises that plastered his face were a kaleidoscope of colours and gave the impression that a small child had attempted to colour in his face and got bored halfway through.

'How is he?' Richard asked nervously, almost frightened of the answer.

'He's doing really well, the nurse replied. 'The operation went better than expected and he's responded brilliantly. There doesn't seem like there'll be any lasting damage, but he'll certainly be a bit confused and groggy in the short term. You might find he doesn't recognise you or gets you confused with someone else. But it's a good job he's a big, strong chap.'

Richard looked at Frances and they shared a relieved smile.

'He needs some rest, but feel free to sit with him.' The nurse then returned to the reception leaving them to sit beside Matt's bed.

The large, high-backed chairs squeaked on the super-clean floor as they moved them into position. Sitting either side of his bed they were at a loss of what to do next. Richard felt uncomfortable and out of place. Frances motioned to him to hold his hand, something that he felt even more uncomfortable and unfamiliar with. But on Frances' insistence he picked up Matt's left hand and felt its warmth. The skin felt rough and calloused from a life of hard, manual work. Richard's hand in comparison, felt small, soft and feminine. He gave the hand a gentle squeeze as he began to speak. It was more for his own comfort than Matt's. 'Hello mate… It's Richie; Richie Chambers. I'm here with Frances… my friend.' Those two words were hard for him to say but right now it mattered little. 'We just spoke to the nurse and she said that you should make a full recovery – that's good news isn't it?' He was aware he was beginning to waffle, but he didn't know what else to say. He wasn't the greatest conversationalist at the best of times, but now he had a one-way discussion that was fast running out of material. Then, just as he was losing the will and about to pull his hand away, he felt the faintest of grasps pulse from Matt's grip. He suddenly felt elated. 'I felt his hand move!' he exclaimed to Frances. She beamed a big smile back and encouraged him to continue. 'I don't know what else to say!' he said flustered. He thought for a moment and gathered himself. 'Errm, th-thank for being my friend,' he continued hesitantly. 'Meeting back up with you has been… incredible, so thank you. Thank you for being there for me this week. For helping me stand up to my parents and for showing me there's a whole wide world out there.' He was now fully focussed on Matt's battered face, looking for signs of a reaction, but in truth the words were now starting to form quite readily and he no longer felt self-conscious. 'You were always the bravest person I knew – You still *are*... I can't wait to carry on with our friendship, to have fun; go down the pub; laugh at stupid things. I'd forgotten how to laugh. You've taught me to laugh again… Anyway, get well soon mate.'

After he finished, he seemed exhausted from the emotion he'd just expelled. He hung his head down, and just as he did so he felt Matt move an indiscernible amount. He looked back up and saw Matt's eyes flicker ever so slightly; and then flicker almost open; and then saw Matt's mouth move as if trying to open. His lips, split from the assault, looked dry and cracked. He fleetingly saw his tongue poke through those lips in a vain, unconscious effort to moisten them. Richard was now transfixed on Matt's swollen face as he willed him back to consciousness. He squeezed his hand a little tighter and Frances, seeing what was now going on, joined him in holding Matt's other hand. Richard flicked an excited look at Frances who returned the look with a raise of her eyebrows and a smile.

When it came, the word was almost inaudible. So low in volume and so distorted by the dryness and swelling of the lips, but Richard heard it well enough. 'Richie,' Matt managed to say as he gave his hand the faintest of squeezes. His eyes fluttered again and for the briefest of moments they opened, only to shut again. And then he drifted back into unconsciousness.

CHAPTER 22

'That was *great*!' Richard said enthusiastically as they walked along one of the many nondescript corridors, on their way out of the hospital. Frances hadn't seen this side to Richard before; excited like a child. Not even when they'd done ecstasy together had he been so animated and euphoric.

Stepping outside into the warm afternoon sunshine, they were left thinking of what to do next. Richard was still beaming a big, broad smile. 'Come on Mr Happy, what shall we do?' Frances said.

'You know what? I really don't mind,' he said casually with a shrug of his shoulders.

Frances thought for a moment. They'd sat on the beach the day before; they'd done their fair share of drinking in the short time they'd known each other; they'd only just eaten and they'd already been tourists around the city. It was such a lovely day that it would be a shame to waste it by just going back to Matt's, but with all the walking they'd done that morning, her feet ached and she was overcome by a sudden wave of weariness. How about we head back to Matt's and enjoy his garden. God knows we didn't have the opportunity yesterday!'

Richard was content to just be with Frances so was more than happy with her plan. He had wondered if she was planning to go to

Jenny's but assumed that she wasn't back from work yet anyway. They flagged down a taxi and ten minutes later they were back outside Matt's house. They paid and thanked the taxi driver who'd been mercifully silent throughout the journey. Weariness had consumed them and it was as much as they could do to not drift off to sleep in the backseat of the cab. Standing blearily facing the door, they swiftly came to their senses.

'Was that lock scratched as much as that before?' Frances asked.

'I don't think so. Looks like someone's had a go at breaking in,' Richard said as he thumbed the scratches. There was definitely some damage to the door frame and some noticeable scratches to the keyhole itself. They looked at one another with a sense of panic. *What was waiting for them behind that door*? Richard gulped, took a deep breath and inserted the door key. It seemed to take him an eternity to turn it and when he did he winced as he slowly and quietly opened the door. He peered around the half-open door and when he ascertained it to be safe, he made his way inside. With his heart beating out his chest, he became frightened to breathe in case it gave him away. He poked his head in the living room then the dining room before creeping silently upstairs. Frances had now made her way inside and was carefully scanning the rooms that Richard had been in for her own reassurance. Her eyes were wide as she tiptoed about. Fear firmly gripped her. Her one thought was that Mike had located her. And as she knew only too well, there was no limit to what he was currently capable of.

Richard pushed opened the bathroom door and was relieved to find nothing untoward in there. He then moved to the spare bedroom. Even before he reached there he could sense something amiss. He took in a large influx of air and puffed out his cheeks as he exhaled. He had decided to confront the looming danger head-on and pushed the door open with his foot. He then rushed into the room and was surprised – and relieved - to find nothing or no one there. But there was definitely something not quite right. He couldn't quite put his finger on it. Puzzled, he looked around the room to see if anything had been taken or been disturbed, but scrutinise as much as he could, he couldn't find anything amiss. Frances joined him in the bedroom. They passed a look of dread to one another before Richard led the way into Matt's room. As his bedroom door was closed he couldn't push it open. Instead, he turned the door handle until he felt it open. He was now as delicate as someone defusing a bomb. He could hear himself gulp loudly as he closed his eyes and gently pushed the door open. Opening his eyes again he saw a sight that astonished him… The tidiest men's bedroom he'd ever seen. It was simply decorated in neutral colours and furnished with quality furniture, but what caught Richard's attention was how everything on show was so precisely positioned. A small pile of clothes lay neatly folded on an armchair. Some toiletries on top of a chest of drawers were evenly spaced and all facing at a particular angle. If there was an intruder in the house they were the most anally retentive of intruders. Richard and Frances breathed a palpable sigh of relief. They both stood there in Matt's bedroom, still frightened to say a word. They knew they still had to check the kitchen downstairs. Seized by a sudden surge of heroism, Richard confidently strode out of the room and bounded down the two flights of stairs, making as much noise as he could and sounding like a man twice his size. If he was going to meet the intruder he was going to give *them* an almighty fright, and not the other way round.

His thundering footsteps stomped on the stairs down to the kitchen. But again, to his considerable relief, there was no one there. After he'd scanned the whole room and found it to be safe, he stopped still and ran his hands through his hair. Frances' head poked down at the top of the stairs as she surveyed the room for danger. 'It's ok. You can come down. No one's here and I can't see any sign of anything being taken. Maybe whoever tried to get in, just didn't manage to do so.' There was more than a bit of shakiness in his voice. The adrenaline that had given him the courage to charge down the stairs was no longer required and he was now in need of a sit-down and a cup of tea. He sat down heavily on one of the stools. 'I think I need a drink after that excitement.'

'Me too,' Frances agreed. A mischievous look then spread across her face. 'I seem to remember there was a bar full of drinks in Matt's summer house. Let's go get 'em… Matt *did* say *his* house was *our* house… Anyway, anything we drink today we can replace tomorrow. I just don't want to go out again today.'

Richard, who was just getting reacquainted with the kitchen stool – a stool he'd spent a fair bit of time perched upon in recent days, dutifully rose and followed Frances out into the garden and across to the summer house. Frances had already opened the fridge and begun to open a bottle of white wine when he joined her. She was frantically unscrewing the cap of the bottle and he could see that she was in far more need of a drink than him. She noisily and messily poured two glasses, handed one to him, said, "cheers," before tipping the contents down her throat in one go. 'Ahhh, I needed that,' she said.

'*Really*, I couldn't tell,' said Richard, dumbstruck. 'Are you alright?'

'I'm better now,' she said as she poured herself another glass. 'That's just really unsettled me. Whether someone's got in or not, someone had at least *tried* to get in.' She vociferously gulped down another mouthful of wine. 'It's him. I know it's him.'

'Who, Mike?'

'Yes, it's definitely him. I just know it.' Although Frances was panicked she wasn't hysterical. The wine had an immediate effect in calming her down.

'We should call the police,' Richard said.

'I've said before, it's not worth calling the police. His dad and his connections within the police force will make sure that anything we come up with against him gets quashed. Besides, it's not even our house. It's Matt's and he's not here. In the eyes of the police, we're as much intruders as Mike.'

Richard could definitely see Frances' point. 'What *shall* we do then?' he asked.

'Get drunk and try to forget about it,' Frances replied waving her glass in the air. 'Have you got a better suggestion?'

Richard didn't so he raised his glass in the air too before taking a purposeful swig. He had to confess the wine tasted good. More refreshing than he was expecting and two more swigs swiftly followed. He raised the glass in acknowledgement and before he could protest, Frances topped him up.

Within minutes they were having their own full-on party. The DJ decks were on and house music was pumping out the speakers. Frances deftly blended one tune into another. These were tunes new to Richard's untrained ears. She encouraged him to dance and as they danced they drank. The fridge was taking a hit but they were doing their best to drown out the fright they'd experienced earlier. Richard could see that Frances' mind was still churning over the thought of Mike having tracked her down, but with every glass of wine they consumed, he could see the worry lift from her. That worry was even further lifted when Frances spotted something on a shelf that took her eye. She went over to take a closer look and, having done so, she smiled mischievously and called out to him, 'Fancy taking this lil' party up a notch?'

He had to squint to see what she was holding up. His vision was fast losing focus thanks to the sudden influx of alcohol. Even with 20/20 vison he would've struggled to see what she held between her two fingers. 'What's that?' he slurred.

'A pill!' she said triumphantly. 'Ecstasy and judging by the symbol stamped on it, it looks to be a Rolex. He's got a whole box of tricks there. Don't worry, we'll pay him back.' She then broke it in half, and without a second's hesitation, popped one half in her mouth. With a swig of wine, she gulped it down and grimaced at the acrid taste it momentarily left behind.

Richard was transfixed at the vision of Frances he saw before him. This Frances was a far cry from the fictitious Frances he'd fantasised over for the past couple of years. She was more carefree and wilder than he'd imagined. He guessed it was hard to build up a complete imaginary personality for someone when all he wanted to imagine was skin deep and lustful. But this was the real Frances and, although she was more than a little traumatised and drunk, he truly loved this version of Frances standing before him.

Frances handed Richard the other half of the pill and looked expectantly at him. There wasn't really a choice he deduced. Hesitantly, he placed the portion of pill on the back of his tongue, took a large swig of his drink, knocked his head back and gulped.

The same grimace was evident once he'd swallowed the harsh tasting chemical, but Frances' beaming smile was all the confirmation he needed that he'd done the right thing.

With the wine flowing freely, the worries they'd shared were now a distant memory. Even in the midst of the alcohol's heady glow he was aware there were things to deal with and fret about; but right at that particular moment, as they danced around the garden in the early evening haze, they weren't a concern at all. The ecstasy took a while to compliment proceedings, but when it arrived it added an even more relaxed feeling within them. Time seemed to drift past. Frances had grown bored of mixing tunes and now preferred to mix drinks. She'd put a DJ mix CD on and the two of them now danced close to one another. Richard was pleasantly surprised how natural he felt doing so. This was still all very new to him. It had only been a week ago that he'd entered a nightclub for the first time and taken ecstasy for the first time. He had to admit that he enjoyed how the drug made him feel. It took him away from himself; completely relaxed him. Like a lot of the things he'd experienced in the past week, it was something he'd wished he'd tried many years ago.

After a couple of hours of revelry, they grew tired and hungry. 'I'm going to order some pizzas,' Frances said through the din of the music. It was the first thing of any note that had been said between the two of them for a long while. She'd reasoned that the hundreds of calories they'd burnt off walking earlier and all the vigorous dancing had given them the right to indulge in some more carb-based fast-food.

Richard still felt the delightful effects of ecstasy working through him, and, with an inane grin and semi-closed eyes, he leaned in closer to hear. He made Frances repeat what she'd said and rubbed his belly in agreement.

Frances had also seen another side of Richard today. He too could be carefree, and, right then, at that moment, he looked as carefree as anyone had ever looked. She couldn't help herself and had to give him a big wet kiss on his sweaty forehead. Richard beamed an even wider smile as she went off to order the pizzas.

By the time the pizzas arrived the music was of a more chilled variety. An old "*Café del Mar*" CD had replaced the thumping funky house. The volume was turned down to a more agreeable level and they sat lazily on the plush lawn with the last rays of sunshine warming the garden before it ducked down behind the buildings.

'That was fun,' said Richard.

'Yes it was. It was good to see you dance again. You've got some moves!' Frances said before she pushed a slice of Margherita pizza into her mouth. The hot melted cheese stuck to the side of her mouth and she was forced to pick up a napkin to wipe herself clean.

Richard was still looking at her with new eyes. The dream woman version of Frances wouldn't have spilt pizza cheese across her face, but he preferred the less perfect Frances. She seemed completely relaxed around him. Something he imagined she'd never been around Mike. As his mind strayed to thoughts of Mike again he was mindful not to let them linger on him for too long. He'd infringed on their thoughts enough already. As he allowed himself surreptitious glances at Frances he could see that the fear she'd carried on her face had dissipated and he was determined for that to remain that way, at least for the remainder of the evening.

'Do you mind if I stay here with you tonight? I'll let Jen know that I'll stay with her tomorrow. I can also help you move tomorrow morning.'

Richard didn't have to think twice before he answered, but he didn't want to appear overly keen. 'Of course!' he excitedly replied. *Oh, well done! So much for being cool!* his inner-self chided. 'I mean, yes, that would be good. I don't like the thought of you making your way anywhere tonight, y'know after…' he trailed off. He knew he was now veering onto the subject of the possible intruder – most likely Mike. The one subject he was trying desperately to avoid. He decided to quickly change the subject. 'You can definitely help me move into my new place.' The sentence made his body stiffen with his own take on fear. It was a small sacrifice though, and he could see he'd gotten away with it as Frances remained smiling.

'Tell me more about your new place,' Frances enquired.

Richard thought for a moment. He'd only seen the place once but the mental picture of his new home was etched well in his memory. 'It's a beautiful place; in Palmeira Square.'

'Palmeira Square? *Very* nice. It's gorgeous round there.' Frances was impressed and that gave him a little shot of pride.

'The living room is a nice size and has a kitchen off the back of it. It's bright and looks and feels so fresh... The bedroom isn't massive but it's cosy. It's got fitted wardrobes too; in fact, the whole place is furnished... Oh, and I'm just a short walk from the seafront.' Richard was suddenly aware he was smiling as he painted a picture of his new home to Frances. *So, what am I so worried about?* he thought to himself. Since he'd signed the lease agreement last week, he'd gone from being extremely excited by the prospect of living by himself, to borderline petrified. He was now starting to see the positives again. Perhaps it was the drink and the ecstasy giving him a more relaxed viewpoint, but he no longer thought how lonely he might be. He was thinking of his independence and not being answerable to his loathsome parents. He'd be able to unwind in his living room, not holed-up in his bedroom. He'd be able to watch what *he* wanted on *his* TV - not some god-awful soap opera or mindless reality show. He could do whatever he wanted.

Frances was smiling too. 'You seem to have warmed to the idea of moving.'

'Mmmm, yeah I guess I have. I'm still a bit scared of living by myself, but I think it's going to be good for me.'

'There's no thinking about it; it's going to *great* for you. You've got to go and live your life as you want to live it. Your life is just beginning... I'm so happy for you.'

Richard couldn't wipe the contented grin from his face. And he didn't want to. With all the drama of recent events - some being far from pleasant to witness – this was a nice moment to savour.

With the pizza rapidly devoured, they tidied up and relocated up to the living room upstairs. There was an air of unease now they were back inside. The feeling that something wasn't quite right had returned, but neither was willing to say as much. They settled on the sofa and felt a noticeable change in temperature from the summer sun that had graced them outside. Frances picked up the discarded blanket that Richard had kicked off earlier that morning and placed it over him. 'I'm just going for a wee,' she said and scampered up to the bathroom. With Frances out of the room Richard really began to feel unnerved. He scanned the room again for any sign of interference, but in truth he couldn't remember how the room was when they'd left it. Rising from the sofa, the blanket still wrapped around him, he looked out the window. His eyes flicked from one side of the road to the other. He wasn't even sure what he was looking for; Mike standing by his car or a masked burglar waiting with his swag bag? He didn't know, but there was certainly nothing untoward out there. He decided to close the blinds and, as he turned to sit back down, he jumped out of his skin… Frances had silently walked back in the room without him realising. He dropped the blanket, leapt high in the air and omitted one of the most feminine screams in the history of feminine screams. And it set Frances off too. She screamed and before they knew it they were two nervous wrecks screaming at one another.

'Christ almighty!' she bawled holding her hand to her chest. 'You gave me a bloody heart attack!'

'*I* gave *you* a heart attack?!' Richard said suppressing the urge to laugh. Raucous laughter soon followed though. Whether it was relief or the build-up of lots of pent-up tension throughout the day, but they couldn't stop themselves laughing. It was bordering on hysteria as they pointed at one another whilst holding their sides.

Once the laughter finally subsided they switched on the TV and searched for something to watch. Despite the gluttony of channels at their disposal there was little of note that captured their attention. They settled on the news and left it on in the background as they hunkered down beneath the blanket. Frances looked endearingly at Richard who was still looking around the room. 'Thanks for a good day,' she said.

'Thank *you*,' he replied, meeting her gaze. 'It's been more fun that it should've been don't you think? I mean, I feel a bit guilty sitting here in Matt's place after the day we've had, when he's lying in that hospital bed.'

'I suppose so. But none of that is our fault. You heard the nurse yesterday, without us bringing him in as quickly as we did, he might not be lying in a hospital bed at all. He might've been lying in a mortuary instead.'

There was some truth in that Richard reasoned, but it still didn't sit comfortably that they were here and he was there. 'If I hadn't encouraged him to confront Jamie he wouldn't have got beaten up in the first place.'

'Now you're just trying to put blame on yourself that has no right being there.' France took Richard's hand in hers underneath the blanket. She kept her gaze upon him but he now looked blankly at the TV. 'Don't feel bad. Matt did what he needed to do. You gave him the inspiration to do something he'd been meaning to do for a long, long time. And he'll get better and the bruising and swelling will go down. He'll be back on his feet in no time. And when he is you'll carry on where you left off… You know, you've probably made as bigger impact on him as you say he has on you. He's obviously missed your friendship too.'

Richard flicked her a look as if what she'd just said had struck a chord. A slightly more satisfied look grew across his face as he turned back to the news. 'Thank you,' he uttered, almost inaudibly.

They sat there for the next half hour not saying much and watching TV, but neither were paying it much regard. Their eyes grew heavier and heavier and when Richard's head lolled forward causing him to jumpstart awake, Frances suggested they head to bed. 'Can you stay in the bed with me?' she asked. 'I don't want to be by myself tonight.'

'Of course.' Richard was too tired to feel in any way sexual, but the thought of curling his body around Frances' was a very pleasing thought indeed. In truth he didn't want to lay alone either. 'I'll just go down and get us some water,' he said as he folded the blanket and sleepily walked down to the kitchen. He was that close to sleep now that he felt like he was sleepwalking. Just as he was about to fill up two glasses from the tap he remembered Matt kept a jug of filtered water chilling in the fridge. Groggily, he shuffled over to the fridge and opened the door. As he leant in to pick up the jug he noticed a small bit of card on the bottom shelf. Curious as to what it was doing there, he picked it up and instantly dropped it… It was Mike's business card.

CHAPTER 23

Richard stood there in the kitchen, shaking; his eyes still transfixed on the card on the floor. It wasn't just a business card. It was a calling card. Mike had been there and Richard presumed he hadn't wanted to be found there. This simple sign of his presence delivered a chilling message; a message he was determined not to pass on to Frances. She'd been through enough and if he could keep this from her, he would. With his heart seemingly in his throat and beating frantically, he took a few deep breaths to try and compose himself. He was about to head back upstairs when he remembered what he'd come down there for. Shakily, he filled the two glasses with the chilled water. His breathing was loud and ragged and his mouth bone-dry, so he took a sip from one of the glasses. The sip became a gulp and before he knew it he'd drained the glass. But his mouth was still dry, and without hesitation he drained the other glass. He refilled them and then replenished the jug before returning it to the fridge. Amazingly, as he closed the fridge door, he spotted Mike's card still on the floor where he'd dropped it. *Idiot!* His hands trembling, he picked it up as if it were about to explode. With panicked eyes he scanned the kitchen for the bin, finding it under the kitchen sink. Screwing the card up as tightly as he could, he pushed it far down the bin so there was no chance of it being discovered. A few more deep breaths and, giving the room one more scan, he turned the lights off and unsteadily made his way back the stairs to join Frances.

Setting down the glasses in the bedroom, he then found Frances in the bathroom.

'I thought you'd got lost down there,' Frances said into the mirror as she applied some moisturiser to her face.

Richard wasn't sure he trusted his voice not to betray the fear he felt, so he offered a simple smile and an indiscernible shrug by way of reply.

'You gotta love a gay man when it comes to beauty products and moisturisers. If there was any doubt that Matt was gay, a look through this bathroom cabinet and you'd know for sure he was. No straight man would have this fine array of products in their bathroom.' France was chirpy considering how weary she was.

Richard was glad. He could play at being too tired to really interact. But his mind was supercharged with thoughts of Mike, and despite the two glasses of water he'd had downstairs, his mouth continued to dry out with dread. Again, he smiled sweetly and manoeuvred past Frances to retrieve his toothbrush. Trying his hardest not to give the game away, he shakily squeezed out some toothpaste onto the brush. He was relieved to have the toothbrush in his mouth as an able prop to disguise his panicked state. He'd obviously succeeded in this covert task as Frances, giving one last look in the mirror, left the bathroom. He thought at a hundred miles an hour. *What if he's still in the house? What if he'd been hiding all the time and was just waiting for us to sleep? How could he sleep? He can't still be here. Even he wouldn't be that patient, surely. Did I make sure the doors and windows were locked completely?* He realised he'd stopped brushing his teeth and was staring blankly at the bathroom mirror. Spitting out the contents and wiping his mouth, he quickly but quietly made his way downstairs. He checked every window was locked and put the door chain across the front door before making his way nervously back down to the kitchen. He was still readying himself for Mike to be sat there as he descended the stairs. Much to his relief he wasn't and he leapt down the last two steps and hurriedly double-checked the French doors before heading back upstairs in the same, silent manner as before. He had to admit, all those years of creeping past his parents' bedroom had served him well. As he climbed into bed next to Frances he found her lying on her side with her back to him. She was almost asleep but reached out her hand for him to take. 'Goodnight. Sleep well,' she said softly.

Frances was asleep in seconds. Her steady breathing more audible; not quite snoring, but not far off. Richard though, could not sleep. He was still adrenalized and feared that Mike would poke his head around the corner of the door at any moment. He sharpened his senses and with every tiny sound he heard, he flinched. After an hour or so, tiredness got the better of him and he too drifted off into a deep sleep. His dreams, when they came, were vivid and tormenting. If he'd been less tired he'd have woken out of them. But tired he certainly was and, despite those dreams, he woke next morning like he was rising from the grave. He looked to his side and found Frances still sound asleep. His heart missed a beat for a moment as dark thoughts invaded his mind. Forgetting that she was still undoubtedly carrying some bruising, he prodded Frances to check she was still alive, and, to his relief, he felt her recoil beneath the duvet. Stretching, he decided to get up and take a shower. Seated on the side of the bed he realised he should've showered before bed last night as he inspected the soles of his feet. They were grass-stained and grubby from all the dancing they'd done in the garden. His calves ached for the same reason, as did his back. His head was a little woolly too and his mouth gummy from copious glasses of wine. All in all, a shower was well needed.

Standing there underneath the shower, hot water raining down on him, he still felt on edge and was listening for any sound of an intruder. He couldn't relax at all, his mind swarmed with thoughts, not just of Mike, but also of his big move. He hadn't arranged any way to transport his belongings, but after a bit of inner reasoning he decided that all his stuff would comfortably fit inside a big six-seater taxi with the back seats dropped down. That was one less thing to worry about, but there was still a multitude of thoughts churning around his head. So lost in his own thoughts he hadn't realised he was doing things on autopilot. He found himself dressed and downstairs in the kitchen, boiling the kettle for a morning cuppa. He'd even forgotten to be scared about walking down there. But as he retrieved the milk from the fridge, the memory of discovering Mike's business card in there was still fresh in his mind. And the thought that that same card was buried deep at the base of the rubbish bin unnerved him; like it was observing them and relaying information back to Mike. As he poured hot water into the mugs he jumped nervously when Frances merrily called, "Morning!" down the stairs. The sudden jolt made him spill boiling water on the work surface which he quickly cleaned up. Frances tottered over to him just as he finished preparing the tea. Masking his edginess, he handed her her tea and looked upon the vision that greeted him. Frances' blonde hair was all over the place. It resembled an eighties rock chick's but lacked the makeup to accompany the look. With an oversized t-shirt – obviously one of Matt's - covering her frame she was in complete contrast to the well-prepared version of Frances that had drifted past him so many times on their journeys to work. He couldn't help himself though; this Frances was the Frances he loved.

Curious as to know what he was thinking as he undressed her with his eyes, she asked him. 'Penny for them...'

Busted, Richard shook himself out of his daydream. 'W, well I was just thinking... I was just thinking how lovely you looked.'

'Don't be silly. I look like the Wild Woman of Wonga. I need a shower. I see you've already had one. What time did you get up?'

'About half an hour ago. I didn't want to wake you. Did you sleep ok?'

'I did. I was exhausted. My head's a bit fuzzy now though. How much did we drink last night?'

'Enough,' he said as he took a sip of his tea. The thought of how much they had actually drunk made his head pound.

'Big day today!' Frances said exuberantly. 'I'll get showered and changed and then you can tell me the plan of attack.' Then, taking her tea with her she marched back upstairs.

Frances re-joined half an hour later. Showered and dressed in an outfit so casual but undeniably sexy, Richard marvelled at the transformation. Her wild hair was now washed, dried and plaited at the back. It was a new look for her and, like every other look, she seemed to carry it off with ease. And there too, drifting on the air, was her scent, filling his nostrils and with it, his heart.

Whilst she'd been getting ready, he'd been busying himself. He'd called the letting agent, Wayne, arranging to meet him at 9:30am outside the flat. He'd also booked a six-seater cab which should be arriving at any moment. And because he had time and was pacing around the place, he decided to completely tidy up and made sure everything was clean and put away. There was no evidence of their little party the previous evening apart from the gaps left by missing bottles of wine in the summerhouse fridge. He stood there with a satisfied look, proud of his efficient use of time.

The toot of the taxi's horn outside shook him out of his momentary self-adulation. Frances flashed him a reassuring look and they made their way upstairs.

After hauling Richard's belongings into the taxi with the aid of the short, stubby and extremely jovial taxi driver, they set off.

'Blimey, is that all you've got?' the cheerful cabbie said into the rear-view mirror. Richard and Frances sat panting next to one another. Neither of their bodies had been ready for the exertions of lifting and carrying. Both felt the fatigue of last night's dancing. The cabbie, who, given his diminutive stature and rather sedentary job, would be forgiven for being the one struggling with those same exertions, was beaming away waiting for Richard's reply.

Richard, for his part, was hoping to get away with pretending not to hear what he'd said, but seeing the happy face looking expectantly at him, knew it was only polite to respond. 'It's all I've got… I travel light,' he smiled.

'It's definitely yours though, right?' There was concern in the taxi driver's voice and in the eyes that stared intently into the mirror. 'I mean you didn't just rob that house and use me as a getaway driver?'

Richard grew worried and then flustered. 'Is that what it looked like? Crikey! I… I.. I…' he stuttered.

'I'm only jokin' wiv yer!' The cabbie said before letting out a seasoned smoker's cackle. 'If you woz burglars you'd be the smartest looking burglars I've ever seen.' He continued to chuckle away to himself as his attention turned to the road. Richard rolled his eyes and looked at Frances who was supressing a smirk.

They arrived outside the flat at exactly 9:30am. Waiting for them, dressed in summery attire, but looking every bit the estate agent, was Wayne. Board shorts and an untucked linen shirt were complimented by aviator sunglasses and loafers. Once they'd paid the driver and unloaded the taxi, they greeted each other. Richard introduced Frances to Wayne and, all grabbing some of Richard's belongings they made their way into the flat. A couple more journeys and the move was done. Wayne went through a few things with Richard as he showed him around again and then he handed him the keys. And just like that Richard had himself a new place to live. He felt strange; like he'd just beamed down onto the planet. He wasn't quite sure what to do next.

'Wanna get some breakfast?' Frances suggested.

Richard gave his new living room one last proud examination and nodded his agreement.

Stepping outside, the dazzling sunshine forced them to simultaneously don their sunglasses. Richard still felt a little awkward around Frances. He still wasn't sure if he could reach for her hand to hold, and as they walked up towards the main road, his arms flailed about superfluously. But just as he was about to dig his hands into his pockets, Frances' hand grasped his. He looked down to see her smiling contently. 'Still friends,' she said smiling.

They walked along the main road for a short while and were about to turn up one of the side streets to a café when something popped into Richard's head. 'Do you mind if we walk along this road a little longer? There's someone I'd like to check up on.'

Slightly puzzled, Frances simply replied, 'Sure.'

They continued along the main road, this time with a little more urgency, as Richard homed in on the destination. He was silent as he focussed on the task at hand.

Frances was beginning to struggle to keep up with Richard. 'Where are we going?' she asked.

'Remember that night when I turned up on your doorstep – when Mike was there?' He wasn't looking at Frances as he spoke. He was concentrating on the way ahead.

'Yes,' she replied uncertainly.

'Well, before that, as I walked along the road, I bumped into – or more accurately, nearly tripped over this homeless guy. He was called Jez and he had a little scruffy puppy, Betty.' The pace slowed as Richard recollected and turned to face Frances. 'I bought them a few items; y'know to…' He didn't actually know why he'd done it. He supposed that it had had a mutually beneficial effect.

Frances looked up intently at him. 'That's a lovely thing to do. So, is that who we're off to see?'

'Yes, but…' Richard started, but as he drew up to where Jez and Betty had been, his face dropped… They weren't there. Instead, a much older chap with a big, wild beard lay in their place. He had a bottle of cheap vodka beside him and, on seeing Richard staring mystifyingly open-mouthed at him, felt the need to challenge him.

'What choo you lookin' at?' he said gruffly.

'I was looking for someone - a chap called Jez. He had a little puppy with him. Do you know where they went?'

The name obviously resonated in the man's booze-sodden brain and he smiled broadly, revealing some less than perfect dentures. 'Ah Jez, yeah I know 'im. 'He gave me 'is patch.' The man spread his arms to signify the space around him, like it was a country estate. 'He's a lovely one he is. Yeah, he said he wanted to see a bit of Britain… Or was it Brighton? I dunno. He looked bloody 'appy though… And clean – like he'd had a bath or something!'

It was Richard's turn to smile broadly as he imagined Jez and Betty strolling off into the sunset on some big adventure. It was probably an overly romantic thought, but he liked it that way. With a warm feeling of pride coursing through him, he took out a five-pound note and handed it to the old man. 'Thank you and take care of yourself.' Unlike Jez, he had no doubt the man would spend the money on booze, but he figured he'd made it this far in life and seemed happy enough with his lot.

'You're just a big softie aren't you?' Frances said as they made their way back towards the café. She no longer held his hand. She had hold of his arm and had pulled herself tight into him.

Sitting in the small, intimate café, Richard continued to sport a satisfied smile. 'I hope he's doing alright,' he said almost to himself.

'Who, Matt?' Frances replied.

'No… I mean yes, Matt too, but I meant Jez.'

It's nice that you're so concerned about him, but in amongst all the worrying you do for other people there's one person you seem to neglect.'

'Oh, I'm sorry I…' Richard panicked as he felt for Frances' hand.

'Not me silly! You!'

'Oh, I'm alright,' he said dismissively.

'I hope you are, but you should put a little bit more onus on yourself. And I'm not just talking about your job situation. I mean, what do you want out of life? What are your goals? It's good to have some sort of plan.'

He was taken off guard. He seldom put himself first or made plans of any sort, so this was going to take a bit of thought before he could deliver an answer. Contemplating what he'd just been asked, he rubbed his chin which was now sporting three days facial hair. He was normally one to keep close-shaved, so the prickliness his fingers now felt upon was a novel sensation. Realising that Frances was still waiting patiently for a reply, he stalled her. 'It's a good question,' he said as he stroked his chin some more.

Frances let out a laugh. 'You look so serious all of a sudden. It's no biggie; just worth thinking about… Just not *sooo* seriously.'

Richard allowed a smile to break across his face too and he let his hand drop away from his bristly chin. 'Sorry, it just got me thinking. I suppose being forty I should have some plans in place, but to be honest, everything is so new to me. This time two weeks ago I was still living at home with my parents and doing the same job I've been doing for god-knows-how-long. I guess I'm just content to go with the flow for the moment.'

'But surely you must have *some* idea of how you'd like your life to pan out… I don't know; would you like children?

'Richard scoffed at the thought. 'I've only just started to take charge of my own life. I'm not sure I'm ready for the responsibility of a child just yet.' He thought for a moment before continuing. 'Who knows though; maybe I'd make a good father one day. Although now I'm forty I'd best get a shimmy on!'

'I think you'd make a fantastic father,' Frances said.

'I can't be any worse than *my* father.'

'What's he like - your father?'

'Honestly? He's a lazy… selfish… spiteful. If I thought really hard, I'd struggle to find a single redeemable attribute my father possesses.'

'Oh, come on, there must be something.'

'Ok, I suppose he *is* exceptionally good at lying horizontally… And he *is* a bit of a wiz at rolling cigarettes, but when it comes to showing love and compassion, he's useless. So is my mother for that matter. It's amazing I'm still alive. They really didn't give a damn about me and certainly shouldn't have ever had me.' A tinge of anger crept into Richard's voice now.

Frances was keen to keep the conversation going though, as she presumed he'd seldom ever talked about his feelings towards his parents. In the time since she'd known him, he'd spoken very occasionally about them and was always less than complimentary, but this was the first time he'd opened up about them. There was definitely some deep-rooted resentment. He'd obviously harboured these entrenched emotions all these years and it amazed her that he wasn't completely messed-up for doing so. For that reason, it resonated with her. That was something intrinsic they had in common. She too had been guilty of holding onto her emotional pain.

'So, tell me how you ended up such a lovely man then? she asked.

Richard smiled and blushed at the compliment; still unused as he was to receiving them. But he'd happily take them, especially from Frances. 'Well,' he started, playing coy; 'I suppose my Gran takes credit for that. It's certainly nothing to do with my folks… I spent more time with my Gran than I did my parents – especially during my teenage years. I think they'd grown bored of me, and my Gran was such a warm, loving person, always making me feel special.' He was starting to feel like he did when he'd opened up to Matt in the pub in what seemed like a lifetime ago. *My god, so much has happened since then,* he thought to himself. With every word he spoke he could feel an invisible weight slowly lift and he loved Frances all the more for being there to listen to the words that fell from his lips. 'From a young age my Gran taught me basic life skills: good manners, etiquette, chivalry, self-respect and respect for others. Obviously, when I went back to my parents, I saw how not to behave. I used them as anti-role models.' He paused for a moment to ponder something before continuing. 'As I grew older I felt a sense of pity for my Gran. I think she'd always carried a degree of shame for the way her son - my father, had turned out; as if it were a reflection on her parenting.'

'Why do you reckon your father turned out that way?' Frances asked. 'It sounds like your Gran was a lovely person and your Dad… well, isn't.'

'I'm not sure. My Gran always blames my Mum; saying that she corrupted him, but I think my Dad was never an angel. My Gran had to bring him up pretty much by herself when my Grandad died. My Dad was just a young boy when that happened. I think he lacked a father figure; someone to put him in his place every now and again. He probably ran her ragged. I was told he was a bit of reprobate at school too.'

'So, what about your Mum? What's she like?'

'Well, you know how most men are mummy's boys? Yeah well, not me. I don't think I'm over-exaggerating when I say that she's just a horrible woman. She's like my Dad… but worse. She doesn't possess one ounce of love for anyone other than herself. Well, I suppose she does love my Father – now there's a bizarre love affair I don't want to think about…'

'But, like you said, they love each other. They obviously have love within them.'

'Yes, perhaps. But none for anyone else. They're selfish together and in truth they're the only people that could tolerate one another… You know, I spent a lot of my life trying to love them in spite of their faults - with no love in return, but as the years went on I became more and more detached towards them; I couldn't *not* be. When you're not shown love for so long, eventually it's going to have an effect. I was always envious of Matt upbringing because his parents really loved him. The relationship he had with his Dad was such a strong one. I mean his Dad *really* loved him and wanted the best for him – you could tell. They did stuff together. The only time my Father and I did stuff together is when he'd give me a whack for not putting the rubbish out or not washing up properly or missing a bit when I was vacuuming. It was hardly the bonding stuff of father/son dreams.'

Frances was about to say something when the waitress brought over their breakfasts. Although this café was different from the previous days', their breakfast choice was the same. They both looked up, said thank you, then leant back in, conspiringly, and continued where they left off.

'So, your Father used to hit you?' Frances said almost in a whisper.

'Oh yes, so did my Mother,' Richard replied matter-of-factly. 'Although neither of them hit that hard. I think it was too much effort for them, and as I grew taller they struggled to reach me to cuff me around the head. But to be honest it wasn't the physical pain of those smacks; it was that they felt the need to do it in the first place. Their smacks could be dealt out for the tiniest of things. I mean, it wasn't as if I was a naughty or mischievous child; I was a good boy - I've always been too scared to be naughty. And like I said, my Gran really taught me right from wrong. I think, given the failing of my Father, she'd made an even greater effort this time round to make sure that I didn't turn out like him…' Richard paused for a moment and took a mouthful of his breakfast. When he'd swallowed he looked earnestly at Frances. 'Do you know the overwhelming feeling they've left me with?.. I feel like I've been bullied.' Just saying those words was like a penny dropping. He suddenly appreciated, after all those years, that he *had* been bullied. He had been belittled and downtrodden, and he'd held it down under the waters of his emotions. It was as if he were coming up for air and he could finally breathe again.

Frances noticed an enigmatic smile creep across his face, somewhere between melancholy and happiness. 'You sound like a modern-day Cinderella,' Frances joked, trying to lighten the mood a little.

'Ha, I suppose I do… So, does that make you my Princess Charming?'

'Sure, I'll take that,' she said with a smile and a wink.

They continued to pick at their breakfasts, but in truth neither of them was particularly hungry. The conversation had got their minds turning. Richard had to admit he felt a lot better after he'd opened up on his past. He wondered if Frances wanted to talk about the subject she'd been avoiding since he and Matt had liberated her. But he didn't want to clumsily prod a nerve and upset Frances unnecessarily. There was certainly a link between them and that was that they'd both been bullied and repressed; him by his parents and her by her husband. 'I suppose that's something we have in common… That we've both endured oppressed lives.'

'Yes, I think you're right,' Frances said after mopping the corners of her mouth with a paper napkin. 'I hate to admit it – that I allowed myself to be so manipulated and controlled; allowed myself to be bullied; and allowed myself to fall so low… I'm a bit ashamed of myself for that.'

Richard reached over the table to take Frances' hand. 'It's not your fault. From what you've told me, he's a very devious and manipulative person… And he's a bully. Bullies have a way – or find a way of getting what they want. I know that from experience… But you're not alone and you've done the hard part; leaving him.'

'Yes… *Again*!' Frances responded. 'God, you'd have thought I'd learnt my lesson the first time! I mean, how foolish am I?!' Frances shook her head in exasperation. 'It won't happen again. Not with him or any other man.'

The last four words stung Richard. He didn't like the thought of Frances with anyone else. He was still struggling to take the backward step of being "just friends" after being so intimate with her.

'I just don't want to be scared of him anymore… And I don't think I am.'

Richard doubted that last sentence somewhat given Frances' reaction the previous day. He, himself was more than a little terrified of Mike; especially after finding that Mike had been in Matt's house. For a split second he pondered whether to reveal to Frances the discovery he'd made in Matt's fridge, but he decided against it. Frances was being positive and that pleased him.

They finished up their breakfast and, with Frances holding Richard's arm, they headed back to his flat. The notion he was going back to *his* place was still a new one, but one that made him feel like he'd finally reached adulthood. There were still a number of life choices awaiting him, but this was one that shouldn't have been so hard. The anxiety he'd felt about living by himself had ebbed away. It was now very exciting and very real. This was the start of a new chapter in his life. In fact, the more he thought about it, this past week or so signified the start of his life. *Better late than never*! Those were words that had been echoing in his mind since his meeting with Charlotte Mulberry. He'd like to think that given all the things that had happened in his life since that meeting, he'd certainly started making up for lost time. But the memory of Charlotte's resonating words brought to the fore the nagging question that had consumed his thoughts over the past week. That of what he was going to do with his work situation. Every part of him didn't want to return to that office. It had absorbed far too much of his life and not given much back. He was still at a loss of what to do instead, but he guessed he didn't have to decide now. He didn't have to decide next week either. In fact, he could take the whole summer to make that decision. He had a large sum of money in his bank account that he'd hardly ever touched. Surely now was the time to take some time to enjoy those savings.

Almost reading his mind Frances asked, 'So, have you given any more thought as to what you're going to do about the job offer?'

'Yes,' Richard said confidently. 'I've decided I'm going to take some time out. I'm not going back to work at the accountants. I'm not sure what I'll end up doing; but I know I don't want to go back there.'

Frances smiled up at him. 'Good for you,' she said, squeezing into him.

En route they stopped off at local supermarket to pick up some provisions. Frances guided Richard as to what he would need, including cleaning products, tea, coffee and other day-to-day necessities. She also bought an expensive bottle of champagne as a housewarming gift. She could see this purchase made Richard beam with happiness. Receiving gifts was something he was obviously unfamiliar with.

When they arrived at the flat, there was a childish excitement in the look Richard gave Frances as he turned the keys on the lock. Taking great pride, he ushered Frances inside with a theatrical wave of his arm. 'Please, enter madam,' he said with a posh butler's voice.

'Why, thank you kind sir,' Frances replied with a small curtsey. She could already see a noticeable change in Richard. The irrational fear had been replaced by a sense of confidence and belonging. It looked to her like their chat in the café had unburdened him of issues that had bogged him down for such a long time.

Kicking off his shoes, Richard savoured the plushness of the new carpet beneath his feet as he walked into the living room. He breathed in the scent of the freshly painted walls and ceilings and marvelled at the cleanliness of everything. This was *his* place. He had finally arrived. Rummaging through the bags of groceries, they began to put items into the bare cupboards, fridge and freezer. Having sorted the shopping, he moved into the bedroom and began unpacking his clothes. It was as he was doing this that he heard a knock on the door. He sprung to his feet and wondered who it could be. Making his way to front door he flashed Frances a puzzled look. Her look in return was one of mild fear and trepidation. It was then that he realised that it might well be Mike. He'd tracked them down to Matt's. It was highly plausible that he'd tracked them down there too. Hesitantly, he opened the door and to his great relief he saw a little old lady standing there with a basket of fruit. 'Hello, I just wanted to welcome you to number seventeen.' The lady's voice was frail but full of kindness. She stood less than five-feet-tall in, what his Gran would've called, a frock, and had a faded pink rinse. She's applied shaky makeup to her face, but this was a lady who had clearly always taken great pride in her appearance. Richard imagined that in her prime she'd stood taller and was a glamorous, well-dressed woman. It was endearing to see her in her autumn years holding the basket of fruit with all the strength that remained in her fragile body. He smiled his thanks and took the basket from her rickety grasp. 'Me and my Brian live just upstairs in flat three,' she said pointing upwards with a crooked, arthritic finger. 'If there's anything you need you just let us know.'

Richard was still just relieved that it was a frail five-foot-tall octogenarian standing before him and not a six-foot-seven bully. The relief was obvious and invaded his voice. 'Thank you; thank you so much! That's so very kind of you. I'm Richard and you are?...'

'Beryl. I'm Beryl, and my husband's Brian. We've been married nearly sixty years – can you believe it?.. Oooh, I could tell you a few stories. We've had a life I can tell you. We've lived her for over forty years – can you believe it? It only seems like yesterday we were moving in ourselves. Oooh, time flies it does; just you make sure you enjoy yourself and live your life. I'll leave you to it m' love, but if you need anything you just let us know… I'm Beryl and my husband's Brian.'

Richard couldn't help but smile as he waved Beryl off, watching her totter up the stairs. *I hope I can live a life like her and Brian have lived,* he thought to himself as he closed the front door to his apartment.

Setting the fruit bowl down on the kitchen worktop, he received a glass of champagne from Frances. 'Cheers,' she said as they clinked glasses. These weren't champagne flutes though; these were normal glasses. Champagne flutes were just another thing he was going to have to acquire in the coming months.

No sooner had he taken a sip than there was another rap on the door; this one a bit more fervent. He gulped back his mouthful of champagne and put the glass down next to the fruit bowl. He had much preferred Beryl's subtle knock on the door to the one just hammered upon it. His hackles were up again as he prepared himself to be confronted with the bulky frame of Mike. Tentatively, he opened the door again, half-expecting the door to be forced open by a heavy foot, but instead, as he opened it further, he was greeted by the sight of two scraggly men in their mid-twenties. Both had wide eyes, wore baggy t-shirts and sported an overpowering odour of marijuana. It was a smell he'd grown accustomed to smelling this past week and these guys reeked of it.

'Yo, what's up bro,' the one on the left said, flailing his arms and hands animatedly as he spoke. He had scruffy hair which seemed to have a life of its own as it stuck out in multiple directions. His face was friendly with a light peppering of facial hair and a warm, genuine smile. 'You moved in ok? If you need anything bro, you just let us know... I'm Ollie and this is Jacob,' he continued, pointing to his taller, more gangly friend.

'Wassup,' Jacob uttered nonchalantly in tone so deep that belied the body it emanated from. Jacob was dressed in clothes that seemed a couple of sizes too big for him. Unlike Ollie, it appeared that facial hair was still a year or two away from making an impression on his long, solemn face. He had long, well-conditioned hair that fell past his narrow shoulders and thin arms that hung low, as if they were too heavy to hold.

'Nice to meet you both,' Richard said politely. An awkward silence then settled between them as they wondered what to say next. Ollie hopped from one leg to another as if he were bursting for the toilet. Jacob looked vacantly through Richard who, himself was at a loss of what to say or do to extend the pleasure of their company. He just stood there with a simple smile and an urge to edge back into his apartment and quietly close the door behind him.

Almost making him jump, Ollie blurted, 'Well, we're just across the hall in flat one, so if you ever want to hang out and, y'know, have a smoke or play Xbox or something, that'll be cool. We're just there.' His over-active hands pointed towards the door at the far end of the corridor.

'That's very kind of you. I'll be sure to swing by some time soon. I'm just unpacking at the moment, but maybe once I've settled in...' Richard was endeavouring to be as gracious as he could, knowing full well he was highly unlikely to spend any time blazing up with these two stoners.

'Awesome,' Ollie said with a big, beaming smile. 'Take it easy bro and we'll be seeing you soon.'

Richard allowed himself another small smile as Jacob and Ollie sauntered back to their flat, leaving the heavy scent they arrived with. Ollie gave an enthusiastic thumbs-up as he drifted inside the door. Closing his own door, Richard almost felt high from the fumes.

'More neighbourly introductions?' Frances said. 'What housewarming gift did you get this time?'

'Nothing this time,' Richard replied. 'But I can pop round to their flat though for a smoke sometime.'

Frances giggled. 'Yes, I can just imagine you doing that.'

They spent the next half an hour unpacking what meagre possessions Richard had brought with him. Richard busied himself, hanging up his new clothing and sorting the rest into the drawers. He was already starting to feel very much at home. He could hear Frances chatting with Jenny on the phone. The sound of her voice and occasional laugh echoing around the high-ceilinged living room gave him a warm, contented feeling inside. She sounded happy and relaxed. Just as she finished her call, there was another knock on the door.

'I'll get it!' Frances yelled out and, excitedly, she scurried to the door. But as he heard the door open he felt a foreboding shudder course through him. Pushing away from the flurry of shirts and trousers he forced himself out of the wardrobe and, staggering into the living room he was greeted with the sight of an unkempt and wild-looking Mike holding Frances tightly by the arm. It was a sight that stopped him dead in his tracks. Any moisture his mouth contained instantly evaporated and his heart felt like it had stopped beating.

'Hope you don't mind. Franny let me in… Well, your stoner neighbours let me in the main door. I said I wanted to surprise you… And, judging by your face and its lack of colour, I'd say I have done just that.' The arrogance was thick in his voice. Despite his shabby appearance Mike still posed an intimidating figure. And as Richard let his gaze flit from Mike to Frances he could see the terror in her eyes.

'I'm sorry,' she mumbled timidly.

Fighting the fear in his own voice, he replied, 'Don't worry.'

'Yes, don't worry Franny. Richard knew I would be paying you a visit. Didn't you my little friend?'

Frances' eyes looked imploringly at Richard.

'I know you found my card,' Mike said with a sardonic smile. 'It was a nice touch leaving it in the fridge don't you think? I can only imagine the look of shock on your face when you discovered it…' A smirk spread across his face. 'Oh, and I can see by your reaction, you didn't tell Franny… Tut, tut, tut. Keeping secrets from one another already. That's not a good sign.'

All the time Mike was talking, Richard was fumbling in his pocket for his mobile phone. Seeing this, Mike said, 'Now now, don't go doing anything stupid. You don't want Franny here to have another accident now do you? Take the phone out of your pocket and place it on the kitchen worktop. We don't want any unexpected interruptions from the police now do we?'

Richard hesitantly did as he was told and set carefully on the worktop.

'Good boy, Mike said patronisingly. 'I can see what you see in him now. He's like an obedient dog. And I must say, I'm pleased to see him with clothes on this time. I still have flashbacks of seeing his *thing* dangling in front of me… Now, I'm sure you're wondering what I'm doing here. Well -…'

'You're here because you want to intimidate us…' Richard's voice was broken and scared and he struggled to make eye contact with Mike, instead choosing to focus on Frances who stood completely static with Mike's strong hand digging into her arm.

'Excuse me,' Mike said, a rising anger tainting his voice. '*Do not interrupt me again… I'm here -…*'

'You're here because you're a bully and you want to maintain some sort of control over Frances…' Richard's voice had found an inner confidence from somewhere deep within and he looked sternly at Mike who met his gaze. 'You've spent a lot of time oppressing her and you think you can continue to do so even after you're separated.'

Frances looked urgently at Richard and shook her head subtly to try to get him to stop. Mike's face was reddening by the second. A fury was boiling up inside of him and he clenched his free hand into a tight fist. The other gripped Frances' arm even tighter causing her to gasp in pain. 'Now, I told you what would happen if you defied me -…'

'Yes, I got that. You'd… Wait, what exactly *was* it you were going to do to me? You never really specified.' Although his voice trembled slightly, there was a resolve in it now. Despite being scared witless, adrenalin had kicked in, giving him the ability to stand up to Mike. He was resigned to the fact that he was about to take a serious beating; there was no getting away from that, but if he was, he was going to take it like a man. He felt an urge to be sick with the sudden surge of adrenalin now rushing through his system, but he gulped it back down and looked stoically into Mike's enraged eyes. He could tell that Mike wasn't used to anyone standing up to him and that gave him some solace.

'You're about to find out first-hand you little shit,' Mike retorted through gritted teeth. He moved menacingly across from the doorway; each step a step closer to Richard's first adult violent altercation. In a week full of firsts this was one he would've quite happily avoided if he could've. He'd had many run-ins with bullies at school but had always managed to get away with just a dead arm or a punch in the stomach. This was altogether different. He knew it was highly likely that some serious damage was about to be inflicted on him. His body tensed, preparing itself for the imminent onset of violence it was about to endure. As Mike lurched forward step by step, it was as if time had slowed down. Thoughts filled his mind of martial arts movies and how the little guy managed to fend off the big guy by moving swiftly. He frantically tried to think of his plan of attack – or rather defence. Should he curl up in a ball and take the inevitable beating lying down or put up some resistance? He wasn't a fighter in any way, shape or form. Unfortunately, Mike looked the sort of person well-versed in pummelling people into fine dust. He tried to gulp but any saliva had long since abandoned his mouth. He could feel himself recoiling, retreating within himself. An image of a tortoise flashed into his head. How he envied tortoises all of a sudden. Fear now gripped his body and, seeing Mike's long reach extend and his free hand coming for him, he felt his t-shirt being wrenched outward. Time slowed almost to a standstill as he observed Mike's other hand, which, a moment ago had been restraining Frances, fly ever closer to his face. He could hear Frances scream a harrowing scream that pierced his eardrums and saw her vainly grasping to stop him, but, with a violence he'd never felt before, Mike's large fist made vicious contact with his eye socket. A kaleidoscope of stars flickered in front of his eyes as blackness invaded his sight. He felt himself falling; his legs buckling under the force of the blow. Time sped up again and, with a sickening thud his head, followed by the rest of him, smashed onto the tiled kitchen floor. And then complete blackness…

CHAPTER 24

'Yo! I think I saw his eyes flicker!'

'How can you see anything under all that blood? It's well grim. Dude, his face is a mess... I mean, *shit*, I thought he was dead for sure.'

'Clear some space boys, the paramedics have just turned up... Rich... Richard, can you hear me?'

Richard could make out Frances' voice as if he were in heaven and she were an angel. His heavily concussed and confused mind tried to make out where he was and what had just happened. Slowly it became apparent that he was lying on his side on a hard floor. He couldn't open his eyes. They felt swollen and his whole head ached like it had never ached before. He felt nauseous and, as he tried to raise his head, he noticed it felt twice as heavy as normal.

'Hey,' Frances said soothingly. 'Just lie still.'

Richard tried to mumble something in response but his mouth didn't feel like it belonged to him. His lips were bloated beyond all recognition. He did as he was bid and settled back down. Hearing the sound of the paramedics arrive, he succumbed to unconsciousness again...

'He's just attention seeking. You know that right? He just wants you to feel sorry for him.'

'Stop it! Don't be mean.' It was Frances' voice again. It was a playful voice this time.

Richard thought hard as to who the other voice belonged to. His eyes weren't ready to open so he only had his hearing to assist him. He was completely disorientated. He was no longer lying on his side. He was lying down on his back on, what definitely felt like a bed. Tightly tucked-in sheets held him secure; not that he was in any state to move much.

'Richie, you big softie, wake up.' There was no mistaking the other voice now. It was Matt. 'I know you want to be like me, but Christ, this is taking it a bit too far.'

He could hear Frances giggle. He tried hard to open his eyes and his right eye opened just enough to make out their blurred images sitting at his bedside.

'There he is... Hey, wakey wakey sleepy head... Listen, you gotta get up. The nice nurses need you outta here. You're taking up a bed that a frail old lady or a cracked-up junkie could be lying in.'

Richard's blurry vision could just make out Matt's smile, barely noticeable through the bruising and swelling his own face still possessed. Confusion reigned in Richard's mind. He still had no idea where he was or why Matt and Frances were there. His eye slowly opened a little more, but his left eye was still firmly closed and he was unable to open it at all. He thought he'd try and speak again. 'W, w, what…What's going on?' The effort it took to mumble that sentence exhausted him and he hoped that was enough to get some answers from the others.

'You're in hospital darling,' Frances said. 'You were beaten up… By Mike.'

Ah, Mike; now it was starting to make a bit more sense. He could remember the hefty, lumbering form of Mike coming at him, enraged and intent on inflicting violence. *Where was that though?... Oh, it was my flat!* His mind was now quickly filling in the blanks. He felt a slight tickle of pride that he'd remembered that, and also at the fact he now had his own flat.

'I think he must've caught you off guard though, right Rich? I think in a fair fight you would've had him, no question.' Matt was enjoying teasing Richard. He'd obviously recovered somewhat since his own beating.

Richard tried to sit up, but his body wouldn't cooperate. His thoughts were still a bit muddled. He couldn't remember his head ever hurting in so many different places before. It felt like it'd been replaced with a cannon ball and raising it for any length of time was arduous. He gulped hard in his aridly dry mouth. 'So, what happened?' he said in a rough voice, using all the effort he could muster.

Frances sighed and with a look of abject guilt moved closer to him. She gripped his hand which took him by surprise. 'I'm so sorry for what happened… It was horrible.' She sighed deeply before continuing. 'After he hit you once, he just kept hitting you as you lie there unconscious... I'm glad you don't really remember any of it. I tried to pull him off of you but I couldn't. Luckily, the boys from down the hall heard me scream and rushed in. The tall, lanky one – I can't remember his name – he just flew at him and somehow knocked him off you. The other one – Ollie I think his name is – thought fast and called the police and then shouted for help outside. The tall lad was somehow stopping Mike from hitting you anymore – I really don't know how - and then Ollie bowled in with another chap he'd accosted on the street and the three of them grappled with Mike and tried to restrain him. I mean, Mike looked wild like he wanted to kill, not just you, but everyone there, but I think he knew he was in trouble by this point and broke free and made a run for it. The chap that had come to help, knew his first aid and rolled you into the recovery position and made sure you were breathing. It was scary stuff though. Your face was broken and covered in blood.' Frances stifled a cry. If anyone deserved to cry it was Richard and she felt too ashamed to allow herself the luxury of shedding tears in front of him. 'They caught him an hour ago. He was sitting in his car; apparently pretending like nothing had happened… Unfortunately, he still had loads of your blood all over him. I think it's fair to say that this time he won't be able to get out of it…' Frances paused for a moment and a quizzical look spread across her face. Not that Richard could make this out. He was still struggling to keep his eye open enough to see anything. '...You knew how he'd react, didn't you?... You made sure he was going to attack you?'

'It was the only way we were ever going to get him out of your life,' Richard said croakily.

'There's your hero,' Matt said beaming with pride.

A look somewhere between sorrow, pity, but overriding compassion, filled Frances' face. She leant over and kissed him delicately on his forehead. 'Thank you.'

'Oh, it was nothing really,' Richard croaked with fake nonchalance.

A doctor then appeared behind Matt and Frances. He was tall, slim and looked far too young to be doing the job he was. He still had traces of acne on his translucent skin, but his face held a sensitive, caring gaze. 'Ah, he's awake,' he said cheerfully, with assuredness. 'How's he doing?' he asked them.

'He's talking. He's a little confused I think... I've just been filling him in with what happened to him. Perhaps you could tell him the extent of the injuries he's suffered,' Frances said.

'Of course... Hello Richard,' he said as he reached down to pick up his notes at the end of his bed. 'I see you've had a heavy concussion so you may feel nauseous and disorientated. I'm pleased to say that most of the damage is superficial. You've got a fractured cheekbone and a broken nose but, from what I hear, that's a lucky escape given the assault you were on the receiving end of. Those fractures should sort themselves out but we'll have a better idea of the damage caused after an x-ray. We're just going to keep you in overnight for observation and check to make sure there's no further complications. For the time being though, just rest up.' He left them with a compassionate smile as he returned the notes back where he found them.

'Awww, bless. It was Doogie Howser MD,' Matt said jokingly.

Richard allowed himself a little smile through his swollen, broken lips. He remembered watching that TV show when he was a kid. 'What are doing you here anyway?' Richard mumbled. 'Last time I saw you you were unconscious.'

'That was two weeks ago mate. You've been in a coma for that long.'

Underneath all the swelling and bruising Richard looked startled, but he could just make out the mischievous look on Frances' and Matt's face as they tried to suppress their giggles.

'Ha ha, very funny.'

'Sorry, couldn't resist,' Matt chuckled. 'The doctors said I've made a miraculous recovery. It normally takes a lot longer to be up and about as I am now. Apparently you can't keep a good man down... But on a serious note, I heard what you said to me when I was lying there. I don't know how. I heard this faraway voice talking to me and I recognised it to be yours… Thanks for being there for me buddy. It means a lot.'

'Don't worry about it. You'd have done the same for me.'

Matt looked down. 'I wish I *had* been mate. At least that arsehole will get what's coming to him now… It was a brave – *and stupid* – thing you did though. Who'd have thought, ol' Richie Chambers would step up and be the hero of the hour. Good on you mate.' He ruffled Richard's hair and, just like Frances had a moment before, planted a gentle kiss on his forehead.

'What happened to Jamie?' Richard enquired; his memory now functioning a little better.

'The police arrested him and charged him with assault. By all accounts he was very remorseful and admitted everything. But I've decided I don't want to press charges. I just want to move on. He's got a kid on the way and he deserves a chance to think of someone other than himself. Who knows, it might be the making of him. I'll just say it was a lover's tiff and they can put it down to being a domestic dispute. That'll be an ironic pill for him to swallow.'

Richard puffed out his swollen cheeks in exasperation. 'That's very gracious of you. I'm not sure I'd have done the same.'

'Yeah, yeah you would. And I think you know you would.'

Richard was pretty sure he wouldn't and he had no intention of dropping any assault charges with Mike. He hadn't gone through all this pain to see him get off scot-free. The effort of thinking and talking had made him suddenly weary. He let his heavy head sag back onto the soft pillows. The last thing his good eye saw before he surrendered to tiredness were the concerned faces of the two people he cared for most in the world. Two people that just over a week ago weren't in his life. Now, they literally *were* his life.

Next morning, after a fitful night's sleep in a ward full of people coughing, moaning, snoring and farting, he rose unsteadily and took a wander. He located where Matt was and, as he approached his bed, found him reading a book. 'Good read?' Richard said by way of getting Matt's attention.

'Not really. It's got some pages missing too, but it's preferable to watching TV… Did you sleep ok?'

Richard wrinkled his nose and shook his head in reply.

'Too many people coughing, moaning, snoring and farting?'

Richard smiled and was reminded of his facial injuries which now felt more uncomfortable than painful. His head no longer ached and his right eye was beginning to open along with his left. He hadn't had the courage to look at himself in the mirror yet but having felt his face he knew it wouldn't be a pretty sight. 'I'm going to be allowed to go home in a short while. They want to make sure I eat some food first but they're happy that I'm ok to leave.'

'Jammy bugger. I've got to stay in for a few more days at least. My memory is pretty much back to normal and I haven't had any bad reactions to the procedure. I even remembered the time Darryl Costello fell off his chair in History class – remember?'

Richard did remember. Darryl was also known by his nickname Sumo, due to his sizeable frame. He also remembered that he always had a big parka jacket on, no matter what the season. On this particular occasion he had been doing what many kids at school tend to do in class, leaning back on his chair. But unfortunately for Daryl a.k.a. Sumo, he leant back a fraction too far and basic physics took control. He fell backwards and hit the floor with such a tremor that a picture fell off the wall. Their teacher, Mr Stanley, let out a shriek of surprise and the whole class turned to see Darryl on his back with his feet wiggling in the air. It'd made Richard and Matt chuckle for a long time since and had gone down in school legend… *"The day that Sumo shook the world."*

Both of them looked heartfelt and wearily at the other. No words were needed. It acknowledged the appreciation, love and respect they both held for the other. In Richard's case, he couldn't thank Matt enough for dragging him, kicking and screaming, into adulthood and into the real world. It had been quite the reunion. Sure, it'd had more than its fair share of drama, as his damaged face bore testament to, but it had also brought a full range of emotions into play. Emotions that enhanced him as a person and now equipped him to take on the world head-on. He now felt alive and much more complete than he'd ever done so before. Although these past ten days had been intense, it had allowed him to fully reconnect with Matt; to pick up where they'd left off. He hadn't appreciated what a massive hole losing contact with him had left in his life. He wondered if Matt felt the same.

Breaking Richard out of his contemplative thoughts, Matt said, 'Go get some food and get yourself out of here. I'll give you a call later to see how you're doing.'

That was typical of Matt, Richard thought; to be more worried of him, despite being in hospital, under medical supervision. 'Ok. I'll see you soon,' he said and he slowly turned to head back the way he came. But after a couple of steps, he stopped, and walked back to Matt's bed and wrapped his arms around him. It was an embrace that came from the heart and Matt needed no encouragement to reciprocate, pulling Richard in even closer. 'Thanks for everything you've done for me,' he said, his voice muffled by Matt's broad shoulder.

When they pulled apart they shared that same knowing look again and, with a tear in his eye, Richard walked back to his bed.

After the doctors were satisfied with Richard's state they discharged him. The medical staff's casual indifference reassured him there was nothing to worry about. Having spent a lot of time in hospitals the last few days, he couldn't wait to get out of there. As he made his way to the entrance, he spied Frances standing there awaiting him. She'd spent the night back at her own house, safe in the knowledge that Mike was in police custody. That was after she'd cleaned up the blood and mess at Richard's flat. She hadn't wanted him to be greeted to that on his return to his new home. 'You look better,' she said on seeing him.

Richard knew she was being kind; he felt grotesque, but he supposed compared to how he was brought in twenty-four hours earlier, he *did* look better. But seeing Frances brought an attempted smile to his face. He couldn't help it, but he loved her. When he thought about it, he conceded he'd fallen in love with her a couple of years ago when he'd first seen her on their way to work. He acknowledged that perhaps that could be more accurately described as infatuation, but those strong feelings had been there from that moment and were only getting stronger as each day passed. The woman that stood before him now was less polished and preened than the "dream woman" version, but knowing her as he did now, this Frances was the real version and his heart melted as he beheld her.

'How did you sleep?' she asked.

'Not that great. I can already feel a nap coming on.'

'Well, let's get you home first. We can make a little nest on the sofa. The taxi is just down here.' She chaperoned him to the awaiting taxi and he slumped heavily into the back seat, spreading himself along its expanse. 'Budge up,' Frances said, urging him to move across.

Setting off, they sat in near silence, both deep in their own thoughts. Richard felt Frances' hand feel for his. She squeezed it tight, and contentedly they both looked out their respective windows, upon the vibrant city as it whizzed by. The weather had treated them to another beautiful day. The sun shone brightly again and, as Richard allowed himself a subtle sideways glance, he could see that Frances' face carried a look that said, *"everything is going to be alright."* As he turned his gaze back out of his window, he could feel a warm glow pervade through him to match the warmth of the sunshine that fell upon his face. He no longer felt the fear, worry and uncertainty that he'd carried around with him for so long. He wasn't sure what would happen with Frances or anything else in his life for that matter, but he knew he was no longer scared to see how things might transpire. Excited, alive and most importantly, happy, from this moment onwards, he would live his life to the fullest.

And, with his heading lolling against the window, and his eyes growing heavier by the second, the same look that Frances bore, crept across his face…*Everything is going to be alright…*

Printed in Great Britain
by Amazon